AFTER THE
FLAMES

AFTER THE
FLAMES

RODERIC GRIGSON

rodericgrigson.com

Dedication

The book is dedicated to the doctors and nurses of the **Burn Unit of National Hospital Colombo** in Sri Lanka who continue to provide world-class management of severe burns in a resource limited environment.

A book of this nature is never the work of just one person and many thanks to my wife Menaka, and to my friends, whose counsel and help I leaned on during the writing of this book.

- Roderic Grigson, December 2017

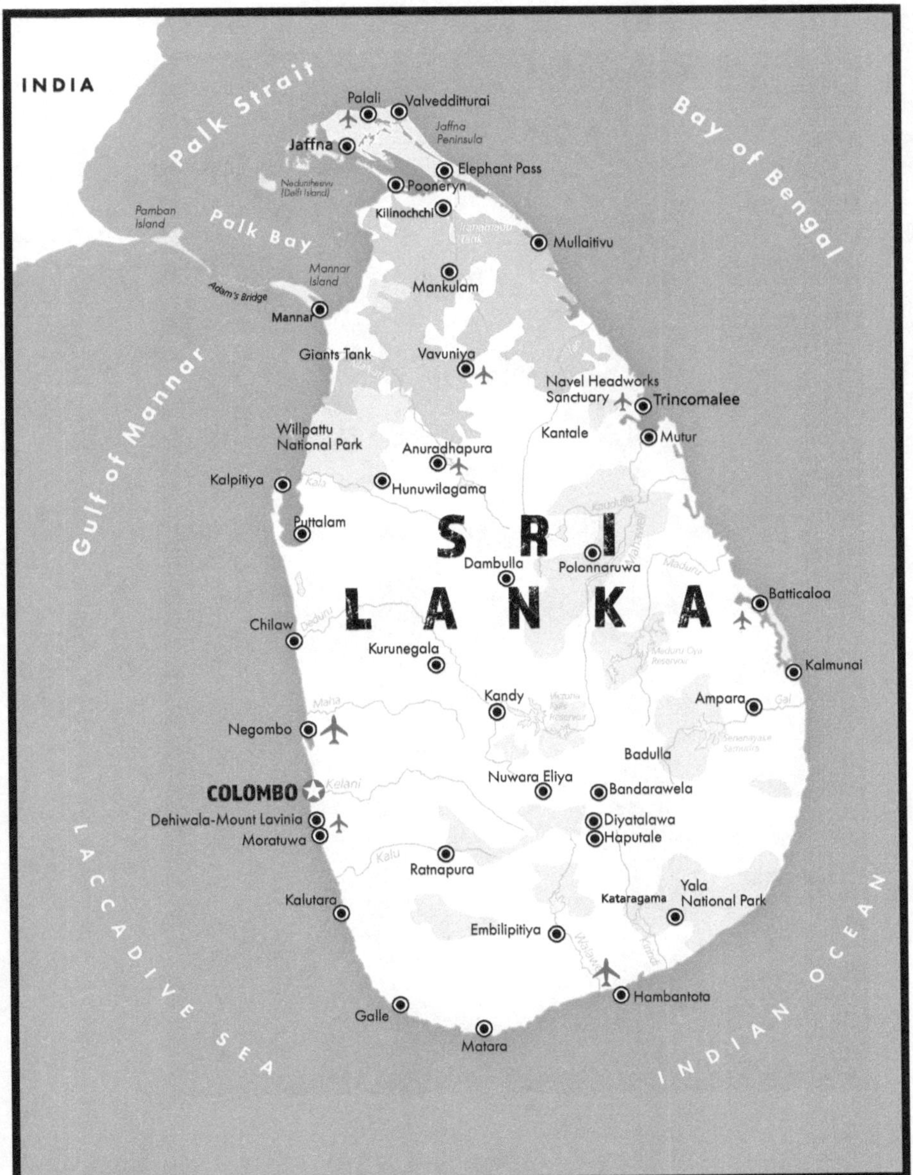

INDIA

Palk Strait

Bay of Bengal

Palali
Valvedditturai
Jaffna
Jaffna Peninsula
Elephant Pass
Nedunheevu (Delft Island)
Pooneryn
Kilinochchi
Palk Bay
Tranmailrad Tank
Mullaitivu

Pamban Island
Mannar Island
Adam's Bridge
Mannar
Mankulam

Giants Tank
Vavuniya
Navel Headworks
Sanctuary
Trincomalee
Kantale
Mutur

Gulf of Mannar

Willpattu
National Park
Anuradhapura
Hunuwilagama
Kalpitiya
Kala

Puttalam

S R I
L A N K A

Dambulla
Polonnaruwa
Maduru
Batticaloa

Chilaw
Deduru
Kurunegala
Maduru Oya Reservoir
Kalmunai

Maha
Kandy
Ampara
Gal
Senanayake Samudra

Negombo
Badulla

COLOMBO
Kelani
Nuwara Eliya
Bandarawela
Dehiwala-Mount Lavinia
Diyatalawa
Moratuwa
Haputale
Kalu
Ratnapura

Kalutara
Yala
Kataragama
National Park

Embilipitiya

Galle
Hambantota

Matara

LACCADIVE SEA

INDIAN OCEAN

S R I   L A N K A

National Parks
Main Cities & Towns
Vanni Area
Airports

0   20   40 km
0   20   40 mi

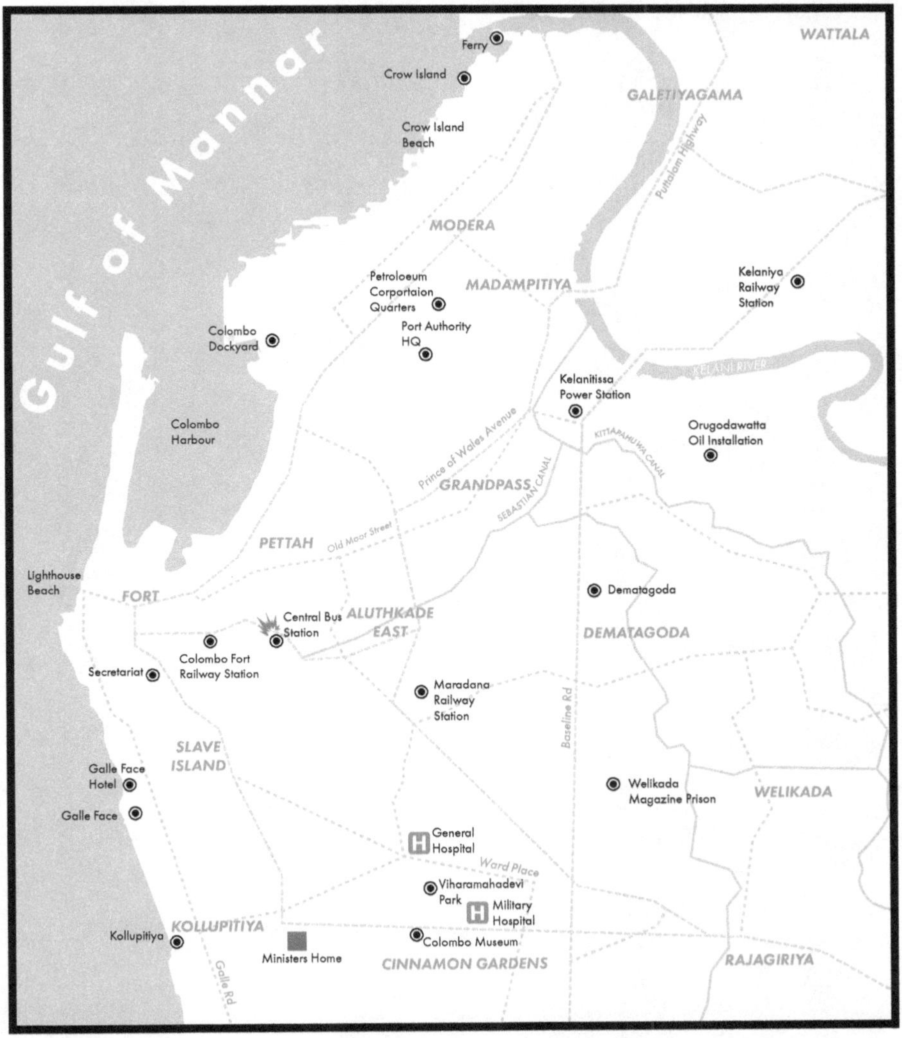

COLOMBO

 Ministers Home

 Hospital

 Significant Locations

——— Main Roads & Highways   **TEXT** Suburbs

CHAPTER ONE

In the northern part of the Colombo a man in a simple cotton shirt and sarong climbed into an old Ford Escort. The faded red car had seen better days. The seats were patched with duct tape and the old, worn out metal springs dug into his back. Large patches of reddish brown rust covered portions of the vehicle's sides but its British-built, steel construction was what made it the ideal vehicle. The rear seat under which the twenty kilograms of explosives were concealed was covered with pieces of galvanized metal, off-cuts of wood and iron scraps he had collected along the way. Two large cans filled with gasoline sat in the boot of the car.

The engine rattled as Nadesan eased the clutch, driving cautiously out of the garage and turning into the busy street running alongside a high wall surrounding the Colombo harbour. Tall cranes and derricks loading and unloading freight from cargo ships, peeped over the wall as he drove past a large dockyard entrance from where containers were transported in trucks around the country. Carefully circling the main roundabout outside the harbour, he stuck to the side of the road.

The heat in the street so late in the afternoon was terrible; the airlessness, the bustle, the stench of the city streets. Nadesan had bathed that morning, cleansing himself thoroughly before wearing the white shirt and sarong he had carried in the car all the way from the east coast. He had worshipped at the kovil in Kotahena, his forehead marked by holy ash when the priest blessed him. He had been at peace with himself. He would soon be joining Radika and Ravi.

The mass of office workers trying to beat the evening rush hour, poured out of the neglected office buildings closer to the city centre, crowding the pavement like ants rushing out of their nests. Some in a hurry to get home, spilled out onto the road, the slow-moving car posing no danger to them.

'I must be careful', Nadesan thought to himself nervously. It would end right here if he bumped into someone.

He swallowed hard knowing he had not far to go. He knew exactly the time it took from the garage where the car had been prepared. He had walked this way a dozen times; many more if he counted the times he had gone over the route in his mind.

The city had intimidated him when he first arrived more than a week ago. The dirt and squalor was everywhere he looked. Even that early in the morning, the streets leading into the city were a cauldron of life. Tired-looking men and women, some with children clinging to their arms, walked on broken pavements avoiding gaunt dogs fighting over scraps of food from overflowing piles of litter. Battered bicycles and three-wheelers jostled one another amid a cacophony of horns, avoiding belching buses and lorries filled to the brim with people and produce.

He was not used to crowds, and how different it had looked from where he had lived and spent his entire life. He missed the fresh sea breeze, the tall groves of coconut and palmyra palms hanging over sparkling blue lagoons, the vast paddies of green rice stretching away into the hazy, jungle-covered mountains, and the roar of the sea as it crashed onto the surf. His home town seemed so far away.

*

That first morning, the air in the city had been overpowering and a stifling and a sapping heat had already begun to rise from the dusty, crowded roads. He was soon soaked in sweat. Nadesan was nervous about the final checkpoint he had to pass to enter the city. The road was one of the main routes leading from the north into the city and the soldiers manning the checkpoint were more experienced than their counterparts in the more rural towns he had passed.

Nadesan was glad that he wasn't required to carry the explosives in the vehicle. He had been stopped half-a-dozen times since his trip from the east coast had begun but since he was not carrying anything illegal, he was always allowed to pass.

The checkpoint on the bridge crossing the Kelaniya river into the northern suburb of the city was busy. A long line of cars, buses and lorries were being stopped, their drivers questioned. Some were asked to move to a separate lane where their vehicles were searched. Vehicles that were waved past did so with an impatient beep of their horns.

Nadesan was unlucky that morning. He was directed to stop behind a lorry overflowing with vegetables. The soldiers were insistent on searching the whole vehicle, getting the driver and his two laborers to move aside cardboard boxes and wicker panniers full of produce so they could search the interior.

The car was getting hot in the direct sunlight. Nadesan wound down the driver-side window while he waited but it made little difference. He slowly arched his back while stretching his legs. They hurt as he'd been travelling for days. Beads of sweat formed on his forehead which he wiped off with a small towel. The threadbare blue cloth faded after many washings helped prevent the sweat forming into little streams and running down his neck but did little else.

Nadesan watched as the search of the lorry yielded nothing. He studied the soldiers impassively as they went about their task. The feeling of anger that always threatened to overwhelm him when he saw one of them was tightly under control. He was only a few steps away from completing his mission. The time would come for him to unleash his anger.

Nadesan was finally allowed to move forward. A soldier carrying an automatic rifle on his shoulder waved Nadesan forward. He was older, more weather beaten than the other soldiers manning the checkpoint and carried himself with an easy confidence.

'ID card,' he ordered, holding his hand out. The man had slicked back hair parted in the middle and a pair of inquisitive eyes, separated by a long narrow nose.

Nadesan handed the soldier his national identification card through the open window. The soldier glanced at the card and then studied it more closely. 'You're not from around here?' The soldier who had two stripes on his shoulder, bent over and looked at Nadesan through the open window, his probing eyes flickering around the inside of the vehicle.

'No,' said Nadesan anxiously. 'I am from Kokkuvil near Batticaloa. I am delivering this car to a garage in Pettah.'

The soldier frowned. 'Why would anyone want such an old car brought to Colombo,' he asked?

'It's for a collector,' Nadesan said. His story about bringing the vintage car from Batticaloa for a car collector in Colombo was usually met with a nod of understanding. But the corporal was a bit more persistent in his questioning.

'Are you selling the car?' he asked, stepping back and looking the car over.

'No, I am just a mechanic. The previous owner wanted me to drive it in case there was a problem along the way. I get paid after I deliver it to the garage.'

The soldier nodded at Nadesan's explanation. 'Open the boot, we want to look inside.'

Nadesan stepped out of the car unhurriedly and opened the boot with a key. Sweat poured off his head as he waited until a soldier rummaged through the largely empty space. The soldiers manning the checkpoint were more alert than he had come across before, making him quite nervous. Only the knowledge that there was nothing in the car which would incriminate him made him stand his ground. These men did not know anything about him ... what he was capable of doing. The soldier completed his search and nodded at Nadesan to close the boot. The corporal who had been watching Nadesan all this time, handed him the ID card and stepped back, waving his hand for Nadesan to drive off.

The address Nadesan had been given in Colombo was a small garage next to a market in one of the busy northern suburbs. It was where he was supposed to meet a man called Deva.

The fresh food market was busy that early in the morning with traders setting up their stalls. Men wandered in and out of the old, run-down building carrying fresh produce out of carts and lorries parked on the side of the road. It was a familiar scene, one that he had seen in every town and city across the island.

Nadesan parked outside the garage and got out of the car looking around. Across the road two early shoppers tried to haggle with an old man who was emptying a gunny bag full of potatoes onto a plastic sheet on the floor of his vegetable stall. The man ignored them as he piled the brown tubers into a large pile.

The garage was a simple structure, wide enough for two small vehicles, with a hard, dirt-packed floor stained black with oil. Nadesan took a few steps into the garage, peering into its gloomy interior.

A wiry, bare-bodied man bent over a bench at the back of the garage, straightened and stared at him suspiciously. 'What do you want?' the man demanded sharply.

'I am Nadesan,' he replied. 'I am looking for Deva.'

The man came forward out of the gloom, wiping his stained hands with a grimy rag. He wore grubby khaki shorts and was bare-footed. A goatee covered the bottom half of a narrow, hawkish face. An aura of menace emanated from him.

'Who wants to know?' The voice was plainly hostile.

Nadesan clenched his jaw when he got closer. The man was obviously annoyed that someone had entered the garage without his permission. Nadesan looked at him warily. He had dealt with these types of men before and knew how unpredictable they were. Since that morning, he had struggled with an uncomfortable feeling which had built gradually since he entered the city. Once again, he wondered who was behind the mission that had brought him into the city. Whoever it was he was thankful he had been given the opportunity. He was not going to do or say anything to change their minds.

'I am from Chenkaladi,' Nadesan said nervously. 'I was asked to deliver this car to you.'

The man studied Nadesan with his penetrating eyes. Nadesan felt uncomfortable at his scrutiny but held his gaze unflinchingly.

'Who sent you?' the man questioned sharply.

It was a question Nadesan had expected, for which he did not have an answer. His instructions were to deliver the car to someone called Deva and follow whatever Deva asked him to do. Nadesan decided to tell the man exactly what he had been told however strange it sounded.

'I don't know,' Nadesan shrugged. 'I was told to bring the car to this place and ask for Deva. I was told that he will tell me what to do. I picked the car up in a garage in Kathankudi.'

'What took you so long? You should have been here yesterday.'

'I took three days to come because I didn't think the car would handle the hill country.' Nadesan explained hesitantly. 'I hope it isn't a problem ...'

The man stared at Nadesan for what seemed a long time. Seemingly satisfied, he glanced up and down the street before motioning Nadesan further into the garage.

'Is that the car?' he asked, gesturing with his chin.

Nadesan nodded. 'Yes, I stopped outside the city last night and came in only this morning.'

'Drive it in here,' said Deva, motioning to one of the car bays. 'We'll have a look at it and have it ready for when it's needed.'

*

That was over a week ago. The garage was a front for a Tamil Tiger cell operating in Colombo. The increasingly aggressive militant organisation had started a bombing campaign across the country in response to a military offensive in the north. Sleeper cells in the islands largest city had been activated to add to the mayhem.

It took a few days for the car to be filled with explosives and rigged to explode once the timer was activated. Nadesan had seen three other men working in the garage but did not talk to any of them. He only dealt with Deva.

The ancient car misfired a few times that morning before the engine caught. Nadesan had been a mechanic all his life and knew that the fuel he was using was probably watered down. The car stank of gasoline, but he didn't care. His target, the central bus station in the commercial district of Pettah was only a kilometre away and he had no doubt the car would make it.

Nadesan felt a sense of nervous excitement because he was about to take the final step in the journey which began when his wife and child had been killed. Their murder had transfused his typical cheerful demeaner, replacing it with cold hate.

This part of the city looked old and decrepit. Grey concrete buildings with rusted metal beams propping them up, hinted of restoration work long forgotten. In less than a few minutes, Nadesan could see the two-storey building he was looking for, standing out from the surrounding buildings. It was Colombo's largest transport hub connecting the entire country with buses coming in and out of it every minute of the day. It sat in the centre of a teeming bazaar noisy with the horns of the buses, three-wheelers and motorcycles. Narrow alleys leading from the bazaar were a labyrinth of closely packed shops selling everything from fast food and vegetables, to clothes and merchandise of every description.

The area around the bus terminal was a mass of office workers rushing to catch their bus home after work. Lines of people snaked around the side of the building, the queues growing longer by the minute. The overpowering odour was that of dry fish and garbage. Men balancing sacks and boxes filled with vegetables and other trade goods on their shoulders, shouted for the crowd to get out of the way. Scavenging crows wheeled above them screaming loudly for a morsel of food.

Nadesan tried to quieten his thudding heart. It wouldn't be long now. He breathed more slowly, more deeply as he managed to edge the car in front of the row of shops which made up the ground floor of the bus terminal. Home going commuters swirled around the car, a man dressed in office clothes thumping the car bonnet in frustration as he found his way obstructed. Nadesan knew that it wouldn't be long before he would be asked to move the vehicle. There were enough policemen hanging around the terminal watching out for pickpockets plying their trade in the crowded bazaar.

The bomb had been rigged by to explode five minutes after it had been armed. 'But don't hang around,' The man assembling the bomb had warned. 'It might go off in three minutes or maybe in ten,' he shrugged, glancing at Deva as he spoke. 'I did the best I could.'

Nadesan remembered looking at the man distrustfully. *What if it goes off immediately?* Nadesan knew that it was an unspoken possibility but decided at that time not to voice his concern. Let them think that if the timer worked as it should, he would have enough time to get away without being blown up. But he would not do that. He was planning to stay with the car.

Nadesan reached down between his legs and pulled up the electronic device which activated the bomb. He pushed the arming switch to the on position hoping that he had triggered the device. The bomb maker had told him that he would not know if the device was armed, just to get out as quickly as possible. Nadesan let the trigger with its red and green wires fall on the floor between his feet, rested his head against the window and closed his eyes.

The events of his life rushed through his mind, one long forgotten memory chasing the other before he could hold onto it. His mind finally fixed on his wife and son. He wondered whether his son had grown at all.

Nadesan bent his head in sorrow thinking of the moment that the soldiers fired into a group of civilians standing at the bus station. The scene was so vivid in his mind.

Radika had wanted to visit her cousin who had given birth to a baby girl. She lived in the next town a short bus ride away. Nadesan left her and his son at the bus stop and had walked into the corner eatery two shops away to buy a packet of crème biscuits as a gift. He looked up in surprise when he heard firecrackers exploding outside the building. Only when a bullet smashed into an aerated water bottle standing on the counter did Nadesan understand what was happening.

Shouts of anger and disbelief punctuated the clatter of automatic gunfire as people yelled and screamed in shock and horror. Nadesan ran out of the eatery and was immediately knocked over violently by a man who was intent on running away from the carnage, away from the screams of the wounded and the dying.

By the time Nadesan got groggily back to his feet, it was all over. The angry shouts of the living grew in crescendo as he staggered over to the pile of bodies by the bus stop. At first, he could not spot the blue saree his wife had worn that morning and for a moment he thought that they had escaped. But then he saw her lying on her back, a widening pool of blood beneath her, their son clutched firmly to her breast. Her torn, blood splattered saree revealed where the high-velocity bullets had torn into her flesh as she tried to shield their son from the murderous gunfire. But her ultimate sacrifice had not been enough to prevent his son from being torn in half by the same bullets that had killed his mother. It was then that Nadesan felt a cold, terrible emptiness; a feeling of silent terror.

A total of twelve people died that terrible day. The soldiers who had caused the carnage had been attacked from a passing vehicle and had returned fire, their bullets slamming into innocent bystanders standing on the side of the road. The government had offered him compensation for his loss, but he had refused to take the blood money, instead walking to Eravur on the northern outskirts of Batticaloa to join the militant Tigers and extract a toll on those who had killed his family.

*

A sharp knock on the car window startled him, bringing him back to the present. 'You can't park here,' a young traffic Police constable in a khaki uniform glowered at him. 'Move your vehicle right away.'

Where did he come from? Nadesan felt confused. He had not seen the constable appear so lost was he in his thoughts. How long had it been since he triggered the device?

It must be at least five minutes … I need more time?

Nadesan wound down the car window taking his time. 'The car won't start,' he said hoarsely to the officer who looked down at him in disgust.

'You can't stop here,' the constable said irritably, looking around. 'I will get someone to help you push the car.'

The central bus terminal was teeming with people waiting to catch their ride home. The constable waved his arm at another policeman lounging against the station wall, gesturing for him to come to the car. Not getting a reaction, he stepped away from the car and waved both arms above his head. Office workers rushing to catch their buses weaved around the car looking Nadesan irritably. The policeman finally managed to attract the attention of the older constable who started walking towards the vehicle. The policeman turned back to the car and gestured for Nadesan to open the door.

Nadesan reached down to the arming device between his legs and pushed the switch off and back on again. Nothing happened.

Nadesan panicked. The bomb must be defective, he thought. The constable will see the wires and arrest me. All this flashed like lightning through his mind. He'd long come to terms with dying but the sight of the policeman and the faulty bomb sent a burst of terror through him in a way he'd never experienced. He was prepared to die but the thought of being captured with a car bomb terrified him. He had heard stories of what happened to people who had been imprisoned by the security forces.; about one man who had been raped repeatedly and beaten with hot metal rods over four days until he had told the Police what they wanted to hear. He was not going to be taken to prison.

Nadesan pushed open the door with all his might knocking the young constable to the ground. The older constable walking towards the car saw the incident, shouted something and began running towards them, pushing office workers out of the way.

10

In his haste to get out of the car, Nadesan's foot got tangled up with the two wires. He reached down to free himself, wrenching at the wires to free his foot. He stumbled out of the vehicle almost falling on the ground. The Police constable was only metres away, shouting at him to stop but he was finding it difficult to get through the crowded bazaar.

Nadesan darted into the crowd, pushing and shoving his way towards an alley he could see in front of him. Bellowing threats, insults and curses, Nadesan forced his way through the choking mass of people. Men and women scattered before him, when they didn't, they were knocked aside, some even falling to the ground, unbalanced by his headlong flight. Home going commuters thinking he was a pick-pocket, shouted and screamed, grabbing at him as he ran past but his forward momentum, fuelled by a panic not to be caught, propelled him into the crowded alley.

CHAPTER TWO

Amanthi had been on duty all day and was looking forward to going home. Her time as a resident at the Colombo General Hospital had come to an end and she was waiting to be assigned to a hospital somewhere in the country. She was completing a surgical residency and had been at the hospital for almost five years. Amanthi had requested to stay where she was but was not promised anything. Hundreds of residents rotated through the General Hospital in any given year in one of many specialties.

The job Amanthi was doing at the burn unit was demanding and very difficult but it was one of the most satisfying places she had worked in the hospital. She had always been interested in looking after sick people ever since her beloved grandfather had been paralysed after a surviving a major stroke. He had been nursed at home until he died almost three years later. The period he was ill had been difficult for the entire family. They were lucky at the time to have secured the services of an experienced nurse who had worked at the Colombo General Hospital for most of his life. Thomis had retired when he found the burden of daily travel from his home town of Gampaha too taxing on his aging body. Amanthi's father, who had once been under the man's care, had offered him permanent employment to look after his paralysed father. Thomis had accepted only after he was allowed to stay at their home in Colombo.

Amanthi realized quite early as a teenager the importance of good care for the sick and elderly. Instead of going out with her friends she would spend time at her grandfather's bedside talking to him, enjoying a level of camaraderie that she had never experienced with him before. Thomis, perhaps sensing her innate ability to work with the sick, had taken her under his wing and taught her everything he had learned in over forty years of working as a primary carer.

The thought of becoming a doctor had never crossed Amanthi's mind until her father mentioned in passing, that she had all the qualities of becoming a good one. It made her think of how rewarding it was, making her grandfather's life a little bit easier and decided that she could see herself working in a hospital and doing it all her life. After much urging, Thomis finally relented one day and with her father's permission, took Amanthi into the General Hospital where he used to work. Amanthi met several carers that Thomis had worked with and spent the whole morning with them, helping them in the linen storage area folding sheets and rolling cloth bandages. What impressed Amanthi most was a sense of the high level of interest and commitment the nursing staff and doctors brought to their jobs.

As a resident Amanthi spent most of her waking hours at the hospital. She had long passed the stage when she did not know how to write orders or fumbled her way through complex procedures, and had become an experienced practitioner in her own right. She was the senior resident on duty that day. No new cases had come in and her time had been filled with examining patients and writing reports which was so much a part of the daily routine of the hospital.

Amanthi looked around the little office she used at the entrance of the ward. The cluttered room irritated her. Drab blue walls badly in need of a new coat of paint, grey government-issue furniture sitting on a grubby linoleum floor, it was all so depressing. She had begun to hate the days when all she had to do was sit around and do paperwork. Amanthi stared hard at the telephone on the desk wishing it would ring. She sighed, breathing in the familiar, sharp odours of the hospital.

The shrill ring of the phone made her flinch in surprise. She smiled at her reaction as she reached eagerly for the phone. It usually meant that she was needed somewhere. It was the charge nurse informing her that a badly burned patient was on the way in from emergency. The hospital burn unit got many transfers of patients who were brought into emergency or from smaller, less equipped hospitals that could not treat severe cases. The General Hospital she was in was a level 1 burn facility with operating rooms, trauma and reconstructive surgeons and specially trained critical care nurses. They normally knew over an hour in advance that a patient was going to come in, but in this case, the patient was from the emergency room in the same building, so Amanthi needed to hurry.

Amanthi picked up the phone and talked to the emergency room doctor who had admitted the patient. From him she learned that the patient was a 22-year old woman with severe second-degree burns to her upper body and one of her arms. The woman was in severe pain and had been prescribed a dose of morphine.

Amanthi felt relieved when she heard those words. Pain meant that the nerve endings were intact. The woman's life was not in danger, but she still needed to be careful. Burns took a few days to declare themselves – some were deeper than they looked, some required surgery. Emergency room and other medical personnel lacked experience and expertise in burns and often made mistakes in assessing the severity of the injury. She had seen patients brought in with large, superficial injuries which were assessed as severe, and small deep burns caused by high-voltage currents as being relatively minor.

Pain was usually a good thing. They could do a lot to manage pain. What bothered Amanthi more was that it was a woman. More than half of the burn victims she treated in the unit were women, many of them the result of domestic violence and self-immolation.

The odour of kerosene and burnt flesh was strong in the windowless room as Amanthi leaned over the distressed woman who moaned softly. Her burnt clothes had been removed and she lay naked from the waist up on a clean hospital sheet, dull from many washings.

Amanthi glanced at the nurse who attended the woman and saw it was Nelum, one of the more experienced nurses in the hospital. She was concentrating on inserting an intravenous catheter into the patient's arm.

'What treatment has she had so far?' Amanthi asked. Burn patients who were brought to the hospital were often treated by medics at the scene to help ease their suffering.

'She was washed in tap water before being brought in,' said Nelum, taping the catheter down firmly. 'Her body has cooled, and the registrar ordered her to be injected with morphine.' Nelum inserted an intravenous line into the catheter and adjusted the flow of saline into the patient.

All the nurses who worked at the Burns unit were specially trained and dedicated to their task. The work they did with the patients was dirty and messy but Amanthi had never heard anyone complain.

The woman's face showed signs of radiant burns but was relatively clear. Amanthi could see that her upper body and arm were severely burnt with burn depths of varying thickness.

Amanthi looked over her shoulder as another nurse hurried over with a bucket of sterilized water and saline immersed with strips of white cloth. Three quarters of severely burnt patients died from the consequences of a severe infection and Amanthi knew that getting the burnt epidermis clean was the main priority.

'How's her back?' If the burns were caused by an accident, the wounds would be localized to the area exposed to the flame. If the burns were self-inflicted, the consequences would be much greater over all her body.

'It's clear,' said Nelum, glancing at Amanthi. Many of the women who came into the burn unit caused their own injuries through self-immolation due to marital problems, stress or helplessness through loneliness and poverty. Although the centuries-old tradition had been banned by the British during colonial rule, some elements of Buddhism and Hinduism tolerated the use of fire to cleanse the soul and it was often used as a form of protest and of martyrdom.

Amanthi nodded as she snapped on a pair of surgical gloves. The next few hours of treatment were critical to the woman's survival and she needed to open the blisters and remove any burnt and loose tissue she could find.

The rattle of instruments in their pans a heartbeat before the building shook took Amanthi by surprise. Through the open door of the treatment room, the rumbling sound of a distant explosion reverberated through the hospital corridors.

That's a big explosion, Amanthi thought, and not too far away. She instinctively looked at the clock on the wall which had slewed sideways for the vibration. It was just after five o'clock. They would have about fifteen or twenty minutes before any victims would be brought to the hospital.

Voices raised in anxiety and fear echoed around the ward. Amanthi closed her eyes briefly, steeling herself for what was to come. She had never forgotten the victims from the communal riots more than a year ago, the feeling of helplessness when the victims flooded in. The staff had been unprepared; nothing in their training had equipped them for the horror and despair they faced when people were burned for being a different race. The hospital had run out of supplies in a few hours and lives were lost that day. She knew that procedures had been put in place after that day and supplies stockpiled for an emergency ... but will it be enough?

Amanthi turned back to the woman on the gurney and began her examination. She knew that she would be needed elsewhere very shortly.

CHAPTER THREE

The long, crowded platforms of the Fort Railway station stretched on either side of Nadesan as he slipped past the ticket collector at the entrance. Built by the British on land reclaimed from the nearby lake, the station was an example of colonial architecture and the main rail gateway to Colombo. Nadesan felt safe amongst the crowd, just one of thousands of commuters going home after work.

Just a short time before, Nadesan had been desperate to get away from the two policemen who were chasing him. He had almost reached the end of the alley when the car bomb exploded.

Nadesan felt the ground heave and was blown off his feet, head first into the dusty pavement. Pungent dirt coated his tongue and he found it difficult to breathe. He tilted his head and spat, then spat again. He felt like he had been run over by a car. Nadesan raised himself to a sitting position rubbing the side of his face, staring wide-eyed over his shoulder in shock and disbelief. He felt detached, a silent witness, like he was watching a silent movie.

A smoky haze covered the devastation the bomb had caused. Pandemonium reigned as stunned pedestrians ran screaming away from the area of the blast, some looking over their shoulders in panic, crashing into each other and adding to the chaos. Others climbed to their feet, dusting themselves and looking in bewilderment down the alley towards the blackened bus terminus which had a large chunk taken out of it. Commuters caught in the blast and parts of the building lay scattered on the ground. A yellow and black taxi blown onto its side had flames pouring out from its undercarriage.

For a brief moment Nadesan felt some remorse at the carnage he had caused. He shook his head to clear the high-pitched ringing noise in his ears. For many years, he had been happily married and content with the life he had. But it had all changed, and his life had taken a different path. He knew that the decision to leave the car and run away would change everything, but he did not yet know what it was going to be like. It was important to concentrate on the task he faced here and now. The original plan was for him to set off the bomb and escape. But he'd never wanted to do that. No one knew that he was planning to blow himself up. Nadesan wanted the people in the big city to understand what it was like where he lived. What it felt like for them to be looking over their shoulders every time they stepped out. He wanted them to be afraid.

The attention of the crowd had shifted away from him. Nadesan managed to move despite a sharp shooting pain down the side of his leg. He didn't want to wait for someone to remember that he was running away from where the bomb exploded. He pushed himself to his feet and stumbled down a cross street, trying not to draw attention to himself. His shirt and sarong had dark streaks down his left side when he was blown off his feet. Twice he bumped into men who hurried towards him, fearful that they had missed the excitement and that there was nothing remaining to see. Storekeepers stood outside their shops pointing towards the mushroom cloud of white smoke rising in the air from the massive blast. Nadesan had learned from the bomb maker that white smoke meant that the bomb had detonated so powerfully and quickly that it had sucked the oxygen out of the air, leaving the plume of white smoke.

Turning a corner, he found himself on a large main road opposite a railway station. The traffic had come to an abrupt stop and was not moving. His hearing was coming back slowly and he could faintly hear the sound of car horns and three-wheelers tooting their horns

Looking around to see whether he was being followed, Nadesan hobbled slowly with his head down trying not to catch anyone's eyes. The pain in his leg was manageable as he limped across the busy thoroughfare and joined the crowd streaming towards the station. Women dressed in simple cotton saris and others in skirts and blouses, mixed with men in white shirts and dark trousers who darted across the road into the railway station anxious to catch their trains home. They kept looking worriedly over their shoulders at the clouds of smoke billowing from the central bus station, just to the west of the railway station.

Nadesan slipped in with the crowd who were anxious to get away. His hearing was almost back to normal and the sound of sirens echoed through the open terminus. A huge column of black smoke from burning vehicles and buildings could be seen drifting skywards through gaps in the ceiling. Office workers milled ceaselessly around the platforms, talking excitedly, pointing at the dark smoke that filled the sky.

'Puttalam Intercity approaching platform A. Stopping all stations.'

Nadesan almost missed the announcement over the hubbub of the station. The amplified voice came from cone-shaped speakers mounted on the steel vaulted ceilings fashioned after a mainline railway station in England. The announcement seemed to galvanize the crowds who rushed at the arriving train using footbridges linking the platforms together. Even before the train came to a halt, they hurled themselves into the trains open doors, rushing to grab empty seats.

Not wanting to get trapped in the middle of the train, Nadesan waited until most of the passengers had climbed on board before stepping onto the carriage and grabbing the brass handrail by the entrance. A whistle blew loudly, and the train lurched forward slowly, gathering momentum as it pulled out of the station.

The smell and heat of the bodies around Nadesan made him feel uneasy. But when he looked around, no one was paying any attention to him. As the train cleared the station building, the large plume of smoke from the central bus terminus became clearly visible.

From where he stood at the carriage entrance, Nadesan could look over the paling fence into the chaos caused by the bomb. The terminus building had been cut in half with piles of debris where the front of the building once stood. The Bank of Ceylon building next to the bus station, its shattered windows looking dark and deserted, had several fires burning out of control. Mangled bodies lay on the ground, many charred and naked, their clothes burnt or ripped away by the explosives. Commuters, their clothing scorched and covered with blood, staggered away from the twisted pile of cars and three-wheelers. A vehicle, almost indistinguishable in the smoky haze, had flames shooting out of all its windows.

Gasps of shock and horror followed by cries of rage filled the carriage as the train accelerated round the bend leaving the horrific scene behind. A woman next to Nadesan sobbed uncontrollably, wiping her face with the corner of her sari.

Nadesan observed the carnage coldly, not feeling any emotion. His masters would be pleased at what he had accomplished but Nadesan knew he had failed at what he had wanted to do. He had been impatient, and he had been a coward. He remembered the locket around his neck. *Should I end it now?* He caressed the piece of jewellery with the tips of his fingers. *No! I will be given another chance.*

The train started to slow down as it approached the next station. The Maradana station was a large railway junction and terminus built by the British for long haul trains. The train screeched slowly to a halt at a dingy platform crowded with people waiting to get on. Nadesan was the only one who stepped off the train. A queue had formed at the exit where an elderly man wearing a khaki railway uniform was collecting tickets. Nadesan suddenly realized that he didn't have one. Neither did he have the money to buy a ticket. He looked around anxiously as he walked over and leaned against the railway station wall a few paces away from the exit. He needed to get out of the station and back to the safe house before dark. He fully expected a curfew to be declared that night.

The wail of sirens outside the station was almost unceasing as emergency vehicles drove past on the road outside. The air was thick with pollution and humidity, the setting sun already beginning to create long shadows across the platforms. An announcement notifying commuters of major delays on all trains from the Fort railway station crackled over the public-address system. Angry commuters on their way home crowded around the station master's office next to the entrance demanding an explanation. The commotion caused by the restless crowd presented Nadesan with an opportunity. He could slip out of the railway entrance without being noticed by the guard.

Edging out of the building, Nadesan warily prepared to cross the road in front of the railway station clogged with rush hour traffic. Over the roar of motor bikes, three-wheelers, taxis, cars and trucks, loudspeakers mounted outside a run-down cinema blared music, inviting customers in. Emergency vehicles, their lights flashing, and sirens wailing were still trying to get through the growing chaos caused by the explosion.

Every time a police car or military vehicle passed, Nadesan's pulse raced, his palms sweated and a terrifying image of being tortured in prison flashed through his mind. He imagined being plucked off the street and plunged into darkness. Nadesan tried to look as innocent as possible, glancing left and right before walking across. He nonchalantly slipped through the crowd that swept and surged past him, turning north towards the river. The pavement was a frenzy of activity as he walked down a long sprawl of motor spares shops, garages and industrial outlets for many large businesses beginning to close for the night. Sleazy hotels, gaudy restaurants and cheap eating houses competed in the warren of narrow side streets leading off the main road.

After walking steadily for half an hour Nadesan noticed with some trepidation that he was in a poorer section of the city. The businesses and houses were in a general state of neglect and decay. He had never been to this area before. Street vendors, some squatting on the pavement, peddled small parcels of food wrapped in newspaper, slices of over ripe fruit, packets of sweets and biscuits, cigarettes, condoms and soap, their loud voices entreating the home going crowd to spend a few rupees. A crippled beggar leaning on his crutches called out loudly for Nadesan to spare him some alms but Nadesan hurried past, not making eye contact. He had to get to Pettah before it was too late to be out on the streets.

The city was disguising itself in the gathering gloom when Nadesan got to a junction he recognised. There was an old and twisted tree growing in the middle of the junction, it's scraggly leaves struggling to breathe in the gasoline polluted air. Nadesan knew he was not far from the safe house and hurried across to the other side. He was perspiring heavily when he finally turned down the street towards the market which was closed for the night. As he approached the safe house, a shadow detached itself from the gloomy interior. It was Deva. He grabbed Nadesan's arm and pulled him into a backroom in the rear of the garage.

CHAPTER FOUR

Amanthi kept moving because she knew she would fall asleep on her feet if she stopped for even a minute. Her stomach was not right by eating the oily food in the hospital cafeteria, but she was still functioning after three days. She couldn't think straight - her mind in a fog through which she had to search for answers. Simple actions she had completed countless number of times took on the weight of complicated procedures.

Finally, some order was being restored to the unit after days of chaos. Doctors and nurses walked rather than ran, talked rather than shouted. No screams, no pools of blood, no mangled and discarded body parts heaped in a pile in the corner.

Amanthi would never forget the first twenty-four hours after the explosion at the bus station. The smell of burnt flesh and smoke was almost overwhelming, the floor of the emergency and burn unit ankle deep in torn paper dressing packets and cellophane wrappers. Victims arrived in ambulances, cars, three-wheelers and even in buses. Each new patient seemed worse than the last. Eventually the triage and resuscitation areas were completely choked. No one knew for certain how many more patients would be coming in. It had taken many hours to separate the living from the dead. It had been a daunting task and Amanthi was not sure whether any mistakes had been made.

Outside in the reception area, the telephones continued to ring incessantly with calls from worried friends and relatives wanting to know about their missing loved ones. The staff couldn't keep up and the phones continued to ring, the constant, repetitive sound an annoying backdrop to the customary stillness in the emergency treatment rooms as they went about their business of saving lives.

According to the latest figures, the number of victims from the bombing exceeded three hundred. Over one hundred were dead, their bodies stacked one on top of each other on the veranda next to the ambulance bay. Most of the wounded were brought to the General Hospital before any treatment could begin. The victims had to be assessed, as the type and severity of the injuries sustained when the bomb went off was a complex mix of wounds, burns and blast injuries. Many of the victims who were closest to the explosive device had either died from the trauma or were carrying all three types of injuries which made treatment very complicated.

The temperature in the hospital had risen to uncomfortable levels with the air-conditioning unable to cope. Huge floor fans chased the fetid air from room to room adding to the discomfort of the patients and staff. Amanthi tailed Dr Perera, the head of the burn unit as she made the rounds, examining all the burn patients spread out across the teaching hospital.

Dr Perera was the reason Amanthi wanted to work in the burn unit. The woman was a pioneer in reconstructive surgery and it was entirely through her efforts that the Burn unit at the General Hospital had been created by a generous grant from overseas. Amanthi never forgot the lecture she attended as a young intern just out of medical school. She could still remember clearly what the doctor had said of her work.

"I respect the ability of scars to do harm. If you don't, you cannot work in this place. You can never treat burns unless you are sufficiently terrified by its propensity to kill but even worse, to scar and cripple you."

There was an intensity to the doctor that Amanthi had never seen before and it was because of her that she had specialized in the field of plastic surgery. They stopped by a patient out in the corridor, his face and upper body concealed by white bandages tinged with red. Amanthi had treated this patient when he was first brought in after the explosion. He was unconscious at the time, his face and upper body had the cherry red glow of medium burns and he was gasping for breath. Amanthi had used a scope to peer down his throat and saw that the soot blackened airway had begun to swell. She had inserted a plastic tube into the man's mouth and down his windpipe to a level below his Adam's apple. The half-inch tube would prevent further swelling from closing his throat entirely and suffocating him. Nelum had inserted an IV line into the man's left elbow. The salt water flowing into his veins was all that stood between him and fatal burn shock.

The medics who had brought him had done a preliminary survey when they brought the man in and their negative finding was accurate. Amanthi had not found any wounds or trauma to complicate the burn injury, though the burns were more than enough to kill him.

They had been able to save him, but he was not out of danger. Infection was the biggest concern and his bandages were changed every twelve hours, the wounds examined carefully for any signs of sepsis. His vital signs, how well his lungs, heart, kidneys and circulatory system were functioning would have to be monitored closely. Plastic catheters were inserted in the femoral arteries near his groin to measure blood pressure, blood gases and blood chemistry. It was important that they knew how much deadly carbon monoxide was circulating in the patient's blood.

Dr Perera motioned to Amanthi to conduct the examination. A petite woman, she had a commanding presence and ruled the unit with ruthless skill and compassion. As the head doctor, she was neat and precise in everything she did, always dressed for action, not appearance, and today was no different. Sweaty in her green scrubs, her face mask hanging around her neck, her hospital greens were badly creased and crumpled by constant use.

The nurse attending to the patient was not from the hospital. One of the many trained volunteers who appeared after the bomb blast, she had been assigned to assist the burn team, and like everyone else, was doing her best. She removed the layers of ointment smeared bandages that swathed the man's body, exposing the burnt skin which gleamed under a thick coating of gel.

Amanthi was tall and inspected the burnt area closely, bending over the patient, using all her senses to assess his condition. He was drifting in and out of consciousness and seemed agitated. She was pleased not to find any signs of infection and reached for the chart to study the record of his vital signs. She was checking his pulse when the young man grabbed her hand.

Amanthi didn't have the heart to remove it. She glanced up at Dr Perera who was watching her closely. 'The patient shows no sign of infection,' Amanthi said, looking down at him. 'But his pulse rate is high and he is showing signs of stress. I treated him when he was brought in and I will remain here until his wounds are dressed.'

Dr Perera nodded at Amanthi before moving away. Amanthi sighed, wondering what the doctor was thinking. Amanthi remembered one of her lectures when the doctor had said, *"my patients many years later would think of me as a friend, but in the acute stage and during rehabilitation I am a terror"*.

Amanthi waited until the nurse completed the messy procedure of re-bandaging the patient. She turned as she felt someone tugging at her arm. The man was dressed in a doctor's coat but it was someone she did not know.

'Doctor Perera wants to talk to you,' he said, gesturing to the corridor.

Amanthi had to focus to understand what he was saying. Amanthi wound her way through the hospital corridor filled with patient beds and medical equipment. Patients with small or medium burns were all evacuated to other hospitals in the area. Patients with more extensive burns with full-thickness skin loss had been assessed, and given that they were working with limited burn care resources, everything was focused on the patients where the most benefit would be realized. Amanthi passed the entrance to the reception area and was shocked by the size of the crowd. A collection of worried, tear-streaked faces stared back at her, unspoken questions clearly etched on their upturned expressions.

Dr Perera waved Amanthi into the office when she saw her standing by the door. She pointed at the chair opposite her desk. 'Sit, sit,' she said, tiredly. 'I wanted to talk to you.' They had both been working with little rest since the explosion and nothing seemed more important than getting some sleep.

Amanthi slumped into the chair completely exhausted. The adrenaline had drained out of her, leaving her feeling like a hollow shell. All she wanted was a shower and to sleep. She wondered what Dr Perera had to say that was so important.

'I have been watching you these last few days,' Dr Perera said. 'You have been doing some very good work.'

Amanthi nodded at the doctor tiredly, acknowledging her praise. As an intern and then as a resident, she had steeled herself. She had hardened herself against the endless hours on duty, against the intolerable and yet endurable lack of sleep. She knew she had given everything she had and was glad that it had been noticed.

'I know you have applied to remain in the Burn unit but we don't have a vacancy for you.' The words did not make sense to Amanthi right away. Then she realized what Dr Perera had said. Amanthi felt a sense of disappointment but she was so exhausted it did not seem to matter.

Dr Perera had not finished. 'We have been given funding to set up an emergency burn team that will go anywhere they are needed', Dr Perera said. 'You will be perfect for that role.' Amanthi looked at the doctor in surprise. Was she dreaming? She had just heard Dr Perera say that there was no vacancy.

Dr Perera smiled at Amanthi's obvious confusion. 'Yes, it's true but it's not the time to discuss it now,' she said, looking at her watch. 'I wanted you to be aware of what we are planning. You will remain with us until the new team is set up. I have worked out a roster and you are off for the next eight hours,' Dr Perera said, rubbing her eyes. 'I want you to go home now and get some sleep.'

CHAPTER FIVE

The rusty, iron-studded gate of the Welikada Magazine prison yard creaked opened slowly. Throughout the year, this side gate remained closed, padlocked and forgotten by everyone within the prison. The light in the short tunnel through the thick, stone prison wall was bare fluorescence, harsh on the eyes.

Tilak could see patches of overgrown grass through the open steel gate. He did not understand why he was there. Two guards had appeared suddenly outside his cell around midnight, banging on the door and ordering him to dress in a shirt and sarong which they threw at him. What's happening? he thought to himself. What was he being singled out like this for?

The day had been no different from any other. The prisoners had been given time in the central courtyard and Tilak did what he always did, walking around the rectangular space fifty times to keep himself fit.

Built by the British as a gunpowder magazine to supply their navy, the large, sturdy structure had been extended over the years by the addition of other buildings and used as a maximum-security prison since the turn of the century. Prisoners roamed about the large, enclosed yard smoking, reading newspapers or kicking a football. Others played cards, huddled in small groups using cigarettes as money. Handmade *beedis* were for smoking but cigarettes were the currency of the prison system. It would buy you anything from a clean cell, food from nearby restaurants and a family visit, to young boys and loose women who sold their bodies every night to the highest bidder. Corrupt prison guards would let them into the prison, singly or in pairs, taking a percentage for themselves, paid in cigarettes or in special favours.

Tilak had been in prison for over five years, convicted for manslaughter. He had watched and learned during the first year of his imprisonment how the prison operated, the men who controlled its daily rhythms, its faults and weaknesses. In those early days, he had been grateful to his family who had disowned him publicly but continued to keep him supplied with money and contraband which made his life in prison much easier. Most of the guards were open to bribery of some kind, allowing deliveries of food and drink to those who could afford it—during the day. But nothing passed through the gate at night.

Over time, it became known in the prison that Tilak had access to money and one of the night-time guards known as the Fixer had approached him with a business deal. If Tilak could arrange a regular supply of cigarettes to be delivered to the gate every week at night time, he would for a price, allow the packets to be smuggled into the prison.

At first it had been only a single pack, dropped off by the side gate which the guard picked up and brought to Tilak's cell. Over the years it had grown to several cartons a week and Tilak's power within the prison grew as a result. On more than one occasion he had been confronted by those who wanted to control the supply but Tilak had managed to fight them all off with the help of the prison guard.

Tilak had changed as a person during that time. He had transformed from a forgotten, pampered, eldest son in a privileged family, to a hard, ruthless man to whom violence was essential for survival. His first real challenge came one day in the dining room when he was standing in line to pick up his food.

Tilak had realized something was about to happen when he noticed the mood in the room had changed. The normal buzz of conversation quietened to almost a whisper and everyone was looking towards the line of men waiting to be served. Not realizing that he was the centre of their attention, Tilak picked up his tray of food and was walking to a table to eat when his way was blocked. Tilak looked up from the tray he was carrying and saw that it was Kuruppu. The man was a thug from the slums north of the Colombo dockyard, who was used to getting what he wanted. He was in jail for the horrific beating of a man whom he had maimed for life and he had begun to assert control within the prison. Kuruppu who had been in prison before, had lorded over the other prisoners since he'd arrived, bending them to his will by intimidation and random beatings. Tilak had wondered when it would be his turn.

'It's time you learned your place here,' Kuruppu snarled, smashing Tilak's plate away, spilling his food on the floor. Dark, cunning eyes set wide across a flattened bulbous nose enhanced the feral grin that plastered his face.

Tilak put up his hands placatingly. The man was bigger than he was and at least twenty kilos heavier. It would not be easy to fight him. During basic training and again at the Officer Training school, Tilak had to learn to defend himself against men who were trained to kill. But he knew that picking the right moment and place would be the difference. Tilak looked around the room to attract the attention of a prison guard but the spot where they usually stood was empty.

'Your bastard family is not here to protect you now,' Kuruppu growled menacingly. 'Any business with the outside must be done with my approval and protection and I have heard that you have such a business.'

It was not the first time Tilak had been challenged in the prison. During the early months of his imprisonment, many men had tried to take advantage of him. Some of them wanted him for sex, others who knew him to be an ex- army officer wanted to exact revenge for some past run-in with the security forces. Everyone resented that he came from a privileged family and the influence he was building with the guards.

'No,' Tilak breathed, shifting his weight to the balls of his feet. The man didn't intimidate him and if he wanted a fight, Tilak would not back down. Kuruppu tilted his head at an angle, his face locked in a fierce glare. 'No?' he thundered. 'Is that all you have to say, you gutless prick. I am not asking you, I am telling you.'

Tilak felt dozens of eyes on him as his guts knotted in anticipation of what he had to do. The challenge Kuruppu had thrown down in front of everyone was about respect and power. Tilak had no choice but to resort to violence and face the consequences that would follow.

His heart rate increased, everything seemed to come into sharp focus. Tilak scanned the room with his eyes. He needed to know whether Kuruppu was on his own. The man usually moved about with two short timers, Kalu and Banda, thugs like Kuruppu who were in prison for petty crimes and assault. Tilak didn't see the two men and realized that Kuruppu was confident he could handle him on his own.

Tilak dropped his arms loosely by his side. A jolt of adrenaline raced through his body. He cleared his mind, the muted sounds of men breathing in the room amplified by his growing concentration.

Kuruppu's eyes narrowed when he realized that Tilak was not backing down from his threats. Kuruppu looked around the room, thumping his chest with one hand.

'I am the only boss of this cell block,' he declared to the silent room. 'This piece of shit now belongs to me. I'll use him tonight and give him to you to do as you will.'

Some of Kuruppu's friends cheered loudly, banging their tin cups on the metal tables.

Kuruppu grinned and turned his head back to Tilak, spitting a thick wad of phlegm in his face. Tilak stared at the man, wiping the mucus from his face. Years of anger and resentment he had been suppressing broke through. The sudden rush of blood to his head made Tilak lose control. It was just like the time he had killed that woman insurgent. Everything slowed for Tilak as he sensed rather than saw Kuruppu take a roundhouse swing at him.

When he was being trained in the army, Tilak had been very good at close combat fighting. He knew what he must do. He stepped forward, fighting against his instinct of stepping back, trapping the man's arm under his armpit.

He pushed up with all his strength, dislocating the man's shoulder from his socket with an audible pop. Tilak continued his forward motion, head-butting Kuruppu on the bridge of his nose and smashing it open in a spray of red blood.

Using Kuruppu's arm as leverage, Tilak smashed his head onto the bridge of his nose, five, six, seven times, finally shoving him away. Kuruppu dropped to his knees, screaming in agony, clutching at his broken and bloody face with one hand. His dislocated hand hung limply by his side.

The room full of prisoners watched in disbelief as Tilak walked over to the man. He needed to finish Kuruppu off so brutally that the rest of the prisoners would remember what he was capable of.

Kuruppu looked up at Tilak with hate-filled eyes, as Tilak moved in close and delivered a powerful right-handed punch with all his power behind it. Tilak felt his knuckles crack as they smashed into Kuruppu's side, at the ninth and tenth ribs. A liver shot was shocking and debilitating, causing Kuruppu to lose his breath. It was also extremely painful. The fight was over for Kuruppu as he collapsed face down onto the floor. But Tilak was not finished. He threw himself at the man, gripping his head with both hands and smashed it into the concrete floor.

Tilak felt himself being grabbed and pulled away from Kuruppu who lay unconscious on the floor, a widening pool of blood forming under his head. Tilak screamed in anger trying to get back at Kuruppu when something smashed into his head from behind.

Tilak had woken up in solitary confinement, his head throbbing from the blow to the back of his head from a guard's baton. His body ached from where other batons had smashed into him. He shuddered, remembering what had happened. A feeling came over him that he'd gotten too close to the edge. It was not the first time. During his time in the army, it had been an effort for Tilak to try and seem normal around the platoon. He had learned to be impassive and to conceal emotion from a very young age when he had discovered his capacity for extreme violence. In prison, it had all changed. With not much sleep and very little food, he felt himself aching to release the demon in him. The day

Kuruppu had accosted him in the dining hall allowed him to show his true self. There was no more hiding in the shadows. Violence was something everyone understood; the prisoners, the guards, everyone. And he had earned their respect. It was never the same again for him. Kuruppu had been transferred to a different wing, his face disfigured by the beating Tilak had given him. The man had been released after serving his sentence, but there was a story making the rounds that he was pushing drugs into the prison from outside and had sworn to get even with Tilak.

Had Kuruppu managed to inveigle himself with his captors to get Tilak out of the prison to have him murdered? He wouldn't put it past the man. Drugs were becoming a major problem and a day wouldn't pass without a drug addict shaking violently with abdominal cramps and moaning all night. Tilak who smuggled cigarettes into the prison, already had a run in with him. The man who had been in Kuruppu's organisation, now controlled the supply of drugs into the prison and used prisoners he had recruited to muscle into the action.

Tilak felt a heady mix of fear and exhilaration that seemed to envelope him in moments of extreme danger. During the five years he'd laboured and languished in prison, he'd lived in a world of swift defensive violence but had tried to keep within the bounds of reason, not allowing the demon he had bottled inside of him to come out again. Where are they taking me at this time of the night? Prisoners were moved all the time but Tilak paid the guards regularly to keep his name off the transfer list.

A shadowy figure stepped into view beyond the gate and motioned him forward. Tilak glanced at the two guards who flanked him but did not move. Tilak had learned to be very cautious in prison. He had heard of prisoners who disappeared during the night never to be heard from again.

The guard on the right grabbed him by the arm and pushed him forward. The other walked behind him, crowding him and forcing him to step through the gate onto the path.

Tilak tensed when the man standing outside stepped forward. He was dressed in dark shirt and slacks and had the erect bearing of a military man.

'Don't be alarmed Lieutenant,' he said softly, speaking in Sinhalese. 'You are not going to be harmed. I am here to take you away from this place.'

Looking around, Tilak could see that the man was not alone. A Police car was parked by the roadway at the bottom of the path, the driver standing at ease next to the vehicle.

Tilak had been in prison for over five years for shooting the leader of a Marxist uprising in the south. He had been at Officer Training College when the bloody uprising took place. The army, who were short of regular officers, ordered him and another officer cadet to go south with an under-manned platoon of volunteer soldiers and clear a district capital of insurgents.

Tilak being the senior of the two officer cadets, was given command of the platoon. He had taken his orders to clean up the mess literally and shot the female insurgent leader in front of his men when she'd spat at him and insulted his family. The woman was the mistress of a powerful priest in the area who used his influence with the government to bring Tilak to trial. After a lengthy hearing Tilak was convicted of involuntary manslaughter and sentenced to ten years in prison.

'What's this about,' Tilak questioned the man. 'Where are you taking me?'

The man shook his head glancing at the two guards who were standing behind Tilak. 'You'll find out soon enough,' he said. He moved towards the guards and handed them a thick envelope. One of the guards looked into the envelope and nodded at the man, who turned and came back to where Tilak was standing.

'Come with me,' he said, walking down the path towards the parked car.

Tilak looked over his shoulder at the prison gate closing slowly behind him.

Tilak felt his energy level rise. He couldn't help but feel a sense of relief walking away from the jail. It was a whore of a place. Intolerable heat and stench, devoid of choice and privacy, embraced in a world of violence, homosexuality, thieving, deprivation, inedible food, boredom and the company of hopeless men and women who would sell their souls for anything.

The roads around the prison were clear of any traffic, the road sweepers busily cleaning up debris scattered across the pavement from the previous day. A couple of men dressed in cotton shirts and sarongs were dozing in their three-wheelers outside the main prison gate hoping to pick up one of the guards completing his night shift.

Tilak had not been outside the prison for over five years. Other than glimpses through the prison gates, his entire world was made up of thick grey walls of dressed stone, heavy wooden doors and metal bars. The car accelerated away from the prison along Baseline Road before turning west towards the Fort. Armed soldiers patrolled every major junction, but the car was not stopped even once as they drove through Maradana, past the imposing Lake House building into the heart of the city.

The car turned into the Police Headquarters complex next to the British-built harbour passenger terminal, the guards waving the car through without stopping it. Tilak was taken to the fourth-floor where he was ushered into a spacious office. Sitting behind a large desk, dominating the room, was the heavily built figure of a Superintendent of Police.

'Thank you for coming at such short notice,' he said, a small humourless smile barely softening his face. 'You will find that your time will not be wasted.' Tilak looked at the man. Who is this arsehole? He must know that I didn't have a choice. What's this about? The officer motioned Tilak to a comfortable looking chair opposite his desk. The man who brought him stood by the door behind him.

'You must be wondering why you are here,' he said, his half-hooded eyes considering Tilak like a cobra would look at a mouse. 'I have read your file and have also spoken to the warden about you. I know what you have been up to in prison. I must say that I am quite impressed.'

Tilak studied the Police officer silently. Hatred and loathing bit deep into him for the men who had put him in those sweating cells, the guards who had spat in his face. Over the years he had risen to a position of power within the prison, but it hadn't come without a struggle. He had the scars to show for it but the men who took orders from him now controlled most of the illegal trade of cigarettes and liquor in the prison.

'The war has been brought to Colombo and people are scared to go out on the streets,' the officer said, looking grimly out of the window. 'We have been ordered to take whatever steps are necessary to stop the bombings.'

Tilak had read about the bombing at the central bus station. Newspaper headlines for the past few days screamed their outrage and graphic pictures were plastered across the entire front and back pages. One picture showed a bewildered and blood-soaked survivor being helped away from the carnage. The victim's shirt hung in shreds, one end of a bloodied bandage wrapped around his head dangled down his shoulder. There were photos of burnt cars and photos of the dead. Bodies lying in the street.

'You heard about the bus station bombing I am sure ... it was unbelievable.' The officer shook his head in disbelief. 'They used a vehicle, a car, to carry the bomb.'

Tilak nodded, the bombing had shocked him too. He didn't understand where the conversation was heading, so he remained silent.

'I have been ordered to form a special squad and I want you to head it,' the officer said, crossing his arms and looking at Tilak expectantly.

Tilak sat back in the chair and looked at the Superintendent carefully. He had learned never to take anything at face value.

'What kind of a special squad?'

The Police officer crossed his arms. 'We have created the Special Task Force to fight the Tigers on their own terms. They are primarily used as a counter terrorist force but they too operate under certain constraints. We want to create a special squad within this organisation who will take orders directly from me.'

'And what sort of orders will that be,' Tilak asked the officer.

The officer steepled his hands in front of his face. 'If I must tell you exactly what your orders will be, you are not the type of person I am looking for.'

You're not going to get away with that, Tilak thought to himself. I am not getting into this without knowing exactly what you want. Tilak raised an eyebrow questioningly and stared at the officer.

The Superintendent sighed and shrugged his shoulders. 'As policemen, we are hampered by the rules and what we can do,' he said, disapprovingly. 'The Tigers take advantage of this and we have lost many good men. We want this squad to work outside the rule of law.'

Tilak studied the man carefully. They want to create a hit squad! Am I reading this right?

'You mean murder them?' It was all a bit too much for Tilak. Less than an hour ago he had been asleep in his cot in the prison and now this overbearing policeman was asking him, no, telling him to head a sanctioned death squad in a paramilitary organisation.

The officer glared at Tilak. 'I think it's sickening what they did at the bus station. Worse than murder, it's bloody inhuman. We should round up the lot of them and shoot them right on the spot.'

Tilak returned the angry stare for a moment. 'Why me?' Tilak questioned. 'There must be others who are capable of doing such things.'

The officer shook his head. 'We don't think so. Not with the combination of skills and experience you have. You are a trained army officer who knows how to take orders. You have shown what you are capable of by quelling the insurgency in Kataragama and then again, your recent activities in prison. You have become an extremely dangerous man. We have a need for someone just like you.'

Tilak slumped in his chair, thoughts tumbling through his mind. It's either go back to that stinking prison or do what the man wants.

After almost six years in prison, Tilak was more than ready to get out. He had often thought about escaping but knew that he would not last long on the run. The only reason he was still alive was because he was bribing the warden to keep him in Colombo. He wouldn't last long if he were transferred to Boossa prison in the south where long-term prisoners were sent. Many insurgents captured during the uprising were being held there and they would show no mercy to someone who killed one of their leaders.

'If I agree to this, how will it be done?' he asked finally, looking across the desk at the Police officer.

The officer nodded his head, reaching for a file which he waved at Tilak. 'The rest of your sentence will be commuted by the President and you will be officially released from prison. First, you will be briefed on what's happening in the north. Names, histories, political and police records. I want you to have a full picture of the leadership within the militant organisations and what we have learned about them.'

Tilak nodded. He had heard a lot about the different Tamil organisations as the prison grapevine was notoriously efficient, but the kind of information the Police officer was offering would not be found in the local newspapers.

'You will be sent to Kalutara for special forces training and then assigned to the east coast. We need you to operate out of Batticaloa for a while. That's where we think these men are being trained.'

Tilak thought about what the officer said. They could hang me out to dry if something goes wrong, but I am not going to worry about that right now.

Tilak nodded his acceptance. *At least I don't have to go back inside.*

CHAPTER SIX

For a moment, Nadesan didn't know where he was. He was sweating, as he always did after a night of bad dreams. Each a vivid snapshot of the carnage at the bus station, interspersed with the faces of his dead wife and child. Each image quickly replaced by another before he could grasp it. Nadesan snapped awake, sick with misery because he knew the dreams reflected his soul. He couldn't hide from them. What he had done at the bus station was unforgivable. He'd panicked! It had all happened so quickly. The policeman ... the crowd trying to stop him ... the explosion ... the mutilated bodies. Every muscle in his body felt numb, frozen in the grip of horror at his memories.

Until six months ago, he had just been a mechanic working in a garage on the opposite side of the country. It seemed like an age since the conflict between the Sinhalese and the Tamils had started.

Nadesan was the son of a mechanical engineer who ran a small metal-working shop on the Trincomalee Road in Kokkuvil, a suburb of Batticaloa, on the eastern coast of the island. His father, Kumaran, was a large man with a hard work ethic. Nadesan's mother, Lakshmi, was the exact opposite of his father. She was talkative and full of life, often chiding her husband for not having a sense of humour. Her family came from Trincomalee where her father owned three fishing boats. Her marriage to Kumaran was arranged and she had moved to Chenkaladi to live with her in-laws. Nadesan had a younger sister who never strayed far from his mother's side. Due to the five-year age difference between them, he was never close to his sister.

When Nadesan was young, he was fascinated by the mechanical lathe that his father had installed in his workshop. Nadesan's father was always busy. He had borrowed money from the People's Bank to buy a more expensive model which could machine both metric and imperial unit parts. His was the only machine shop in Kokkuvil which had the ability to produce parts in both standards and he always had customers.

From a very young age, Nadesan hung around the shop after school, watching his father work on the machine. When he got older, his father gave him odd jobs to do around the shop. Nadesan found that he enjoyed working with his hands, putting together vehicle engines like giant jigsaw puzzles after his father machined a bearing or a screw that needed replacement. After Nadesan left school, he started working full-time in his father's shop. He learned how to dismantle an engine and break it down to its different components. His father machined the parts that needed replacement and Nadesan put the engines back together again. His father sent him to a technical school in Batticaloa where he became a fully-qualified auto technician. Working with his father who concentrated on machining parts, the little business flourished.

Nadesan's father although quiet at home, often commented about the inequality the Tamil people suffered at the hands of the Sinhalese when they were together in the workshop. He'd always have the shortwave radio on, chiding Nadesan to stop what he was doing when the news was on.

'I was brought up during the colonial period', he often used to say, 'Many of us were educated in English-speaking mission schools and we did well under the British. But we are being excluded from government positions as English was no longer an advantage after Sinhalese became the official language.

Nadesan had known for a while that his father's family had not been one of the privileged class. Many Hindu Tamils reacting against the anglicization of their culture had established their own schools, temples and societies. Increasingly, Tamils like Nadesan's family had thought of themselves as a separate and distinct community.

One day after a broadcast of a debate from the parliament as to whether the Sinhalese, who considered themselves as the original people on the island, would share parliamentary representation with the other minorities on the island, Nadesan's father threw down his gloves in anger.

'This is worse than I thought,' he said unhappily, dabbing his face with a cloth he carried on his shoulder. 'We've had to put up with the Sinhalese moving into our lands and now they don't want us in the government either.'

Nadesan had always kept quiet when his father started talking politics. But he had begun to feel troubled when his father had started to complain how he had begun to lose his Sinhalese customers and even the arrangement he had with the Sri Lankan Transport Board had recently come under review. Only the lack of a Sinhalese- owned, metal workshop in the area prevented the Transport Board from cancelling his contract.

Despite his previous reluctance to understand what was happening in his community, Nadesan started to pay attention to what his father was saying. The two of them would often take their lunch break listening to the Tamil news broadcasts coming out of India.

Nadesan also started to pay more attention when at least once a week, usually on a Friday, close friends of his father visited him in the evening after the shop was closed. They sat around in a group, drinking arrack from a bottle his father produced from a cupboard at the back, discussing what was going on in the country. His father always sat on the floor, his back against the lathe, listening to what was being said.

One of his father's friends was a teacher who often read out long articles he'd collected in magazines and documents. They learnt that with the support of a large Tamil diaspora in India and the west, a militant separatism based on the ancient South Indian Chola empire had been developed by Tamil intellects which had led to the rise of a number of radical Tamil groups.

After one such reading, the idea of self-government was discussed by the group. The teacher argued that it was important to win this right through the political process. But others in the group brushed away the argument and talked about the necessity of an armed struggle.

Acts of violence between the various Tamil groups, fighting against each other to gain control, seemed to intensify. The news was full of reported bank robberies, assassinations, strikes and acts of sabotage against government installations. Various Tamil groups killed each other as ferociously as they targeted Sinhalese police and army personnel.

Rumours began to filter through that the Indian government was sympathetic to the Sri Lankan Tamils plight and were training militants in dozens of hidden camps located in India. It was whispered that large quantities of money were being collected internationally and were helping to fund the purchase of weapons and ammunition which was gradually being moved by boat into Sri Lanka.

He remembered that his father did not say much during these gatherings, content to let his friends talk about what was going on. But that all changed one day when a deadly ambush of an army patrol in the Jaffna peninsula by a group called the Tamil Tigers killed thirteen Sinhalese soldiers. Angry mobs of Sinhalese roamed the streets of Colombo and other large towns across the island, dragging Tamils from their homes and businesses and beating them to death.

The news was full of the movement of large numbers of Tamils from the south who were fleeing by road and by boat. Many of them went back to their homes in the north of the island while others were shipped in boats sent from India. Tension arose as the flight of so many refugees stirred up the Tamil Nadu government who started to call for Indian intervention.

'This is not good for us,' Nadesan's father said glumly, listening to a Tamil radio broadcast from India. 'We're not united as a community and although we are fortunate to be living in the east, these riots are going to make things very difficult for everyone.'

His father's words were prophetic as open warfare broke out between the Tamil militant groups. Massacres and revenge killings escalated while increased brutishness, kidnappings and torture became routine events. Fanatics from one group seized supporters from another group, many of those abducted dying or vanishing, their bodies never to be found. The Tamil Tigers quickly rose to prominence. They were disciplined under a single leader, well-motivated and determined to protect not just their ancestral homeland in the north but also their families. The largely ceremonial Sri Lankan army were ill-equipped to counter the confident young Tamils who were trained by the vastly superior Indian army.

Tamil businesses were targeted by the Sinhalese majority and the once profitable businesses suffered. Nadesan's father was unable to keep up his monthly payments and it was only a matter of time that the lathe would be seized to pay the outstanding amount owed to the bank. His father started to drink and worked even harder, taking on small jobs that he would not have had time to do before. He often slept in the shop without coming home when he had too much to drink.

Nadesan tried hard to help in any way he could. He could see the toll it was taking on his mother and worried for her health. Late one evening when they were working on the hitch of a single axle, two-wheel tractor, a man dressed in dark shirt and trousers, carrying a rife over his shoulder walked out of the darkness into the machine shop. His eyes were hard as he looked at them. Nadesan noticed that a thin black moustache almost blended with his dark upper lip. He introduced himself as the leader of a militant Tamil cell in the area and offered to pay the debt owing on the lathe if Nadesan's father agreed to do some work for them.

Desperate times demanded desperate measures and Nadesan's father agreed to the militant leader's demand. The banks debt was paid and the valuable lathe became the property of the militants who used Nadesan's father's knowledge to machine parts for their guns, and to manufacture gun barrels out of steel rods. Business improved for a while and this was the time that Nadesan met Radika.

That was over five years ago but the war continued. Twenty kilometres from where he lived, the port of Trincomalee had become an armed camp, crammed with troops and equipment. The government's grip on the predominantly Tamil north and east had tightened with the police and army arresting those suspected of siding with the militants. People were scared but had adapted to the situation.

Nadesan and his family had adjusted to the conditions and lived a comfortable life. But his life turned upside down when a group of soldiers who had been shot at from a passing vehicle indiscriminately fired into a group of civilians standing at the bus station, killing his young family.

The horror of losing his young wife and son had changed Nadesan. His life was never the same again. They had been there for each other for as long as he could remember and now she was gone forever. Every thought ended with an image of his wife or his son, every dream ending with their torn and broken bodies. He hardly slept and avoided his friends, hiding in his home until they too stopped coming around, driven away by his feverish eyes and his wasted face.

One day he had woken up from a dreamless sleep, his sadness had retreated like a wave, leaving him with one thought only. He would not go on living like that. He needed to focus his sadness and anger into some purpose. He had no idea about what it had to be. All he knew was that everything had to change. He was someone different now and he was not sure it was good.

*

Nadesan felt his eyes begin to water but he blinked back his tears. He had taken his hurt away to a private place. It would do no good to show these men how he felt. They treated any form of emotion as a weakness, one that must be erased. Brought up by his father to value the non-violent philosophy of *Ahimsa*, the pain Nadesan felt in his heart only lessened when his thoughts turned to revenge.

Nadesan lay still with a sense of dread. The sound of voices forced him to reluctantly open his eyes. The room was empty. Nadesan rolled off the thin mattress and got to his feet. He shook his head, trying to clear the images in his mind. Through the open door he could hear snatches of Deva talking. '… received orders … wait a few weeks … must not compromise safe house.'

Nadesan ran his fingers through his hair and shuffled to the doorway rubbing his hip and thigh. A dark bruise covered his hip extending halfway down his thigh.

Deva and two of the men who worked in the garage were huddled around a table pushed up against the wall. Against the opposite wall, a kerosene stove stood on an upended wooden packing case next to an open cupboard containing bags of rice, spices and several cooking implements. A door next to the cupboard led out to a tiny courtyard containing a tap and a squat toilet.

'Ah, Nadesan,' Deva said, seeing him standing in the doorway. 'Come here and join us.' The room smelt of sweat and other odours given off by men stuffed too long in close quarters. It was also tinged with a hint of something.

The men watched him as he came into the room. They were hard men; he could see no charity in their faces. But he sensed that he had won their respect. One of them, Baala, stepped aside leaving Nadesan room, by the table.

Deva inspected him, staring into his face intently. His mouth was drawn into a tight-lipped smile, his black eyebrows arched over eyes like hard steel. Nadesan could see the toughness; the meanness and detachment that coursed through the man. He felt nervous around him.

'The papers are still full of the bombing,' Deva said, tapping an open newspaper on the table. 'It's better than we expected. You've done well.'

The morning sunlight pouring through a small open window made him squint at the stark black and white photograph plastered across the front page. Thoughts chased each other through his head as he looked at the carnage caused by the explosive. It was what he'd wanted to happen but he was not expecting to have been alive to witness it. He felt again the pang of regret and self-contempt for running away. The desire to flee was not always wise and the thought of letting down his wife and son had begun to eat into him from the moment he realized what he had done.

Nadesan raised his pale and almost mournful face, making no reply. It was not just the army's watchful eyes he had to worry about. The Tigers were unforgiving to combatants who had doubts about what they were doing.

Deva was watching him expectantly. Nadesan nodded slightly, acknowledging the order of things. It would do no good to upset him or any of these men. He needed their protection.

'Have you heard anything about another mission?'

Nadesan had spent the last twenty-four hours worrying about this. He wanted another opportunity to do what he should have done in the first place.

Deva stared at Nadesan before shaking his head. 'We are to remain hidden and not draw any attention to this place,' he said. 'When the time is right, we will be informed.'

There was something unsettling about how casually they talked about what had happened and what they were going to do. Nadesan felt his heart rate accelerate, his face flush and his palms begin to sweat. He suspected that their thoughts were not for the victims of the bomb blast but with their own families in unmarked graves across the island. His own thoughts turned to his wife and child and wondered if what he had done would make them sleep easier. He didn't think so but all he could deal with was today.

*

Deva came into the room at the rear of the garage to listen to the news. It was three days since the bomb went off at the bus terminus and the news was reporting that a cell of Black Tigers had infiltrated the city and that they were responsible for the bombing. It had sent everyone into a panic and the city had been locked down. The radio, which was constantly tuned onto an all-news station, had been reporting that a massive manhunt was underway across the city. The authorities were appealing to the public to help track them down.

Nadesan sat on his mattress, his hands shaking with nervousness. The thought of being captured still ate into him but it was tinged with a sense of guilt for what he had done. Photographs of the victims being treated in hospital had appeared in the newspapers every day since the bombing. One showed a masked female doctor and a nurse, both gowned in hospital attire, bent over a hospital bed examining one of the victims wrapped in stained bandages.

'What has got into you?' Deva looked at Nadesan searchingly, his lips twisted into a mocking smile. 'You did what you were meant to do! Are you feeling sorry that it happened?'

Nadesan felt compelled to answer but as he opened his mouth to speak, Deva's attention shifted to the radio. He gestured at Nadesan to remain quiet as he leaned forward, his head tilted to one side as the announcer talked about measures the government was implementing to keep the city safe from bombing. They wanted all residents living in Colombo to register with the Police.

'Huh!' Deva grunted, looking up, his face screwed up in concentration. 'I bet they will only be registering the Tamils.' He thought for a moment. 'This is actually quite good …. it will bring more of us together.'

Nadesan remained quiet as Deva, distracted by the what he'd heard, left the room. Nadesan sat for a long time in the same place while the news droned on, his thoughts going back to when he met Radika.

It was fate that had brought them together. Attacks by the Tigers against the government were growing in the east and armed patrols roved the streets. Tamils were being singled out and searched for weapons, some even arrested and taken away for questioning. He was watching from the shadow of the workshop when a patrol of armed soldiers stopped a young woman in a light blue sari, ordering her to open her bag and display its contents.

Nadesan had seen her a number of times walking past the workshop. Every evening she stood waiting at the bus station feeding scraps of bread to a flock of pigeons. He noticed that she wore the same light blue sari every day and had wondered who she was. That day she missed the bus and she was still standing by the side of the road when he'd finished work for the day.

It was getting dark when Nadesan crossed the road and stood next to her at the bus stop. He looked at her, stared really. He had noticed that she had a dark complexion but he did not expect her to be so beautiful. Her long black hair was parted in the middle, a hint of homemade kohl on her eyes and light powder on her face. Apart from the black *pottu*, no other make-up. She seemed to be deliberately looking away from him.

Nadesan shuffled his feet, looking around, uncertain what to do. A few people stood waiting for the bus. A woman negotiated with a man who stood behind a handcart covered with large green striped watermelons. A light breeze brought the smell from an open drain next to the shops. Nadesan studied the girl from the corner of his eye. He couldn't help himself. She was taller than he expected, only slightly shorter than him. Her sari wrapped around her in the breeze accentuating her slim figure.

After a while, she looked up at him. He met her eyes, then watched as she looked nervously away. His interest in her was building and he made up his mind to talk to her.

'Vanakkam, I am Nadesan,' he said. 'I work in the garage and see you going home every day. Where do you travel to?'

She looked at him with lively, intelligent eyes before responding. 'My family lives in Eravur,' she said.

Nadesan smiled at her, raising his eyebrows in surprise. Eravur was the suburb next to where he lived and he had never seen her before. She blushed and quickly looked away.

'I live in Chenkaladi and have never seen you,' he said. 'Have you always lived there?'

She shook her head. 'No, we lived in Trincomalee and moved to my uncle's house after ours was burnt during the riots.'

Mobs assisted by navy personnel from the naval base, incensed by the ambush that killed thirteen Sinhalese soldiers in Jaffna, had rioted attacking Tamil and Muslim shopkeepers and burning their businesses. Nadesan remembered his father closing the workshop for three days after receiving death threats but nothing ever came out of it. It was the first time he had seen his father concerned about their future.

'Do you work around here?' he asked.

She hesitated. 'I work in the hospital.'

'Are you a nurse?' Nadesan remembered asking.

'Not yet,' she shook her head. 'I am a trainee nurse.'

'How long is your training?' Nadesan wanted to learn as much about this girl as he could.

'Three years. I am finishing my second year.' she said, proudly. 'I have only one year left.' Nadesan realized that the light blue sari he had always seen her in, was her nurses uniform.

It was only when the bus pulled up at the stop did Nadesan realize he had not asked her name.

'I am Radika,' she said, smiling shyly. 'What's yours?'

They had sat next to each other on the bus, not too close to each other but close enough. The flowery smell of her talcum powder mingled with her perspiration drifted to Nadesan. He learned that she had one brother and two sisters. Her father worked as a bus conductor while her mother stayed at home and helped run the household. Before long they reached the stop at which Radika got off the bus. It was two stops before his. He followed her out.

'I will walk from here,' he said, when Radika looked at him strangely. 'I am just two stops away.'

Nadesan watched her walk away in the deepening gloom. He felt strangely elated and couldn't understand why. It was not that he had never met and talked to girls before. But there was something about this girl that was different.

At home that night he tried to read the newspaper but he couldn't concentrate. His thoughts kept coming back to Radika. His mother, who had been watching, wiped her hand on the cloth she was carrying and sat next to him. She offered him a glass of milk tea.

'What's the matter,' she asked, putting her hand on his shoulder. 'You're not your normal self. Did something happen at work?'

'Nothing happened,' he said unconvincingly, looking across at her.

His mother raised her eyebrows. 'It doesn't look that way! What's wrong?'

Nadesan shook his head. 'Nothing's wrong ammah, but I met this girl.' He had always found it difficult to keep anything away from his mother. She always seemed to read his deepest thoughts.

His mother grabbed his arm with both her hands excitedly. 'Oh, who is she?'

'She's a trainee nurse at the hospital. I've seen her before walking past the shop but I only met her once,' he said lamely. 'Only today.'

His mother beamed at him. 'You must tell me who she is so we can find out more about her and her family background.'

'Her name is Radika and she's from Trincomalee.' Nadesan felt relieved that he didn't have to keep his meeting a secret. 'She lives with her uncle at Eravur.'

'Why that's so close,' she said beaming at him. 'Did you speak to her?'

'Of course, I spoke to her,' he said irritably. 'Otherwise how would I know her name?'

'I will talk to your father. He thinks you're not ready for marriage.'

'Who's talking about marriage ammah. I only just met this girl and I don't even know whether she likes me.'

'You know Nadesan, there are people already enquiring about you and here you are looking for one of your own.'

The period that followed was the happiest in Nadesan's life. He did not see Radika at the bus stand the next day and could not sleep that night thinking that she was avoiding him. But he was thrilled when he saw her the following evening, walking down the street towards the workshop. She looked in as she went past and they both smiled at each other.

Nadesan had not stopped thinking about her since he had watched her walk away two days before. Her face had intruded in his thoughts during every waking moment. She was standing at the bus stop when Nadesan got there.

The evening was warm and moist. It was raining lightly giving the wet surfaces a metallic sheen. Radika looked surprised when she saw Nadesan hurrying towards her in the rain. He stopped next to her and smiled. 'I thought I'd go home early today.'

Radika began to smile, her eyes dancing in her face. 'You don't have any work to do?' she asked, lifting her umbrella, inviting Nadesan to share the little shelter it gave from the rain. 'You don't usually leave so early.'

Nadesan smiled gratefully as he stood next to her. 'I have a job to do but it's getting dark and I can finish it in the morning.' He could smell her; a mild soapy smell with faint traces of jasmine.

Radika grinned at him and looked away. Nadesan stood quite close to her, the cotton of his sleeve brushing her arm making him nervous. She looked even more beautiful than he remembered. Nadesan found himself tongue tied. He saw her looking at him from the corner of her eyes.

'I would like to spend some time with you,' Nadesan blurted out. 'We can take the bus on Sunday morning and visit the temple in Trincomalee.'

Radika tilted her head at Nadesan, looking at him shyly. 'I would like that but I have to tell my parents.'

Nadesan nodded vigorously. 'Yes, yes ... I understand!' he said. 'I told my mother that I met you.'

'You did?' Radika asked looking at Nadesan in surprise. 'What did she say?'

'She was very happy that I met someone like you,' he said. 'She wanted to know all about you.'

Nadesan thought back to the first time he had realized that he was in love with Radika. After a few weeks of seeing each other, he could see himself having a serious relationship with her and marrying her one day. His mother had spoken with his father and they had made enquiries about Radika's family through a relative who lived in Eravur.

'We have found she comes from a good family,' his mother said. 'Your father still thinks you are too young to marry but he won't stop you if you decide she's the one.'

Nadesan had fallen in love for the first time—but his elation didn't last long. Three months after their marriage, his father had a massive heart attack and died.

Nadesan felt a sharp pain. His bladder was full and he pressed his legs together, tightening his groin muscles, which brought him back to reality.

'Do we have to register ourselves?' he asked Deva who was hunched over the store dipping a tea bag into a steaming mug. Nadesan shifted uncomfortably from one foot to another as he waited for Deva to respond.

'Not everyone,' Deva said, looking over his mug at Nadesan. 'We'll send Yogi. He's from Colombo and won't be suspected.'

A dark thought, which he tried to push away, came to him. 'The police conducted house to house searches in Batticaloa looking for Tamils,' Nadesan said, shuffling slowly towards the courtyard door. 'They might do the same here.'

Deva nodded, watching Nadesan leave the room. 'I am aware of that but we don't have a choice. We must not show how many live here. Only Yogi and Jagan will work in the garage. You and I will remain here in the back until things get quiet.'

Nadesan did not respond as he went in the toilet and closed the door behind him. He didn't like this growing feeling. He never felt that he had to justify what he was going to do; the rage and the hatred had made sure of that. But revenge was one thing; this had simply been murder. He had never thought about it before as he was so focused on killing himself at the same time; to become one of the victims and join his family.

He put his face in his hands. What a terrible thing have I done, he thought to himself. But it was too late to change anything. He was weeping now as he thought of the life he once had, the life he had worked so hard for, the lives he'd destroyed. He sobbed quietly for several minutes. The police would eventually track them down. He needed to be extra careful not to get caught. He shuddered at the thought. They would not treat him well if they did.

CHAPTER SEVEN

Tilak watched the snake emerge from under the log not more than a meter from where they were hiding. He spotted the movement as its head emerged, its tongue flickering as it tasted the air. Tilak crouched on one knee a few steps behind the instructor whose name was Mike. The man knelt behind the log watching a squad of men moving stealthily away from them down a narrow trail.

They were on a training exercise, in a heavily wooded area of the sprawling base in Kalutara which housed the facilities of the Special Task Force. The exercises were designed by former members of the British Special Air Service who provided specialized training in counter terrorist and insurgency operations. A month of training had gone quickly. Tilak sensed that Mike liked him as he followed orders without hesitation. Mike must have known something about Tilak's army background as he made Tilak the leader of a squad.

Mike had ordered him to join him on the exercise. 'Tilak,' he called out. 'I want you to follow me on this one. Maybe you'll learn something.'

The men being trained in the camp came from different parts of the country. The faces were mostly of young men in their twenties although one or two looked a bit older. They were required to wear an olive drab, one-piece jump suit with no insignia. There were no ranks during training. Only the instructors could wear badges of rank. And only first names were used. Anonymity was guaranteed.

Tilak held a Chinese-built assault rifle and carried a fighting knife on his belt. They had been briefed when the course started on dangerous wildlife they may encounter during training, and venomous snakes were high on the list. The southern province had more than its share of them. The one he watched looked dangerous, as it slowly slithered out from under the log.

Although Tilak was used to seeing snakes, he had an instinctive dislike for them. This one was large with a triangular head, a little less than a meter long but Tilak could not make out its colour or markings in the darkness of the forest canopy.

Mike stirred, angling his body to look further down the trail. Tilak saw the flicker of the snake's mouth as it sensed his movement. The snake turned towards Mike and started to coil its lower body as it drew back its head to strike.

Tilak had to go for his knife. The gun was useless as it was loaded with training rounds. He fixed his eyes on a spot just behind the snake's head and reached for his knife.

Reach, draw, strike! His hand was a blur of movement as he used all the power he had in him, driving forward with the knife against the body of the snake, aiming at a point behind its head.

Mike was thrown forward as Tilak crashed into him. 'What the fuck!' he grunted, angrily looking over his shoulder.

The snake was pinned to the side of the log, the handle of the knife protruding from behind its head. The body and the tail of the snake thrashed against Tilak's arm, curling around his forearm.

Mike's eyes widened when he saw the snake. 'That's a viper,' he said staring at Tilak. He pushed himself up from where he had fallen. 'I heard they're not so common here but they can kill you just the same.' He pulled a knife from its sheath hanging upside down on his chest harness. Reaching forward carefully to avoid the snake's open mouth, he sawed off its head just at the point where Tilak's knife pinned it to the log.

Tilak was trembling. His hands were beginning to shake. Mike picked up the snake's head with the point of his knife and stared at it closely. 'Daboia russelii, the Russell's Viper,' he said softly. 'It's the most dangerous viper in the Indian sub-continent.' He shook his head and looked at Tilak. 'That was well done,' he said. 'I owe you one.'

The men they had been watching had disappeared down the trail. The exercise forgotten, Mike and Tilak headed back to the barracks.

The camp in Kalutara was not an easy place to find. The compound tucked away in a remote corner of the sprawling southern military base, housed the training facilities for the paramilitary Special Task Force. A base within a base, the high security training centre was marked by fences and signs warning people away.

During the first week, they were subjected to various trials to assess their health and endurance. The lead instructor called Mike came from Britain, it was obvious from his accent. He had four other men from the same country who assisted. They woke them during the night and made them run around the training ground, armed and with full packs, as if they were in the field.

After a week, they were taken out into the field, into rubber and coconut plantations that surrounded the camp. They ran like a pack of animals with no semblance of order in total darkness, down dirt tracks shaded by the tall trees, up and down hills and every meter cost an enormous effort. Extremely demanding and very difficult, Tilak had never done such hard training in his life. In prison, he had tried to maintain his fitness but nothing had prepared him for this. Some of the men got hurt, one fell and broke his leg another ran into a ditch and cracked his pelvis.

'You have to learn to move quickly in the dark. Like an animal. Darkness will be your best friend and you have to embrace it. It's your lover, your partner. It will keep you alive.'

They learned how to orient themselves at night. The instructors took them out in the middle of the night in trucks dropping them in the middle of the rubber plantations and wanted them to find their way back. They had to load their rifles, pack their gear all in the dark. Even in the barracks, the windows were covered by heavy wooden shutters. They went to the toilet, showered dressed, dismantled and cleaned their weapons all in the dark.

After that came the target practice. They were asked of their skill with weapons and whether they had any combat experience. Tilak found himself in the group who had very little or no combat experience. They spent hours in the shooting range using different types of weapons. Tilak learned to shoot different weapons with reasonable skill. Survival training came next, followed by unarmed combat.

Mike called out from his cubicle at the back of the barracks. 'Tilak, the Boss Man wants to see you right now!'

Tilak had just come back from a run with a couple of others and had lain on his cot after a quick shower. He groaned as he got out of the cot and changed into his fatigues.

The commander's office was spartan. Nothing of a personal nature adorned its space. Tilak saluted and stood to attention in front of the old wooden desk.

A large man with broad shoulders, the commander sat on his chair at attention, his back straight as a ramrod. Another man in the room dressed in civilian clothes sat slouched on one of the chairs.

'At ease Lieutenant,' the commander had a deep and well-modulated voice. He sounded like a film star. He had seen the commander on a few occasions when he had addressed the group. He'd never been introduced to him.

'How are you handling the training?' he asked Tilak. 'I have read the reports but I'd like to hear it directly from you.'

Over three months had passed since Tilak arrived in the camp. 'I am handling it well sir. I am learning quite a lot.'

Tilak did not believe that he had been called to the commander's office for some idle chit chat. There had to be something else.

The commander looked at a file on his desk. 'Your instructors have placed you in the top ten percent,' he said looking up at Tilak. 'That's pretty good going for someone who has never had any kind of training for quite some time.'

Tilak did not realize that he had been rated so highly. 'Thank you, sir!' he said straightening his shoulders. The Commander's eyes narrowed. 'I guess a smart fellow like you must be wondering why he has been called into the commander's office suddenly.'

'The thought did cross my mind sir.'

'This gentleman,' the commander said, waving at the civilian, 'wants to have an off the record conversation with you.' The commander looked at Tilak questioningly. 'You know what off the record means don't you?'

Tilak nodded glancing at the man. 'Yes sir, I do.'

The commander continued like Tilak had not spoken. 'What it means to me is that this conversation never took place. I will deny it ever happened. And our friend here; well you'll never find out who he is so he wasn't here either.'

Tilak looked at the civilian who finally showed some signs of life. 'This is not an official meeting,' he said looking at Tilak thoughtfully. 'We want to keep it simple. You okay with that?'

Tilak nodded. 'Yes sir,' he said warily. The man who looked like he was in his late forties was neatly dressed in shirt and trousers. He had a handsome face with thick brows and penetrating dark eyes. A small moustache adorned his upper lip.

'We have been waiting for your training to be complete and the commander believes that you are ready,' the civilian said. 'You will be based in the east and will from time to time be asked to take orders from me.' He studied Tilak carefully. 'You have any issue with that?'

Tilak's life had completely changed when he was sent to prison. More than the physical hardship and danger he faced in prison, the uncertainty of not knowing what would happen to him when he was finally released ate at him constantly. He had built a wall around him and he didn't realize how much he missed being part of the world outside. He was not going to let anything change that.

Tilak shook his head. 'No, I have no issue with that,' he said, looking at the commander. 'I assume that I will be a part of the regular force structure?'

The commander studied Tilak with singular intensity. 'Yes,' he nodded. 'You will be deployed to the east with a team.'

The civilian leant forward conspiratorially. 'Good. We have been watching with great interest at what is happening in the north and east.' He glanced at the commander. 'The Tigers are getting stronger and it seems that the Indians are in the game and are playing a major hand. We don't think their motives are as pure as they make it out to be.'

Tilak studied the two men, every movement, every emotion, their faces, eyes, voices. The two men had an advantage over him, or so they thought. But he wouldn't allow them to control him. He'd learned the hard way that people who let others control them always ended up the loser.

'That's possible, sir.' Tilak decided not to say too much.

The civilian looked at Tilak with raised eyebrows. 'That's possible, is that all you have got to say?'

The man was beginning to annoy Tilak. 'What do you want me to say sir,' he stared at a point above the Commanders head. 'I've been in prison and only read what's in the newspapers.'

The civilian looked at Tilak intently. 'We have plans to use you,' he said. 'In more than one capacity but it's something you should not take for granted.'

Tilak stared at the man but remained silent.

The civilian glanced at the commander. 'Perhaps it's best that we spell things out now so there's no misunderstanding.' He sat forward on his chair. 'There are militant cells in the area you will be operating in, that need to be eliminated. And by eliminated, I mean just that,' he emphasized. 'We want to send a strong message to them to keep their hands off the east. Is that something you are prepared to do?'

Tilak was not under any allusion as to what was required when he had agreed with the Police Superintendent back in Colombo. They wanted him to take orders without question even if that meant killing someone.

'And what do I get in return for being your gundog?' he asked staring at the civilian.

The man sat back in his chair, a small smile spreading slowly across his face. 'What do you want Lieutenant? Money, women ...' he paused, looking at Tilak curiously, 'young boys maybe?' he grinned. 'After all you were in prison.'

Tilak felt his face flush. 'Don't insult me,' Tilak spat out angrily. 'The last time this happened I ended up in jail. What prevents it from happening again.'

Tilak heard a chuckle from the Commander. 'I told you it won't be that easy.'

Tilak tried to control his growing anger. He glared at the officer. They seemed to think it was some sort of a game.

'You are in no position to negotiate,' the civilian said smugly, steepling his fingers together. 'You can always go back to prison you know, and this time I'll make sure it won't be to Colombo.'

Tilak was not the same man he had been before entering prison. He had learned the hard way that people in positions of authority often resorted to threats and intimidation to get what they wanted. But many did not know how to handle it when put in a similar position.

Tilak half-turned and took a step towards the civilian putting him within easy striking distance. The man saw the look on Tilak's face and flinched back involuntarily, his eyes opening wide in disbelief.

'Your threats don't intimidate me,' Tilak said softly, leaning forward threateningly. 'If you send me back to prison I will find out who you are and where you live. That much I will promise you.'

Tilak's sudden change from deferential trainee to intimidating convict had taken both men by surprise. The commander pushed his chair back preparing to rise but stopped when Tilak put both his hands up and stepped back. Tilak needed to assert his authority over this man but knew not to step over that invisible line where he would be considered too dangerous to be manipulated.

The atmosphere in the room suddenly became electric. The civilian sitting in his chair was staring at Tilak like he'd just seen a ghost.

'I am in no mood to be played around with,' Tilak said, staring at both men in turn. 'I appreciate you getting me out of prison but don't think for one minute that I will only play by your rules.'

The commander took a deep breath. 'Ok, ok! Let's calm down,' he said. 'No one's going anywhere.' He reached down and waved a piece of paper in the air. 'This is your official release from prison. Your sentence has been commuted for good behaviour and you are a free man.'

Having been released from his sentence made Tilak feel better but it would not help him in the future. He needed more information about who was running the show to protect himself.

Tilak reached out and took the sheet of paper the commander was holding out to him. He folded it and slipped it into his trouser pocket without looking at it.

'This will do for now,' he said, glaring at the civilian. 'But before I agree to anything, I want to know your name, your organisation and who you work for. Once I get that information I will be your man.'

The civilian looked at the commander nervously. 'I will have to get permission from my superiors,' he said, licking his lips. He levered himself out of his chair, stepping away from Tilak, putting the chair between them. 'I'll let the commander know what their decision is.'

Tilak nodded reluctantly. It was the most he could expect given the situation. But he now knew there was someone higher up the food chain who was pulling the strings.

The Commander stood up as well. 'That will be all Lieutenant. You may leave now.'

Tilak saluted the commander and left the room, his mind buzzing with uncontrolled thoughts.

CHAPTER EIGHT

Amanthi walked in silence, hands thrust deeply into the pockets of her white coat making no attempt to protect her sandaled feet from the damp grass in the park. She needed to get away from the hospital, to clear her sleep-deprived head and lungs.

It had been almost three months since the attack at the central bus station but the work had not slowed down. It felt like it was even busier than those first three days after the attack, but that couldn't be possible. The plague of bombings and shootings had kept up its headlong pace and new patients were being brought to the General Hospital almost every week. She was exhausted by the long days and nights, against the pressure and fear of making a mistake, against the horror of mutilated bodies and the naked grief of the bereaved.

Amanthi slumped on a bench under the shade of a large flame tree. She had changed as a person during this time. She noticed that she was paying more attention to the news on the radio and listening to the gossip that circulated around the hospital. She had never been interested in politics or anything that distracted her from her goal of becoming a doctor before all this started.

The midday sun shone brightly on the gleaming white columns and dome of the colonial-era town hall building rising above the surrounding trees. Amanthi had always treasured the beauty and ugliness that she had grown up in and had never wanted to live anywhere else. She loved living in a culture which was an amalgamation of multiple religious and ethnic groups with massive social influences from their colonial past. Her family was by no means wealthy but they were educated members of Colombo's intellectual class. She had grown up in a comfortable suburb in Colombo, gone to a private girl's school and lived the privileged life that her upbringing had given her. But beneath it all was a more frightening Colombo – a city hiding war and bloodshed. Her city had become a place of terror. The sounds of distant bombs and wailing sirens a constant distraction, always intruding into the calm and sterilized rooms of the burn unit.

Of course, she knew about the war in the north and was well aware of the growing number of armed soldiers that seemed to hang around at every major junction in the city. Her focus had always been tending to the burnt bodies of men, women and children being brought in by traumatized people and she paid scant attention to anything else.

A line of school girls dressed in white crossed the park in pairs, walking towards the squat brown Colombo public library in the corner of the park. The school girls chattered amongst themselves, peals of laughter ringing out as they followed their teacher.

The scene reminded Amanthi of her time in school. She could clearly recall her time as a teenager, dressed in the same white uniform and walking hand in hand with her best friend to the library. It was on one of these trips to the library that her whole life had changed.

They had just arrived at the library and were standing in front of a pile of books deciding which one to read when she heard a loud crash through the open windows. People yelled and she heard a long-tortured wail unlike anything she had ever heard before. She ran over to the library window with her friends and watched as a man stumbled out of a burning car which had been hit by a lorry. The small vehicle had erupted into flames, smoke pouring out of its open windows. The man's clothes were burning off his body. He tried hitting himself, contorting his body while trying to beat out the flames.

Why doesn't someone help him? she thought.

The man threw himself to the ground and rolled around the grass screaming in agony, smoke coming out of his charred body. Smoke swirled around as passers-by ran to him, beating him with shopping bags and rolled up newspapers in a desperate attempt to beat out the flames. After a few minutes, they stepped back, leaving the man sprawled lifeless on the ground, wisps of smoke still rising from his body.

A man dressed in a white coat suddenly appeared, pushing himself through the crowd and crouching over the semi-conscious man. Amanthi watched as he leaned over trying to comfort the man, motioning to the growing crowd to give them room. The man on the ground suddenly started to spasm, his body arching off the ground. The white-coated man whom Amanthi assumed was a doctor, went down on his knees, pushing his shoulders to the ground, gesturing at someone in the crowd to grab his feet. He blew air into the burnt man's lungs and pounded his chest. A man handed the white-coated man a bottle of water which he held to the burnt man's mouth, pouring the rest on his face before handing the bottle back for more. Sirens wailed as an ambulance screeched to a stop next to the still burning car. People pointed as the paramedics hurried over, carrying a stretcher with a blanket which they used to smother the burnt man on the ground. Amanthi watched as the badly burned man was bundled in the blanket, the paramedics abandoned the stretcher in the rush to get him into the ambulance which took off, red lights flashing, sirens blaring.

The man in the white coat who had attended to the accident victim remained on his knees for a few minutes, his head down as if in prayer. A woman in a sari approached him and gently touched him on his shoulder, bending down and talking to him. The man looked around and got to his feet, pushing aside the woman's helping hands. His white suit was streaked with black reaching up his arms. For a moment, he looked in Amanthi's direction, his face expressionless, almost carved out of stone, before turning and pushing into the crowd, disappearing.

For days afterwards, Amanthi could hear the screaming in her sleep. And whenever the wail replayed in her mind, she would squeeze her eyes shut and shake her head. But the image of the doctor helping the burn victim stayed with her.

When her grandfather was paralysed after his stroke, Amanthi would come home from school and spend time with him, often doing her homework in his room. The two of them developed a close relationship and over time she felt the urge to help her grandfather in any way she could. Thomis his nurse, who slept on a reed mat in her grandfather's room, taught Amanthi little ways to make his life more comfortable. Amanthi's world got smaller as she found herself spending more and more time with him. An emptiness opened in her life the day he died and it was not long after that, her father asked her what she wanted to be when she left school. The memory of the man from her childhood still haunted her and she felt a sense of responsibility to do all she could for the helpless.

Her father followed her wishes and pushed her hard towards a career in medicine. Her mother, who realized that having a daughter who was a doctor was not a bad thing, changed her mind and proudly paraded Amanthi in front of her friends whenever she could.

For a while, Amanthi could not decide on a specialty in medicine. It took a severely burnt woman to stir her passion. Her initial contact with the woman who had poured kerosene on her body and set herself alight, was both traumatic and heart-rending. But once she got past the hopelessness of the woman's condition and realized that there was a human being beneath all that horror, she was determined to help in any way she could. Ironically, the other young doctors with whom Amanthi had been to medical school with no desire to take up a specialty where the outlook for patients was so grim and the work so challenging. Their plan was to pick a fashionable specialty that would allow them to begin a private practice and lead an affluent life.

Once Amanthi had decided on her specialty, she threw herself into it, spending hours at the bedsides of her patients, trying to soothe the agonizing pain of their burns and ease their fears about dying, or worse, of living. She was lucky to have a mentor in Dr Perera who constantly stimulated Amanthi, encouraging her to consider what might be possible caring of the severely burnt.

As a resident on duty, Amanthi rarely had a chance to sit down. Whenever she could, she tried to get away from the hospital and spend a few minutes in the peace and quiet of the park. Her mind, freed from the constant pressure of emergency procedures and treatments even for a short time, turned to the situation she found herself in.

It had been four weeks after the bus station bombing when Dr Perera had called Amanthi into her office. The head of the burn unit had come in that morning and done a quick round of the ward with her senior staff, scanning each patients chart for any change in their condition. This was her usual practice and only then did her day begin. For her staff, there was always a sense of relief when she was in the unit … they were reassured by her presence.

Dr Perera was dressed in her surgical greens. 'Funding has finally come through for the emergency response team,' she said, looking up from a pile of papers on her desk. 'We need to discuss who'll be on the team with you.'

As a part of her training to lead an emergency response burn team, Amanthi had been working in the emergency treatment unit of the General Hospital. She knew that picking the right people was critical to building an efficient team. The staff that Dr Perera had surrounded herself with were all very capable and committed. The attending residents, the nurses, the therapists and other support personnel were all handpicked and specially trained to handle a variety of burn injuries. The work was both physically and emotionally draining. Long, gruelling days, hour after hour of witnessing unspeakable agony and suffering, and too many sad stories were all part of the job. Amanthi had developed a healthy respect for them all.

'Do I get to choose from any of the main teams?' Amanthi asked, looking at the doctor hopefully. The specialized staff in the unit were divided into two teams who between them covered the different hospital shifts.

Dr Perera steepled her hands. 'I am not going to send you out there on your own,' she said, thoughtfully. 'But I also don't want to weaken any of the teams. Is there someone you have in mind?'

Amanthi hadn't thought that she would get any of the experienced nurses but knew which one she would pick if she was given a choice.

'Yes,' she nodded. 'Nelum and I work well together.' The experienced nurse had been a big help when Amanthi started working as an intern in the unit, patiently leading the young doctor through the difficult procedures when a burn victim was brought in. People often mistook her pleasing presence for softness, but when she needed to be, she could be as strong and authoritative as a magistrate.

'I haven't spoken to her about it though,' Amanthi said hastily when Dr Perera raised an eyebrow.

'I didn't think you had,' Dr Perera said smiling at Amanthi's apparent discomfort. 'I am actually pleased with your choice as she was the person I had in mind.'

Amanthi's face cracked into a wide grin. Having Nelum on the team would make her job that much easier.

'Don't be that pleased,' Dr Perera grumbled. 'You'll need another nurse and I can't spare anyone else.'

Amanthi was so pleased at getting Nelum that she didn't care. She knew that most of the nurses in the hospital came from poor backgrounds and there were many good ones at other hospitals who aspired to work at the main teaching hospital. She remembered the young nurse who had volunteered and worked with some of her patients. Not everyone was cut out for working in the burn unit but Shanthi was different. She took direction well and got along well with the other nurses.

'There was this nurse, Shanthi,' Amanthi said looking at Dr Perera. "She showed up on the day of the bus station bombing and helped for many days. I would like to look for her.'

Dr Perera nodded. 'Yes, I remember her.' She made a note on a pad she carried with her. 'Ok, I'll find out where she came from. We'll have a record of who helped. Let's bring her in and talk to her.'

That was two months ago. Dr Perera had managed to find Shanthi and the nurse accepted a junior position at the Burn unit working under Nelum.

Amanthi looked at her watch and realized she needed to get back. In the emergency treatment unit, Amanthi was treated like just another resident. The senior residents and the various specialists who came in from time to time ordered her around. But she came into her own when a burn patient was brought in. They often knew that a burn patient was being admitted, and they were informed that was one coming in this afternoon.

Nelum and Shanthi were preparing to change the patients dressing when Amanthi hurried into the unit. This patient had come in from the Ratnapura General Hospital where they didn't have the facilities to treat severe burn victims. The patients' gender was indeterminate although Amanthi knew from the paperwork that it was a woman. Her body was distorted by the burns, the trunk bloated, the face swollen and covered by a mosaic of wounds and patches of hair. She was in a drugged coma–like sleep, a twilight zone controlled by a morphine drip injected directly into her veins.

Nelum was letting Shanthi take the lead. Shanthi adjusted her face mask and pulled on a pair of long rubber gloves before she began unwrapping the patient's bandages. From the time they started the procedure, it would take them two hours. Every inch of the patient's body needed to be inspected. They needed to note every wound, remove any dead skin, check for bed sores, for signs of infection.

Amanthi checked the patient's temperature. It was not unusual for a patient to arrive at the unit with a low temperature. Even with the constant heat and humidity in Colombo, burn patients had to be kept warm. Amanthi noted on the patient's chart that her temperature was just a degree below normal.

Next Amanthi checked for signs of infection. Hospitals were full of infectious bacteria which was not a major issue for patients with intact skins. But once that protective layer was breached, burn patient's immune systems found it difficult to cope.

Amanthi sent some tissue samples and blood to the lab for testing knowing that they would come back positive. This patient had been moved twice, she noted from her chart. Once from a clinic on a tea estate where she was treated first, and then from the Ratnapura hospital emergency room. Neither very sterile environments. Preventing burn infection with this patient was a major challenge that Amanthi would have to face.

CHAPTER NINE

Nadesan sat in the corner of the room frustrated. He was watching Baala strip the weapon and put it back together after cleaning it. It was something Nadesan had learned to do after he joined the militants. He knew how to assemble and fire a whole range of weapons and handle various explosive devices.

The last few months had been difficult. Nadesan had rarely gone out at first and had become irritable and morose, sitting in a corner of the backroom staring into space. The last set of orders they had received were to act normal and do nothing. They would be contacted when they were required. The daily newspapers still carried articles about the search for the bus terminal bomber and almost weekly there were incidents when security forces clashed with militant sleeper cells they had uncovered in the city.

Only after the others in the garage had complained about Nadesan had Deva relented and allowed him to spend some time in the market outside the garage. At first, they had looked at him like some sort of a hero but Nadesan could see the way they looked at him, and hearing the whispered comments between them, that they thought he was going insane.

Not that Nadesan wanted to leave the safety of the garage. He was afraid of being picked up by the security forces and it had taken him many weeks before he could step out of the shadows at the rear of the garage.

Having time on his hands, Nadesan's thoughts skipped randomly between the carnage he had caused with the bus terminal bombing, the journey that had brought him to this place and what his future would be. He woke up every morning from a tortured, broken sleep, irritable, ill-tempered, and looked at hatred at the room. But however much he tried to justify what he'd done at the bus terminal, he just could not. He knew that by deciding to run, instead of remaining in the car, he had charted a course for himself which he would have to deal with.

And yet all these questions were not new ones. Dealing with the police after his wife and child were killed had been the worst days of his life. The police had taken the bodies away after the massacre and when they finally responded to his pleadings to hand over the bodies, he was told that they had been cremated and the ashes scattered. Nadesan had been inconsolable, almost speechless for days.

When Nadesan finally was able to talk to a police inspector, he was made to look like he had done something wrong by leaving his wife and child alone at the bus station

His frustration and anger at the way they treated him grew day by day until he couldn't control the hatred that had coiled around his heart. He knew then what he had to do. He would strip away the feeling of helplessness and hatred, and replace it with anger.

Through the militant contacts he dealt with in the workshop he was able to get the address of a Tiger safe house in Trincomalee. The person who gave him the militants location warned him about the dangers of joining the hardcore group but Nadesan shrugged it off. He had made up his mind. He would make the occupiers pay for what they had done to his family.

The night sky was clear and a light wind lashed his face as he turned away from the street that ran by the dockyard fence. There were no street lights in the warren of shops, dockworkers homes, brothels, tea rooms and eating houses; Just the dim glow of hurricane lamps seeping between shuttered windows and beneath closed doors. The stench of cloying spices and cooking hung in the sloping alleyways leading away from the harbour. A lone generator chugged away somewhere in the dark.

Nadesan kept walking deeper into the sprawling slum on the city's edge where he was to meet a man. The narrow lanes and alleys were filled with rotting rubbish and furtive movement in the shadows kept Nadesan's nerves on edge. The address he was given was not hard to miss. It looked out of place in the run-down neighbourhood he had just walked through. A battered concrete wall pasted with fading Sinhalese and Tamil movie posters surrounded a house shrouded in darkness. Nadesan looked around. He felt like he was being watched but could not see anyone on the street. His heart pounded as he pushed open the yellow metal gate and walked up to the front door hidden in a pool of darkness.

The door was a shadowy outline in the gloom when he stepped onto the covered porch. The door creaked open inviting him to enter. Nadesan stepped forward tentatively, stopping just short of entering the darkened room. He tensed at the sound of a movement from behind him. A hard shove catapulted him into the cold darkness.

Nadesan fell forward onto the unyielding floor, his lungs emptying with the impact. There were people around him, holding him down roughly. A hand on his head forced his face into the dusty floor. His fear escalated to absolute terror. He struggled to breathe and roll over to his side.

A knee thudded into his ribs. 'Stop moving,' a voice whispered in his ear. 'Who are you? Who sent you here?'

'I am Nadesan from Chenkaladi …,' he gasped. 'From the metal workshop on the Trinco road. I came to join you.'

'How did you find us?' The voice insisted. 'You knew where to come … we have been watching you.'

'I was given this address …' Nadesan took a deep breath, dust flew up his nostrils triggering a coughing fit. 'Kumar gave it to me …'

A muttered curse and the weight on his back shifted. Hands patted his body for weapons. The weight on his back shifted, hands hauled him to his feet holding him upright. He bit his lip to stop himself from coughing. A rough cloth was thrown over his head and his hands tied behind his back. Nadesan was dragged forward and walked down a set of steps. He could sense he was outside the house. Branches brushed against his face as he was hurried through the garden. The men pushed him into a vehicle, forcing him to lay on the floor. He felt someone sitting next to him, his feet on Nadesan's back. The door slammed shut and the vehicle drove off slowly.

Through the suffocating cloth Nadesan could hear the men's conversation. He could identify three different voices. They were taking him to see someone they called the leader. Nadesan began to relax. They were not going to kill him. He had heard how ruthless these men were and only his desire for revenge had made him take a chance. The motion of the vehicle was constant, its progress uneventful. Minutes stretched into what felt like hours and Nadesan felt himself dozing.

A jolt snapped him awake. The vehicle had turned onto a bumpy track. The air Nadesan breathed was thick, tasting of petrol fumes and he began to pant for air. The undulating road tossed Nadesan around on the metal floor making his body ache. Just once they stopped for a short time and he heard voices, a rapid exchange, before the van was moving again. After what seemed like an hour the vehicle stopped and the engine cut.

Nadesan was half-carried out of the vehicle onto the hard ground. A voice ordered him to be brought inside. Nadesan tried to get up but his frozen limbs refused to cooperate. Coughing and heaving, he struggled to his feet with the help of one of the men. The cloth was whipped off his head and he was pushed forward. A light, brilliant, blinding, flooded over him. Nadesan blinked in the harsh light. An unfocused shape materialized in front of him, growing clearer as his eyes focused.

A tough-looking, middle-aged man wearing an unbuttoned military jacket over a sweat-stained brown t-shirt and faded green pants stared at Nadesan. On the wall behind him hung a flag with a tiger on a blood-red background. The man was unshaven and smelt of stale perspiration.

'So, you want to fight, hey … why?' he barked. Nadesan detected a note of derision in the man's voice.

'My wife and son were killed by the army,' Nadesan replied. 'I want to avenge their memory.' He was hungry and tired and was intimidated by the man's aggressive attitude.

'Ah, I have heard about you,' the man stated, his voice softening. 'I was told that you ran a machine shop?'

Nadesan looked down and nodded wordlessly. 'Yes, we made parts for cars and trucks, and also for the bus company in Batticaloa.' He noticed that the man was wearing boots. Hard, roughened, unpolished and cracked with wear. 'I am a trained mechanic.'

'Do you understand what you are asking for,' the man asked. 'You have to live like an animal in the jungle. You will have to sacrifice your life for your departed wife and child. Is that what you really want?'

Nadesan nodded without saying anything. The wound inside him was still too raw and tears came unbidden into his eyes every time he thought about them.

The man stared into Nadesan's eyes. 'We will teach you to control that emotion and anger you carry inside you,' he said. 'We will teach you how to kill them as they kill our people.' He snapped his fingers. A young man in a dark brown uniform rushed over. 'Show him where he can sleep tonight. Tomorrow he can join the others.'

Nadesan slept that night without any of the dreams that had been haunting him since the shooting. He wanted revenge for what had happened and he had finally found the way to get what he was looking for.

*

What first confronted Nadesan was the heat. Sometimes like a scorching blast from a hot oven, sometimes sticky and damp under the jungle canopy. All his life Nadesan had lived close to the sea, with its constant sea breezes which kept the temperature to a bearable level. The heat and increasing humidity of the monsoon meant that his skin was always wet from perspiration which made for uncomfortable days and many sleepless nights.

Their first training camp was a clearing cut into the jungle. Shelters of branches made of four corner-posts, a floor of parallel posts raised some centimetres off the ground and cross branches overhead spread with green sheets of plastic making a sloping roof. Open on one side, there was just enough room for three or four men lying side by side in close proximity.

The rigorous training program lasted almost three months. Discipline was vigorously maintained and a strict code of conduct followed, allowing no distraction from the training. Marriage, relationships and sexual activity were banned and celibacy was enforced ruthlessly. Smoking, drinking and gambling was not tolerated and anyone who strayed from these rules were punished severely.

Nadesan did not enjoy the physical exercises, where elbow skin turned into calluses and the trainees bathed in their own sweat and in the powdery dust of the dry zone. Where he excelled in was the theoretical and practical exercises on weapons and explosives.

Given his experience as a mechanic, he learned to use and maintain communication equipment, how to handle explosives, electronics and weapon technologies. Others specialized in the use of light and heavy weapons, field medicine, counter surveillance, intelligence work and hand to hand combat. Their studies were always at night. The classroom was a hut, poorly lit by an overhead bulb hanging off a long frayed electrical cord. Garden lizards darted between the cracks on the mud walls, flicking tongues and swallowing insects. Men and women were segregated and trained separately, the women taught to provide battlefield-aid, field nursing, communications and supply.

Much of the physical training was structured around the need for securing food which was limited and they often ate only once a day. The quality and quantity of the food depended on access and frequency of the supplies. Often this meant only one cup of rice and dhal cooked without salt, onions and chilies, for a midday meal. The recruits tramped through thick snake-infested jungles to collect food supplies brought by boat from India and unloaded on desolate beaches. They would carry 50-kilogram sacks of rice, dhal, flour and other vital rations on their shoulders into camps deep inside the Vanni jungles.

Water too was scarce in the dry zone and strictly rationed. Available underground, adequate supplies of water could only be collected by digging deep wells. The trainees laboured for days gouging out rock and earth to depths of fifteen metres or more before the precious fluid would ooze out of the ground providing water for drinking and bathing.

Fresh bread was baked in underground bakeries whenever flour was available. In earthen bunkers camouflaged by woven coconut leaves, a chest-high oven made of clay was filled with burning coals. The flour was first hand-mixed with water on flat tin plates, the dough flattened into round cakes which went into the oven. The cooked bread that came out of the ovens was collected by one of the young boys or girls who worked in the camp as helpers, and piled neatly onto banana leaves which were wrapped and tied with bark stripped off banana trees. These packs were then taken away to be distributed to other camps and sentry posts in the area.

They were woken early that morning by Jeevan, one of the instructors, to go on a mission. Nadesan was one of ten trainees who had been chosen. They were issued dark blue shirts and trousers and rubber sandals for their feet. Nadesan was glad to get rid of the torn shirt and trousers they had been training in. Even after constant washing they looked old and dirty.

The Chinese T-58 rifle Nadesan carried came with a satchel full of ammunition which he carried slung across his shoulder. He'd become familiar with the weapon during training although he had only fired it once. Nadesan had endured the three months of training although his heart was really not in it. What he wanted was to act, to do something which would hurt the regime that had taken his wife and child away from him. It consumed him like a slow-cooking fire, filling his thoughts when he was alone. But he had been told that he would be called when the time was right. Until then he needed to be patient and learn to be a fighter.

'This is not a training mission,' Jeevan warned, regarding at each of them individually. 'They shoot at anybody they can see so we must be careful to avoid their sentry posts.'

He reached into a cloth bag slung over his shoulder pulling out a handful of kuppies. 'You are now one of us,' he said, handing a capsule, contained in a glass ampoule, carefully to each of them. 'The gifting of one's life is a weapon that must be used selflessly. Only use it when you don't have a choice left.'

Nadesan knew the significance of the cyanide capsule every Tamil Tiger wore around their neck; to commit suicide rather than be captured.

'Make sure you can raise it to your lips when you tie the kuppie around your neck,' Jeevan said using his own to demonstrate the action. 'You won't have much time if you are caught.'

Nadesan draped the glass vial which hung from a green string, around his neck, pushing it under his collar. He felt a hammering in his head and the familiar ache. It would be so easy to join his wife and son when he was ready.

*

Their transportation was a trailer attached to a farm tractor. The forest roads they took were made with tree trunks placed lengthwise. To stop the trunks from moving, wooden logs were positioned across them, the spaces filled with sand which were rammed in. The trailer shook as they rumbled over the uneven surface until Nadesan's head began to hurt from the constant shaking. Most of the time they were hidden under the jungle canopy making them feel secure from any prying eyes. There were moments however, when the tractor travelled through a clearing or through open fields making them anxiously scan the skies, hoping not to be seen by a passing military helicopter.

Nadesan had fallen into a stupor when the tractor finally stopped. His head hurt from the vibration and the bright sunlight made him squint. Nadesan looked around. They were still concealed under the jungle canopy but ahead of them the track wound next to an open rice paddy before re-entering the jungle.

'This is it,' Jeevan called out. He'd been riding on the back of the tractor next to the driver. 'We walk from here.'

Nadesan stumbled and almost fell as he jumped from the trailer. His legs felt weak. He walked around, stamping his feet on the ground until he felt the circulation return.

They walked in single file, through water-logged paddy fields that were overflowing with young, green paddy shoots. The jungle lay about two hundred metres away; a ragged dark green wall disappearing into the distance. Behind the dense growth, jungle-covered mountains, their tops wreathed in mist, rose into the clear blue sky. In the far corner of the rice paddies, a thatch-roofed hut dwarfed by tall palmyra palms, sheltered it from the heat of the burning sun. Water-filled channels snaked through the muddy fields carrying their precious cargo. Herons walked in the fields, feeding on tadpoles and water insects that darted among the green shoots. It was a scene that Nadesan had witnessed countless number of times.

It was after midday when they crossed a dirt road and climbed to the bund of a large wewa next to a rusted sluice gate. Schools of tiny fish darted in the clear water behind the barrier. The lake was fairly broad, with clumps of tall trees rising out of the water. Starved for water in the dry season, these trees were engulfed by the rising waters of the monsoonal rains, shedding their leaves which had collected in large piles by the edge of the water. Cormorants sitting on the leafless branches, their white throat feathers clearly visible against their black bodies, squawked and fluttered their wings, spreading them out to dry in the sun.

On one side of the lake, tall trees tilted over the water, their large canopies providing shade to masses of tiny water lilies. Branches swished as they pushed into the undergrowth, a sharp hiss from Jeevan warning them to move quietly.

The forested area they were in was narrow, opening out to a series of small rice paddies and gardens overgrown with weeds. Rotting plantain trees, their dry leaves hanging forlornly over an occasional pumpkin creeper filled with bright yellow flowers. Jam fruit bushes growing wild between the neglected plots, reached up to almost waist height.

'Why are these fields not tended?' The trainee next to Nadesan whose name was Jegan came from a village further south. He was shaking his head in disbelief while looking around.

'People won't come to work the fields,' another trainee called Easan hissed angrily. 'They are frightened by the army who don't want anyone wandering around outside the protected areas. In my village, they mined the tracks and killed the water buffalo we used to plough the fields.'

Nadesan looked down, shifting uneasily. He didn't want to step on a mine and loose a leg.

Jeevan knelt and motioned them to gather around him. 'We will rest here till this evening,' he said. 'The army camp is on the other side of that plantation. There is a sentry post next to that hut. They sometimes have a sniper on this side so we must be careful.'

Across the abandoned rice paddy, a mango orchard was in fruit. Birds called to each other as they flittered through the leafy branches. Through the trees, the mud walls of a hut could be seen. Its cadjan roof had large holes in it and one of its walls was completely missing. A large hibiscus in full bloom partly obscured the rest of the building.

'This post is the furthest from the main camp,' Jeevan said, looking around at them. 'It has a wide-open space in front. They laid mines in those vegetable gardens so we have pulled back to these trees. Our job is to create a diversion here. Our main attack will come from the western side.'

Jeevan studied the sentry post, raising himself cautiously to peer over the bushes. 'The army also use dummy positions to prevent us from attacking. There are a couple to the right of that hut. We shoot at them occasionally to make them think we don't know they are empty.'

'How strong are the positions?' Easan asked, raising himself to look.

'Be careful,' Jeevan warned, pulling Easan down. 'Don't stay up too long. They watch constantly and will shoot at you.'

'Can't we use the RPG to take them out?' Easan had trained with the rocket propelled grenade launcher and fancied himself a bit of an expert.

Jeevan shook his head. 'We have tried but the sentry posts are very strong

... even the dummy ones. They stack railway sleepers and trunks from the coconut trees and use many sandbags to protect them.'

The sun started to dip below the trees behind the sentry post. The sky looked like it had been painted red, the white clouds tinged with the same colour. A white heron flew across the open fields heading back to its nest.

Darkness descended quickly as the sun disappeared. Stars began to twinkle, the brightest first and then thousands of others. A peacock screamed, its strident wailing filling the darkness with its sound. Food parcels were opened and they shared the contents between them.

'Remember this is a diversion,' Jeevan warned them, as they checked their weapons. 'Short bursts only. Don't fire everything at once. We have to make them think the main attack is coming from here.'

Nadesan remembered what he had been taught. We are not a state, we don't have a lot of resources. Every bullet we use must kill an occupying enemy soldier. We must avoid the wasteful use of arms.

A gentle breeze fanned across the trees, rustling the branches as they advanced quietly to the edge of the field. Moonlight lit up the abandoned plots creating shadows that stirred in the wind. The men spread out preparing to fire their weapons. Two of the men carried grenades in cloth bags across their shoulders. They would advance closer to the sentry post before throwing them. Nadesan peered out into the darkness clutching his rifle. He was scared.

This was not what he expected when he signed up to fight. His heart burned in revenge for the death of his wife and child. But prowling about in the night was not what he wanted. He turned his head and looked at where Easan was hiding about twenty metres away. He had moved forward, out of the trees and into the open where he could get a good shot at the sentry post.

Jeevan cupped his hand to his ear, listening. Nothing broke the stillness of the night. Even the night birds seemed to sense something was about to happen and were keeping quiet. The moon disappeared behind a cloud plunging everything into darkness. The faint flicker of a fire was visible from the direction of the sentry post. Nadesan settled his rifle on his shoulder and aimed it towards the light.

The faint sound of a whistle could be heard in the wind, growing louder for a few seconds before dying away.

'It's time,' Jeevan hissed. 'Open fire.'

Nadesan saw Easan climbing to his feet and lifting the rocket launcher to his shoulder. He steadied for a minute taking aim through the reticule before pulling the trigger. The rocket roared out of the launcher trailing sparks, heading in the direction of the hit.

Nadesan held his breath watching the projectile on its short journey. The rocket hit the building exploding in a loud crash, flames and debris visible for a second as they cascaded into the air. Gunfire erupted around Nadesan reminding him to pull the trigger on his automatic rifle.

Screams, shouts and flashes of gunfire erupted along the tree line where the army sentry post was located. Bullets whistled through the trees, thudding into tree trunks and shredding branches, showering them with twigs and leaves. A flare shot up into the sky from behind the army lines bathing the area in light. The cacophony of sound increased as loud flashes of light from exploding grenades added to the mayhem.

Another rocket propelled grenade arched into the sky as Easan fired his weapon. Bullets whizzed around Nadesan as the army targeted his position. Nadesan crawled behind a tree trunk which barely covered his body, pushing his rife forward over an exposed root. The rifle clicked on empty forcing Nadesan to change the magazine. He couldn't remember having fired a whole clip.

A loud grunt and thrashing in the bushes as a man was hit close to him by incoming fire. The first ten minutes was total chaos. Mortar shells started raining down on them shaking the ground with their explosions. Blast waves of the explosions, hammered his eardrums, filling his lungs with smoke and choking dust. A deep-throated metal clatter of a heavy machine gun began as the army brought up reinforcements. It's deeper, more frightening tone was continuous as leaves, twigs and broken bits of branches rained down on him.

Nadesan curled up behind the tree as bullets thudded into its trunk, chewing off chunks of wood.

Almost as suddenly as it began, the firing slowed down from both sides. Sporadic gunfire still erupted from one side or the other but the rate of fire had dropped down to almost nothing. Flares still shot up into the sky and the high-velocity crack of sniper rifles convinced Nadesan to keep his head down.

Nadesan's ears rang, his teeth and ears felt gritty, his nerves uncoiling slowly after the barrage. Nadesan rolled on his back, his eyes tightly closed. He dared not raise his head.

'Prepare to pull back.' Nadesan heard Jeevan shout. 'Give them everything you got.'

Firing intensified as the men responded to Jeevan, one of them screaming loudly and firing his weapon on full automatic towards the enemy. Nadesan's throat was dry as he emptied his final clip at the army position. Adrenaline still pumped around his body making him acutely aware of what was going on. Flashes of gunfire still sparkled along the tree line opposite them. A huge gout of fire framed the trees about a kilometre away as a large explosion lit up the night sky. The main attack had kicked off.

'Ok, that's it,' Jeevan yelled hoarsely. 'They've started their attack. Help anyone who is wounded and let's get out of here.'

Two of the men were missing, their bodies nowhere to be found. Three of them had received wounds and Easan was dead. The army had targeted where the rocket propelled grenades came from shredding his body to pieces. Despite his exhaustion and thirst, Nadesan helped carry one of the wounded away from the scene of the action. It was slow going especially since they had to hide from the helicopters that were circling the camp, machine gunning anything that moved.

*

Two days after the attack, Nadesan was called to the hut which the camp leader occupied. Gopu was sitting on the roof of a sand-bagged bunker next to the mud-walled shack, his bare legs stretched out in front of him. Jeevan sat on his haunches on the sand next to the hut, whittling a stick with a pocket knife.

As part of their training program, Nadesan and a few of the trainees had built this very same bunker. It had three levels and could hold up to twelve fighters. The deepest section where a man could stand upright was damp and suffocating. Roofed with thick coconut trunks with a layer of sandbags and earth on top, it was the safest section to be in. A third of the bunker consisted of a waist high section lined with planks of wood on which supplies were stored. The front end of the bunker was covered with thatched palmyra leaves which could be pulled over to conceal the entrance.

Nadesan had heard from others that the attack on the army camp had been partly successful. Two suicide bombers had entered the camp and blown up an ammunition storage bunker and a petrol dump, but the sudden appearance overhead of two helicopters had prevented the camp from being completely overrun.

'Jeevan tells me that you handled yourself well in the attack.'

Nadesan looked at each man without saying anything. He had gone over in his mind what had happened that night and could not remember much. What he could vividly remember was the mind-numbing terror of being shot at by machine guns and being slammed into the ground repeatedly by explosions, but nothing much else. He had come back with his satchel of ammunition empty with only a vague recollection of firing his weapon.

'This was a test to tell us how you perform under fire. You have passed the test and now you have a choice to make,' Gopu said, looking at him intently. 'I've been ordered to send you to Chenkaladi for the next stage in your journey but if you want to stay and fight with us, it can be arranged.'

Nadesan could not think of anything worse. The heat, the humidity, the flies and insects combined with the back-breaking work of digging trenches and cutting tree trunks for bunkers was not what he wanted. He had nothing common with the other trainees who came from farming families and did not have the mechanical knowledge and skill that he had. He couldn't understand why they wanted him to stay, but the taste for revenge was with him every waking minute and he wouldn't get it here in the jungle fighting against an unseen enemy. He decided honesty was the best way forward.

'I am a trained fitter and mechanic,' he said. 'If the movement thinks I am better off here, then so be it. But I want to do something big, something significant for what they did to my family and I am not sure this is the right place to do that.'

Gopu studied Nadesan before replying. 'You have shown an aptitude in your training for repairing weapons and for bomb making,' he agreed. 'So, I can see why they want you somewhere else.' He glanced at Jeevan before addressing Nadesan. 'There's a tractor leaving early tomorrow to collect supplies. You make sure you're on it.'

Nadesan was relieved by the leader's decision. He didn't want to get on the wrong side of him. Nadesan nodded at the two men, trying hard not to show any emotion. The hatred he felt for the people who had killed his family made his ache for revenge. He would get back into the built-up area along the coast and find a way to hurt them. He didn't care if he had to die in the process.

CHAPTER TEN

Amanthi felt wrung out and tired, but sleep eluded her at every turn. Last night she had woken to the ringing of the phone and had been called in to treat burn victims from a traffic accident. She hated working on children and this time was no different. Fortunately, the child had not suffered major burns, protected in her mother's arms by the raging fire caused by the exploding petrol tank. Her mother was not so lucky and Amanthi had spent the night and most of that morning trying to save her.

The warmth of the sun wrapped around Amanthi as she tucked her feet into the rattan armchair that her father used to lie on. Her mother would have objected saying that it was unladylike, but she was beyond caring.

Amanthi washed her hands in the bowl of water that the servant had held out to her. Then she dried them on the soft cotton hand towel before picking up a metal spoon and fork placed on the table for her use. Growing up she had always used her fingers to eat. There was something satisfying about feeling the texture of the food in your hands, squishing the food between your fingers and placing selected morsels in your mouth with the tips of the fingers. However, she eschewed the use of her hands to eat since she had started going to medical school.

Amanthi hadn't realized how hungry she was until the plate of food was placed in front of her. Amanthi had asked the old *ayah* to serve her food on the plate like she used to do when she was a child. The woman had been with them since her father had brought her from a poor village in the south to look after Amanthi when she was born. The woman took care of all the chores around the house and cooked their meals for them.

Her mother had watched as Amanthi ate, hungrily spooning the mixture of rice, dhal and vegetable curry into her mouth. Her mother never understood why Amanthi had become a vegetarian and Amanthi did not have the heart to tell her mother that the smell of cooked flesh had turned her off eating meat forever.

'How are things at the hospital?' her mother had asked. She disapproved of Amanthi working in the Burn Unit, telling all her friends that she worked at the General Hospital.

'Very busy,' Amanthi said, spooning a dollop of chutney onto her plate. 'We're up to twenty beds now.' After the bus station bombing, the burns unit had been extended and doubled in size. Beds were no longer crammed into the hospital corridors and hallways and the unit was properly air conditioned to a steady temperature to keep the burn patients comfortable. It had made all the difference to those working in the crowded unit.

'I don't understand why you are still working there,' her mother said. 'All of your batch have joined private practices. I am sure *thaarthi* would have wanted you to go private!'

Amanthi shook her head. 'I am happy with what I'm doing,' she said, glancing at her mother. 'I'm sure he would have understood.'

Amanthi remembered her father with fondness. She missed him. A big strong man who loved to party and tell stories, his job as the Forestry officer in a group of low country tea estates kept him away from home for days, but he always brought something back for her. Her mother had met her father when they were at university together in India. He'd swept her off her feet and after a short courtship, married her and brought her back with him to Colombo.

'But it's ruining your social life,' her mother said peevishly. 'You never have time to go out with anyone. When will you have time to find a husband?'

There was an awkward pause as Amanthi chose not to answer. This was not the first time her mother had raised this with her and recently it had ended in them arguing. All of Amanthi's school friends were married, some had children, and they all seemed very happy with their big houses, new cars and servants to do their bidding. However, much she despised them for their wealth and middle-class values, she'd almost become like one of them. But it wasn't the life Amanthi wanted for herself. She was happiest doing what she did and had recently been spending some of her free time at the hospital. There was no adventure, romance, success. This was it. Life was mundane and dangerous at the same time, and the realization of it made her melancholy.

The reality was that Amanthi was lonely. She hated meeting with her friends. She was not interested in talking about how well their husbands were doing or how their children were growing. Didn't they know that a war was going on in the country and people were dying by their hundreds? She hated to gossip and had recently started making excuses about how busy she was to avoid meeting with her friends. She had not had a serious relationship since medical school and she missed the intimacy. But she had chosen to lead this life and she was content.

Dr Perera had been satisfied with the training Amanthi and her team had completed, and everything was in place for their first emergency response. Boxes had been packed with medical supplies which could be transported by road or by air. They had been assigned an ambulance which had a supply of medicines and bandages needed for burn victims.

They had even met with army surgeons in the Colombo military hospital not far away from where the General Hospital was located and worked out a procedure which would be put into effect whenever a soldier was severely burned. Amanthi and the emergency response team would be flown out to the patient if the soldier was too sick to be moved.

Amanthi leaned back and stretched. Thinking back through the past few months, Amanthi was amazed at how things had fallen into place. She felt as ready as she would ever be. Both Nelum and Shanthi had become good friends and worked well as a team. She had also found two senior medical students who had volunteered to be the team orderlies.

Grey clouds began to drift across the sky above the garden. They would gather quickly, in an hour perhaps, and the afternoon's rain would roll in.

But not yet, thought Amanthi. She could sit for a while longer. She hadn't felt like resting in her room as her mother had insisted. There was far too much going on in her mind. Her mother always rested in the afternoon these days. Amanthi knew it was a convenient excuse. They used to talk of so many things, but after her father died, her mother had retreated to a hidden world of darkened corners that only she would enter.

Amanthi looked around the garden and pulled out a cigarette from her coat pocket. She still felt guilty, having started to smoke at work. The enjoyment she got during the time she spent away from the unit, surreptitiously enjoying the nicotine laced smoke that filled her lungs, certainly made up for it. Lighting up she inhaled deeply. She felt relaxed as she looked up and exhaled a cloud of smoke into the air. She knew her mother would be upset when she found out.

A military helicopter thundered overhead, flying quite low to the ground, startling a flock of roosting birds into flight. The noise had become a common occurrence in the capital since fighting in the north had intensified and no one paid much attention to them anymore. Dark clouds framed the green machine as it disappeared from sight behind the neighbours' buildings.

The bold headlines on a folded newspaper lying on the table caught her attention. 'Army and Airforce continue offensive in Jaffna – Foreign Minister in Discussions with India'. She picked up the broadsheet, scanning its contents before tossing it back on the table. Amanthi shook her head in disbelief. The whole country was affected by what was happening in the north and she blamed the government for creating the situation the country now faced. Marginalizing a whole race of people based on their ethnicity was abhorrent. Wasn't the country big enough for both the Sinhalese and the Tamils to live together peacefully. More and more people being brought into the burn unit were victims of the bombing campaign the militant Tamils had begun in retaliation to discriminatory policies being enforced by the ruling party. And now we're bombing them. When is it going to stop?

The relaxed atmosphere she had been used to in Colombo had changed since the bombings had begun. Suspense hung heavily in the air, none more so than at night when the streets which were usually full of people and traffic, lay quiet and empty. People were scared to go out fearing of being questioned or picked up by the heavily armed soldiers who patrolled the streets at night.

There had always been a class division in the country between the rich and poor. After all she experienced it in her own home every day with the three servants who lived with them ever since she was a child. But she couldn't comprehend how people could be treated differently due to race or religion. It just didn't seem right.

The drop of rain on her upturned face was not unexpected. There was the smell of rain in the air. Taking a couple of puffs, she stubbed out the cigarette, hiding it under the garden soil as she went into the house. She wasn't needed till morning so she changed into a long t-shirt, kicked off her slippers and lay on top of the bedspread, staring at the faded ceiling. A gecko scampered across intent on stalking a fluttering moth, dancing around a beam of light filtering through the lace curtains.

Heavy drops of rain on the roof tiles drowned out her thoughts as she fell asleep. For the first time in a long while, it was deep and untroubled, taking her far away from the world which she now lived.

CHAPTER ELEVEN

The shade offered him little protection. It was suffocating in the stinking, brutal heat. Tilak's shirt was soaked with sweat under the straps of the heavy pack which chafed his shoulders. His hips ached with the weight of more than fifteen kilos of belt kit, ammunition, jungle knife and two water bottles. The standard issue Armalite rifle in his hands was heavy and slippery in his hands.

The jungle was full of the sound of insects and the haunting bird calls from high in the canopy gave a surreal sound to the concealed world they were moving in. The eight-man patrol was following a narrow trail in the Sinharaja Forest, a virgin tropical rain forest in the south-western lowlands of the country. The team were well spaced out, about ten metres apart, the men moving with caution along the trail in the dim light of the afternoon. A few thin shafts of light that managed to get through the dense canopy did little to illuminate the path or the surrounding jungle. The deep shadows in places would be ideal cover for the men they were hunting.

Tilak stumbled from tiredness at the rear of the patrol. Tired legs, sore feet, heaving chest ... they must have been on the trail for over three hours. He was listening hard, trying to interpret the sounds of the jungle. All he could hear was the call of a bird far overhead and the bark of a monkey. He moved with care past vast tree trunks shooting fifty metres into the sky, past saplings, around outcroppings of tree roots and dense bushes trying not to slip on the damp leaves and rotten logs. He was trying to make as little noise as possible while trying to keep the man in front in sight all at the same time. It demanded a lot of concentration.

They were on their final training exercise. He was guaranteed to pass out tomorrow, but he didn't want to make any mistakes and incur the wrath of Mike. Tilak paused as he watched the man in front come up to a large rotten log. The trail had narrowed even more, the ground sloping up more steeply on either side.

Tilak felt the hackles rise behind his neck. Mike and the two trainers were out there somewhere preparing to ambush them. He sank to his haunches and cautiously peered around the surrounding undergrowth. Tall trees grew straight up, creating a canopy which made the area shadowy. The saplings and bushes growing on the slope were an indistinct dark grey or black in places.

The normal jungles noises were muted, seemingly coming from further away. It didn't feel right. The man in front began to move when the jungle erupted in gunfire. Tilak froze. The crackle of automatic fire, the ear-numbing bangs of explosive devices echoed and rebounded off the trees. Men shouted and began to return fire. Tilak dived next to the log and wrestled free of his pack. He began to fire up the slope.

The little gully they were in was the perfect place for an ambush. Thick smoke from an explosive device began to fill the ravine as more explosions sounded. They needed to get out of the killing zone. Tilak gathered his feet under him. They had been taught that the best way to get out of an ambush was to attack it. He looked around, and through the drifting smoke saw the soldier ahead of him, signalling with his arm in the air. Tilak repeated the gesture hoping that the only soldier behind him was watching. A whistle sounded and he scrambled to his feet and charged, weaving up the slope towards the firing. He fired from his hip as he ran, sensing the others in the patrol around him doing the same. Slipping on the wet floor he almost fell, grabbing a leafy sapling to prevent crashing to the ground. Recovering his balance, he panted up the hill, firing short bursts from his rifle.

Tilak saw a couple of shadowy figures about twenty metres away and began to run towards them, frantically changing a magazine as he ran. The next thing he knew he was flat in his face. A tripwire had dumped him face down in the damp leafy floor of the jungle. He lay there for a moment stunned and exhausted, panting for breath.

'Bang, bang, you're fucking dead.'

Tilak looked up into the face of an instructor who grinned at him cheerily. His face was covered in green and black stripes, his camouflaged uniform blending almost seamlessly into the jungle undergrowth. He winked at Tilak and slithered back out of sight like a reptile hiding under a pile of leaves.

A dull animal rage boiled within him as one by one, the sound of gunfire died down. Tilak sat on the ground sullenly and waited for the whistle to blow to mark the end of the exercise. He felt almost helpless. It was a feeling he was not used to and did not like. He had never had to deal with anyone so capable. He shook his head at the ingenuity that the ex-SAS instructors displayed. This was the first time they had used a combination of smoke and trip wires and the patrol had blundered straight into it. Each one of the trainees had led a patrol and everyone had been ambushed, each ambush site different to the previous one, some sprung soon after they left the camp, others, hours later as they finished their patrol.

The whistle blew and he made his way down through the bushes and trees to collect his pack and join the other men. The young police sub-inspector who had led the patrol was getting a severe talking to by one of the instructors. It was clear to Tilak that the instructor was not impressed with how the sub-inspector dealt with the situation and was telling him so.

'I am glad these exercises are finally over,' exclaimed one of the men. 'These bastards can hide under a banana leaf. I didn't even see the one who got me.'

Tilak nodded. He didn't want to say anything knowing it would come out wrong. He wiped the back of his right hand across forehead still feeling the anger bubbling in him.

The patrol had gathered in a group. Some of the men were drinking water while one or two of the men squatted on the ground smoking. Tilak wiped his head with his neck cloth. It kept the insects and other nasty creatures from crawling down the back of his collar. He was wet and filthy from the humid damp, his own sweat and the repeated crawling in the wet earth. They looked like a heavily armed bunch of bandits.

They had all been trained on how to respond to an ambush, how to direct fire and escape the killing zone. They had been taught to navigate within the dense and seemingly featureless jungle very quietly, disturbing nothing and leaving little indication that they had passed. But again, and again they had been caught and ambushed as they played cat and mouse with their cunning teachers.

But the lack of sleep and the short breaks they had been given in the intense heat and humidity totally exhausted them, made them react slower and make mistakes. They should have been more aggressive. The front and rear sections should have moved very quickly off the trail while the middle section laid down heavy covering fire.

They were ordered to form up and prepare to head back to the camp. The instructor stood off to the side and watched as they staggered to their feet and lined up on the trail. There was a collective sigh of relief as a command was given to move out. The instructor set off at a fast pace heading for the camp about five kilometres away.

*

The white minivan dodged through rush hour traffic on the Galle Road filled with all manner of vehicles. The driver swore as he braked hard to avoid a dirty Leyland bus which stopped suddenly in the middle of the road. Office workers desperate to get on board, rushed from the pavement, pushing each other to get into the bus which had started to move after disembarking a passenger.

Tilak had woken that morning to the insistent rapping on his cubicle door. A sergeant dressed in a crisp new uniform informed him that he was to report to the Commanders office right away. Still half asleep, Tilak struggled to get into his uniform and splashed some water on his face before having a quick shave. In his shaving mirror, he saw a face burned deep brown by three months of fierce tropical sunshine. His eyes were bright and clear, the constant jungle training had left his senses sharpened and on a high edge of alertness. He felt fit and hardened and looked forward to another day of training. As he finished shaving he grinned broadly at his reflection in the mirror. In that moment, he was as happy as he had ever been in life. Getting out of prison had been a huge change. He didn't have to be always on guard, always looking over his shoulder in case someone stuck a knife into him. Also, the well prepared, nutritious food and constant exercise were both physically and mentally cleansing. He felt he had finally cast off that fearful burden, that inner demon that had so long been weighing on him and all at once there was a sense of relief and peace in his soul.

The commander looked up when Tilak entered the operations room. He waved Tilak over and motioned him into his office, closing the door behind him.

The commander was not in a mood for pleasantries. 'We have found the terrorist cell that blew up the central bus station in Colombo,' he said. 'They are located in a safe house not far from the river. It's being raided tonight and we want you there.'

Tilak had known for a while that this day would come. His training had ended a week ago and he was wondering why it was taking so long to be deployed to the field. Tilak had been briefed on which organisation he was working for. It was the Special Branch. He still did not know who was pulling the strings but realized it was all the information he was going to get.

'This will be an undercover operation so you're to dress in civilian clothes,' the commander said, waving his hand at Tilak. 'Get changed and have something to eat. Pick up a concealed weapon for yourself from the armoury. I want you ready to go in an hour.'

Tilak nodded and left the room. *It must be pretty serious if they are issuing weapons.* Like everyone else in the country, he had heard about the bomb at the central bus station that had killed over a hundred people and injured a few hundred more. For days, the newspapers dedicated a whole section to what had happened and the search for the bombers.

The hard-looking man leaned against the minivan smoking a cigarette. He was tall and dark skinned and wore a simple white shirt with sleeves folded over strong forearms. A dark sarong was wrapped tightly around his slim hips. Tilak had never seen him before.

The man stubbed his cigarette on the ground while watching Tilak walk over to the minivan. Tilak had dressed in bush shirt and dark slacks. A pair of sandals completed his attire.

'I am Chandra,' he said in Sinhalese, extending his hand. 'I will accompany you today.'

'Are you with the Special Branch?' Tilak enquired in the same language, shaking Chandra's hand.

Chandra nodded without speaking. His hooded eyes examined Tilak carefully taking his measure. Tilak held his eyes for a few seconds before breaking contact. He would not be intimidated by these men.

Tilak got into the back of the minivan behind Chandra.

They drove out through heavy gates that were set in a barricade of close-set steel posts with coils of barbed wire over the top. He closed his eyes and must have fallen asleep as the next thing he knew they were already in Colombo.

Tilak stared out the window of the minivan. It had been many years since he had been to this part of the city. Some of the buildings which remained a legacy of the country's colonial rulers had long fallen into disrepair. Neglected by its new owners, the old white buildings were streaked with decay and tarnished by the choking pollution of the crowded streets. Stray dogs, their ribs starkly prominent on their thin bodies nibbled around the edges of piles of rotten vegetables and over-ripe fruit. Hundreds of people swarmed the narrow, crowded streets as the minivan edged its way forward, its horn honking loudly.

Chandra leaned forward and tapped the driver on the shoulder. 'Stop there,' he grunted, pointing to an open bazaar overflowing with people. The bazaar which sold vegetables, dried fish and fruit stood at the corner of two busy streets. A double-parked line of three-wheelers with their drivers calling out to shoppers, jammed one side of the market.

The minivan coasted to a stop, the busy crowd eddying around the vehicle. Chandra gestured with his chin towards a garage about fifty metres across the road junction. A three-wheeler lying on its side on the hard-packed dirt floor of the garage was being worked on by a bare bodied man wearing oil-stained khaki shorts.

'That's the place,' he said, glancing at Tilak. 'We have been watching it for a few days. At least three men live there and we have seen others going in and out. The three-wheeler came in yesterday and we think it may be used to transport another bomb. We'll wait until tonight before going in. We don't want to risk anything with so many people around.'

Not more than a car length wide, the wooden structure which was the garage was held up on each side by the walls of adjoining shops.

'What if they move the three-wheeler today?' Tilak asked, trying hard to look into the shadowy interior of the garage.

'We have people standing by to block off the streets if they move the vehicle.' Chandra nodded at the driver who opened his door and slipped into the crowd. 'Kirthi will do a walk-pass to see how many of them are there.' Chandra gestured at the small eatery next to the bazaar. 'Let's go to the kade and get something to eat. We'll not get any food later.'

Tilak got out of the vehicle and stretched. His back was aching, probably from just sitting in the minivan. For the first time since leaving prison Tilak felt invigorated and alive. His nerves were tingling with the prospect of catching the bus station bombers.

The day of the bombing was still fresh in his mind. He had heard the distant thud of the explosion in his prison cell but thought nothing about it until later in the evening when they were lining up to enter the prison canteen for their evening meal.

An ear-piercing shriek as shrill as a wild-pig, pulled him around to see one of the guards grabbing an inmate by his hair while another kicked him repeatedly. Tilak recognised the man they were assaulting. Not much was known about him but it was whispered in the hallways that he was a political prisoner from the north, a senior member of one of the militant Tamil groups. Inmates scattered as more guards poured into the room, pushing them aside as the man was bundled out of the room screaming something in Tamil at the top of his voice.

Order was quickly restored when the guards pushed the prisoners back into line, wielding their batons if someone showed any signs of resistance. The room was abuzz with whispers as the inmates were hustled into the canteen to be served.

A bomb in Pettah ... hundreds killed ... bus station ... Tamil Tigers ... curfew! Tilak's blood ran cold as harsh whispers circulated the room. An emergency broadcast on the radio had announced the bombing at the central bus station during evening rush hour, with initial reports putting the dead in their hundreds. The radio was appealing for people to donate blood and for medically trained volunteers to go to the Colombo General Hospital. A red haze clouded his thoughts as years of pent-up prison anger he'd buried in the back of his mind burst through. How could they do this to ordinary people?

A liquid anger, thick and red threatened to overwhelm him. Tilak hated that he was in prison when he should have been out there looking for these bombers. It was what he had trained for as an army officer. To protect his country and its people. The men standing next to him edged away, looking at Tilak strangely as he tried to control himself. One of the guards stared at him intently, tapping his baton against his leg as Tilak tried to pull himself back from the abyss. Tilak took a deep breath and forced himself to relax. If I ever get a chance I will make them pay!

The promise he had made to himself that day was fresh in his mind as he swivelled his head, looking around the market. It was brimming with goods and shoppers but no one paid them any attention. Now that they were close to their target he felt that all too familiar intensity building up inside of him. No amount of training would ever replace the sense of imminent danger which always worked as a fast-acting drug on his senses.

'Hmm …' Tilak thought, his mind now fully focused on what was to come. He caressed the reassuring bulk of the automatic pistol he carried, tucked into his trouser under his shirt.

CHAPTER TWELVE

A loud electronic tone from the public-address system indicated an announcement was imminent. The system which had been installed after the bus station bombing was usually reserved for Code Blue and other major emergencies. Amanthi paused in her writing to concentrate on the broadcast.

'Code Red Emergency, repeat Code Red Emergency. First response teams to report to their stations immediately.'

Amanthi froze in shock for a moment. She had waited for this moment to come and finally it was here. She pushed past Renata, knocking the nurse's clipboard to the ground.

'Oh, I am sorry Renata. I didn't mean to do that.' Amanthi glanced back at Renata.

'Don't worry about it,' Renata said, waving her away. 'You take care!'

Amanthi walked quickly down the ward to the small office she used. She grabbed the emergency medic pack lying next to her desk and rushed out of the room. The corridor was filled with supplies being delivered to the hospital and she navigated around the boxes and cartons like an athlete negotiating a hurdle course. The ambulance bay was crowded with people when she rounded the corner. Dr Perera stood next to the registrar looking down at a sheet of paper. She glanced at Amanthi as she bustled down the corridor, focusing back again on the paper she held. Nelum and Shanthi were already in the ambulance looking anxiously in her direction. Amanthi dumped her pack next to them, giving them a nervous smile of reassurance.

Dr Perera waved Amanthi over. 'The security forces are raiding a house where a Tiger cell is located. They believe this is where the bus station bomber is hiding', she said. 'It's next to a busy market and they want our team on standby in case there's an explosion. The ambulance will be parked a few streets away until you are needed.'

Taking a deep breath, Amanthi nodded wordlessly. This was her first real emergency. They had drilled for this moment many times but somehow this seemed different. Amanthi hoped that she would perform the role she had been given.

Dr Perera perhaps sensing Amanthi's uncertainty, turned to her and took her arm. 'I have every confidence you can do this,' she said, looking at Amanthi directly. 'You are a capable surgeon with an experienced team behind you. We're only minutes away if there is something you cannot handle. You'll be fine.'

The vehicle roared to life as Amanthi got in to the passenger seat. It was stuffy inside the ambulance. The driver whose name was Sunil looked at her, his fingers drumming on the steering wheel, waiting for her permission to move. Amanthi nodded and the vehicle moved forward slowly, easing into the traffic on Kynsey Place.

Amanthi turned and looked back at the two nurses. They had spent several days inventorying and restocking the two-bed, extreme care ambulance that had been acquired by the burn unit. The ambulance coasted to a stop on a busy street in Pettah. Small garish shops and emporiums carrying goods of every description lined both sides of the noisy thoroughfare. Fruit and vegetable sellers selling their dusty produce out of wooden crates and flat bottom barrows, sat on mats spread on the narrow uneven pavements. Two or three men dressed in cotton shirts and sarongs were sitting in their three-wheelers on the edge of the road talking to each other while fume-belching lorries and buses passed within touching distance. Scrawny barefooted men with cigarettes pinched into the corners of their mouths were loading a lorry with sacks of coconuts while unhealthy looking stray dogs crawled around under parked vehicles looking for food.

A Police inspector accompanied by two armed constables walked up to the ambulance. The noise and smells of the street filled the ambulance when Amanthi rolled down the window. The inspector leant in through the open window and looked inside.

The inspector was an older man, with the tired, cynical look of a city-bred local. 'What are you doing here?' he asked in Singhalese. 'This area has been cordoned off for a police action.'

'I am a doctor and we've been placed on standby in case of any trouble,' Amanthi explained. 'We're from the burn unit of the General Hospital.'

The inspector studied her carefully and then seemingly satisfied, he looked around. 'This is not a good place to park,' he said. 'Follow me.'

The inspector guided them down a narrow lane leading off the busy street. The laneway had a wooden barrier across its entrance and was empty of any traffic. 'Park here,' he said. 'This road will give us access to the market if we're needed.'

The lane was being used by the police as a staging area. A group of heavily armed men wearing bullet proof jackets and metal helmets were lined up on one side against a wall checking their weapons. They were being spoken to quietly by a sergeant.

Amanthi felt both excited and apprehensive at the same time. This was the first time she had been involved in anything like this. What if it all went wrong and the market was blown up. Amanthi shuddered, remembering the burnt and dismembered bodies she had to work on after the last bombing. She felt her nerves threaten to overwhelm her but she shook off the feeling. She shouldn't worry about things she could not control. The police had a job to do and so did she. Amanthi felt the ambulance move as Nelum moved to the front of the ambulance and looked over her shoulder at the armed men outside.

'What are they doing,' she asked, her eyes darting between the men in the laneway and Amanthi's face.

'They found the place where the Tigers are hiding,' Amanthi said reassuringly. 'These men will be the one's going in after them.' Amanthi turned and looked at Nelum. 'We're here in case something goes wrong.'

Nelum's eyes flickered a tiny, hopeful smile in response. She moved back deeper into the ambulance and sat on a gurney opposite Shanthi. Amanthi understood how Nelum must be feeling. She thought about the people who were causing all this chaos. What had driven them to do what they had done. Were their lives so bad that they would resort to murder on such a large scale. Amanthi watched as the armed men moved purposely down the lane, away from the ambulance. She wondered how many of them would survive the day.

CHAPTER THIRTEEN

Nadesan walked across the road into the crowded market. He had been helping the other men repair a car and had forgotten to have lunch. He wanted to get something before the small eatery in the bazaar ran out of food. Even though he had been treated like a returning hero by the men who worked at the small garage, he could not shake off the feeling of guilt at running away at the bus station. He was in a wasteland of grieving and sorrowful shame. What would he give to hold his young son in his arms as he slept, stroke his wife's long black hair and delight in her beautiful smile. But here he was, still alive, not even wounded.

Nadesan felt ashamed when the leader of the cell passed on a message from the head of the organisation congratulating him on the success of his mission. Nadesan just could not handle the admiration and respect he received from the others without thinking of his wife and son. He could see in the men's eyes that they did not understand why he had retreated behind a wall of silence, finally leaving him alone to wallow in his self-pity.

One day became seven days and one week turned into a month. The Tiger cell had not been given any missions since the bus station bombing and Nadesan couldn't understand what was causing the delay. Everyone was restive and agitated by the long wait.

Because it was judged too dangerous for Nadesan to leave the safe-house, he remained in the back room lying on his mat, sinking into a deepening gloom. All that grief and soul searching took such a toll on him that he lost weight. His cheeks grew hollow and there were black hollows under his eyes.

Deva spoke to him from the doorway of the room one day. 'What's going on with you?' he questioned, staring at Nadesan intently. 'The men are all complaining about you moping around the place. I have noticed it too and I want you to snap out of it.'

Deva was calm, and he seemed to be completely relaxed, but his face betrayed the tension that he was feeling.

'It's nothing,' Nadesan sighed, offering him a small smile in return.

'Come on,' he insisted. 'Let's have it.'

Nadesan looked at Deva and lowered his head. It occurred to him that if their roles were reversed and one of his men was behaving with such disturbing preoccupation, he too would have brought it up.

'Well, it's just a bit of soul-searching I guess. It's been almost three months since the bombing, and I'm getting crazy just sitting around. Do you know why we don't have another mission?'

'They are keeping us for something special,' Deva shrugged. 'It's not like I like waiting either.'

'What could be that special?' Nadesan asked. 'Don't they know how difficult it is?'

'I only know it's an important target and they don't give a shit what we think. Anyway, there's nothing we can do! We've run out of explosives. I am expecting another shipment but I don't know when.'

'I don't like it,' Nadesan whispered, shaking his head. 'It's been too long. I need to get out of this place.' The frustration, the dread, the worry was getting too much for him. Most nights he was haunted by recurring nightmares. He would wake up in a bath of perspiration when one of the others sleeping in the room would throw something at him.

Deva stared at him in silence before replying. 'I agree. I think I have kept you in here too long. Go outside into the market. No one knows who you are but clean yourself up before you go. There is a price on all our heads but they don't have a description of any of us. We would have heard by now if they did.'

Deva watched Nadesan as he struggled with what he had just heard. 'How do you know this?' he finally asked.

Deva shook his head. 'I don't know this for sure but we would have heard if they were looking for a particular person. The only way you are going to find out is by going out. It's not that difficult.'

Nadesan did not leave the garage for a few more days. Deva left him alone to brood until one-day Nadesan decided he had enough and walked across the road into the market. At first, he thought that everyone was looking at him and wanted to run back to the garage but then he saw Deva watching him. It took him almost an hour to overcome his fear and realize that no one was interested in him. From that day, he went into the market at least twice a day to buy food for the people in the garage.

Gradually Nadesan's mood began to change. He took care not to draw attention to himself by wearing a loose white shirt over a plain sarong and not entering the market until it was busy. The vendors in the market got used to seeing him and some even called out greetings to him. But he walked along quietly and sedately, without hurry, to avoid being noticed. He scarcely looked at any passerby, tried to escape looking at their faces at all. His confidence began to increase and though his nightmares came less frequently, he never lost the paranoia he had about being captured and always kept a close watch on what was going on around the market.

That morning, he had been busy helping the men remove the head gasket of a car engine. It was a major repair and he did not pay much attention to what was happening in the market. Nadesan helped them to drain the oil and coolant from the engine before removing the cylinder head from the engine block to reveal the damaged part.

With a newspaper-wrapped rice parcel in his hand, Nadesan walked along the potholed street back to the garage when a white minivan with three occupants coasted past him and parked beside the side of the busy bazaar.

Coming up to the rear of the vehicle, his suspicions were aroused when he noticed all three men in the vehicle looking intently towards the garage across the street junction.

Nadesan acted without thinking. Turning abruptly, he dodged a cyclist and an empty three-wheeler and walked hurriedly across the road away from the minivan. Looking over his shoulder he saw the driver's door open and a man slip into the crowd, disappearing from sight. Nadesan stood next to a shop selling plastic goods, partially concealed by a stack of plastic laundry baskets. He glanced around the shop-lined street to see whether he was being observed by anyone before switching his attention back to the minivan.

Nadesan's fear of being caught that fateful evening had never left him. He had not once thought that he would have to remain in Colombo, committing himself to his mission totally. But after what happened, he had asked to remain and be given another mission.

The minivan door facing away from him opened and two men got out of the van. Nadesan's whole body tingled with anticipation and dread as the two men looked up and down the road before crossing it. The men although indistinguishable from others in the crowd stood out like beacons to Nadesan. Their posture and bearing clearly revealed to him that they were both from the Police. He had spent enough time in the Police station when his wife and child were killed, so that he was able to recognize a plain-clothed policeman when he saw one. That in itself was not surprising as Nadesan knew that off-duty servicemen away from their bases were not allowed to wear their uniforms. But when coupled with their interest in the garage, it told a different story. He watched as the two men went into a little eatery opposite the bazaar.

Nadesan wondered whether he was getting too paranoid. Was he imagining all this? But taking extra precautions and staying one step ahead of the Police was his only hope of not being captured. He wanted to warn the others but he would take the real risk of being spotted and followed. Not knowing what to do, Nadesan looked around again to see whether anyone was watching him. He fingered the locket around his neck nervously. Inside it was the cyanide capsule he had been given after his training. If the garage was under observation, they would have seen him enter the bazaar. But he never went far and always returned before too long. He didn't see anyone watching him so he wedged himself against the side wall of the shop and opened his rice parcel. He might as well eat while he waited.

CHAPTER FOURTEEN

Kirthi lounged back in his seat but sat upright when Tilak and Chandra climbed into the minivan. 'What's happening?' Chandra asked the driver.

'They're still working on the three-wheeler,' the driver said. 'I saw three men when I walked past. There was one other man according to Jagath but he went into the bazaar and has not returned.'

The three-wheeler was upright, facing the garage entrance with a man working in it. No one else could be seen from where they were parked.

'Did anyone follow the man who went into the bazaar,' Tilak asked, looking around at the shoppers outside. 'We need to capture the whole cell.'

'I don't think so,' Kirthi said, glancing at Chandra. 'We don't want to tip them off by following them. The ones we have been watching have all come back to the garage eventually.'

Tilak looked at Chandra who shrugged. 'It's a decision that's been taken at a higher level. We will throw a cordon around the whole area when it's time and make sure everyone is questioned.'

'Look,' Kirthi said pointing at the garage. Two men were lifting a wooden box into the back seat of the three-wheeler while the other supervised. The crowd had thinned out as vendors in the bazaar packed up their goods making the garage clearly visible from the van.

'They could be targeting another rush hour crowd,' Chandra said, pulling a walkie-talkie from his pocket. 'Are you seeing this?' he spoke into the device.

'Yes, we are,' the reply came back. 'Hold your positions until we get the order to move.'

Chandra reached under his shirt and pulled out his hand gun indicating to the others to do the same. He held the gun below the level of the minivan windows and chambered a round while holding on to the walkie-talkie.

The two men had finished tying down the box on the back of the three-wheeler and were standing back to admire their work. The other man walked towards the back of the garage, disappearing from sight.

'Ok, we've got permission to take them down,' the walkie-talkie squawked into life. 'Wait until we block the roads and go on my signal.'

Two 4-wheel drive vehicles entered the road behind the minivan. One stopped, blocking the road while the other drove past the minivan, stopping at an angle across the middle of the junction.

'Go, go, go...' the radio, squawked into life. 'Take them down!'

Men carrying handguns seemed to erupt from everywhere. Four heavily armed Special Task Force soldiers scrambled out of the back of the 4-wheel drive blocking the junction and took up positions covering the garage entrance. Shoppers in the streets surrounding the market stopped and stared at the chaos around them. The sound of a helicopter close overhead made everyone duck their heads.

Chandra and Tilak were out of the minivan and running towards the garage before the walkie-talkie stopped transmitting. Tilak saw a plain clothes man club one of the workers in the garage with a solid blow to the head, pouncing on him as he fell to the ground. The other man didn't wait to be told, falling onto the ground with his arms raised in the air.

Tilak was close behind the first responders, jumping over the two men wrestling on the floor. His eyes quickly adjusted to the gloom inside the garage. The entrance to a narrow passageway led to the back of the structure. A movement at the far end caught his eye as he turned towards the doorway. His left foot slid out from under him on a patch of engine oil and he crashed to one knee.

A burst of automatic fire from inside the passage way sent bullets whizzing over his head and out of the garage entrance behind him. The slip had saved his life. Tilak dived onto his stomach firing his handgun into the passageway before crashing into a toolbox and coming to a stop. Bullets thudded into the toolbox, the metal tools absorbing the rounds and stopping them.

Tilak flexed his knee and risked a quick peep around the side of the toolbox. He could not see anything from where he was. He poked his gun over the toolbox and fired three quick shots into the passageway hoping to keep the gunman off balance. He knew the longer they took to kill or capture the terrorists the more difficult it would get in the warren of rooms and passageways behind the garage. And if the terrorists had any explosives hidden in the back, they wouldn't hesitate to use them putting everyone at risk.

A pile of oily rags in a corner gave him an idea. He rolled out from behind the toolbox and scrambled to the pile.

'Give me your lighter,' he shouted at Chandra who was hiding behind the tree-wheeler. Chandra nodded his head and reached into his trouser pocket digging out the butane-filled lighter. He tossed it at Tilak who grabbed it with one hand.

Rolling a few rags into a ball, Tilak set fire to them with the lighter. When the ball was well alight he tossed it as far as he could into the cement lined passageway. The terrorist kept shooting in bursts indicating that the man had some military training. The rags burnt with a thick cloying smoke which quickly filled the passage way. Tilak changed the magazine in his pistol and crawled on his stomach into the passageway under the layer of smoke.

The man coughed giving Tilak an idea of his position. He fired five shots at the sound, aiming the first one low and moving up as he went. The clatter of a rifle hitting the floor and a thump made him jump to his feet and charge into the smoky passageway. The passage led into a large room with two doorways. Through the smoke, Tilak could see a man on his back in a growing pool of blood across the entrance to one of the rooms. The man shuddered as he saw

Tilak and reached for something behind the door. Tilak fired twice hitting the man in his head to kill him instantly.

Tilak felt someone behind him and pivoted on one foot, sweeping his weapon around in a half circle. Chandra who had entered the room behind him put up his hand when he saw Tilak's pistol in his face.

'Don't shoot,' he said, hoarsely. 'It's me.'

Tilak nodded and put his finger to his lips. He pointed at the two rooms leading off the passage asking Chandra to cover him. One room had mats on the floor with clothes hanging on hooks from the wall. A door opened into a small enclosed courtyard with a squatting toilet in the corner. The other room was smaller and filled with wooden boxes. One of the boxes which had its lid on the floor contained pouches stuffed with grenades and automatic rifle magazines. The man had been reaching for a grenade when Tilak had shot him. 'Good work,' said Chandra, after a bout of coughing. 'We've captured two of them, which should lead us to a few others.'

Tilak nodded but did not say anything. He was totally committed to finding the terrorist cell. Drawing a deep breath, he pressed his hand against his throbbing heart. He had never been shot at before and had always wondered what it would feel like, would he be afraid? But he was not afraid, his mind even occupied by irrelevant matters, but by nothing for long. He turned and walked down the passageway and out into the street.

Faces stared at him from the bazaar across the street. He suddenly remembered the man who had gone into the bazaar. Was he one of those looking at him? It was a shame they didn't take down the whole cell.

CHAPTER FIFTEEN

Nadesan watched the raid progress, shrinking into his hiding place as the sound of gunfire erupted from inside the garage. Bullets hit the side of the market. A man was hit and crumbled to the ground. People ran away from the gunfire screaming in fear as Nadesan slipped from his hiding place and joined the frantic throng.

At the top of the street, a few Police constables tried to form a cordon to stop the crowd leaving the area, shouting at them to get into a line but their efforts were useless. The crowd burst through the cordon taking Nadesan with them as they went.

Nadesan did not want to draw any attention to himself and kept to the edge of the pavement, ducking behind a cart full of bags of vegetables. The cart was rocking against the press of the crowd and a bare bodied man in a sarong was desperately trying to keep it from toppling over. Nadesan moved next to him, putting his shoulder against a stack of gunny bags and steadying the cart.

'Thanks!' the vendor acknowledged Nadesan's help with a nod of his head. The crowd was beginning to thin, some of them rising off the road and dusting themselves after having fallen to the ground. Two of the Police constables who had grabbed a couple of frightened shoppers as they rushed past the cordon were being shouted at by sections of the crowd who wanted them released. A lorry that had been stopped in the middle of the road by the panicked shoppers was blowing its horn trying to edge past the crowd. No one was paying Nadesan any attention so he walked quietly down the road away from the chaos.

Only when Nadesan reached the Prince of Wales Avenue did he begin to feel safe. The immediate sense of survival had taken over his mind. It was frightening, the isolation he felt. He was truly alone now. Without friends and accomplices and with just a few coins and only the clothes on his back, he wouldn't last long in the city.

Nadesan tried to shut himself inside his little world and avoid eye contact with the people around him. He belonged to no part of them. He would have to walk to the safe house across the river in Wattala. There he would find someone who knew the hidden places where ammunition and materials were stored, how to contact other militant cells in the city and the list of targets they would have been given. Separated into their action cells, junior militants like Nadesan were barred from knowing the identity of others in the cell, the location of safe houses. It was essential procedure. Only he had been lucky.

Nadesan knew of the safe house across the river. It was a lapse of security on Deva's part letting him know the area where the safe house was located, but he was thankful that he knew of it. He didn't know exactly where, but he would find it. He had to.

CHAPTER SIXTEEN

The strong smell of freshly made curry powder greeted Amanthi as she entered the centre courtyard of their home. The paved area, dominated by a medium sized temple tree, was enclosed on three sides by a wide veranda with carved wooden pillars.

Amanthi's mother was seated on a rattan lounge chair, watching a servant girl kneeling by a granite mortar. She looked up hearing Amanthi enter. 'Ah, I didn't expect to see you till later,' she said. 'It's a good day to make a batch of curry powder.'

The eldest of three children, Amanthi's mother was the matriarch of the family. Ever since Amanthi was a child, she remembered her mother making her own curry powders and doling the precious mixture to all her relatives.

'Stir it gently,' she admonished the servant girl who was vigorously stirring the aromatic mixture of carefully measured quantities of sun-dried coriander, cumin, fenugreek, fennel and mustard seeds. 'It doesn't need to be beaten into submission.'

Amanthi smiled at the scene. She remembered hearing the same scolding when she was a young girl.

'I brought a tin of powdered milk,' Amanthi said, placing the package on a table by the door. 'I tried to get two but they are rationing them until the emergency is over.' They had run out of powdered milk and her mother had asked Amanthi that morning whether she could buy a tin of milk on her way back from work.

Amanthi's mother waved her thanks, turning her attention back to the servant girl who was using a four-foot wooden pestle to pound the mix. She would pound the seeds to a fine powder before sieving the mixture and pounding it again. Once the seeds were pounded to her mother's satisfaction, she would do the same to a combination of cloves, cardamoms, turmeric, dried red chilies and rock salt before mixing it well with the powdered seeds. The mixture would be dry roasted in a frying pan and put in an airtight container to be used when needed.

'Is it a meat or vegetarian day?' Amanthi asked, not wanting to leave so quickly. Amanthi did not get to spend much time with her which she regretted. 'I am thinking of making a mutton poriyal,' she said, glancing at Amanthi. 'You used to love eating it when you were a child.'

Before she started working at the burn unit, Amanthi loved to eat all types of meat, and the mutton dish her mother made was one of her favourite. Her mother had taught her cooking from a very young age. She remembered rubbing the meat with ground coriander, cumin and dried red chilies with a sprinkling of salt, turmeric, cinnamon powder and crushed cardamom pods, and mixing it with pureed tomato to cut through the fat, before placing it in the refrigerator to marinade overnight.

Amanthi breathed out in exasperation. 'Let's not start that again.' Her mother had never really understood her becoming a vegetarian and took every opportunity to remind her of her previous meat-eating habit.

Amanthi's mother shrugged unapologetically. 'I will prepare the meat tonight and cook it tomorrow. Today is a holy day and I am making a seer fish curry and vegetables.' Being a staunch catholic, her mother did not eat any meat on a Friday or a saint's holy day.

Amanthi nodded gratefully. She had been eating a lot of canteen food and having her mother's fish curry would be a real treat.

'I'll try and make it back for dinner tonight,' she said. 'But I'm not sure what time I'll be able to get away. Could you serve me a plate and keep it in the oven, please?'

Her mother looked at her questioningly. 'What's happening?' she asked. 'The emergency is going on for so much longer this time. Are there going to be more bombs?'

'I don't know, mother. I heard they found another Tiger cell and are searching for the men.'

'I don't know what this country is coming to,' her mother said. 'Your father would have been very upset by all this. He strongly believed that everyone should get along.'

Amanthi remembered her father well. He was a boisterous, good looking man with a head of thick, curly, dark hair and a strong square jaw with a pronounced cleft in his chin. His nose was long and aristocratic, a sign he used to say laughingly of his Royal Kandyan lineage. Their home was always filled with friends her father seemed to collect, almost at random, on his many nature visits to the far corners of the island. They came from all walks of life and they were always welcome in their home. After the government nationalized the tea estates, forcing him to leave the central highlands and find work in Colombo, her father had become quieter and more introverted, always despairing at the direction the country was taking.

He had died before she had passed out as a doctor, killed in a head-on crash with a lorry on a lonely up-country road. She missed her father, his loud laugh, the smell of his aftershave when he wrapped his arms around her.

Amanthi shook her head trying to erase the image in her mind. She couldn't sit here day dreaming with everything that was happening.

'I've got to leave now,' she said, bending over to kiss her mother on the cheek.

'Try not to be too late for dinner,' her mother said, reaching up and caressing Amanthi's cheek as if she knew Amanthi was thinking about her father.

Amanthi nodded, her emotions choking her. Her mother exasperated her at times but Amanthi knew that she still mourned for her father and the love they had shared together. She hurried out of the house, the image of her father still etched in her mind.

CHAPTER SEVENTEEN

Tilak snapped abruptly out of a deep dreamless sleep aware only that something had changed around him. On his back, staring upward into the velvety blackness, hearing only the sound of men sleeping, Tilak realized that this unusual silence was the reason he was awake. It was wrong.

The room he slept in was part of the Police sub-station in the northern outskirts of Batticaloa. The building was an old colonial country house, its eight rooms linked together like a chain around a centre courtyard. The building was worn and crumbling, the pillars holding up the outer veranda showing signs of age and neglect. The rooms could be accessed down a corridor that surrounded the courtyard which had a fungus covered stone bench and a few tired roses in concrete pots. A broken wooden trellis which sat on a low wall, separated the corridor from the garden. Everything looked like it badly needed a coat of paint.

Militant activity had been growing in the eastern province and the Police Special Task Force had been deployed to keep control of all major towns and villages along the coast. Tilak had arrived with his squad a few days before to strengthen the outpost and was settling in to the routine of the station.

Sleep still heavy and confusing to his eyes, they adjusted to the darkness allowing him to dimly make out the blades of the ceiling fan overhead. They turned gently, the wide blades slowing. The power was out. Judging by the still turning blades it had cut out less than a minute ago. That was what had awakened him, the sudden cessation of the ordinary rhythms of the Police station at night.

The night was still and warm. As he lay there with the gentle snores of his men sounding loud in the stillness, he wondered why he still felt edgy. Having lived in a prison dormitory for many years, his senses were attuned to anything unnatural around him. Once he had woken to see a man with an object in his hand standing over him. Only the quick jerk of his head saved him from being stabbed in the throat by the sharpened toothbrush.

Somewhere close by a dog started to bark. Tilak pushed his sheet away and slipped quietly out of his cot. He stood in the middle of the room for a time, listening for anything out of the ordinary. Power cuts were a common occurrence in the country. So why did he feel so jumpy? Lithe on his bare feet, he padded across to the window and looked out through the dirty glass pane. The corner room faced an open stretch of grass which ended at a barbed wire fence by the edge of a grove of coconut palms. A family of domesticated goats kept mainly to prevent the thick grass from growing too tall, usually wandered the area, but they were not to be seen.

Normally this area would be lit up by floodlights mounted on the roof of the station but with the loss of power, the only illumination came from the moon, making it difficult to pierce the darkness beyond the fence. The rumble of a generator being started vibrated through the building. The floodlights came back on again, burning with much less intensity than Tilak had seen before. The light didn't quite reach the fence, creating a menacing darkness that raised the hackles on Tilak's neck. He stepped away from the window. The Police station was in a predominantly Tamil area and he couldn't shake the feeling that someone was out there, watching.

The dog's barking got louder. The minutes ticked by slowly. A goat bleated from somewhere outside. A shape, low to the ground, materialized out of the darkness near the barbed wire fence. For a moment Tilak thought that it was a goat, but the shape was wrong. Tilak's heart rate increased steadily as it moved closer, inching forward until he could make out the shape of a man crawling forward on his stomach.

Tilak moved without thinking. He slipped silently over to his cot, grabbing his automatic rifle leaning against the wall. The light in the corridor cast a checkered shadow on the bodies of his sleeping men. He crossed to the cot next to him and shook Chandra's shoulder.

'What, what …' the man groaned. Tilak knelt next to him, his arm across his chest.

'Wake up,' he whispered in the man's ear. 'We're under attack. Get your weapon and wake the others. I will try and hold them off.'

Tilak moved back to the window, crouching as he approached the rectangle of light. The sound of movement and whispering in the room behind him as his men came awake reassured him, but was it too late?

The man crawling outside had almost reached the side of the building. Tilak could clearly see him now. He was dressed in dark clothes and was pushing a canvas bag ahead of him.

It's a bomb, Tilak realized, raising the rifle to his shoulder. If it was detonated against the side of the building there wouldn't be much left of the police station. His body tensed in anticipation as he flicked the safety off with his thumb. His hand shook slightly as he lined up the sights and fired through the windowpane aiming for the man's torso. The man's head exploded in a spray of red mist as the bullets stitched a line up his body.

Tilak watched the still form for a few seconds and switched his attention to the fence line looking for any movement. He felt calm, totally in control with his emotions. This is what he'd been trained for.

For a moment, there was total silence. Then everything seemed to happen at once. A loud explosion from the other side of the building shook the room violently, shattered roof tiles cascading down in a shower of broken pieces. A man screamed in agony and gunfire erupted from the darkness beyond the fence.

'Chandra, take Wimal and Saman to the other side,' Tilak shouted over his shoulder. His men were well trained and wouldn't need to be told twice. 'Athula, bring me my ammo pouch.'

Bullets thudded into the side of the old building as Tilak returned fire, aiming at the muzzle flashes from beyond the fence. A flash of fire followed by a streak of flame trailing sparks connected with the side of the building. Then came the blast waves of the explosion, hammering on his eardrums and throwing him backwards off his feet. Tilak found himself lying across the room still clinging to his weapon, his head ringing from the blast. He had been lucky. The rocket propelled grenade had hit the side of the building blowing out the wall. If it had come through the window as the Tigers had intended and exploded in the room, he wouldn't be alive.

The room was filled with smoke and dust. Tilak crawled through the door leading into the station. Athula followed, dragging a pouch filled with rifle magazines and grenades. He was bleeding from a cut on his face.

'Wait here,' Tilak mouthed the words while pointing at the doorway, not sure whether Athula could hear him. 'Shoot anyone who comes in.'

Athula nodded as he unslung the rifle around his shoulder and settled in one corner of the doorway facing the wide opening in the wall created by the rifle propelled grenade. He placed three magazines and two grenades next to him, pushing the canvas pouch to Tilak.

'Don't worry,' he said grimly. 'The bastards won't get through here.'

Tilak slung the ammunition pouch around his shoulder and looked around. The inside of the station looked like a scene from hell. The outside wall of the building had been blown in, the roof only held up by a large cross beam sagging from its weight. Two of his men had taken positions inside the station covering the large opening, the third could not be seen.

Firing from the front of the building indicated that the policemen manning the station were returning fire. Tilak scrambled into the front room of the station where the charge desk was located. The two shattered front windows were each manned by policemen carrying automatic weapons. The sub-inspector in charge of the sub-station was crouched behind the large wooden charge desk speaking into a radio telephone.

Tilak squatted next to him. 'We're going to need help,' he said. 'We're wide open at the back. I've got my men covering the two breaches but they have got a rocket propelled grenade launcher.'

The sub-inspector nodded. 'I got through and they're sending help,' he said. 'But it's going to take some time. We'll have to hold out for twenty minutes, maybe more.'

Tilak took a deep breath and massaged the back of his neck. 'We're not going to hold on for that long,' he said. 'We need to get out of this building.'

'What do you mean, get out of the building?!' The sub-inspector looked confused. 'How the hell do we do that?'

Tilak knew that all it would take was for one of the satchel charges to explode inside the station. 'We can't stay here,' he said, grabbing the sub-inspector by the arm. 'They have satchel charges. We're better off out there.'

The sub-inspector nodded numbly. 'You alert your men,' Tilak said. 'And get ready to go out the front. We can use the vehicles as cover and move out to the street.'

Tilak scrambled to the back room. Chandra and Wimal were firing randomly through the opening in the wall to keep the Tigers away. But Saman was still missing.

Tilak called out to them. 'Get ready to move out through the front entrance,' he said, making sure each of the men heard him. 'I'll look for Saman.'

The corridor to the room on the east side of the building was filled with smoke and dust. The ceiling had collapsed, with heavy roof rafters lying in odd angles across the passageway. Flames flickered out from within the room.

Tilak clambered over the rafters and looked into the room. A figure lay motionless, face down on the ground next to the doorway. The room was filled with smoke, the flames getting stronger, dancing over the man's body. As Tilak bent over next to Saman a tongue of flame flicked out, burning him on the side of his neck.

'Shit,' he said, grabbing at his neck. It hurt like hell but he had to get Saman out.

Tilak reached down and grabbed Saman by his legs, dragging him away from the flames and out into the corridor. The man's shirt was still smouldering from the heat and charred bits of cloth stuck to his body when Tilak turned him around.

Tilak checked his neck for a pulse. A brief flutter against his fingers told him that Saman was still alive. A burst of firing from where Tilak had left Athula brought him to his feet. Tilak moved cautiously down the corridor and across to the backroom.

'Athula,' he called out. 'It's Tilak! I am coming through' Tilak didn't want to get shot by suddenly appearing in the doorway.

Athula lay in a pool of spent cartridges where Tilak had left him. 'They tried coming through the wall,' he called out, seeing Tilak. 'I got them both, but I think they're up to something.'

'Let's not hang around to find out,' Tilak said, pulling out a grenade from the pouch hanging on his shoulder. 'Come with me. I need help to get Saman out of here'. Tilak pulled the pin and threw the grenade underhand through the gaping hole. 'This will slow them down.'

Tilak and Athula flattened themselves against the wall as the grenade went off. A man screamed in agony as the two of them scrambled down the short passageway into the station.

Tilak pointed to the corridor where he left Saman. 'He's in there.'

Saman had recovered consciousness and was groaning gutturally when the two men approached. 'Grab his right arm,' Tilak said, gripping his left. They lifted Saman up as gently as they could and half-dragged, half-carried him into the main area.

'Bloody hell,' Chandra said, his eyes wide in disbelief at seeing his friend. 'He looks like shit.' Wimal took a quick look before firing a burst through the destroyed wall.

'We're going to take him to the front room,' Tilak said, adjusting his grip on Saman. 'You better watch this entrance as we're wide open at the back.' Chandra nodded, shifting his position to cover the back entrance. Between the two of them they would have to keep the Tigers from entering the station.

Tilak laid Saman next to two Police constables who had been injured in the attack. One of them looked like he had taken the full force of a blast, his mangled upper body showing no signs of life. The other had been hit in the upper body, a field dressing stained with red covering his torso.

'What's the status of the relief force?' Tilak asked the sub-inspector, still clutching his radio telephone. The officer shook his head fearfully. 'I don't know. I haven't heard.'

Tilak cursed under his breath. He still felt trapped inside the station and wanted to get out in the open but it would be difficult to do it with the two injured men. They would have to make a stand at the station and hope the reinforcements came quickly.

The rate of firing from outside increased as if the Tigers knew they were running out of time. A loud explosion shook the back of the building where most of the firing was coming from. Tilak crawled to the back not knowing what to expect. A thick fog of smoke and dust raised by the explosion filled the room. The muzzle flash of a gun firing told him that at least one of his men was alive.

A shadowy figure holding a gun almost crouched in two, suddenly appeared out of the fog in front of Tilak. Tilak fired instinctively from his prone position, hitting the man who spun around and collapsed on the ground.

Bullets peppered the wall above Tilak as he tried to push himself into the cement floor to try and make himself as small a target as he could. Tilak fumbled in his pouch, his hand clasping the last grenade. Remaining in his horizontal position, Tilak pulled the pin from the grenade and flung it sidearm across the room towards the opening in the wall. The grenade went off with a sharp crack, shrapnel peppering the room walls.

Tilak changed the ammunition clip on his rifle, realizing that there were only three more clips left in the pouch. The ammunition was stored in a locked room at the back of the station which would be impossible to get at. They would have to manage with the ammunition they had.

The firing suddenly died down, almost as quickly as it had started. The rumble of approaching vehicles vibrated through the floor that Tilak lay on. They're here, he thought to himself, laying his head down in his arms. Other than a few cuts and bruises, only the burn on his neck would need attention. But Saman was injured badly and he didn't hear Wimal firing. He wondered whether he'd lost another of his men while he waited for the soldiers to relieve them.

CHAPTER EIGHTEEN

The antiquated air force Bell helicopter lifted off from the helipad opposite the Ramada Renaissance hotel in a flurry of dust and sand. Amanthi and the two nurses clutched the metal sides of the canvas bucket seats nervously as the helicopter's nose dipped and moved forward slowly, flying low and gaining speed over the crowded, red-tiled slums of Slave Island.

They were being flown to Batticaloa on the east coast where a Police station had been attacked overnight. Many men had been injured, one of them was badly burnt. An urgent request from the Director of the Military Hospital to provide specialized burn care to the soldier was responded to immediately.

Dr. Perera called Amanthi into her office before she left. 'Remember that you are going to a war zone,' she said, studying Amanthi carefully. 'Being a doctor will protect you to a degree but don't take anything for granted.'

The three of them had been handed large padded headphones which kept the noise of the rotor blades to an acceptable level. They could hear the pilots talking as the helicopter climbed steadily away from Colombo. A European with a distinctly British accent sat next to the Sri Lankan air force pilot, quietly instructing the young man as they flew away from the city.

The built-up areas of the suburbs gave way to orderly rows of coconut and rubber trees interspersed with open fields of rice paddy. Roads full of traffic wound towards the central highlands where British-built tea estates dotted the landscape. Amanthi was both nervous and excited at the same time. She had never been in an airplane let alone a helicopter before. Her nerves were on edge during the safety briefing, overlaid by the urgency to get to the injured soldier as quickly as possible.

Amanthi quickly forgot her nervousness, amazed at how beautiful the country looked from the air. Cultivated land changed to lush jungle before the helicopter flew over a sprawling city she thought was Kurunegala, and then turned east towards the coast which she could see in the distance.

'Medivac flight zero one zero approaching Batticaloa airport. Request permission to land.'

Amanthi was surprised when she heard the pilot's voice through the headphones. She was so enthralled by the view that she didn't realize that they had arrived at their destination. The helicopter began to descend and slowed, touching down with a gentle bump.

The small airfield was surrounded on three sides by a lagoon. The area was encircled by a chain-link wire fence in various states of disrepair. Watchtowers built of coconut tree trunks, perforated steel planking and sandbags were situated at every corner.

An officer dressed in a camouflaged uniform whom Amanthi had never seen before met them as they disembarked. 'I am captain Munasinghe,' he said, waving them towards a small yellow building next to the tarmac. 'I'll take you to the hospital where the injured soldier is being treated.' Two soldiers dressed in similar uniforms lifted the boxes holding their medical supplies out of the helicopter and followed close behind them.

'Is the hospital close by?' Amanthi asked the officer. She was anxious to get to the patient as soon as possible.

'Yes. They're in the Batticaloa General Hospital,' the officer nodded, holding the door open for them. 'It's just across the bridge in the middle of town. We can be there in ten minutes.'

The officer was right when he said the hospital was not far. The centre of Batticaloa was located on a small island cluttered with buildings of all shapes and sizes. They passed an old catholic church in faded blue and pink before they turned into the main hospital car park. The open area in front of a wide doorway marked 'Emergency' was filled with army vehicles. Soldiers carrying weapons stepped aside as the officer led them into the unit.

They were greeted by a harassed looking doctor in a white coat. 'I am glad you're here,' he said, without introducing himself. 'We don't have any facilities to treat patients with such severe burns.'

Amanthi and the two nurses were taken into what looked like a waiting room with a hospital bed in the middle. A faint smell of coffee mixed with antiseptic solutions floated in the air. A set of open windows and a door led out to a wide veranda at the back of the room. Empty chairs lined the walls. A man dressed in khaki t-shirt and torn camouflaged trousers lounged on one of the chairs, a white bandage covered one side of his face and neck. After sparing him a glance, Amanthi walked over to where the injured soldier was lying face down on the bed, a nurse from the hospital standing next to him. An intravenous drip hung off a metal frame and a trolley full of medical instruments and bandages stood next to the bed.

'He was brought in early this morning with severe burns to his back and to the right side of his body,' the doctor said, handing Amanthi a clipboard. 'He also has shrapnel injuries to his face and chest but they're not too severe. We stopped the bleeding and stabilized him with a saline solution,' the doctor explained. 'I prescribed five milligrams of morphine for the pain but have not attended to his burns as yet. I decided to wait until you arrived.'

Amanthi scanned the chart and handed it to Nelum who stood by the side of the bed. Shanthi was busy behind her opening boxes and unwrapping sealed packages.

'How's his breathing?' Amanthi asked, bending down and looking at the soldier's face. She knew that a majority of burn victims suffered from respiratory problems caused by toxicity in the smoke they inhaled.

'His lungs are clear and his breathing is okay,' the doctor said, waving his hand at the soldier lounging in the chair. 'I was told by the Lieutenant that he was lying unconscious on the ground during the fire. That probably saved him from inhaling too much smoke.'

Amanthi glanced at the Lieutenant who was watching her intently. 'Let's put him on oxygen just to make sure.' She was pleased that fluid had started being given to the patient. It was important to stabilize burn patients right away, even before they arrived in hospital.

Nelum checked his temperature and recorded it in the chart before showing it to Amanthi. The soldier's temperature was below normal. He was leaking heat through the burnt parts of his body. They had to be careful not to let it get lower. She walked over to the open windows and shut them, firmly closing the door to keep the coolness of the morning out of the room.

Nelum and Shanthi prepared bandages for the patient, soaking them in a saline and anti-bacterial gel solution that they mixed in plastic buckets they'd brought with them. But before the bandages could be used, every inch of the patient's body had to be examined, all burnt fabric or skin removed and the flesh scrubbed.

Amanthi used her stethoscope to confirm that the patient's lungs were clear. It was not that she didn't trust what the Doctor had reported. She followed a process she had developed working at the Burn Unit on hundreds of burn victims and she hardly if ever deviated from it.

The soldiers back looked like a tattered shirt, a patchwork of red and white, black and brown covering his arms and upper torso. Amanthi noted that the patient had a combination of reddish swelling and small blisters, fiery red patches of skin with large blisters containing yellowish fluid and a tightening, shrivelling and thickening of the skin. But what concerned her most was the patches of black skin with a hard, dry crust that had formed when the skin and the flesh underneath with its veins, arteries and sinews had burnt and dried.

Amanthi instinctively knew that the soldier was out of immediate danger. Whoever had treated him, right after he had been burnt, had known what to do. Most of the burns were on the torso of the patient. The most dangerous burns involved the head and face, with the eyes, groin and genitals all having been spared. The soldier would have to undergo a series of painful skin grafts which would replace the skin on his body over time. The biggest danger he would face during this time was infection. But she still had to make sure that he was being given enough fluid.

'Do you know how much plasma he's been given?'

'This is his second bag,' the Doctor said, looking at his clipboard. 'He'd been given a bag before he got here and we gave him a second.'

Fluid resuscitation was vital to stabilizing a badly burnt patient. Burn patients who did not get proper supportive care often suffered the consequences of shock, up to and including death. Burns often caused the body to leak fluid out of blood vessels into the surrounding tissue. This fluid which was mostly water included vital minerals and sugars. Some of this fluid seeped from the wounds but most of it was taken up by the tissues like a sponge sopping up a spill. The waterlogged tissue interfered with the movement of blood by pressing on blood vessels, narrowing and even collapsing them. At first the swelling concentrates around the burned area but after an hour or so the leakage spreads until the body grotesquely swells.

There were signs that the fluid shift had begun in the patient's body. The swelling at the site of the burn was prominent and Amanthi could see that even the unburnt and distant parts of the body had begun to retain fluid.

Amanthi knew that by the time burn victims got to have specialized care they would have litres of fluid pumped into their system. She also knew that the sickest patients were the ones for whom resuscitation was a matter of life and death. As the Doctor in Charge, she was responsible for calculating the formula that would be used on the patient. She calculated the amount of fluid and infusion rate in her head, using the patients approximate age, weight and the percentage of body surface that was burnt. It was not totally accurate but it was close enough until they got the soldier back to Colombo. She would need the soldier's medical history to make an accurate assessment.

'Could you make a request for his medical file to be delivered to me in Colombo?' she instructed the Doctor, who nodded and made a note.

Amanthi bent over the patient to make sure he was asleep. The morphine was doing its work and after checking his pulse, she nodded at Nelum to begin.

*

Amanthi stepped out of the room onto the veranda leading off the waiting room. She felt drained after the procedure but knew that with the proper care, the soldier would recover from his injuries. She lit a cigarette from the packet she carried in her pocket, fumbling with the lighter and dropping it on the ground after she did.

'Here, let me help you.' The Lieutenant who had followed her into the veranda, bent down and picked up the butane lighter, holding it out to her.

Amanthi took the lighter, slipping it and the packet of cigarettes into her coat pocket.

'Thanks,' she said, sucking deeply on the cigarette and blowing out a stream of smoke into air. The officer had remained in the room during the whole procedure and Amanthi had been conscious of his eyes on her while she worked.

He was slightly taller than Amanthi, with broad shoulders and slim hips. His thick curly hair framed a handsome intelligent face, the bright and animated light brown eyes looking confidently at her. A dressing spotted with blood covered one side of his face and neck. He leaned against the post holding up the veranda. 'My name is Tilak,' he said. 'Thanks for looking after Saman. Will he be alright?'

'Yes, he'll be fine,' she said, sprinkling ash from her cigarette into the flower bed. 'The burn will take a few months to heal.' Amanthi looked at him. 'What happened to your face?'

Tilak raised his hand and touched the dressing on his face. 'I got burnt pulling him out of the fire,' he said, grimacing with pain. 'The doctor said it's only superficial.'

'You better let me look at it,' Amanthi said, taking a deep pull from her cigarette before stubbing it in an ashtray lying on the ground. 'Burns get infected quickly if not treated correctly,' she explained, ushering Tilak back into the room.

Tilak's burn was superficial as the doctor had said and Amanthi could find no fault with what he had done with the wound. 'It looks fine,' said Amanthi, taping a new dressing over the wound. 'Keep the dressing on it for a few days before exposing it to the air.' Amanthi walked over to one of the medical boxes they had brought from Colombo. 'Here's an ointment you should apply twice daily,' she said, holding out a tube to him. 'It will prevent any scarring.'

Tilak took the tube slipping it into his trouser pocket. 'Thanks,' he said. 'I don't even know your name.'

'Amanthi.' The name slipped out before she could even think. She felt strangely attracted to the Lieutenant and realized that she wanted him to know her name. Amanthi watched as he walked away, lean-hipped with broad shoulders sloping into long arms.

The hospital doctor walked into the room and came towards her. 'I have arranged for the patient to be transferred to the Military Hospital with you when you leave,' he said, handing her a sheaf of papers. 'We'll send you by ambulance to the airport.' Amanthi nodded, leafing through the paperwork. The soldier would be well looked after in Colombo.

They began preparing the soldier to be transported and started packing up their medical gear and supplies. The injured soldier was lifted onto a gurney provided by the hospital and wheeled out by a hospital orderly. Amanthi felt a sense of disappointment when she looked around and didn't see the Lieutenant. He must have slipped out when they were preparing to leave. Amanthi sighed as she realized she didn't even know his family name. Maybe she'd bump into him one day.

CHAPTER NINETEEN

A pair of eyes stared out from under wooden rafters holding up the corrugated-iron roof. They were perfectly still as they looked across the ramshackle rooftops and into the narrow alley. From where he hid, Nadesan could watch the entrance to the safe house in Wattala without anyone knowing he was there.

It had taken him many days to get to this place, he'd lost count. He had spent hours of anguish staring at roof just a few centimetres away, going over and over in his mind what he'd done at the market. It still tortured him and numbed him. He could never have imagined such carnage and the very thought of triggering a bomb in a place crowded with civilians felt nauseating to him. Having seen pictures and read in the newspapers about the suffering he'd caused still gave him nightmares. He felt soiled by his actions and often wondered what Radika would have to say.

Nadesan was tired and weak, the heat from the steel roof making it feel like an oven. With his weariness had come no sense of defeat, no will to cringe and concede. Only a confusion as to whether he'd gone too far and what was still expected of him.

Nadesan was slowly coming to the realization that he wanted to survive and complete his next mission, whatever it was and however long it took. But he did not want to become the person he had turned into. How could he face his family as a person who had caused such horror? I must find a way to make it right! The thought kept going around and around in his mind.

For the first time since the raid on the garage, he felt safe. He was still afraid; afraid of being alone in this big city; afraid of being captured alive and tortured but there was also something else. An exhilaration of risking everything to survive.

Trying to remain invisible was exhausting. Getting across the river had proven to be a major challenge. Both the Police and the army had guard posts and checkpoints on the two bridges which he would have to walk past if he crossed by foot. He had watched from the side of the road as they stopped and searched people at random. He wouldn't be able to explain why he was not carrying any identification papers and would be thrown in jail as a suspected terrorist.

Nadesan was scared. He fingered the locket around his neck. He had nothing but the clothes on his back and a few coins in his pocket. He had to get out of the city which was turning into an armed camp. From where he sat he could see another checkpoint at a major junction leading to the city. It had been set up only a few hours after he had walked past the junction. He was trapped between the soldiers at the junction and the soldiers on the bridge, in an area of shanty dwellers living under the structure.

Diesel and petrol fumes from the automobiles, trucks, buses and three-wheelers passing within a few feet of where he sat, wafted over him, sending him into a kind of stupor.

The tinkle of a coin in front of Nadesan brought him out of his deep trance-like state. A woman dressed in a saree, carrying a bag of groceries had dropped a coin in front of him thinking he was a beggar. Nadesan, although a Hindu, knew that Buddhists believed in accumulating goodness and often gave alms to beggars on the street. By evening he had collected enough money to buy a hot tea and a meal at the eatery beneath the bridge. It had solved the problem of finding food but he still had to find a way across.

Nadesan walked down through a double row of dilapidated shanty huts under the enormous structure to the river's edge. The miserable shelters were patched together from corrugated siding, sheets of plywood, bits of wood, plastic and paper. Some had miniature fences surrounding tiny plots of land where chickens roosted. The dwellings slumped together, attached to one another with narrow lanes winding between then. Nadesan had removed his shirt, wrapping it around his waist and hitching up his sarong. He didn't want to stand out from the other shanty dwellers. Some of them looked at him curiously when he walked past, but he was not stopped or questioned.

Street lights from the bridge reflected on the slow-moving river. Children splashed in the shallows beside mothers bent at the waist washing clothes or kitchen utensils. A pair of mangy dogs snarled at each other on the water's edge. Nadesan watched a large piece of foliage from a tree upstream float past.

Judging by the size of the debris, the river current was much stronger in the middle than it was at its sides. He realized it would not be wise to swim across. Nadesan did not want to walk through the shanty town again so he turned into a side alley bordering the slum which was foul as only a poor Colombo street could be. It hadn't been swept for days, perhaps longer. The air was rank, inhabitants of the neighbouring shanty's adding to the stench by heaping waste onto piles that dogs rooted in, spreading the refuse across the alley like a cancer. He avoided a series of dark puddles no doubt fed by some leaking sewage pipe before walking back to the road leading to the bridge.

Nadesan huddled that night beside an empty shop boarded for the night, his mind trying to think of ways of getting across.

The solution came to him much later that day while he watched the traffic on the bridge. The street was as jammed as the day before, but Nadesan noticed a pattern in the way the soldiers at the roadblocks carried out their searches. They would stop every vehicle coming into the city, searching it thoroughly for weapons or explosives but did not pay as much attention to vehicles that left the city. Nadesan decided to hide in the back of a lorry that was leaving the city. To do that he would have to find one he could climb into without being seen.

Slowly making his way down the main avenue towards a petrol station that lorries often stopped at, he paused realizing that he would have to pass a checkpoint on the city side of the wide road. The soldiers at this entry point checked everyone trying to get through. He wouldn't get through. He was trapped.

Nadesan decided that he'd have to take a chance. Hanging around like this would only bring attention to himself. As he sat on the pavement, a three-wheeler taxi stopped in front of him. After dropping a woman who clutched the hand of a child, the three-wheeler driver accelerated towards an eatery where there were many parked three-wheelers. This gave Nadesan an idea. He casually walked up to the eatery and bought a loaf of bread in a plastic bag. He noticed that the three-wheeler driver had joined a group of other drivers at the back of the eatery and was busy talking to them. This was his chance.

It was easy for him to start the two-stroke engine with his mechanical background. He wheeled the machine around and drove up the road and onto the access road to the bridge. Nadesan knew he had no choice but to go for it. He slotted himself behind a bus, next to another three-wheeler carrying passengers and drove onto the bridge coming up to the first roadblock. The soldiers manning the roadblock stopped the bus but waved the rest of the traffic through, not even glancing at Nadesan as he drove past. The soldiers at the second roadblock by the roundabout across the river did not even bother to look at them as they crossed onto the other side of the river.

Nadesan drove into the busy suburb on the northern side of the river, following signs onto the Negombo Road which carried traffic to the international airport at Katunayake. He ditched the three-wheeler after driving a few kilometres, leaving the vehicle outside a bank at a crowded junction and disappearing into a narrow side street.

It took him another two days to find the safe house. He had started at one end of the suburb, walking down every street until he found it. Nadesan knew it was the right street, by the roadside shrine under a tree next to a petrol station. He had only been here once before with Deva when he had first arrived from across the country.

Nadesan's feet were raw and dirty by constant walking but he did not want to approach the house. He wanted to make sure it was not being watched. So, he had crawled into the roof of an empty warehouse close by which gave him a good view of the street from across the junction. He bought two loaves of bread, a comb of bananas and filled an empty plastic bottle he found discarded on the street, with water. All of which he carried up to his hiding place.

In the heat of the roof space, he fell asleep, curled on his side with his knees pressed up against his chest. His mind closed to all around him, his breathing calm and regular. He would remain here until he was sure that no one was watching the safe house.

CHAPTER TWENTY

From far back in the trees, Tilak watched the house. He waited all evening for the man to show himself, but except for the dog, the place looked empty. The yard round the house was cleared and covered with a layer of smooth raked sand that was fenced. The land extending out from the palm groves and patches of thick wild vegetation, was bordered on three sides by a sea of rice paddy. A rutted dirt track winding through the trees was the only visible access to the property.

It was dark, and water dripped from the trees on his shoulders. Tilak knew the man was called Rajadorai; knew that the man was a farmer; knew that he lived in that house. But the house seemed empty.

Behind him Chandra was waiting. Tilak had received a phone call that morning that an mid-level militant leader had been identified. While the military controlled the towns along the coastal highway, the hinterland was all militant territory and many of them came from the towns and villages along the coast.

The voice on the phone sounded like the man from the Special Branch that Tilak met in the Commander's office. 'We want him eliminated,' the man said. 'Chandra has the details and will take you to his location. Remember our agreement. We don't want you to forget the consequences of failing.'

Tilak went looking for Chandra but could not find him. He finally showed up a few hours later. 'We have information that this was the man who ordered the attack on the Police station,' said Chandra. 'There have been other attacks in the area so eliminating him will remove an important resource for the Tigers.'

Three times in the last month, they had been given information which led them to a militant sympathizer. But this was the first time they had been asked to eliminate the target. Hurting someone and threatening his family was considered enough up to now. They could always visit the person once again if he was foolish enough to not listen.

Tilak knew that Chandra was a Special Branch operative that was placed in his squad to keep an eye on him. Tilak had no reason to complain as Chandra was very capable and had proven himself during the firefight at the Police station. Tilak touched the burn on the side of his face which had started to itch. He had taken the doctor's advice and kept the bandage off after a couple of days, using the ointment she gave him. Tilak wished that he had met her under different circumstances.

The shadows had retreated as the sun set, the building no more than a blackened outline, indistinct in shape, difficult to focus on. Around him the noises of the night were gathering, swelling until it became a chorus. There was no light from inside the house, no fire had been lit to cook any food. Only the dog knew they were there.

Tilak turned his head and spoke over his shoulder. 'What do you think?' he asked. 'Should we come back tomorrow?'

'Let's wait a bit longer,' replied Chandra. 'He will come back eventually to sleep.'

Tilak paid attention to what Chandra said. He would have had more experience dealing with these types of covert operations.

Tilak did not move. Darkness carpeted the night, throwing its blanket over the fields and plantation. The barking of a far distant dog and the ever-present drone of mosquitoes was the only sound he could hear.

Chandra was proven to be right. Around midnight the dog started barking and by the sound of his bark Tilak knew that the dog was greeting his master. A flickering light in the window confirmed that the man had come home.

Tilak felt Chandra next to him. The man moved like a ghost. 'Let him settle down and think he's safe. I'll go around and approach the house from the paddy field. You cover the front of the house.'

It was a clear night with the moon almost full. Tilak gave Chandra time to get to the rice paddy. He pulled out the automatic pistol from where he had tucked it in his waist before he began his advance. The ground in the coconut plantation was an obstacle course of foot-deep holes, muddy bunds and slippery tufts of grass. Unchallenged, Tilak arrived at the fence of thatched palm leaves. The house was dark. The light they had seen having been extinguished. Tilak hoped it meant the man had gone to sleep. Tilak hesitated at the fence. The dog was going to be a problem and Tilak did not want to hurt the animal.

Tilak cocked the automatic pistol, easing back the slide so it wouldn't make a sound. He was about to open the wooden gate when the dog, sensing someone's presence in the yard, erupted from the house, barking loudly. To Tilak's surprise, the dog ignored him and ran barking angrily to the back of the house where Chandra was making his approach. This spurred Tilak to action. He slipped the retaining wire over the fence post, opening the gate and moving quickly towards the darkened front of the house.

A movement at the door and a man emerged, a dark shadow against the stained yellow wall. Tilak saw the pistol in the man's hand. Short and stubby, a black barrel, same as the colour of his arm. Tilak charged. He did not think, he went on instinct. As he hit the man, shoulder against stomach, he heard a shot being fired. The man went down. They fell on the ground together. Tilak smelt curry on his breath as he grabbed the man by his shirt and smashed his right knee into the man's groin. One hand holding him by his shirt, Tilak punched a short- arm jab into the man's face with his pistol, heard the crunch of his nose bone shatter.

Tilak pushed himself up. The man groaned gutturally. He had dropped the gun and his hands were over his groin. Dark blood streamed down his face. Tilak kicked the gun away and spun around when he saw a shadow turn the corner.

'It's me,' Chandra said nervously. 'Don't shoot.'

Despite all that had happened Tilak could only think of one thing. 'What happened to the dog?' he asked Chandra.

'I shot him,' Chandra said, looking strangely at Tilak. 'I had no choice.'

Tilak realized that the shot he had heard must have been when Chandra shot the dog. He shrugged in disappointment, the death of the dog affecting him more deeply than he thought. He turned back towards the man on the ground who was moaning in pain.

Chandra stepped around Tilak and looked at the man. 'You did a number on him,' he said quietly, glancing at Tilak. 'I'll look inside in case there are more.'

Tilak's heart pounded. He slumped against the wall, the effects of the adrenaline rush making him feel weak. He was familiar with the effects of a life or death struggle. In prison, he had killed the man who had tried to stab him in the neck while he slept, strangling him with his bare hands. It had taken a lot out of him but it had made his reputation in prison as a dangerous man. No one ever came near him after that.

Chandra came out of the building. 'It's a shit hole,' he said, kicking the man on the ground. 'Let's finish him off and get out of here.'

Tilak's heart hammered in his ribcage. This was too much like what occurred before. How the hell did I get myself into this situation? He had already done one prison term for manslaughter and knew that if he didn't complete the job the chance of being sent back to prison was very high, pardon or no pardon. He couldn't show any weakness or hesitation in front of Chandra. He didn't want to end up in a maximum-security prison again.

Tilak's stomach knotted as he stepped up to the man whose eyes widened when he realized what was about to happen. Tilak fired two shots, their impacts lifting the man off the ground.

Chandra nodded, a small smile forming at the corner of his mouth. 'That's the job done,' he said. 'Let's get out of here.'

Tilak was drenched in sweat, and not just because of the heat. He took a deep breath. He needed to control himself. He looked back at Chandra and nodded without saying a word but his heart was thumping and his mind churning with unbidden thoughts. A feeling of loathing surged up within him growing stronger by the minute. What am I becoming? He stood for a moment lost in thought as dark agonizing ideas rose in his mind ... am I mad? He felt at that moment he should to be doing something utterly different from what he was doing now.

Chandra gestured impatiently from the gate forcing Tilak to move. Dimly conscious of his surroundings he realized he still held the gun in his right hand. He hastily tucked it back into his waistband and walked over to the gate, pushing past Chandra. A passing cloud obscured the moon briefly as they left the scene together, making no effort to conceal what they had done.

CHAPTER TWENTY-ONE

Amanthi had just finished a late lunch at the hospital canteen when an orderly informed her that Dr Perera wanted her to come to the burn unit immediately.

Dr Perera was standing next to her desk wearing a hair mask and surgical scrubs. A disposable mask hung around her neck. 'Listen to me carefully,' Dr Perera said. 'A senior army officer has been badly injured in an explosion and is being brought here. I would normally attend to this matter but I am in the middle of a difficult procedure and I need you to handle it.'

The morning newspapers had reported the commencement of a major military operation in the north and the burn unit had been put on standby.

'I'll get the ambulance ready to leave for the airport?' Amanthi said. The procedure they had put in place with the military was to meet any seriously wounded soldiers at the military airport at Katunayake.

'No,' Dr Perera shook her head. 'It was a bomb here in Colombo. Get your team together. He'll be brought here shortly.'

Amanthi nodded and hurried out of the room. As she changed into her surgical scrubs, the hospital public address system announced a Code Red emergency. Amanthi pushed her handbag into the desk drawer and slammed it shut, locking it with a key she slipped into her pocket. She hurried out of the room and quickly walked the short distance to the emergency treatment room.

More information had come in about the bombing. The officer had been sitting in the passenger seat of a military SUV when a man riding a motorcycle had blown himself up next to the vehicle. The explosion had crushed the side of the lightly armoured SUV causing severe burns and injuries to its occupants.

By the time the officer was pulled out of the burning vehicle, he had lost a lot of blood from wounds to the left side of his body.

Amanthi stood under the glaring bright lights, leaning over the blood-soaked gurney that held the officers shattered body. She had seen her share of horribly wounded men and women but the raw brutality of modern explosives had been quite a shock. She had adapted to it during the bus station bombing but none of the patients she had treated approached the savagery of this officer's injuries.

The left side of his face was a lurid red mask, the skin shiny and taut, his hair and the top of his ear singed, both his eyelashes and eyebrows swept away by the heat of the explosion. The skin on his upper body was a patchwork of healthy and burnt skin. The officers lower body seemed to be free of burns but his trousers were torn and saturated with blood by wounds suffered the trauma of the bomb exploding so close to him. Only the side walls of the lightly armoured SUV had prevented him from being blown to little pieces.

The officer was unconscious and breathing hard as if he had just finished a hurdles race. There was no blood pressure to record and Amanthi couldn't feel a pulse on his wrist, only a thin reedy apex beat palpable in his left chest. Amanthi saw that an intravenous line going into his right arm oozed dark and thick blood out of his half-collapsed vein.

'He has lost a lot of blood and is going into shock,' Amanthi snapped over her shoulder. 'There's no time to check his blood group. Get me two bags of group O blood.'

Amanthi moved to the other side of the gurney and lifted the officer's arm. Her body felt heavy with the increase of adrenaline as she worked feverishly trying to get a second line into the man's left arm. Amanthi breathed a sigh of relief as she felt the needle enter the vein. She had done enough of these procedures to know when it worked. She moved quickly and attached both lines to the two bags.

'We have to stop his bleeding. Have you found all his wounds?'

The officer was showing no signs of improvement. No pulse on his wrist. A weak flutter on his neck. He was still bleeding. They had missed a wound somewhere.

The team worked feverishly to stabilize the officer. Nelum elevated his legs by placing pillows under them. Anything to get blood to his vital organs.

'Dammit! He's got a wound on his back that has reopened,' Kumudu called out. 'Help me turn him on his side so I can stop the bleeding.' The boyish-looking emergency room doctor whom Amanthi had worked with before had a deep voice which belied his looks.

A large ragged gash in his lower back was bleeding profusely. The medics had stuffed gauze pads into the wound which were soaked red. Kumudu removed the useless pads and swabbed the wound. Blood poured out of the deep laceration.

'He's bleeding from an artery,' Amanthi said. 'You'll need to clamp it.'

A wave of dread washed over Amanthi. The burns though serious were not bad enough to kill him. To Amanthi's practiced eye, the burns looked partial thickness, but it would take a few days to make sure how deep they were. But all the signs showed that he was suffering from serious blood loss and that was far more likely to kill him. She moved across to the two tubes feeding blood into his body and increased the flow.

'We will need more blood soon,' she snapped over her shoulder. 'We need to get his blood type quickly. Ask one of the officers out there to get if for us. It should be on his military records.'

The first priority in any emergency department is to save a life by any means possible. There is no time to locate the next of kin and the hospital undertakes all measures to preserve life. With this officer, it was touch and go. Tubes and wires snaked all around him hooked up to a battery of pumps and monitors. One tube down his throat helped him to breath. Intravenous lines went into both arms and another needle was being inserted into his groin. The burn was not being attended to but Amanthi knew that they couldn't ignore it for too long.

'Got it.' Kumudu looked up with a triumphant grin. He had managed to find and clamp the torn artery. 'Have we stopped all the bleeders? Check him again.'

The team worked tirelessly on the senior army officer, speaking quietly amongst themselves. Amanthi worked on his swollen face and upper body, debriding burnt and melted pieces of skin and applying layers of ointment while Nelum covered the burnt areas with solution soaked bandages. The emergency room doctor worked with one of the trauma nurses on teasing lumps of jagged metal and melted plastic away from the charred and bleeding muscles.

A circle of sweat had formed on the back of Amanthi's uniform when she finally stepped away from the patient. They had been working on the patient for almost three hours. His vital signs were looking better. His blood pressure had come up and Amanthi could feel his pulse had gotten stronger. The patients correct blood type had been phoned in by the army medical service and he was on his fifth bag of blood. A senior army doctor was on his way from the military hospital to monitor his condition. His wounds had been assessed and a thorough burn diagram filled in. Dressings soaked in a silver nitrate solution had been put on carefully and samples of his fluids had been sent off to the lab for analysis. Nelum checked the patient's temperature and covered his body with a quilted foil blanket. It was important to keep him warm so he wouldn't lose heat from the burnt areas where he had lost his skin.

Amanthi felt good about the patient. Everything they had done for him had worked and she was confident he had a very good chance of recovery. She thanked the team and walked into the adjoining change room. After cleaning up and changing into a fresh set of scrubs, Amanthi remembered that sometime during the procedure, Dr Perera had come into the emergency room and had watched the team working on the officer. She had caught Amanthi eyes before nodding and leaving the room.

Dr Perera was in her room talking to an army officer. She waved to

Amanthi when she saw her looking in.

'Ah, Dr De Silva. Come in, come in.' This is Major Doctor Karunaratne from the army medical corp. He wants an update of the General's condition.'

Amanthi looked at the two of them in surprise. She was not aware that the officer she had been working on was so highly ranked.

Amanthi walked into the office and leant against the office wall feeling exhausted. 'The patient has been stabilized but has severe trauma and burn wounds to the left side of his body. He was agonal when brought in. The biggest concern was the loss of blood from deep shrapnel wounds to his lower back and legs. We had to pump him up with five, no, six bags of blood and his blood pressure is back up, but he has some ways to go before—'

The Major cut her off. 'I am perfectly aware of his condition. I read the medics report. However badly injured, he needs to be under twenty-four-hour protection to prevent another assassination attempt. It's almost impossible to do that here. Is he stable enough to be moved?'

Amanthi glanced at Dr Perera before responding. 'I don't think it'll be a good idea to move him just yet. Where do you want to take him?' She was craving for a cigarette and was wishing she had not gone looking for Dr Perera.

'To the military hospital in Cinnamon Gardens,' the Doctor responded. 'I am the Medical Director there.'

Amanthi had heard of a highly secure military hospital in Colombo where government VIPs and senior officers from the security forces were treated.

'Amanthi, what do you think?' Dr Perera responded, looking enquiringly across at her.

The army doctor turned to face Amanthi. 'It's not far from here and we have all the facilities to treat him. We'll be able to better protect him there.'

'Do you have nurses who know about caring for burns?' Amanthi asked. 'He can be moved once his vital signs settle but I'm concerned about the treatment of his burns. He'll require someone who knows what they're doing.'

Amanthi was certain that the hospital would have all the latest equipment, but what her patient required was experienced nursing care. The burn unit at the general hospital had the best burn care nurses in the country. They did most of the hands-on care for the patients, helping them with meals, bathing and personal care, checking temperature, blood pressure and so much more. Even with a relatively small burn and the best of care, the chance of an infection was very high.

The Army Doctor shook his head. 'We don't have nurses who are as experienced as the ones here,' he said. 'But they have treated burn patients before and know what to do.'

'The General has been burned badly on the left side of his face and upper body and is going to require very special care,' Amanthi said. She had learned through experience that the healing process began almost immediately after a burn and it was all about timing. Making sure the delicate balance between destruction and construction was managed properly was her biggest concern. 'Proper care for his wounds is my biggest worry.'

Dr Perera nodded. 'I agree with Dr De Silva. It's too risky if you don't have properly trained staff. I suggest you assign a doctor and two army nurses to work with us for the next few days and we'll train them on how to take care of his wounds. Once we feel comfortable they know what they're doing, we'll release him into your care.'

The Army Doctor didn't look happy but he must have realized that if he pushed too hard he would undermine the relationship he would need to have with the two of them.

'Ok,' he said, standing up. 'I'll have a medical team sent over here shortly. You'll also have to put up with extra security while the general is here. There's no getting around it.'

'Just keep them outside the burn unit,' Dr Perera said. 'We need to maintain a sterile area around the general.'

Dr Perera motioned for Amanthi to remain as Major Karunaratne left the room. She leant back in her chair tiredly and waved at Amanthi to sit down.

'It's been a very long day,' she said. 'How are you coping?'

'The team's done well,' Amanthi said. 'I just need some fresh air and some food.'

'I think you better stay here tonight and keep an eye on him.' Dr Perera said. 'I've already got a call from the Minister.'

Amanthi nodded. She had nothing planned for that evening. The phone on the desk rang, startling her. She got to her feet and left the room as Dr Perera picked up the handset.

Amanthi walked to the ambulance bay where she lit a cigarette and looked up at the darkening sky. It was going to be a long night. She could feel the pressure, the constant burden ever since she was put in charge of the Emergency Response Team. She couldn't lose it and had to remain in control. Her team depended on her. She could feel the glances, the stares, as they looked to her for the strength and support they needed to go on.

Other than the officer she had worked on, there were no critical cases in the burn unit which would give her a chance to rest. Amanthi remembered that very same spot not two weeks ago when she had gone out on her first emergency call. So much had happened since then.

CHAPTER TWENTY-TWO

Trincomalee was not one of Tilak's favourite places. With its volatile mix of Sinhalese, Tamils and Moors all detesting each other, the tension often flared into widespread communal rioting. His parents had brought him to the town many years ago during his school holidays and they had been caught up in a riot near the entrance to the massive harbour. Only the timely arrival of a shore patrol of blue-clad navy seamen wielding batons had allowed them to escape the violence.

The army's northern offensive had made Trincomalee the major collection point for war displaced refugees. Hidden amongst these refugees were militant sympathizers who disappeared into the local Tamil community, only to reappear as armed militant cadres. Attacks on nearby Sinhalese and Muslim villages had intensified, putting pressure on the authorities to do something.

It was late evening and the street was almost empty. The shops were all shut except for one teahouse where they sat. Ever since the incident at the farmers hut, Tilak had been conscious of an inner turmoil which seemed difficult to pin down. For over six years, while he was in prison, he had been on constant alert never allowing himself to let his guard down. He was always a heartbeat away from some violent action, either from the guards, from the prisoners or by himself. Living on the edge for so long had taken its toll but recently he had become more relaxed, still attuned to his immediate environment but not on edge as he used to be.

'It's time,' Chandra murmured, glancing around the room. The last customers were sitting on broken-backed chairs, arguing furtively over drained glasses. The debate was far too engrossing for any of them to notice the two of them slinking quietly up the street.

The aroma of highly spiced food made Tilak hungry as he stood outside a shuttered shop in the heart of the town. The buildings were old and dilapidated, stone facades once splendid and impressive were crumbling, grimed and patched with haphazard necessity. The shop was no different to many others on the road, only a hand painted sign saying 'Suminda Stores' indicated to Tilak that he was at the right address.

Tilak rapped on the door and took a step back. Chandra lounged against the shop wall which was plastered with advertisements for cigarettes, toothpaste, powdered milk and different types of biscuits. They had been ordered to meet with a man who was one of the leaders in the local Sinhalese community.

Tilak could sense someone looking at him through a peephole in the wooden shutter. He waited patiently for it to be opened and rapped on the shutter again with his knuckles when it didn't. Tilak glanced over his shoulder at Chandra, he was getting impatient. He banged on it again, thumping the wooden shutter hard with his fist. This time he heard some movement. A bolt was withdrawn and one of the wooden shutters was pushed aside creating a narrow opening.

'What do you want?' a gravelly voice asked from inside. 'Can't you see we are closed for business?'

'We're here to meet with Suminda,' Tilak said into the opening. 'He's expecting us,' Tilak heard some whispering and more bolts being withdrawn. A second wooden shutter was removed and then another, creating an opening for Tilak to go through. Chandra remained outside on the street.

The inside of the store was dark. Tilak sensed more than one person in the room. As his eyes adjusted to the gloom the same gravelly voice asked. 'Who sent you?'

'The man who sends you money and looks after your children.' Tilak had been asked to say those exact words.

An exposed light bulb hanging by two wires above Tilak, came on suddenly bathing the room in a harsh light. He blinked in the sudden glare, at a heavy-set man standing behind a solid wooden counter a few feet away. Two other men in sarongs and t-shirts stood on either side of him. The room was filled with glass cabinets and boxes containing household consumables of all kinds.

'I am Suminda,' said the man from behind the counter. 'What do you want?' Suminda looked to be in his fifties with a halo of grey-white hair, and white bushy eyebrows.

'The man who sent me has a message,' Tilak said, glancing around. 'But only for you.'

Suminda waved his hand irritably. 'You can speak in front of them,' he growled. 'Nothing I do can be done without them.'

Tilak shrugged. 'Ok,' he said. 'I have been asked to tell you that the Indians are putting pressure on the government to sign some sort of an agreement with the Tamils. As part of that agreement, the army will have to withdraw all troops in the field to their bases. I don't need to tell you what that will mean to you and the rest of the Sinhalese people in the east.'

When Tilak had heard what was going on, he felt angry that their powerful neighbor to the north would interfere and force the government to accept such conditions. He had heard stories whispered while in prison that the Indians were training the Tamil Tiger cadre in camps in India and had considerable influence with some of the militant groups operating in the island.

'How can they do that?' Suminda asked, raising his voice. 'They're abandoning us to these dogs from the north.'

Tilak shook his head. 'Not totally,' he said. 'The military will be ordered back to their bases and since Trincomalee is one big military base, you'll remain under their protection. But what happens outside the town will be another matter.'

Suminda pondered at what Tilak had said. 'That makes sense but there's something you want done,' he said shrewdly. 'Otherwise you won't be here.'

Tilak had wondered who Suminda really was and how much control he had within the Sinhalese community. He was about to find that out.

'We want you to make sure that the entire town remains in our hands,' he said. 'We cannot give the Indians any reason to come in and take over. We, the government, don't trust them. This means you will have to keep a tight control of your people. No rioting, no looting and no killing.'

Suminda nodded thoughtfully. Tilak could see that he was processing what he had just heard. 'But before all this happens we want to make sure that all the Tamil militants in the town are eliminated,' Tilak continued. 'For that we require your help.'

'That makes sense,' Suminda said, nodding understandingly. 'Ok, what do you want us to do?'

'We want you to send your people out to identify where the Tigers safe houses are, where their weapons and explosives are hidden. You don't have to do anything except lead us to them. We will do the rest.'

'And we do this for what?' Suminda asked, looking at Tilak searchingly. 'You want me to risk my people to gather this information. What if it does not work? We will have to live with the consequences.'

Tilak had been expecting this question. 'I have been authorized to tell you that you can give me a list of all your competitors,' he said. 'Once this matter is concluded you will control everything in this town.'

Tilak had mixed feelings about what he was being asked to do. He hated the idea of having the Indians come into the country in any capacity and that feeling was foremost in his mind. He had learnt from a young age how the ancient Sinhalese Kings had resisted numerous Indian invasions over two thousand years of history and had developed a sense of pride that the island had never been conquered by them. He knew that he was just a pawn in a greater political battle being fought at an international level and regretted the part he had been asked to play in it.

When Tilak had first heard what was being offered, he realized that the person he was being sent to meet was more than just a community leader. He must be one of the men who controlled the illegal activity in the port.

'I give this list to you?' Suminda asked, looking curiously at Tilak.

'Yes,' Tilak said. 'To me. We have been asked to take care of the matter.'

'You and that killer outside,' Suminda said, grinning at Tilak, looking pleased with himself. 'I wondered what he was doing here.' Suminda paused for a moment and glanced at his two men before nodding. 'We cannot do this by ourselves. We will use our Muslim friends to help us. We will need their permission to pass through their areas. But leave that up to me. Tell your boss that I will do as he asks.'

'But we don't have much time,' Tilak nodded in agreement. 'We need those lists quickly.'

*

Tilak yawned, stretched, scanning the messages that had come in to the operations room overnight. He took a pencil out of a chipped mug stuffed with writing instruments and drew a line through two names on a list he pulled from his pocket.

Suminda had kept to his end of the bargain and provided a list of militant hideouts and arms caches his men had discovered in Trincomalee. The military had raided many of them and had been surprised at the quantity of arms that had been found. The modern weapons had included a shoulder fired surface to air missile, which along with the other weapons were sent to Colombo for analysis. The list of competitors Suminda had provided was relatively short, containing seven names of which there were just two remaining. The others had been eliminated one by one and Chandra had gone out early that morning to a part of the city that the remaining two men frequented.

The Inspector in Charge of the Trincomalee Police station walked into the room with a mug of steaming tea. He was a big burly man from Colombo whom Tilak got along with quite well. He motioned Tilak into his office.

'The government has finally signed a peace accord with the Indians,' he said, tapping a report on his table. 'They have deployed troops in Jaffna and opened direct negotiations with the militant groups and all our military forces are restricted to their bases.'

'It wasn't unexpected,' said Tilak. 'It was going to happen but the big question now is how the people in the south will react to this. I am personally against it because I don't trust the Indians.'

'I know what you mean,' the Inspector agreed. It's bloody shambles. I heard that the Cabinet was divided and the President pushed it through. What pisses me off is that we have to release all the militant prisoners we have caught since all this started. That's over 2000 of them,' he said angrily. 'We lost many good men catching that lot.'

Tilak hoped that the politicians knew what they were doing. Letting the Indians in was a mistake and nothing good would come from it.

The telephone on the Inspector's desk rang loudly. He scowled at it irritably before picking up the handset. 'What is it?' he barked into the phone. 'Can't you see I am busy?'

The Inspector listened to what was said on the phone before placing the handset gently down on its cradle. 'There's rioting in Colombo,' he said, thoughtfully. 'It is against the accord.' He stood up and reached for his peaked cap. 'I have been asked to deploy my men and prevent any protest meetings.'

Tilak was not surprised by the news. In fact, he would have been surprised if his countrymen had accepted what the Indians did without some form of protest.

Chandra was in the operations room when he left the Inspector's office.

'How did it go,' Tilak asked Chandra. 'Did you find them?'

Chandra shook his head. 'I cannot find the last two men on the list. I think they have realized what's happening and have gone to ground. It will take some time to locate them.'

'It was bound to happen,' said Tilak. 'I'd better go and give Suminda an update. I don't want him to think that we didn't keep our side of the bargain. If he finds out where they are hiding he can send word to us.'

Chandra nodded. 'That's not all,' he said. 'We've been ordered back to Colombo.'

'Were you given a reason?' Tilak was surprised that they would be pulled out at such a crucial time in the operation. There were still a few militant safe houses and caches on the outskirts of the city that needed to be cleared out. And then there was the matter of the two men that had to be found.

'No,' Chandra shook his head. 'The commander just wants us to leave today.'

'Ok,' Tilak shrugged. He'd better go and talk to Suminda before leaving.

CHAPTER TWENTY-THREE

Nadesan approached the safe house cautiously. He had been observing the laneway and the surrounding houses for two days from his hideout in the warehouse. He was lucky that the warehouse was empty and that he could get in and out through the broken cladding at the back.

He had not seen anything out of the ordinary and felt reasonably confident that the Police did not know its location. But he had felt the same way at the garage in Grandpass and only his need for food had saved him from being captured.

That morning, Nadesan had watched as Deva entered the house for the first time. He knew that the leader of the militant cell wouldn't be there if the place was under observation. One of Nadesan's concerns was that he wouldn't be recognised by the safe house occupants and be denied access, or worse. But with Deva there, Nadesan felt confident of gaining access.

The lane was almost empty of people. A woman in a hijab, four doors down, was hanging her washing on a line outside her front window. The safe house was just like the other houses on the street, only the number twenty-eight identifying it as being the one Nadesan wanted. The front door opened right onto the lane, only a wide concrete slab over a deep drain separating it from the road. A narrow, barred window next to the door was half-shuttered and curtained from the inside.

Nadesan rapped on the door, taking a step back after he did. The curtain moved slightly as someone looked out. A bolt was drawn back, the door swung open. Nadesan looked up and down the street before stepping in.

A lamp threw out a dull light from a table in the corner and the stink of kerosene was strong in the small room. From the deeper shadows of the doorway leading to the rear, he saw the gleam of a rifle barrel aimed at his chest. Nadesan slowly and very carefully raised his arms. He heard breathing close to him, someone grabbed his collar and the barrel of a weapon was pressed hard into the back of his neck. The door shut with a loud thump behind him. Hands patted him down. He was pushed into the doorway leading to the back of the building.

'Put your hands on your head,' a voice whispered. 'And keep them there.'

A scurrying movement behind him and the lamp was lifted, allowing him to see into a corridor with two doors leading off it. A thin man with shrunken cheeks held out a hand grenade, its pin removed. His eyes glittered with madness. A rifle hung from a sling down his side.

'I am looking for Deva,' Nadesan said nervously in Tamil. 'I know he is here.' 'Who are you?' the voice behind him muttered tersely into his ear. 'How did you know to come here?'

'I am Nadesan from the safe house in Pettah,' Nadesan said anxiously. These men didn't know him and he needed to establish his credentials quickly. 'We were raided four days ago. I escaped and have been looking for this place.' The man behind him cuffed him across the side of his head with his weapon. 'How did you know to come here,' he repeated angrily. 'Were you followed?'

Nadesan shook his head. 'I was not followed,' he said, clutching his ear. 'I came here once with Deva before the bus station bombing.'

The man pressed the gun barrel hard into Nadesan's ribs. 'Don't lower your hands until I tell you to.' The man pushed Nadesan forward to an open doorway. The room was lit by a lamp, three half-eaten plates of rice and some sort of curry lay on a table in the middle of the room. The room stank of food and kerosene.

The man pushed Nadesan into the room, turning him so he faced the doorway. Deva walked into the room carrying an AK-47. 'I thought you'd been captured by the Police,' he said, looking at Nadesan suspiciously. 'Where have you been all these days?'

'Trying to get across the river without being caught,' Nadesan said irritably. He had not washed himself in days and he felt filthy and tired.

Deva stared at Nadesan before nodding at the man behind him. Nadesan glanced over his shoulder before removing his hands from his head. The man stepped around Nadesan, tucking a handgun into his waist. He was a heavy, thickset man who looked like he could break a person in two.

Deva crossed the room and stacked his rifle against a wall. 'You better put the pin back,' he said to the man with the grenade. The man fumbled with his clothing and inserted the pin into the explosive device, giggling and dropping the grenade into his pocket.

'So, tell me what happened.' Deva said, stepping forward towards Nadesan. 'We have kept away from the other side of the river.'

A woman hung back in the doorway staring at Nadesan. She was young, in her twenties. Her glossy dark skin and intelligent eyes reminded Nadesan of his dead wife.

Nadesan stretched his arms by his side, shaking them to get the circulation going. 'I was lucky to be in the market when the Police raided. There was firing and people in the street were shot. I had to steal a three-wheeler to get across the river and find this place. It took another two days to make sure no one had followed me or was watching.'

'You've been watching us? From where?' Deva turned and barked at the two men, glaring at them angrily. 'I thought you said no one was watching this place.' The men looked at each other, squirming uneasily. They glared at Nadesan as if he had done something wrong.

'They couldn't see me. It's across the junction, but you can watch the house from there,' Nadesan said soothingly. 'I will show you. It's a good spot.' He didn't want to get these men upset with him. Somewhat placated, Deva sniffed, stepping back from Nadesan. 'You stink,' he said, fanning his hand in the air. 'Take him to the back and show him where he can have a bath. And get him some fresh clothes.'

The men's names were Kumar and Geethan and the woman's name was Sita. The two men stayed indoors all the time while Sita did the shopping. The area was a mixed community of Tamils and Muslims and they were careful not to show their neighbours that so many people lived in the house. The house was sparsely furnished, with reed mats on the front room floor and cots and oil lamps in the two bedrooms. The only piece of furniture was in the kitchen where a large wooden cupboard held an assorted selection of battered pots and pans, a large bag of rice and various spices and condiments. A kerosene cooker with two burners sat on a low table. Water came from a single tap at the back of the house.

A wash from a bucket and a change helped Nadesan push back the tide of exhaustion that had gradually engulfed his body. After his close escape at the garage, he wanted to be more involved with what was happening around him. He was still frightened of being caught but was feeling more confident in his abilities to live and survive in Colombo. The big, chaotic city did not terrify him as much as it once did.

'What plans do you have to use me,' he asked Deva, uncertain of what his future would be. 'If I am not needed I would like to go back to Kathankudi where I can be of more use.'

Deva shook his head. 'No, we're going to need you here. I have still to hear about what they want us to do but I suspect it's a hit on someone important.'

Nadesan looked at Deva questioningly. 'What do you mean someone important?'

'Some target,' Deva said studying Nadesan suspiciously. 'Why do you want to know?'

Nadesan paused uncertainly. A warm burst of heat bloomed in his head. He realized he'd gone too far with his questions. These men were already on edge after the raid on the garage.

Nadesan shrugged. 'I would like to know, that's all.' He looked at the others in the room. 'Don't you want to know?'

Both Kumar and Geethan were scowling gloomily while Sita sat cross legged on her sleeping mat, looking down nervously, clasping and unclasping her hands in her lap.

'That's none of your fucking business,' Deva said stepping forward, looking angrily around. 'You all know the rules. We stay hidden until we are needed.'

'They will be looking for us,' Nadesan said. 'What if they find us here?'

'What has become of you?' Deva sneered heatedly. 'You were not like this before.' His eyes were like black lasers.

Within the quiet, and the dim light in the room, Nadesan experienced the same feeling he had earlier, uncertainty bordering on hopelessness, crossed with fear.

'I can't just sit around doing nothing,' Nadesan pleaded. 'You know what happened in the garage. I'll go mad.'

Deva studied Nadesan for a few moments. 'You are a smart fellow, no!' he said, the heat seemed to have gone from his voice. 'You're a mechanic and you can drive a three-wheeler. I have an idea. I will give you some money to rent a three-wheeler. You can use it as a taxi and get to know the city. It will come in useful one day, I am sure.'

Nadesan looked at Deva in disbelief. 'You want me to drive around the city in a three-wheeler?' he said incredulously. 'I will need an identification card and a license to do that.'

Deva waved his hand in the air. 'That's easy,' he said dismissively. 'I'll take care of it. I'll give you some money tomorrow to find a three-wheeler you can use. There's a place at the junction that rents them. Get one that is old and cheap to rent and fix it up.'

Nadesan warmed to the idea the more he thought about it. Hiding in the house for weeks or months was not an option for him. His escape across the river had made him realize that he could move in the city without anyone knowing who he was. It was like hiding in the jungle. He would blend into its streets and alleys and look just like anyone else. The only danger was living in the safe house. It was the only thing that connected him to the Tigers. If the police found the safe house like they did at the market then they would find him.

What Deva was suggesting was a way to get him out of the house. He would learn the city and patiently wait for the right moment to strike. Nadesan nodded his consent. He would do whatever it took to succeed the next time.

*

Nadesan enjoyed the freedom the three-wheeler gave him. Renting one from the petrol station was easier than he had expected. All the petrol station owner wanted was the entire rental fee paid upfront and money to reserve the same vehicle for the next day.

The narrow, crowded streets of Colombo made Nadesan feel safe. He was just one of the hundreds of three-wheeler drivers in the city and no one paid any attention to him. The only danger came from the noisy, overloaded buses and trucks who didn't seem to care what mayhem they caused as they forced their way through the pedestrian and vehicular traffic.

The owner of the petrol station came out of his office and watched Nadesan tune up the two-stroke engine on the three-wheeler until it was running perfectly. Nadesan had worked on two-stroke motors before and had learned that it had the potential to produce twice the amount of power than a four-stroke motor of the same size. It used a mixture of oil and gasoline to generate power and getting that mixture right was the secret to getting the best performance from the engine.

'Are you a mechanic?' the petrol station owner wanted to know. 'That engine sounds pretty good.' The man spoke Tamil and wore a taqiyya on his head.

Nadesan nodded. He didn't want to get into a discussion with the man in case he asked Nadesan where he was from. He felt very insecure after what had happened and did not want to draw attention to himself.

The man waved his arm at two rows of three-wheelers lined up on the other side of the yard. 'I need these machines in proper working condition every day,' he said. 'Otherwise I am losing money. I'll pay you for each machine you work on?'

Nadesan had not accepted the man's proposal right away although he was tempted. Having a job would earn him some money and get him out of the safe house. He might even be able to find a place to live on his own. He told the petrol station owner that he would think about it and let him know when he brought the three-wheeler back that evening.

Driving around the city, familiarizing himself with the roads and landmarks of the northern suburbs, Nadesan was only stopped twice. Once by an army roadblock and then by the Police. The national identification card everyone was required to carry in the country identified him as Basheer Marzook, a Muslim resident of Maligawatte. Neither the soldier nor the policeman paid attention to him, waving him on after cursorily scrutinizing the card which Deva had given him. On more than one occasion Nadesan had been hailed by people wanting a ride but he had resisted the temptation. He wanted to learn to drive a three-wheeler in the city. One thing he was careful of was not to go back to the safe house. He would keep his distance from the sleeper cell until he was needed. It was the only place that connected him to the militants. Maybe he could try and get away but he needed time to collect some money. The only person who had access to any money was Deva and he would want to know what he needed the money for. Nadesan would bide his time, be patient and get to know the city first.

CHAPTER TWENTY-FOUR

Amanthi was nervous. It was the day of the island-wide strike and she had been warned by her colleagues not to go into work.

A Sinhalese insurgent group known as the People's Liberation Front who had risen phoenix-like from an abortive insurrection in 1971, had become a powerful factor in local politics. The group who drew their main support from amongst the workers, students and unemployed elements in the country had attempted and failed to use the democratic process to gain power. It was reported recently that the leaders of the Front had begun to build a cell system in the Sinhalese areas of the south and started training their cadre with the idea of waging an armed struggle against the government.

Amanthi had just started going to university during the time of the first uprising and remembered that period with dread. She had to endure university closures and the sudden cancellation of classes and exams until the trouble had finally died down. It had added almost an extra year of study to her degree. Acts of violence had been slowly building up across parts of the country, accelerating recently after the Indian Peace Accord gave rise to a wave of protests by the Sinhala masses who were opposed to letting the Indians in. Almost daily the newspapers reported politicians and government officials being killed and their houses burnt. It had been reported that the Front had infiltrated supporters into the ranks of the Police and army who seemed helpless to stop the killings.

A reign of fear gripped the island, with threats against innocent citizens, the imposition of island-wide strikes called 'hartals', and unlawful curfews, resulting in immense hardship to everyone. Political killings led to assassinations of senior Policemen, families of senior military officers, members of the Buddhist clergy, prominent citizens and businessmen. A campaign to strangle the economy of the country by crippling the island-wide transportation system, disruption of power supplies, burning of factories and destroying produce led to disruption and chaos. Worst effected were the tea plantations where factories were razed to the ground, strikes fostered, superintendents of tea estates killed and pay packets robbed.

She had woken up that morning to the sound of her mother's footsteps walking down the corridor leading to her bedroom. The house was built in the shape of a horseshoe around a central courtyard and her room was at the very end of the corridor. Her mother laid Amanthi's cup of coffee on the dressing table and drew the curtains aside.

'Are you going to work today?' her mother asked. It was unusual for her to bring Amanthi's coffee, generally leaving the servant girl to attend to Amanthi's needs.

Amanthi knew what she meant. News reports the previous night said that a hartal had been declared for that day. Various groups and trade unions were demanding a day of protest to mark the killings in the north by the Indian Peace Keeping Force.

The Indian government had sent troops as a part of the Peace Accord but they had behaved more like conquerors, killing, raping and pillaging the local villages.

The Tamil militant groups including the Tigers announced that they would enforce the demands that everyone boycott work. They did not want anyone on the street and ordered that no lights or televisions be turned on.

'Yes, of course,' Amanthi said, getting out of bed.

Her mother frowned and looked at her disapprovingly. 'It's not safe with all these killings. Can't someone else do the job,' she asked questioningly?

'Why does it always have to be you?'

'Because if I don't, someone else will have to,' Amanthi murmured, sipping her coffee. 'And anyway, I am presently in charge'. Dr Perera was overseas, attending a conference and had left Amanthi in charge of the unit.

Amanthi's mother pursed her lips in disbelief. 'I knew you'll be stubborn about this. Can't you see what will happen if they find out you went to work?'

The radio had reported that in the south, the insurgents had resorted to burning the homes of people who did not support their movement.

Amanthi shook her head. 'That's all propaganda to make us scared,' she said. 'And it's only happening in the south. They won't dare resort to such tactics here.'

Her mother looked searchingly at Amanthi before grunting her displeasure as she left the room. Amanthi walked to the open door, cradling the coffee mug in her hands and watched as her mother walked away. She could understand why her mother was worried. Every day the newspapers were filled with stories of people being murdered, homes and businesses burnt. Military units were being recalled from the north to put down the insurgency in the south leaving the Indians to manage the demands of the Tamil militants. The whole island seemed to be coming apart at the seams.

It was a warm morning. Showers were predicted for the afternoon making the air hot and humid. A magpie robin stationed itself outside her window and filled the room with its morning melody. Amanthi finished her coffee and went back into her room to get ready. While she was in the shower she thought she heard the phone ring. She was drying herself when the servant girl brought her a message. The note was in her mother's handwriting.

Amanthi was needed in the hospital to attend to a child who had been brought in with severe burns to her body. The only staff in the hospital were nurses from the previous evening shift who would remain on duty until relieved. There was nobody at the hospital to handle an emergency burn admittance.

Amanthi quickly changed into her hospital greens, shrugged on her white coat and stepped out onto the road outside her house, after pecking her mother's cheek. Amanthi was glad that she had not brought up the subject of her not going into work again.

The roads around her home, normally crowded with pedestrian and vehicular traffic were quiet. Only Police and army vehicles filled with armed men patrolled the empty streets. There were no taxis or three-wheelers in sight. Amanthi started walking in the direction of the hospital. She didn't go far before an army jeep slowed down and stopped next to her.

An officer armed with a sub-machine gun got down from the vehicle. 'What's the problem doctor,' he asked. 'Can I be of assistance.' Two armed soldiers at the back stood up, looking up and down the street.

'I need to get to the General Hospital quickly,' Amanthi said. 'They are bringing in a burn victim, a child, and I have been called in to attend to her.'

The officer did not hesitate. 'We'll take you there,' he said, stepping back and motioning her to the jeep. 'Get in the front. I'll sit at the back with my men.'

The entrance to the hospital was unusually quiet. Normally a busy place in the evening with people coming and going, there was nobody in the admittance hall. The hospital was dark, no lights had been turned on in the hallways. Only the wards had lights burning at the nursing stations.

The army officer offered to walk Amanthi into the burn unit but Amanthi declined his offer.

The nurse in the burn unit looked tired. Her name was Nandini and she had been on duty since the previous day. 'The patient was just brought in, doctor,' she said. 'She is with her mother in the emergency room.'

Amanthi nodded at the nurse and hurried into the emergency room. The patient was being attended to by a doctor from the General Hospital Emergency Unit. A woman dressed in a blouse and long skirt stood by the head of the bed, stroking the patients face. The doctor glanced up hearing footsteps, a look of relief sweeping his face when he saw it was Amanthi.

'Amanthi, thank God you are here,' he said, turning to the patient. 'I have stabilized her with a saline drip and given her a small dosage of morphine to manage the pain.'

Amanthi stood next to the gurney and studied the patient. The young girl, not more than ten years old, lay quietly on her side breathing irregularly. She had been wrapped in a damp sheet that was soaked through with blood and other body fluids.

'We need to remove that sheet,' Amanthi said. Medics attending to burn victims often wrapped the patient in a wet sheet or bandage in a misguided attempt to cool the burnt area, risking severe and potentially fatal hypothermia. Amanthi knew that a burn victim who was very young or very old was at a far greater risk of dying from burns unless treated immediately.

Amanthi snapped on a pair of gloves and started to peel off the sheet gently from the child's body. She was so intent on her work that she was startled when the portable heat lamps in the emergency bay snapped on suddenly.

A shadowy figure in the back of the room came into the light. It was Nelum. Amanthi smiled at her gratefully. This was going to be a complicated case and having part of her team around her was comforting.

'Shanthi is here too doctor,' Nelum said. 'We came together. She's getting the bandages ready.'

Amanthi choked up. She was lucky to be working with such dedicated nurses. She looked down at the patient who was showing signs of distress. Amanthi turned the knob on the IV drip a notch sending a higher dosage of morphine into the patient's small body. Getting the dosage right for children was always tricky. Too much could send them into a deep coma and too little would bring the pain back. Amanthi watched the child's body relax as the morphine took hold. Her breathing became less shallow and her skin was dry to the touch.

Amanthi stepped aside and let Nelum take her place. She needed to talk to the child's mother to find out what had happened.

It was after midnight when the intricate dance of admitting a burn patient into the unit was completed. The child whose name was Kasuni was in a faraway place, embraced by powerful drugs that would hold the pain at bay. The wounds on one side of her body were clean, the burnt skin and bits of clothing removed carefully by Amanthi. She had been wrapped by Shanthi and Nelum in solution soaked bandages and injected with strong antibiotics to stop any infection.

The girl's distraught mother told Amanthi that the child had been playing in the kitchen and had knocked over a kerosene lantern which had doused her with flaming liquid.

Amanthi knew that they had done all they could for the girl who would face many months of painful grafts and healing to replace the burnt skin on her body. They wheeled the emergency gurney with Kasuni into the ward, transferring her onto a vacant bed next to the nurse's station.

The hospital corridors were dark and empty as the three of them walked to the canteen down the hallway to get something to eat. The large room, normally bustling with doctors, nurses and orderlies was empty, the kitchen counter shuttered tight.

'Let's go outside and get some food from the kade,' Nelum said. 'They usually stay open all night.'

Amanthi craved a cigarette and her senses were heightened by the emptiness in the hospital. Her nerves were on edge as they walked down the long corridor towards the hospital entrance. She wished at that moment that the General had not been moved to the military hospital. While he was being treated in the burn unit, there were armed soldiers stationed at both ends of the corridor and also at the entrance to the burn unit.

The admitting room where patients were first brought to the hospital looked empty as they approached, the overhead lights not turned on. Only the light from the street outside, shining through the glass doors and floor to ceiling windows, cast a pale light into the large room. She wondered whether going out was the smart thing to do when she saw movement outside. Through the doors, the dark shapes of two men stood silhouetted against the street lights.

An icy chill clenched Amanthi's stomach. She grabbed the two nurses before they left the darkness of the corridor. 'Don't go out there,' she whispered, her heart thumping hard in her chest.

Hidden in the dark shadow of the corridor she peered out. From where she was hiding, Amanthi found it difficult to make out who the men were. One carried what looked like a shotgun while the other carried a large club on his shoulder. They were joined by another man also carrying a gun. He looked like the leader, talking and waving his hand at the two men. One of them turned and peered into the admittance hall through the glass door.

Amanthi remembered the warning they'd been given, not to go to work, that the day of protest would be enforced if anyone broke it.

'We'd better go back,' Amanthi whispered to the two nurses who looked scared. 'They don't look like they want anyone here.' The three of them retreated slowly back down the hallway, their footsteps echoing in the empty corridor. They almost ran the last few yards to the burn unit, closing and locking the door behind them in relief.

'We better jam the door shut,' said Amanthi, looking around. Shanthi ran over to a heavy metal cabinet on wheels used to store drugs and other medicines. She released the wheel locks and rolled the cabinet against the door, locking the wheels in place so that the cabinet could not be moved.

'I'll stay here and watch the door with Shanthi,' said Amanthi. She felt a sense of responsibility to her team. 'Nelum, can you check on our little patient.' Amanthi remained awake watching the door until daylight started creeping through the windows, slowly lighting up the dark ward.

By sunrise, the normal hustle and bustle of the hospital coming to life pushed the nights ordeal to the back of her mind like a bad dream. She would check up on her patient before going home to sleep.

CHAPTER TWENTY-FIVE

This had to be the worst job he'd ever done. Tilak sat outside the well-lit house in a Mitsubishi Pajero while the Minister for National Security screwed his mistress. They had been assigned as bodyguards to the man after a bomb attack at a party meeting in the parliamentary complex killed one Minister and injured a number of others. Other senior government officials had been assassinated on their way to work or in their homes.

The armed revolt across the southern and central regions by disaffected Sinhalese youth had broken into open conflict. The police and military were locked in a fierce struggle and revenge killings from both sides grew in intensity. Young Sinhalese men disappeared across the island, thousands were murdered and thousands more were thrown in jail under terrorism charges. This made the Minister a prime target for retaliation by the insurgents.

Tilak and Chandra had been following the Minister around for almost a month and he had refused to change his habits despite the possible threat to his life.

A document released by the insurgents which was circulating openly, warned that any politician who had supported the India-Sri Lanka alliance would not be safe. The document had stated that 'we will target all those who whitewash the destructive acts of the Indian Army and describe them as a peace keeping force.'

Chandra materialized out of the dark. The man moved like a ghost. He had gone around to check on the rear of the house.

'It's clear,' he said quietly, when Tilak looked at him questioningly. 'These houses all have high walls and it'll be difficult for someone to get in from the back.'

Tilak hunched down in his seat and ran his finger around his collar. He hated the feel of a tie around his neck but there were times when it was necessary. Tilak glanced at his watch. It was almost ten in the evening. If the Minister stuck to his normal schedule he would be leaving in the next few minutes. It had been a scorching day and the night was no better. Tilak scanned the neighbouring houses. The gardens were shrouded in darkness and the windows closed.

Tilak sighed in boredom. His life had gone from being in prison, to being trained by ex-SAS soldiers, to assassinating Tamil militants, all in the space of a few months. And here he was, sitting in a parked car on a darkened street waiting for a politician to finish with his mistress. His thoughts strayed to the Doctor he had met in Batticaloa … Amanthi! He had watched her work on Saman and been impressed by her quiet confidence. I wonder if I will ever bump into her again he thought to himself.

Never short of female company until he went into jail, Tilak had resisted the urge to pay for a short time with the prostitutes who frequented the prison even though he had the opportunity. He had been tempted many times but it was the penalty he had imposed on himself to pay for losing control and killing that woman.

After a while his thoughts drifted, and he found himself reliving the moment he killed the insurgent leader. When they were sent out of the Officer's Training School to quell the Marxist uprising, a change came over Tilak. He had been put in charge of an under-manned platoon and ordered to recapture the town from an estimated two hundred insurgents. Normally a relatively cool and easy-going person, Tilak had through necessity turned almost overnight into a ruthless and feared officer.

The woman who had been the insurgent leader had been a beauty queen in her time. She was in her late twenties, loud and abusive, calling them, among other things, fornicators of animals and sons of whores. She had been identified as the person who had personally killed two policemen in front of the local post office and when she spat at him his resolve crumbled. Tilak grabbed her by the hair and dragged her outside the police station, kicking the woman out into the yard before pulling out his revolver, and shooting her twice at point blank range. When Tilak came to his senses she was twitching soundlessly on the ground, a pool of her blood snaking towards the edge of the yard. It was then that he had realized what he was capable of. That killing rage had served him well in prison, the inmates recognizing the devilish fury in him.

The lights of a car turning into the street made Tilak sit up attentively. It was not a through road; only cars on the street were those of residents living there. Chandra disappeared into the shadows by the side of the road. Tilak reached under his shirt and pulled out an automatic pistol, chambering a round and releasing the safety. He quickly scanned the houses down the street. They were still dark but how long would they stay that way?

The car drove slowly up the street towards them. Tilak could not make out who was in the car and ducked his head below its tinted windows as it passed, not wanting to be illuminated by its headlights.

The Minister decided to leave at that moment. The porch light switched on and the door opened, framing the Minister in its glare. The man paused at the doorway and looked over his shoulder, speaking to someone who was out of sight.

The car which had passed and was about three houses down, switched off its lights and accelerated to the end of the street. Tilak had a bad feeling about this. He opened the Pajero's door and slipped out of the vehicle, keeping the vehicle in his sights.

Tilak couldn't see where Chandra was, hoping that he would get the Minister away from the porch light and into the house. Tilak saw the car's brake lights come on when it turned into a driveway, reversed out back onto the street and stopped. Something was not right and he couldn't put his finger on it.

Then it came to him. If whoever was in the car knew the Minister's habits, they would also know about his bodyguards. Tilak whipped his head around and looked back up the street. His eyes searching the darkness for anything out of the ordinary.

There! A movement two houses down. A shadow detached itself from the garden hedge and moved closer, disappearing into the darkness only a house away. Tilak realized that the car was a diversion and they'd almost fallen for it. Tilak guessed there were more men on the street whom he couldn't see.

The front door clicked shut and the porch light flicked off, covering the front of the house in darkness. The Minister was nowhere to be seen. He must be in the house.

That placed Chandra in the garden. He must have warned the Minister. Tilak retreated until he felt the fence line behind him. From there he could keep his eye on both the car and whoever was coming up the street.

The man on the street was the biggest threat. And Tilak was convinced that there was more than one. A minute passed, then two. Tilak saw someone peering out from behind a bush, looking into the garden trying to spot where the Minister had gone. A branch moved to Tilak's left, not more than a car length away. A shadowy figure stepped into view, a pistol in his outstretched hands. It was the second man who had come to take out the bodyguards.

Tilak didn't give the man a chance to get up to the Pajero and discover that it was empty. Tilak raised his handgun and lined it with the man's head, squeezing the trigger twice. The muzzle flash from the gun blinded him for a moment as he ducked away from where he was standing.

Constant movement in a gun fight will keep you alive. Mike's words echoed in his ears. Tilak glanced at the man on the ground who did not move. He'd been too close to miss.

Tilak moved quickly towards the parked car leaving the other man for Chandra to handle. The car up the street suddenly moved, gaining speed as it came towards Tilak. The driver's face was a shadow in the front windscreen when Tilak fired three shots, shattering the glass into a thousand pieces. The car swerved to the left almost hitting Tilak before crashing into the parked Pajero.

The driver was barely alive when Tilak looked in the car. A big chunk of his throat had been torn out by the bullet, blood pulsing from his severed artery. A semi-automatic machine pistol lay on the seat next to him.

Tilak reached in and took the weapon, slinging it over his shoulder. He ejected the clip from his pistol and replaced it with the one he carried in his hip pocket. Tilak crouched by the two vehicles, his eyes searching the surroundings for any danger. The loud gunshots and the crash had woken the neighbourhood. Dogs barked and lights came on in some of the houses but no one came out onto the street.

A figure in the garden waved at him, signalling him to come over. From its shape and size Tilak knew it was Chandra. Tilak jogged over, still alert for any danger.

Chandra stood over a man lying on his back. Dressed in dark shirt and trousers, the man stared sightless to the stars, the haft of a fighting knife sticking out from the base of this throat. Chandra bent and picked up a gun which he examined and stuffed into his belt. He nodded at Tilak and looked at the house where the Minister was hiding.

'Let's call this in,' he said. 'The Minister is not going to be happy about his nice new Pajero.'

CHAPTER TWENTY-SIX

Nadesan felt relaxed; more relaxed than he had ever been since coming to Colombo. The northern suburb he was living in was a melting pot of people of all faiths and from all walks of life, allowing him to move around without being noticed.

With the fares, he made using the three-wheeler as an un-metered taxi, and the money the petrol station owner gave him for keeping the other three-wheelers on the road, a job he had subsequently accepted, Nadesan could leave the safe house and find a room of his own. The petrol station owner whose name was Mahroof, had a storeroom in the back of his property filled with junk and when Nadesan approached him about using the room to sleep at night, Mahroof had not hesitated in saying yes.

The room was fifteen paces long and nine wide. There were no windows and only one door. Nadesan had cleaned out most of the rubbish and pushed the rest aside giving him ample space to lay out a mattress to sleep on. He bought his food from the buth kade next to the petrol station and used the station outhouse as his toilet.

One morning, Nadesan saw Deva on the street outside the petrol station. Deva looked around and motioned for Nadesan to join him. Looking over his shoulder to see whether Nadesan was following, he went down the road and entered a small tea kade located in a lane off the main street. It was mid-morning and the shop was almost empty. Nadesan paid for a glass of milk tea at the counter and sat at the corner table next to Deva.

Deva scrutinized Nadesan. 'You look well,' he said. 'How are you managing on your own?'

'I am fine,' said Nadesan. He waited until the waiter placed a glass of frothy tea in front of him. They quietly spoke in Tamil as Nadesan didn't want to draw any attention to the two of them. 'Have you received any instructions?' he asked, looking at Deva pointedly.

Deva shook his head. 'No, nothing,' he said. 'A number of our people were arrested or killed after the incident. They will have to find others to bring the messages.'

Nadesan nodded unhappily. He would have to be patient. There were rumors circulating almost daily of militant cells being raided and of gunfights on the street. Just the previous week a bomb had exploded in a bus going to the Fort, killing many passengers. The Police had doubled their presence on the street and were questioning anyone who looked like a Tamil. Nadesan had been stopped twice and released after the Police checked his identity card which identified him as a Muslim.

'Stay away from the house,' warned Deva. 'I don't want to have too many coming and going from the house. Geethan and Sita have gone back. The Police have informers everywhere. I'll send Kumar to get you when I hear something.'

Nadesan walked back to the petrol station deep in thought. It looked like nothing was going to happen for a while. He would continue to maintain the fleet of three-wheelers owned by Mahroof and drive one whenever he wanted to. The arrangement he had with the business man was good for both.

It was the normalcy which was coming back into his life that frightened him. The grief he carried for his wife and child was still there, burning inside of him, but it wasn't consuming him as it once did. Did that make him unworthy as a husband, a father? He had come to Colombo on a mission which he had every intention of completing but he had panicked at the very end and that shamed him. Did he want to go through that again?

Nadesan paused, checking the traffic before crossing the road. He didn't know what to do. He had enough money with him to get on a bus and disappear, but where would he go? Back to his home, which would only remind him of his wife and son? They will find me if I run away ... I'd rather die here.

Death had never terrified him. Just the pain he would have to suffer if he ever got caught. He had been unwavering in the commitment he had made to the cause since he started the journey and pushed aside all thoughts of weakness.

No, he would remain in the city and complete whatever mission they wanted him to do. But he needed to prepare for that day. He would learn everything he could about this terrible, crowded place. Get to know it's thoroughfares, its warren of streets and alleyways, and get to know its secrets. I don't want to end my life as a failure!

CHAPTER TWENTY-SEVEN

Tilak was frustrated. After the attempt on his life, the Minister had insisted that Tilak and Chandra be assigned to him permanently. When Tilak objected, he was ordered to keep quiet. The senior Minister was in the Cabinet and carried a lot of clout.

The Minister's detail had been beefed up, and a squad of specially trained troopers provided all around protection to the man and his family. But the Minister only wanted the two of them with him when he went to visit his mistress.

Tilak and Chandra had been sent on a close protection training course in Kalutara run by an ex-British soldier. The intensive crash course was conducted when the Minister went to London for a conference. They spent the time learning about protecting VIPs who left the safety of their homes and places of work. Much of the training was geared around the fact that most of the attacks occurred when the target was in or around their vehicle. They learned how to protect the VIP, and just as importantly the limousine driver. The terrorist mindset was stop the driver, stop the motorcade. Keep the target in the kill zone until he is eliminated. A close protection detail should not let this happen.

Today the Minister was attending a parliamentary meeting at the government complex in Kotte and Tilak was feeling bored. The politician lived in the heart of Cinnamon Gardens and Tilak passed the General Hospital many times a day when driving the Minister around. Tilak often thought about the doctor who had attended to his face in Batticaloa, wondering how she was doing. He once again recollected how he had watched as she attended to Saman, a small frown of concentration on her forehead, her expressive eyes intent on what she was doing.

'I am going to see someone,' Tilak said to Chandra who lounged against the Pajero. 'I won't be back for a while so if he comes out and asks for me, tell him that I am busy.'

Chandra glanced at Tilak without saying anything. He watched as Tilak left the Parliament Complex and hailed a three-wheeler back into the city.

The drive to the hospital at Ward Place did not take long. Tilak wondered whether the doctor would even remember him.

Coming in from the street, his eyes took a little time to become accustomed to the cool shadow of the admittance hall. Tilak hesitated. She may not be on duty, he thought to himself. He didn't even know her last name. But he had come this far and decided to go in and ask for her.

'Dr. De Silva,' the woman behind the counter breathed, smiling at Tilak. 'Yes, she's on duty. Do you want me to tell her you're here?'

Tilak nodded, still feeling uncertain that he was doing the right thing. The receptionist pushed back her chair, leant over and whispered something to her colleague who glanced at Tilak.

The admittance hall was crowded with visitors and patients waiting to be called for treatment. Tilak wandered through the crowd, feeling nervous, not knowing why. He barely understood this sudden compulsion to see the doctor. He saw the receptionist come back into the room and look around for him, waving when she spotted him.

'The doctor is busy right now and cannot come out,' the receptionist said. Tilak nodded at her uncomfortably. It had been a mistake coming. 'But she wants you to come in and wait for her in her office,' she continued with a smile. Tilak followed the woman through two swinging doors into the main hospital corridor. Doctors and nurses moved purposefully in all directions, intent on whatever task they were on. The receptionist pushed open a large door under a sign which read 'burn unit' and pointed to a small office next to the entrance.

'Stay here,' she said. 'The doctor will see you when she is ready.'

From where Tilak stood he could look into the unit, past a number of empty bays filled with medical equipment. At the far end of the room, a group of Doctors and nurses huddled around a bed absorbed by whatever they were doing.

Tilak sat on the chair in front of the desk and looked around the room. It had two visitors' chairs in front of a stark grey desk unit. A four-drawer filing cabinet and a framed medical chart on the wall were the only other furniture in the room. A green flak jacket and a metal helmet lay thrown untidily on the floor in the corner. Other than a white coat hanging on a stand by the door with a partially obscured nametag, it was devoid of anything that would have identified the owner.

Tilak was contemplating looking at the nametag when someone spoke from behind him. 'Lieutenant, I am sorry I kept you waiting. One of our patients had a small emergency which needed to be taken care of right away.'

Tilak turned guiltily. The doctor in her hospital greens stood by the door her hand outstretched. Her hair was a bit longer, but her light eyes which contemplated him amusedly were just as intense as he remembered.

'Hello doctor,' said Tilak, shaking her hand. 'I was passing the hospital and thought I would drop in and thank you for treating Saman.' Tilak glanced into the ward. 'But if you're busy I won't take any of your time.'

'No, no,' the doctor said. 'I need a break. How about we get out of here and get something to drink?' She hurried behind the desk and pulled a handbag from the drawer, slinging it on her shoulder. 'Let's go into the canteen,' she said. 'I need to be close in case I am needed. And stop calling me doctor. My name is Amanthi.'

Tilak couldn't take his eyes off Amanthi as he followed her deeper into the hospital. She looked so open, so beautiful. He realized at that moment that he wanted her to like him, but he carried a secret that she did not know. What would she think of him when she found out?

The canteen reeked of food as they stood at the food counter and ordered. He carried the tray with two cups of steaming hot tea and four sticky buns, to the table she directed him to.

'What are you doing in Colombo?' Amanthi asked, delicately sipping the hot tea. She watched him openly, not hiding the interest that shone out of her light grey eyes.

'I have been assigned to a Cabinet Minister as a personal bodyguard,' he explained gloomily. 'It's not what I want to do but these are strange times.'

'What do you normally do?' she asked guilelessly. 'I mean, what do you do when you are not a bodyguard?'

Tilak squirmed uncomfortably. 'I am an officer in the Special Task Force.' He didn't want Amanthi to think badly of him because many people considered the STF to be a bunch of paramilitary thugs.

Amanthi looked at him frankly over the cup of tea she held in her hands. 'You said that as if you feel ashamed to be part of the force. Is it something you have been forced into doing?'

Tilak looked at her in surprise. She was reading him like an open book. 'Eh, yes! I mean no … I don't know,' he ended lamely. He couldn't believe he was behaving like a teenager on his first date. It was true that he hadn't had a proper conversation with a woman for many years. But this was ridiculous.

'Do you want to talk about it,' Amanthi asked. She looked at Tilak carefully. 'Or you can tell me it's none of my business. We can still be friends.'

Tilak stared into the cup of tea on the table. Ever since he'd come out of prison, he felt alone. His parents were distant with him and he visited them rarely, feeling that they did not enjoy his company. He had no one to talk to and now this woman, whom he hardly knew, was asking him to tell her what he was going through.

He started at the very beginning. His aspirations to be an army officer, the insurgency of 1971 when he was ordered as an officer cadet to take a platoon of part-time soldiers and recapture a town with over 300 armed insurgents. His killing of the woman who was the insurgent leader, the publicity it was given in the press, his trial and conviction for manslaughter, the treatment he received from his family and his time in jail. He watched Amanthi as he spoke, searching her face for some indication of revulsion or horror.

CHAPTER TWENTY-EIGHT

Amanthi caught herself staring at Tilak. She was attracted to him no doubt. The lines around his eyes framed his clear dark eyes. There was strength, and intelligence, and warmth, and the hint of possible anger in them. But there was something else. A sadness that touched her heart.

The story he told her was incredible and she believed every word. He talked expressively, using his hands to display emotion, surprise, anger and resignation. She noticed that the left corner of his mouth tightened bitterly when he spoke of certain things.

Amanthi drew a sharp breath when Tilak finished, aware of a feeling she wasn't used to. A pleasurable warm glow spread throughout her body. She had not had a relationship with anyone for many years, she had always felt that she didn't need it. She had just turned thirty, was a doctor who had committed herself to help people suffering from burns. The discipline and self-denial had come to her more easily than she had imagined. She had hardened herself not to get too close to anyone. For her, sex was a physical thing, a pleasant diversion which happened once or twice in university. She had been careful not to get involved. But that was a long time ago.

Tilak was watching her. He looked uncertain by the lack of any reaction to his story. The sadness which she had seen in his eyes was now clearly visible. He frowned, his hands clenching into fists, expecting some form of rejection.

Amanthi started to say something then stopped. She wanted to put the right words together, didn't want to lose the moment. She wanted to learn more about him as a person and hoped in the process to get to know about the world he lived in. She wanted him to know that she cared but something had shifted in her consciousness and she was surprised and shocked at how uninformed and naïve she was.

'You think your life has been harsh and it probably has been for you,' Amanthi said compassionately, reaching out and placing her hand on his. 'But not until you have seen and felt the pain of people who come to this place for help will you understand the true meaning of the word.'

Tilak looked at her in surprise. Amanthi felt him relax a bit, his clenched fists softening under her hand.

'Do you feel any guilt for what you have done?' she asked, looking into his eyes.

Tilak held her gaze and nodded. 'Yes,' he said without hesitation. 'Killing that woman was wrong. I have come to accept that guilt and will carry it for the rest of my life. But what's happening now is different, I think. We are at war, and I haven't been given a choice.' He looked at her closely. 'Do you have to make choices like that in your job?'

Amanthi remembered the time when the victims of the bombing in Pettah were brought into the hospital and how they had chosen to work on those who had a greater chance of living. It was a decision taken at the time based on what they could cope with at the hospital.

'Yes, we... I have,' she said. She remembered the endless stream of examinations, the assessments they had to make. The choice they had was to use all their resources on those with the greatest chance of success. She remembered it wasn't such a hard decision at the time. She was still saving lives.

Tilak nodded understandingly. 'I thought as much,' he said. 'Doctors are no different to the soldiers on the front lines. They have to face choices between life and death all the time.'

There was an awkward pause as they looked at each other hesitantly.

Amanthi removed her hand away from Tilak's as though suddenly realizing what she was doing.

Amanthi decided to be direct. 'Why did you come here today?' she asked Tilak.

'Because I wanted to see you,' Tilak said, looking embarrassed. 'I watched you work on Saman that day and hoped that I would get to meet you in different circumstances. If you want me to leave ...'

'No, no ... I didn't mean it that way,' Amanthi said hurriedly. 'I am glad you came.' Amanthi felt herself blushing. She was usually not so bold with men. But she didn't want him to leave without knowing that she was interested in him.

Tilak looked at Amanthi with light dawning in his eyes. His face looked even more handsome than she remembered. She thought it prudent to take the conversation to safer ground. 'How long are you going to be in Colombo,' she asked.

Tilak took a deep breath before answering. 'I am not sure. Things sometimes change overnight,' he said, shrugging his shoulders. 'The Minister has requested the two of us to be assigned to him so it'll be for a few weeks longer I think.'

Amanthi stared at her watch, realizing how much time had passed. She looked at Tilak regretfully. 'I have to go now,' she said. 'I am off tomorrow afternoon. We can meet if you are free.'

Nelum looked at Amanthi curiously when she came into the ward. 'I saw you with that handsome soldier from Batticaloa,' she said, smiling at her. 'I came into the canteen but you two were so absorbed in each other that you didn't even know I was there.'

Amanthi blushed, looking at her friend. 'He came looking for me and we are meeting for dinner tomorrow.'

'About time you started going out with someone,' Nelum said smiling. 'You can't afford to get too absorbed in this job. It sucks the life out of you. You need a few distractions and a good-looking man is a wonderful one.'

Amanthi nodded happily. She was already looking forward to seeing Tilak the next day.

CHAPTER TWENTY-NINE

Nadesan came around the bend and saw rusting oil drums placed across the narrow road. Clustered around the red and white barrels were six Special Task Force troopers in their distinctive camouflage uniforms and dark green berets, fat sunglasses covered their eyes. They were armed with a menacing array of automatic rifles and pistols. Nadesan slowed down, wondering why they were there. He came this way often and it was the first time there had been a checkpoint.

'What's going on?' The passenger in the back of the three-wheeler was sitting forward nervously, looking over Nadesan's shoulder.

'Don't worry,' Nadesan responded. 'It's just a roadblock. They will check our IDs and let us through.'

Nadesan was an expert on roadblocks but he couldn't stop his stomach constricting when he saw who was manning the blockade. He had been through a countless number of them, both during the day and night, manned by the army, the navy, the air force and the Police. But the roadblocks manned by the STF always made him nervous. The paramilitary Special Task Force was highly trained in counter insurgency operations and had a reputation as being hard-bitten and dangerous.

They coasted to a stop behind a car which had been held up at the roadblock. A solidly built trooper with his rifle held across his chest, watched them impassively from the side of the road. Nadesan noticed that the occupants in the car ahead of him were all asked to get out, the car searched thoroughly by two of the troopers before the occupants were allowed back into the car.

The car was waved on, squeezing between two barrels before vanishing up the quiet street. Nadesan was waved forward and stopped opposite the trooper who had motioned him to move.

'ID cards!' The soldier snapped. He had three stripes across his shoulder and wore a yellow and red campaign ribbon on his chest.

Nadesan nervously handed him the ID card he always kept in his shirt pocket. The sergeant studied it before bending and looking at Nadesan's passenger who was anxiously fumbling around his clothing.

'Come on, hurry up! We don't have all day.' The sergeant was getting impatient.

Nadesan turned and looked at the man sitting in the back. His eyes narrowed when he saw that the man was nervous, sweat pouring off his face. He had hardly glanced at him when he stepped off the curb with his hand raised. The man was dressed in shirt and trousers with sandals on his feet. He carried a woven cloth bag which was bulging from the sides. Not finding what he was looking for he was digging around inside the bag at his feet.

'Ah, here it is,' the man said, looking relieved. 'I remember taking it out to show the bank and must have put it in the bag.'

The sergeant who looked like he was about to order the man out of the three-wheeler, grabbed the ID card. He studied it carefully, looking at the photograph on the card and the man's face a number of times.

'Where are you from?' the sergeant grunted.

'I am from Wattala,' the man answered with a tremor in his voice. Nadesan could sense that something was not right but couldn't put his finger on it.

The Sergeant looked at Nadesan. 'Where did you pick him up from?'

'Near the Pettah market, sir.' Nadesan responded. His heart was beating fast and he could feel the palms of his hands get sweaty.

'Get off the vehicle,' the sergeant ordered the man. He motioned to one of his men. 'Search him and the bag.'

'You,' he addressed Nadesan. 'Where are you from?'

'I am originally from Batticaloa sir, but I am now living in Wattala.'

Nadesan tried hard not to lower his eyes, looking into the man's sunglasses which reflected his image back at him. The sergeant stared at Nadesan for a few seconds, then glanced down at the identity card he held in his card.

'You're a Muslim!' The sergeant said dismissively, handing the card back to him. Nadesan nodded not trusting himself to say anything.

The sergeant turned to Nadesan's passenger who had been patted down by the STF trooper and was nervously watching his bag being searched. The trooper pulled out a package from the bottom of the bag and waved it in the air. The package was the size of a book, tightly wrapped in old newspapers and tied with a piece of string.

'What's this,' the trooper asked.

'I don't know, sir,' the man said fearfully. 'I don't know how it got into my bag.'

The trooper held the package to his nose and sniffed it. He grinned and looked at the sergeant. 'It's ganja,' he said, sniffing the package again. 'And it's the good stuff.'

The sergeant took the package held it to his nose, inhaling the scent like a connoisseur. He held the package in his hand and waved it at the man who was shaking in fright.

'So, you don't know what this is,' he asked. 'It's not yours?'

'No, no, Sir,' the man babbled fearfully. 'Someone must have put it in my bag.'

The sergeant nodded in mock agreement. 'Ok, then,' he said. 'You can go.' He looked around at his men who had broad grins on their faces.

'But, but sir, what about the package.'

'We will keep the package until someone comes to collect it,' the sergeant smiled with his teeth. His eyes glinted like hard pebbles.

'Ok, sir, I understand.' The man nervously picked up his bag and got into the three-wheeler.

The sergeant stepped next to Nadesan. His dark sunglasses made him look bug-like and menacing. 'You keep your mouth shut,' he said threateningly. 'I know who you are and where to find you.'

Nadesan nodded, not trusting himself to speak. The sergeant stared at him for a moment before motioning him to move. Nadesan negotiated the oil drums and roared off down the road. He was in a bath of sweat. He looked through his rear-view mirror at his passenger who was looking distressed. Nadesan didn't feel sorry for him. He was lucky that the troopers at the roadblock had been crooked. Nadesan didn't fancy his chances if the man had been arrested for possessing drugs. He too could have been arrested as an accomplice and put in prison. He had been lucky. It was a very close call.

*

Nadesan sat in his three-wheeler and smoked a cigarette. He had given up smoking many years ago but had started the habit again. He had parked opposite a food stall selling hoppers and kotthu roti. Business was good as a constant stream of vehicles pulled in to collect their packets of food. The kotthu man made a loud drumming noise as he pounded the hot skillet with two sharp-edged metal plates, cutting the large, flat roti's into small edible pieces before mixing them with cooked meat, vegetables and a beaten egg.

He was waiting for a hire with the other three-wheeler drivers by the side of the road next to the petrol station. The traffic out of the northern city suburbs was chaotic that morning due to an accident on the bridge.

Nadesan had just eaten a par-boiled and roasted corn cob, coated with salt, chilli powder and drizzled with fresh lemon juice when he noticed a man standing at the entrance to the alley watching him. It looked like Kumar. He knew that Kumar wouldn't be there unless he had a message for him.

Kumar emerged from the alley after a few minutes and stood next to Nadesan, looking at him expectantly. Nadesan knew what he wanted. He offered Kumar the cigarette pack from his shirt pocket from which he extracted a cigarette. Nadesan handed him his half-smoked cigarette which Kumar used to light his own, holding the glowing tip against the tip of his unlit cigarette and sucking air in deeply. Kumar studied the glowing tip of his cigarette while handing Nadesan's one back to him.

'Deva wants to see you at the house,' he said, glancing around to make sure no one was listening. 'He's received a message and has something to tell you.'

Nadesan had been waiting for this day to come. After his initial fear of driving around the city with forged papers, he had realized that they were good enough to get him through any checkpoint without being questioned. Perhaps being identified as a Moor helped allay any suspicions that he was a Tamil militant from the north. His fear of being captured and tortured no longer seemed to be a real threat. As long as he drove the tree-wheeler around the city he felt safe. There were so many of them on the road that it was like hiding in plain sight.

'When does he want to see me,' Nadesan asked. Kumar was one of the men living in the safe house with Deva.

'Tomorrow, but early,' he said. 'We'll leave a white towel hanging on the line outside if it's safe to enter.'

Nadesan nodded. He would also use the spyhole in the warehouse roof to make sure that there was no one observing the safe house. 'Ok, tell him I'll be there.'

Kumar glanced around and walked away down the street. Nadesan watched him thoughtfully. Nadesan worked in the garage repairing the three- wheelers and drove his three-wheeler taxi sixteen hours a day for six days every week. He was always exhausted. But he dared not slow down. He was constantly beset by the torment of not fulfilling the promise to his dead wife and son. Only when he was working did he not think about them

*

Nadesan had been watching the street since before daybreak and had not seen anything that looked suspicious or out of place. Feeling reasonably sure that the safe house had not been compromised, he knocked on the front door next to where a white towel was flapping in the breeze.

Kumar opened the door and stepped aside, letting Nadesan enter. When his eyes adjusted to the gloom, he saw Deva sitting at the table with a sheet of paper in his hands.

'Ah, there you are,' Deva said tersely looking at him. 'You took your time.'

Nadesan made eye contact with Deva. 'I was just making sure no one was around,' he said. 'What have you got for me?'

'We have been asked to be prepared to hit another target in the city,' Deva said, holding Nadesan's gaze. 'You'll deliver a package but I don't know as to where and when.' Deva looked down at the sheet of paper he held. 'They sent us a list of what they want us to get,' he said. 'We also received a box which is at the back. We've been asked not to touch it.'

Nadesan said nothing. Deva took his silence for acquiescence. 'They are sending someone to put it all together,' he said. 'I was not told when he'll be here.'

'When will we know the target?' Nadesan asked. They would need time to work out the best way of delivering the bomb without being stopped.

Deva shook his head. 'All I know is that we will be told what the target is by the man who is coming.'

It was not ideal but it would have to do. Nadesan knew that the Tigers withheld information so that no one person knew the details about a specific operation. But he couldn't understand why they had wanted to see him.

'So, you asked me to come here just to tell me that?' Nadesan asked Deva angrily. "I thought you were concerned about the neighbours seeing different people coming and going from the house?'

'You had to come because I want to show you this,' Deva said, holding out the sheet of paper to him. Nadesan looked down at the paper which had a sketched drawing of a three-wheeler. What was unusual about the drawing was the vehicle had been drawn with a pannier underneath the driver's legs.

Nadesan immediately knew what it was for. He had always wondered how he could use the three-wheeler as a vehicle to deliver a bomb. There were thousands of them in different shapes and colours buzzing around the city. It would be easy to hide amongst the swarm. The pannier that had been crudely drawn would hold the bomb and if the driver wore a sarong it would not be easily seen.

'You want me to prepare a machine like this?' Nadesan asked. It would be relatively easy to build the part in secret and hide it amongst all the other spare parts in the yard until it was ready to be used.

Deva nodded. 'Yes, we want you to be prepared. But there's something else.' He leaned forward conspiratorially. 'The head of the army was targeted by another cell but was not killed,' he said in a low voice. 'According to the radio, he was badly hurt and is being treated in a special military hospital somewhere near the General Hospital.'

Nadesan raised his eyebrows without saying anything.

Deva studied Nadesan for a moment. 'I want you to find out where it is.'

'You want me to find the hospital?' Nadesan felt his spirit lift. *Finally, I am being given a target.*

'Yes,' Deva nodded firmly, sensing Nadesan's interest. 'If we find the hospital we'll find him and finish the job.'

Nadesan frowned as he pictured the area in his mind. He knew the neighborhood around the General Hospital quite well as it was an area that three-wheelers could find fares easily. But he couldn't remember ever seeing a military hospital.

'Ok,' he nodded at Deva. "I'll find out where it is.'

Nadesan left the safe house glad that he had something to do to keep himself occupied. Now that he had a target he could prepare. He needed to be patient as it wouldn't be too long now.

CHAPTER THIRTY

Tilak awoke rested. It was still dark. He still couldn't believe that it had happened. He had often thought about meeting someone special especially when he was in prison, but the opportunity had never been there before he joined the army.

Amanthi had turned out to be everything that Tilak had ever wanted in a companion. Tilak picked her up at her home in Borella and was surprised to see a poised young woman dressed in an elegant black kurthi with decorative bands of coloured silk over a pair of jeans open the door at his knock. Amanthi wore make up, her kohl shaded eyes making her look very Indian. Tilak had never seen Amanthi in anything but her hospital greens and the beautiful woman in front of him just took his breath away.

Before Tilak could greet her, a shorter, older version of Amanthi dressed in a dark green sari peered around the door, looking at Tilak critically. 'I wanted to see for myself who was going out with my daughter,' the woman said, glancing at Amanthi. 'It's been such a long time, dear.'

Amanthi blushed, the colour rising in her flawless skin. She looked over her mother's head at Tilak, her eyes pleading with him to understand.

Tilak smiled at the old lady, bowing slightly from the hips. He was dressed in collarless shirt and trousers, a stylishly cut jacket fitting snugly around his shoulders. He had gone to his parent's home that morning and rummaged through his old clothes. He was lucky to find something that fitted.

'Good evening, Mrs. De Silva,' he said graciously. 'It's my pleasure to take your daughter out for dinner. I owe her a debt of thanks for looking after one of my men who was badly burned. You must be proud to have such a beautiful and accomplished doctor as a daughter.'

Amanthi's mother frowned at Tilak. 'So, you're the boy that went to jail for shooting that terrorist in Kataragama,' she said, wagging her finger at Tilak. 'I always said that she deserved what she got ... behaving like that,' she added irreverently. 'I'm an old friend of your mothers though we haven't met for many years. How is she doing?'

'Ah, mother is fine,' Tilak said, looking at Amanthi who stood behind her mother with her hand over her mouth, her eyes round with shock. 'I'll tell her that you asked.'

Amanthi pushed gently past her mother who looked like she wanted to say something more. 'We have to go now mother or we'll miss our booking,' she said, looking anxiously at Tilak. Tilak smiled at Amanthi understanding her concern. He sometimes felt the same way about his mother who could be overpowering at times.

Tilak brushed away Amanthi's apology when they got into the car. 'It's okay,' he said, amusedly. 'She didn't mean any harm. She looks like a person who speaks her mind.'

'Yes, that has always been my mother,' Amanthi said, grimacing at Tilak. 'She used to scare away all my boy friends when I was in school.'

Tilak took Amanthi to a little courtyard restaurant, close to where his parents lived. The building was a square colonnaded quadrangle open to the sky in the middle which had been tiled with bricks in various patterns. Cooking was done in the traditional way, using earthenware pots, blackened with age, over open fires. Two strings of colourful Vesak lanterns crisscrossed the courtyard providing shaded light to the patrons.

'I didn't even know this place existed,' Amanthi said, her eyes glinting in the light. 'How did you find out about it?'

'My mother,' he said, smiling at her. 'She's a bit of a socialite. When I told her I wanted someplace nice for dinner she suggested I come here.' His mother had done much more than that, wanting to know whom he was going out with and for how long he had known Amanthi.

The evening slipped away unnoticed for Tilak. The meal was excellent. Neither of them drank anything alcoholic. The conversation ranged from politics to the cinema. Tilak couldn't keep his eyes off Amanthi. He thought she sensed his interest in her and wished the evening would last forever. Tilak's heart sank when Amanthi's pager went off. She reached into her bag and pulled out the little device, reading the message that scrolled across the screen. She looked up at Tilak and smiled at the expression on his face.

'It's nothing,' she said. 'They are just giving me an update on a patient's vitals. I don't have to go in,' she reassured him. She put the pager back into her bag and looked at him warmly. 'I am enjoying myself too much anyway.'

Tilak looked into her eyes for evidence of a lie and couldn't find it. Her eyes were clear, bright and unwavering. He touched her hand. There'd been few gestures of intimacy between them so far. Tilak knew little of love. There had not been much of it when he grew up. The old ayah that looked after him said that his parents loved him but they did not show it like he had seen other parents do with his friends. His parents were more intent on furthering their careers and keeping up appearances.

Tilak was a little nervous. Amanthi was very different to any of the women he had known before. Watching her work, he had seen that she had control and could have described it even as authority. She was intelligent without arrogance and did not reveal her thoughts easily. Her quick and curious mind stimulated his own and he realized that he had found someone that was very special.

'I don't want this to end either, Amanthi,' he said softly. 'I thought meeting someone like you was never going to happen to me after what I did.' Tilak studied her face as he spoke.

Amanthi's clear grey eyes regarded him seriously. 'We have been thrown together by extraordinary circumstances,' she said, holding his gaze. 'What you did in the past was wrong, but you've accepted it, and you served out your time.'

Tilak shrugged dejectedly. He felt a mix of emotions and could not speak. He wanted Amanthi to like him but he also was miserable that his past would be a barrier to having any sort of fruitful relationship.

Amanthi looked into his face and smiled. 'We all make mistakes in life but it's how we handle it afterwards that really matters.' She hesitated before continuing. 'I think this should be the last time we talk about it. I'll be happy to go out with you again but don't rush me. Let's get to know each other first before we decide on what happens next.'

Tilak nodded gratefully. It was more than what he had expected.

*

Tilak and Chandra left Colombo early that morning, long before the roads leading out of the city got too congested. The main road narrowed past the southern outskirts of the city, never straying too far from the railway line which hugged the sea coast. Tall coconut palms, some leaning precariously across outrigger canoes lined up on the sandy beach, framed a cloudless blue sky full of wheeling seagulls chasing a fishing boat pulling in its morning catch.

They had finally been released from their Ministerial bodyguard duties and were on their way to meet the senior ranking Police officer for the district. Attacks against government officials had started to die down mainly due to the increased involvement of the military who had been redeployed from their bases in the north. The officer had requested the services of the Special Branch and they were going to Galle to get their orders.

Tilak had said goodbye to Amanthi before he left. He had found her at home entertaining guests when he went looking for her. She looked at him disappointedly when he told her that he was leaving for the south the next morning.

'Will it be a long assignment?' she asked, stepping out onto the porch and closing the front door behind her.

'I don't know,' Tilak said. 'We were just informed to report to the Galle District commander first thing in the morning. We'll only find out then what they want us to do.'

'Try to be careful,' she said. 'We are Buddhists but we seem to have forgotten that we are. This war we are fighting amongst ourselves isn't like any before. Things are much more complicated now.'

Amanthi stood on tiptoe and, slid both arms around his neck and turned her face up. 'Kiss me,' she breathed. 'I don't want you to go without knowing that you have become very special to me.' Tilak pulled Amanthi to him and lowered his face. She had lean hips and a flat belly, her buttocks round and tight like an athlete. Her lips were soft and sweet as they parted under his tongue. They stood like that for a while until Amanthi pushed him away.

'I have to go now,' she said breathlessly. 'Amma will be wondering where I am.'

Tilak nodded wordlessly. He reached up and brushed a lock of hair that had fallen across her face. 'I promise I will be back,' he said. 'I have something to live for now.'

Amanthi held his gaze as she half-turned and opened the front door. She smiled at him before slipping through the entrance. She waved at him as she gently shut the door leaving him both happy and sad under the flickering porch light.

CHAPTER THIRTY-ONE

The solid grey walls of a well-preserved colonial Fort appeared on their right as Tilak and Chandra entered the busy town of Galle. Red-tiled roofs peeped over stone and coral ramparts first built by the Portuguese in the 16th century. Fortified by the Dutch and occupied by the British, it housed a community of over five hundred families.

'You want us to do what?' Tilak almost snapped at the Police Assistant Superintendent sitting behind his desk at the district headquarters. They'd found the Police building surrounded by barbed wire and heavily armed sentries and had been ushered into the Assistant Superintendent's office by a junior constable.

The officer frowned at Tilak. 'We want the two of you to infiltrate the Boossa prison camp and kill this man,' he said, tapping a photo on the table. 'What's the problem with doing that?'

'I can think of many things that are wrong with doing that,' Tilak said. 'You're asking us to pretend to be criminals, be incarcerated in a maximum-security prison full of real militant cadres and kill this man. Why don't you just pull him out and do it yourself?'

'We will start a riot if we do that,' the officer said. 'He's their leader and he's running a campaign against us from inside the prison. I have been asked to eliminate him but we'll have to get through the other prisoners first. That'll take too many men and resources. You'll be able to slip in, do the job and get out without anyone noticing.'

Tilak couldn't believe what he was hearing. This moronic officer wanted them to commit suicide. He glanced at Chandra who was looking at the man stone-faced.

'No,' he said, glaring at the Assistant Superintendent. He turned to leave the room grabbing Chandra by the arm. 'Let's get out of here before this idiot thinks of something even more stupid.'

The Assistant Superintendent jumped to his feet. 'Whom are you calling an idiot?' he blustered. 'I will have you kicked out of the force for saying that.'

Tilak didn't even bother to answer as he left the room with Chandra. How could this man be the senior ranked Police officer for the Galle District? On his way out of the station, he stopped at the booking desk.

'How come that ASP Mendis is the senior ranked officer for the district,' he asked the grizzled looking Police sergeant. 'He seems a bit out of his depth.'

The sergeant looked over his shoulder towards the rear of the station before answering. 'The Superintendent was shot in his home last week,' the sergeant said, shaking his head gloomily. 'He's a good man and lucky to be alive. He's recovering in the Police hospital in Bambalapitiya.' He glanced back again before continuing. 'ASP Mendis was in charge at Hikkaduwa which is just a sub-station looking after tourists. He has been given temporary command of the district. His uncle is the MP from the Hikkaduwa electorate. He's trying to make a name for himself ... at the expense of others. He wants to get a transfer to Colombo, I heard.'

Tilak nodded sympathetically. He had experienced similar problems when he was in the Army. Politics played a big part in the appointment of senior positions and it didn't come as a surprise to him.

He thanked the sergeant and joined Chandra who was waiting outside. Tilak explained what he'd learned from the sergeant.

'We better call this in,' he muttered to Chandra. 'I am sure he'll be calling his uncle as we speak.' Tilak realized that Chandra had not said a word the whole time they were in the Police station. 'You have nothing to say?'

'I would have said something if you didn't,' the man growled. 'You were doing just fine.'

*

The Special Branch commander was somewhat unsympathetic to Tilak's plight. 'The man needs to be eliminated,' he growled. 'It's the price we have to pay to get some important information about the sleeper cells in Colombo.'

'How does that work?' Tilak asked sceptically. His interest was aroused once he heard that the real target were the militant cells in Colombo.

'We have opened a line of communications with a high-level militant leader in the east.' The commander explained. 'If this man is eliminated, he will give us some vital information we can use to track the sleeper cells.'

'Are you sure?' Tilak questioned. 'Why does he want him killed?'

'Some sort of vendetta but I don't really care.' The commander snapped. 'You're not to question your orders. Just get it done quickly.'

Tilak walked over to the Pajero where Chandra was smoking a cigarette. 'They want us to kill him one way or the other. It's the price they have to pay for getting some important information about the militant cells in Colombo.'

Tilak was not completely surprised at what he had been told. He understood from his time in prison that there was a price for everything. 'Let's drive down to the camp and figure out something.'

The Boossa Detention Centre was located a few kilometres outside Galle, adjacent to an Army and Navy camp. It was a prison where the most hardcore convicts, Tamil militant and insurgent prisoners were held in separate sections of the camp. When Tilak was in prison, he had avoided being transferred to the maximum-security prison knowing that his life would have been in danger from the insurgent prisoners in the camp.

Understanding the prison system as he did, the only way to target someone inside the prison without causing a riot would be with the help of the prison guards. At any one time, even though there were hundreds of dangerous criminals and terrorists locked in a prison like Boossa, only about thirty to forty guards were ever on duty. If they could find one guard who would be willing to cooperate with them it would solve their problem.

The more Tilak thought about it the more he realized that the answer to his problem was in Colombo. When he was serving his term in the Magazine Prison in Colombo, he had dealings with one of the guards who was known as the 'Fixer'. His tentacles spread across the prison system and he could get anything done for a price. Maybe he could get the man transferred to Colombo?

Tilak explained his plan to Chandra and they drove back to Colombo that afternoon, planning to meet the guard when he finished his shift.

Even standing outside its high gates, ringed by walls and watch-towers, Tilak could smell its kitchens and lavatories. The scent of a community in confinement was unmistakable. He shuddered at the thought of entering those gates and decided to wait outside for the man.

The guard whose name was Munidasa was startled when he saw Tilak sitting on a bench outside the prison under a street light. He was a short stocky man, with strong arms and legs. He was dressed in his prison uniform, a canvas bag slung across his shoulder.

'What do you want?' Munidasa asked, looking carefully around. 'I heard that you got a pardon.'

'Yes,' Tilak said. 'I now work for the government.'

Munidasa looked at Tilak shrewdly. 'Hmmm, you want something done. Something you don't want to do yourself,' he said thoughtfully. 'Something nasty I think.'

Tilak had never underestimated Munidasa. When Tilak had controlled one of the gangs in the prison, he had always made sure that Munidasa was well looked after.

'Yes,' Tilak said. 'But first we have to bring someone here from Boossa.'

'That's going to cost you more,' Munidasa said, his eyebrows rising. 'But you knew that already.'

Tilak nodded. 'Yes, I knew that,' he said. 'You're quite predictable you know.'

'Look who's talking,' he said. 'I can remember the time when you first came in and depended on your Mummy's money to keep you out of trouble,' Munidasa sneered at Tilak. 'But I underestimated you then ... what do you want?'

CHAPTER THIRTY-TWO

Amanthi was trailing Dr Perera through the ward. The doctor was reviewing the patients who had come into the Burn unit when a fire in a shanty town caused a number of badly burnt victims to be admitted during the night.

Amanthi was exhausted after being called in to attend to the more severe cases. She was writing down Dr Perera's observations on each patient but her thoughts were drifting. She missed Tilak. It had been a few days since he had left and she already missed his smile and the way he crinkled his forehead when he was thinking.

'Did this patient come in last night?' Dr Perera turned and looked at Amanthi strangely. 'I don't think I've seen him before.' Nelum standing across the bed from Dr Perera had a wide grin on her face.

'Err, yes, he did come in last night,' she said, color rising in her face. Amanthi flipped a few papers on the clipboard, reading what was written on them. 'He was treated by the ETU Doctor on duty.'

Dr Perera studied Amanthi for a moment and turned back to the patient. The man's hands were severely burnt, his left arm to above his elbows. One side of his face was very red, especially around his mouth and one eye and his eyebrow and hair were singed on the same side. Many of the burns on his arms looked like second degree burns and the man's left arm had puffed up and was three or four times its normal size. The bed was adjusted so that his head was elevated and his hands were splinted to keep them immobile. Dr Perera bent over and looked at the man's face.

'This patient has a bad burn on his face which has not been treated properly,' she said irritably, straightening up and glaring at the Doctors and nurses around her. 'We are the best Burn unit in the country and must provide the best care for everyone. This is not acceptable!' she snapped.

The medical team around Dr Perera fidgeted and looked down at their feet as she swept her eyes over them. Her eyes stopped at Amanthi. 'You were called in last night to treat these patients. You were the senior doctor here. He should not have been left to be treated by the ETU Doctor without someone from our unit reviewing his case. If you were too busy then we have a problem with our admission procedures.'

Amanthi's face burned with embarrassment. She had been the senior doctor in the Burn unit and she felt responsible. By the time she had come in to the unit after being called in after midnight, the admission room was in total bedlam. Emergency workers rolled in burn victims wanting to know where to take their patients. Relatives who had accompanied them or followed the ambulances, wailed over their loved ones. Policemen taking names and checking the victims' identifications, interrupted staff from both the Burn unit and the emergency treatment unit who were trying to assess each person's injury. Amanthi had taken charge and eventually brought some semblance of order to the place but she knew it had been at the expense of the treatment of some of the patients.

Dr Perera took Amanthi's silence as an answer. 'Come and see me in my office after you attend to him,' she said, her eyes full of disapproval. 'I want to know exactly what took place here last night.'

Nelum stayed with Amanthi as Dr Perera and the group of doctors, residents and nurses who accompanied her every day on her rounds, moved away from the patient.

'Don't take it too badly,' she said quietly, seeing the look on Amanthi's face. 'I don't know why they did not call me.'

Amanthi nodded wordlessly, snapping on a pair of gloves. The fire that had broken out in the shanty town had only been declared a level two emergency by the first responders. The mistake had been made when they had not realized the true nature of the fire that raged through the tightly packed wooden dwellings, trapping whole families sleeping in their huts. Even after the fire was raised to a level one emergency, no one at the scene had bothered to inform the hospital.

The burns on the patient's face did not look severe and was showing no sign of infection when Amanthi examined him. She stepped back from the bed and stripped the gloves off her hands. Dr Perera had spotted something which did not look right to her but Amanthi could not put her finger on it. She knew that it sometimes took days for a burn to reveal itself, some burns were deeper than they looked and might require surgery to heal.

Amanthi bent over the patient again studying him carefully. While she watched, a drop of clear liquid oozed out from under his swollen left eyelid. Amanthi suddenly realized what Dr Perera had seen. She had been focusing too much on the burnt skin that she had ignored the patient's eyes.

'We need to have an ophthalmologist examine his left eye,' she said, looking up at Nelum. 'Can you call the Eye Hospital and get them to send one right away.'

Amanthi stayed with the patient until Nelum made the call. 'I'd better go and see Dr Perera now,' she said to Nelum who nodded sympathetically.

Dr Perera was in her office and waved Amanthi in, leaning back in her chair. 'Well?' she said questioningly, studying Amanthi intently.

It was a loaded statement and Amanthi knew she had to have an answer. 'His left eye,' Amanthi said guiltily. 'We did not have it checked.'

Dr Perera nodded. 'Yes, you didn't,' she said matter-of-factly. 'I have spoken to a few people about what it was like out there this morning and can understand what happened. But it's no excuse. We have to be better than that.'

Amanthi nodded. She knew that she could say that they were under-staffed and she did not have time to look at every single patient but that would just be making an excuse. Dr Perera set high standards and expected everyone to follow them.

'I will revisit how we handle emergencies at night,' she said. 'We'll have to have some sort of security on call and someone from administration to manage the admissions. We can't have our Doctors and nurses filling out forms and dealing with the public.'

Amanthi was convinced that with more resources the problems she had faced the previous night could be avoided. She felt weak and shaky and wondered whether she was coming down with a cold.

'Is something the matter?' Dr Perera asked Amanthi. 'You seem a bit distracted these days.' Amanthi blushed at the doctor's candid observation. She had been thinking about Tilak often and wondered whether she'd fallen in love with him. She had never been interested in anyone and he kept intruding into her thoughts. The nurses had noticed that Amanthi was getting distracted and had been teasing her about it.

'Err, not really,' she said, looking at the doctor who raised her eyebrows not believing what she said. Amanthi sighed. The doctor would find out soon enough. 'Well,' she began. 'I treated an officer in Batticaloa a few months ago when we were on a medivac. He showed up here last week and asked me out,' she said. 'It's sort of getting serious.'

Dr Perera looked at Amanthi interestedly, 'A soldier?' Dr Perera asked. 'What kind of soldier?'

'He's a Lieutenant in the STF but works for the Special Branch I think,' Amanthi explained. 'He was assigned to a Cabinet Minister's protection detail.'

'I see,' Dr Perera said. She studied Amanthi before continuing. 'So, what's bothering you?' she asked. 'I would think that you'll be happy.'

Amanthi shook her head. 'It's nothing,' she said. 'I've never had a serious relationship with anyone. I just need to get used to the idea.'

Dr Perera looked at Amanthi. 'Ok,' she said. 'I don't think you are telling me everything but you must make sure it won't affect your work.'

Amanthi left Dr Perera's office knowing that Dr Perera would not let her off so easily next time. She needed to focus on her job and try to push all thoughts of Tilak out of her mind.

CHAPTER THIRTY-THREE

The morning traffic was still heavy as Nadesan crossed the bridge into the city. The checkpoint at the main thoroughfare into the city always made him nervous but the soldiers manning the roadblock waved him through when they saw that he was not carrying a passenger.

Last evening, Nadesan had picked up a short fare from the General Hospital; a mother and her daughter who wanted to be taken to an address in Cinnamon Gardens. The suburbs shady boulevards, flanked by stately homes, art galleries, cafés, and historic buildings was home to the countries elite. The street he turned down was flanked on either side by old colonial-era residences. Nadesan knew it only as where all the wealthy people lived. As he dropped them at the entrance to their home, he noticed an army ambulance driving down the street. Nadesan watched interestedly as the vehicle slowed about 30 metres away, turning into a property not visible from where he was parked.

Nadesan collected his fare and drove up the street, past where the ambulance had turned in. He didn't want to draw any attention, only glancing casually at the metal gate protecting the entrance. Tall trees peeked over the unusually high brick wall preventing him from looking into the property.

The place intrigued him. Why would an ambulance be going there? Nadesan had been driving around the area ever since Deva had asked him to find the hospital where the General was being treated. But he had not been successful. Was this the place?

A mixture of old and modern vehicles filled the main thoroughfare creating a haze of polluted air. Nadesan parked his three-wheeler at the General Hospital carpark a few streets away and approached the area on foot. He surveyed the road carefully from the corner. The tree-lined street was relatively quiet, only a few cars speeding through to bypass the congestion at the main junction a few streets away. The pavements were deserted except for a man sleeping in a garden doorway. No police cars or any military vehicles could be seen.

Nadesan realized that walking down the street was risky. He'd look out of place and would only draw attention to himself. Looking around, he noticed the overhanging branches from a flame tree on the opposite side of the street provided an expanse of shade from the mid-morning sun. Nadesan crossed the road and sat cross-legged on the cool ground, his back against the stained parapet wall. He would be patient and watch what went on in the street.

This was his favourite time of day. The morning rush hour was over and it was nearly always quiet. It would get busy again soon, at lunchtime, and then again when the schools emptied in the early afternoon.

Luxury cars, SUVs, three-wheelers and the occasional van, turned into the street, most speeding past the gate he was monitoring, others turning into residences along the street. Nadesan reached down and picked up a small piece of glass, rotating it in his rough hands. It had been almost two months since he'd come into the city. It was a bright clear day and for the first time since the explosion at the bus terminal, he felt alive. Everything was happening exactly at it ought to. Nadesan had come to the realization that killing all those people at the bus station was wrong. It was something he was deeply ashamed of doing.

He couldn't bear the thought of looking into his wife's innocent eyes again knowing what he'd done. She'd be horrified. She wouldn't want her death avenged in such a fashion. Nadesan had agreed to bring the car to Colombo and trigger the bomb at the bus-station because he didn't want the people in Colombo to ever feel safe again. Why should they lead their insignificant little lives in peace and quiet while his people were being killed for no reason? And without any repercussions to the people who were doing the killing.

He had been so consumed by anger and rage that he'd not realized what the consequences were. Didn't care really. The bomb was a manifestation of a decision he'd already made. It was going to be his ultimate sacrifice. But having the general as a target gave him a way out of this predicament he'd got himself into. When he triggers the device that ends the life of this general, he'll do it not because he wants him dead, although he cannot deny that he does, but because the soldiers this man commands have robbed him of the most precious things he had ever known. His own chances of escaping the repercussions of this assassination were non-existent. He'd make absolutely sure of that.

Nadesan blinked. He'd been waiting a long time. A group of schoolboys dressed in white walked past. None of them even glanced in his direction, so intent they were on their conversation. A black Pajero, an army pennant fluttering from its bonnet turned into the street. It passed him and the group of schoolboys, picking up speed as it moved down the street, it's black-tinted windows giving no indication of its occupants.

Is this it? Nadesan clenched his fist in anticipation, the piece of glass he had been turning over in his hand digging painfully into his palm. He opened his hand, his eyes fixed on the vehicle, hearing the small sound as the fragment returned to the ground.

Nadesan tensed as the Pajero slowed and turned, stopping in front of the residence he was watching. The metal gate rolled slowly sideways for a short distance and stopped. An armed soldier stepped out of the narrow gap it left, moving to the driver's side of the vehicle. Nadesan watched as the soldier spoke to the driver before signalling for the gate to be opened completely. The vehicle drove in slowly, the heavy gate trundling shut behind it.

It was impossible for Nadesan to see into the compound from where he was sitting. He couldn't even see over the boundary wall, it was so tall. He watched a while longer, waiting for the vehicle to re-emerge. More and more school children some with adults accompanying them turned into the street. One of them looked at him suspiciously, hurrying her charges past with a pat on their backs.

Nadesan realized staying there would only draw more attention. He pushed himself to his feet and stretched, dusting himself before moving slowly back to where he had parked the three-wheeler. As he walked, he noticed that the sky was beginning to darken. A few drops of rain hit his forehead, dripping down the side of his neck.

He was almost convinced he had found the place he'd been looking for. It was unquestionably a well-protected, military establishment with its strong gate, thick high walls and well-armed soldiers. The ambulance he saw going in the previous day made it likely to be a hospital.

Nadesan picked up a fare the moment he climbed into his three-wheeler. Two school girls wanted to be taken home before it rained any harder. As he drove them to the other side of the park, he decided he would monitor the place on his visits to the area to make sure it was what Deva was looking for.

CHAPTER THIRTY-FOUR

The prison door creaked open and a hand waved them in. The Fixer had come through, his curt message delivered by a taxi driver, that asked Tilak to be at the side gate of the Magazine prison at midnight.

Tilak had mixed feelings about going into the compound where he had spent so many years as a prisoner. He hesitated before crossing under the arched stone doorway, his legs almost refusing to step forward. A creeping coldness numbed his heart when metal slammed on metal behind him, the keys jangling and turning in the lock. He felt his body clench like a fist and somewhere deep inside of him his heart beginning to thump with dread.

A prison guard standing in a dark shadow of the wall motioned them to a doorway inside the prison grounds. Tilak forced himself forward, glancing sideways at Chandra. He was glad to have the operative with him. He felt more secure with him around.

Tilak knew where they were. The dimly lit room was where visitors were checked before they were allowed inside the prison. The high-ceilinged space was about twenty paces long and ten paces wide with barred windows overlooking the prison yard. A tall steel barrier divided the room in half, preventing easy access to the prison. On either side of the room, tall wooden shelves filled with stacks of colourful plastic containers sat behind a long wooden table where a second prison guard stood. Tilak looked around. As a long-term resident of the prison, he had been into the room many times, washing its floors and cleaning the squat toilet that visitors used. The room had not changed in all the time he had been incarcerated. He suspected it had remained the same since the prison was built by the British when they were in power.

The guard standing behind the table gestured them over. Tilak recognised him immediately. It was one of the guards that he had known while in prison. The man was squat and overweight, squeezed into a uniform at least two sizes too small for him.

Tilak was wearing his uniform and the guard took a moment to recognize him. His eyes flickered in surprise. 'I heard you were with the Police.' He spoke loudly, glancing at the other guard standing by the door. He looked at Tilak resentfully, tapping aggressively on the table. 'Are you carrying any weapons? You know the rules. They must be handed over.'

Tilak was not surprised by the guard's behaviour. To him Tilak was just another prisoner to be bullied. He nodded and unclipped the holster from his waist motioning to Chandra to do the same. Prison rules on weapons were strictly enforced. No firearms were ever allowed to be taken into where the prisoners were held.

The guard walked to the barrier and opened a gate framed in steel. He pointed towards an archway that led into the prison's interior. 'The man you are looking for is being held in the infirmary. Do what you came to do and then get out.'

Tilak nodded and gestured to Chandra. 'Watch my back,' he said. 'I don't trust any of these pricks.'

Tilak walked through the archway into a long narrow corridor. There was a hard-right turn halfway down the corridor leading to a wide veranda. The prison infirmary was the second door to the right.

The room held eight beds. Only one was occupied. A wide bladed fan rotating slowly on a long metal pipe hung from the ceiling. Light spilled into the room from an over-sized, barred window next to the doorway. Chandra stood by the door while Tilak walked slowly to the bed. The man's eyes were closed. He lay on his back, both of his arms and legs strapped tightly to the bed. An IV line from a plastic bag of saline suspended on a stand, ran into a cannula in his arm. A capped syringe lay on the bedside table next to his head.

Tilak glanced at Chandra who nodded and moved into the room. Tilak moved to the infirmary entrance and looked out. When the commander had given them the order to kill the insurgent leader, Chandra had volunteered to carry out the hit. Chandra had no qualms about killing the man who had given orders to kill the families of police and army officers who had refused to resign their positions in the force.

In less than it took for Tilak to look around the empty prison yard, Chandra was back standing next to him. Tilak glanced at Chandra and raised his eyebrows. Chandra nodded, his eyes flicking over Tilak's shoulder into the prison yard.

Chandra's eyes narrowed and he pulled Tilak against the wall. 'There's someone out there,' he said. 'We better get out of here.'

Tilak looked out but couldn't see anything. The prison administration building shadows concealed pools of darkness that anyone could be hidden in. They moved out into the veranda, pulling the infirmary door shut behind them. They walked swiftly towards the corridor leading back into the visitor's room when they heard the running slap of feet behind them.

'Quickly,' Tilak called out, pushing Chandra ahead of him. He risked a look over his shoulder and saw three men in shorts running towards them. Tilak recognised them immediately as prisoners. One even looked familiar.

Someone must have tipped them off that we're here. The thought came tumbling into his mind. Tilak realized that they wouldn't have time to escape.

The men were too close and gaining on them. They needed to find a place to defend themselves.

'Into the corridor,' he shouted. The long narrow corridor would be the ideal place to hold them off until the door was opened. Tilak cursed the guards.

Chandra dived into the corridor quickly followed by Tilak. The prisoners from the yard had gained on them and crowded the doorway behind him.

Tilak was so focused on the men behind him that he didn't see Chandra had stopped and ran into his back. 'What the fuck?' Tilak shouted. 'Keep moving.'

'I can't,' Chandra said calmly. 'I need to clear out some vermin first.'

Over Chandra's shoulder Tilak saw why he had stopped. Three prisoners carrying wooden staves were in the corridor, blocking their way forward. Tilak suddenly realized that they were trapped between the two groups of men and would have to fight to get out. He looked around but none of the guards could be seen.

Tilak turned to face the men from the yard. They all carried wooden staves studded with nails and bits of glass, and shivs fashioned into knives out of lengths of metal and plastic. Tilak knew these prison-made implements were as deadly as a proper knife and had always treated them with respect.

One of the men he recognised. Joseph! He was a long-term prisoner who controlled illegal gambling and drugs in one of the buildings. Tilak had refused to take orders from him. He remembered the time they had come for him in his cell. He had been prepared after receiving a warning from one of the prisoners and had used a shiv on the man, disfiguring him and almost killing him. Tilak had made a life-time enemy and only his stature in the prison system had kept him out of the man's clutches.

Joseph recognised Tilak, his scarred face rapidly cycling through hatred, fear and rage. 'It's him!' Joseph screamed, taking a few steps forward.

Tilak realized that they were in a fight for their lives. He refused to believe that it had finally come down to this, it was all going to end in a dimly-lit, prison corridor.

Amanthi's face came unbidden into his mind. He concentrated, his uncertainty slipping away. He had something to live for now. To fight for! There was a taste, thick and bitter at the back of his mouth. Tilak struggled to swallow and then he remembered. It was the taste of hatred he had carried while in prison. Hatred for himself for doing what he did, for the guards who preyed on him, for the prisoners who had made his life miserable and the rest of the world who had once put him there. Prisons were hell holes where the devil preyed.

If you did not sell your soul to the devil you would never come out alive. Tilak had sold himself many times and he would do so one more time.

Joseph crouched in hungry anticipation, two others taking station on either side of him. Tilak's initial thought was confirmed. These were not normal prisoners. They were either former soldiers or hardened prisoners. They were trained for the assault. Joseph motioned at Tilak and crooned softly. 'When I heard you were here I couldn't believe it! I hoped that my prayers had been answered.'

His men laughed and whistled, dragging their weapons along the stone walls. Tilak knew they expected him to hesitate, to show caution at their greater numbers. Instead he advanced straight ahead. There was a brief instant when surprise registered on Joseph's face, a tightening of the skin, a warping of the scar rising from his jawline. Then Tilak struck.

He slipped easily under the right-hand attacker's swing. Tilak was then too close for the staves to do any good as they risked striking each other. He uncoiled so fast the leader did not even see the two strikes, a fist to the centre of his chest over his heart and the other to the side of the man's jaw, high up towards his temple. The man was unconscious before he was fully aware of having been hit.

Tilak used Joseph's body as a shield against the left- hand attacker and aimed a kick for the most vulnerable point, his testicles. He let the leader drop and twisted the stave from the man's fumbling hands. Swinging around, his entire body a whip, he aimed a blow at the now uncertain man to his right. The attacker barely blocked the strike with his stave, the piece of wood he carried recoiling back, the embedded nails opening a wound on his face. Tilak channelled his own momentum and spun around, rapping the man on his left on the forehead, hearing the sound like the cracking of an egg.

His right arm burned as he felt a shiv rip down his forearm, slicing through his sleeve into the flesh beneath. Tilak grabbed the man's arm and pulled him forward, head butting him on the bridge of his nose. The attacker fell back, raising his forearm to his face and giving Tilak an opening. Tilak aimed his kick at the man's ribs, his boot-clad feet smashing into the man's body, snapping the bones with a loud crack. The man screamed, dropping to his knees in agony. A blow to his head knocked him on his back, silencing his scream abruptly.

Only then did Tilak become aware of the din that surrounded him. Chandra had dispatched both his attackers who lay moaning in the corridor. A guard who had heard the commotion and opened the door to the visitor's room, was struggling with another prisoner. Tilak watched as Chandra kicked the man behind the knees and delivered an elbow to the top of his head.

The guard looked shocked. The corridor seemed to be filled with bodies. 'Come quickly,' he gestured, taking a step back. 'You must get out of here before the Captain comes.'

Tilak could feel a trickle of blood run down his cheek from a gash on his forehead when he head-butted the man. He was breathing rapidly, his clothing drenched in sweat. Tilak paused and looked down at Joseph. This was the second time the man had almost got him. He had no doubt in his mind what would happen to him if he was in the man's clutches. Tilak waved at Chandra. 'You go ahead and keep the guard distracted. I have something to finish in here.'

Chandra stared at Tilak and then down at Joseph. He nodded and stepped over the bodies, disappearing into the visitor's room.

Tilak reached down and picked up a short-bladed knife lying on the ground. He noticed blood dripping from his arm where he had been cut. Tilak stepped over to Joseph and bent over the man. He was gasping for breath, his face beetroot red.

Tilak hesitated as a feeling of loathing surged up within him growing stronger by the minute. What would Amanthi think of him. The thought flashed unbidden into his mind. He panted, not knowing what to do. Shreds of thought swarmed into his mind making him lose focus. So wrapped up was he in his feelings that he was dimly conscious when someone dashed into the corridor behind him shouting at the top of his voice. His mind cleared knowing he had only seconds to act. He brought the shiv down on the man's face, slashing him from his jaw to his hairline, opening his cheek and cutting his nose in two.

At that moment Tilak realized that something had changed inside him. He had wanted to kill the man but he had held back. He rationalized his action with the thought that he would have to answer to the commander. The insurgent leader's death could be written off as a stroke but a dead prisoner would automatically open an inquiry. Too many questions would be asked but that was not the reason he'd hesitated.

Tilak threw the knife on the ground, his hands sticky with blood, and walked quickly to the door. It clanged shut behind him, the guard throwing two bolts to secure it shut. The prison was quiet as they collected their weapons and were hurried out of the side gate.

*

The sounds from the street were muted as Tilak watched as the coffin made of fresh rough-cut timber was lowered into the unmarked grave. Unlike in other Buddhist countries, Sri Lankan Buddhists always buried their dead because in the poorer villages outside Colombo, a family could not afford the cost of wood for cremating a body.

The Fixer had come through. He had extracted a high price but the militant leader was dead and it was all that mattered. Tilak would have liked to know how news of his being in the prison had spread so quickly. It had to be one of the guards who had let them into the prison. He would have been the one to tip them off. The wound on his arm was not deep and only needed a few stiches. If Joseph had known he was coming and had time to prepare, he would have used more men.

Chandra sat quietly next to Tilak as they drove back to Colombo. Tilak was glad that Chandra was not with him when he had hesitated in the prison corridor. It wouldn't have been easy to explain. But Tilak felt good about what he'd done. He felt relaxed, like a weight had been lifted from his shoulders.

Tilak glanced at Chandra wondering whether he had ever heard Chandra say anything more than a few words at a time. He tried to amuse himself while driving by thinking of what Chandra would say under different circumstances.

He chuckled when he thought of something really silly, glancing at Chandra when he did. Chandra was studying him with a bemused look which made Tilak laugh out loud.

Tilak was meeting Amanthi for dinner that night. He was taking her to the Mount Lavinia Hotel. It's old colonial charm and view of the city at night from its outdoor terraced restaurant would make it a very romantic spot for dinner. He had reserved a room for the night and would drive straight there.

The Galle Road was buzzing with impatient motorists, mostly buses and school vans. Pedestrians scurried along the sidewalk occasionally risking their lives by dashing madly across the road. They arrived in the outskirts of the city in the late afternoon heat. Schoolboys dressed in white crossed the road from a private college near the road leading to the hotel. An old steam train with clouds of smoke belching from its funnel, thundered under the bridge at the entrance to the old colonial hotel.

Amanthi had not been sure what time she would get off work and said she would take a taxi to the hotel. It gave Tilak time to have a swim in the calm sea behind the hotel. The warm water making him sleepy, He took a nap with the windows open, the gentle sea breeze blowing over his naked body. He woke up when the sun was a red orb slowly sinking into the sea opposite the hotel.

It was after seven when Tilak saw Amanthi walk out into the restaurant. He was sitting at the bar which gave him an uninterrupted view of the city coastline. She saw him and waved at him, negotiating the tables and chairs arranged around the half-moon bar.

Amanthi was dressed in an elegant red salwar with a wide gold border, a colourful scarf casually draped over both shoulders.

'Hi.' Tilak smiled and stepped off the bar stool to greet her. Amanthi offered her cheek. Her hair was short and bobbed in a modern style, and when she smiled it was reflected in the glow in her eyes. She smelt fresh and alluring.

'I am sorry it took so long,' she said. 'The traffic is getting worse every day.'

Tilak gestured to an alcove with a cushioned settee and a small square table. 'Let's sit over there,' he said. 'What would you like to drink?'

'Just passion fruit juice for me please,' she smiled at him. 'Without sugar.' Amanthi walked over to where Tilak had pointed while he ordered the drink from the bartender. Tilak looked at Amanthi while he waited for the drink to be poured. He couldn't believe that the doctor he had watched working on Saman those many months ago was the same person.

Tilak took the drink back with him and placed it in front of Amanthi. He was captivated by her bright eyes, clear complexion, glossy hair and glowing lips.

'What are you staring at?' she asked, smiling with her eyes as she sipped her drink.

'You look so beautiful,' he said, admiring her features in the ambient lighting of the lounge. 'I can't help but stare.' Tilak watched Amanthi blush which made his heart race even more.

Tilak toasted her with his glass, they touched with a clink. Her presence made him feel light-headed and for the first time since he could remember he felt relaxed and comfortable.

Amanthi watched him with those alluring eyes. 'What are you planning for dinner?' she asked. 'I have not eaten anything all day and I am starving.'

Tilak sat forward embarrassedly. He had been lost in her completely. 'I was thinking we could go to the terrace upstairs,' he said. 'They have an ala-carte menu and a themed buffet as well.'

Amanthi nodded happily, collecting her handbag before standing up with her drink. They walked into the garden overlooking the beach. They were shown to a table against the balustrade where they could look out on the ocean and watch the lights of the shipping vessels lining up to enter the port of Colombo.

The lapping sound of the small waves on the beach just below came clearly up to them in spite of the noise in the restaurant. They ordered from the menu, freshly grilled fish for both, just caught that morning off the beach behind the hotel. The dark chocolate mousse they ordered for dessert was light and divine. The meal was a great success. They chattered without a thought to the time. Tilak was curious about her and the work she did and Amanthi talked about the feeling of fulfilment she got helping people who were badly burnt.

Hotel guests and visitors were drifting in and out of the terrace as the evening progressed. The light from the candlelit table created a romantic cocoon around them as a jazz band playing softly from the other side of the swimming pool. 'Tell me something about yourself I don't know,' she said, looking at him across the table.

'Hmmm,' he said, looking at her. 'Something you don't know.' Tilak thought about the question for a moment. 'Well, I have always wanted to travel. My plan was to go to England, to Sandhurst when I became an officer. It was all arranged but that didn't quite work out as you know.' He shrugged unhappily. 'Maybe I'll get to go overseas one day,' he said looking at the ships out at sea.

She looked back at him thoughtfully. 'You shouldn't feel sorry for yourself. You were sent into a nasty situation half-trained, and you overreacted. If that happened today no one would blame you.'

Tilak stared at her. He had never met anyone who spoke to him so frankly.

'I used to think like that but I don't like the person I've become.'

'What do you mean?' Amanthi studied him over the rim of her wine glass.

Tilak's mind was churning in circles. 'I have this aggression, this violence in me which I find difficult to control,' he said. shrugging his shoulders resignedly. 'I was never like that before.' He was conscious of a terrible inner turmoil. He was afraid of losing his self-control.

'It's probably your training.' Amanthi said soothingly, reaching out for his hand. 'Soldiers are conditioned to acts of violence without any thought. It undoubtedly got worse when you were in prison.'

Tilak nodded reluctantly, not sure what Amanthi would think of him.

'I have to deal with people who resort to burning themselves,' Amanthi said, a faraway look in her eyes. 'For a long time, I thought it was because they wanted to die but I now know that in some cases it has little to do with suicide.'

Amanthi shook her head, like she was clearing her thoughts. 'People can be severely traumatized by high levels of emotion and stress in their lives which cause severe psychological damage. They resort to burning themselves to make a statement. You have been trained to kill and although you weren't prone to violence, you used it to defend yourself. You can't just turn that off. It will take time.'

Tilak felt a sudden sense of indescribable relief He looked at Amanthi who was studying him thoughtfully. She was right. It was time to let his past go.

'Yes,' he nodded. 'You are right. It's time to put it all behind me.' A faint and even pleasant shiver ran down his spine as Amanthi smiled at him but did not respond. There was a moment of quiet. Only the sound of the waves crashing on the shore as the tide came in.

Tilak looked at the moonlight glinting on the ocean. 'Why don't we go for a walk? There are some rocks over there and sometimes there are fishermen catching fish.'

Amanthi nodded and they walked down the balustraded staircase to the beach. Amanthi quickly took her sandals off and dug her toes sensually in the still warm sand. 'Come on. Take your shoes off. It's wonderful.'

Tilak tried to balance as he took off first one and then the other shoe and sock. He rolled up his trouser legs and followed Amanthi who had already set off down the beach. Tilak held out his hand and she took it, her cool slim fingers gave him a complete sense of well-being. Above them the night sky was almost clear, the shadows of clouds on the horizon reminding them that it was the monsoon season.

They did not speak and soon came to a cluster of rocks that jutted out into the water. Tilak found a flat rock facing the sea they could climb onto. They sat next to each other, their arms touching. Tilak put his arms around her and she lay her head on his shoulder, half turning her head and looking at him. He leaned over and kissed her gently, feeling her body respond to his lips. She turned to him and put her arms around his neck, opening her mouth to his caress. Amanthi moaned softly and forced her mouth more firmly on his.

Tilak's blood was racing. He felt himself grow but there was nothing he could do. He couldn't reach down and adjust himself.

Amanthi pulled away breathlessly. 'Mmm, that was nice,' she murmured leaning back in his arms. Tilak stroked her head as they sat quietly watching the light glimmer off the black sea, lifting and dancing on the small waves.

They kissed again, this time more urgently. Tilak became bolder, gently kneading her breasts through the silk top of her kameez. His hand started to wander lower but she pushed it away firmly. 'Let's go to your room,' she said softly against his face.

CHAPTER THIRTY-FIVE

From behind the hotel, the morning sun shone brightly on the buildings along the city skyline. A large container ship, its high sides reflecting the light from the rising sun, powered its way towards the breakwater at the entrance to the harbour. But the ominous dark clouds gathering threateningly on the horizon promised another afternoon of monsoon rain.

From beneath the sheet, Amanthi looked out into the bright airy bedroom, shafts of dusty light streaming through its lofty casement windows. She hadn't been aware of Tilak leaving the bed. He possessed the ability to move with remarkable stealth and agility. She had sensed his absence rather than felt it.

She thought about their lovemaking the night before. How tender he was at times, yet he could be brutal as though he was trying to bury some sense of anger deep inside her. She heard the shower start and stretched luxuriously against the crumpled sheets. She slid off the bed and went into the bathroom, joining him under the rain shower that cascaded water down on them.

'Ah, sleepy head.' Tilak looked at Amanthi in delight. 'I was wondering when you were going to wake up.'

They soaped one another under the warm shower, exploring each other. Amanthi teased him with her fingers, cupping him and stroking him while he tried to kiss her slippery body. They soon reached a point that they could not wait any longer. They almost ran to the bed, soaking with water and fell onto it.

She guided him and then clutched him, giving a low moan of pleasure as they came together.

They moved as thought it was a familiar rhythm, rocking gently together. Amanthi stared straight into his eyes, her mouth slightly open, her hips driving into him. She climaxed, gasping and clutching at Tilak as she felt his warmth wetness in her. Amanthi fell back, her heart pounding wildly. She tried to catch her breath and tilted her head to watch Tilak who had his eyes closed.

'Wow,' he said, opening his eyes and looking at her. Amanthi smiled at him languorously, licking the sweat off her upper lip. Tilak's eyes opened wide at the sexy motion and reached for her again.

Amanthi did not hear her beeper go off. Her muffled cries as Tilak drove hard into her drowned any sound except the hammering in her brain. She climaxed twice before she felt his release, her heart pounding in her chest like she had run a marathon. Amanthi had never known she could feel the way she did. Her previous sexual partners were inexperienced and never made her feel anything like she was feeling just then. She felt sore, but it was a delicious soreness. Something to remind her of what it had been like.

The beeper sounded loud in the quietness in the room. Tilak who had been dozing raised his head, startled by the strange sound. Amanthi slipped out of bed and padded across the wooden floor to the chair where she had left her belongings. She fumbled in her bag and pulled out the device.

'There's been another bombing,' she said. 'They've called a level one emergency and want me in the unit right away.'

Tilak raised himself on one arm and looked at her. 'You're going to hit rush hour traffic,' he said. 'Let me call a taxi for you while you get ready.'

Amanthi nodded as she rushed into the shower. She couldn't go to work smelling of sex. By the time she was ready, Tilak had organized a taxi which was waiting for her downstairs in the hotel courtyard. She kissed him hard on the lips before she wrenched herself away and almost ran down the corridor, ignoring the creaking ancient lift and taking the wide wooden staircase two steps at a time.

The drive into the city was quicker than she had expected and she breathed a sigh of relief when the taxi pulled up outside the hospital entrance. The entrance was crowded as it always was at that time of the day. She noticed two ambulances that were parked next to the entrance, the paramedics nowhere to be seen.

Amanthi ran down the corridor into the unit, grabbing her white coat from her office before hurrying into the busy ward.

Nelum who was attending to a patient looked up as she walked into the assessment room. She was about to say something then shut her mouth, seeing the look on Amanthi's face.

'Tell me,' Amanthi said. 'What happened?'

'A bomb went off in a bus at Maradana,' Nelum said. 'So far they have only brought two people.'

Amanthi stepped around Nelum to look at the patient. It was a woman who had been dressed in a sari, the silk cloth having fused to her skin by the heat from the explosion. Nelum and Shanthi had started soaking the burnt areas in saline, peeling off the coloured bits of materiel and charred bits of skin.

Leaving the two experienced nurses to handle the woman, Amanthi went looking for the second patient. The closed screen around the gurney was ominous. She parted the curtains and saw that a sheet had been pulled up over the patient's head.

Amanthi found Dr Perera in her office talking on the phone. She motioned Amanthi into the room, raising her eyebrows at Amanthi's attire visible under the while coat. Amanthi smiled sheepishly, knowing she would have to answer a million questions about why she was dressed like she was going out for dinner. She sighed when she realized the rumour mill would be going into overdrive. She'd have to talk to Tilak about cutting back the time they spent together and be more careful in future!

CHAPTER THIRY-SIX

Nadesan studied the vehicle from all sides. The compartment he was building for the three-wheeler was finally ready. In some vehicles, especially the early models built in India, the space under the driver's seat was empty. He had decided not to construct a pannier as he'd been instructed. It was easier for Nadesan to construct a compartment of thin sheets of steel which he welded to the vehicle's frame under the seat. The compartment could be opened from behind the driver's legs where Nadesan had installed a hinged door with a clasp.

Nadesan decided not to modify the vehicle which he drove around in. He worked on one that had been discarded at the back of the lot which no one wanted. The machine was old and looked like it was on its last legs. Nadesan replaced the old two-stroke engine with one of the more modern four-stroke engines, taken from a new three-wheeler which had met with a bad accident. Looking at the modified machine, no one would ever guess that it ran better than most of the other three-wheelers in the yard.

Deva showed up at the yard a week later and Nadesan followed him to the tea stall they had used before.

'The man will be here in two weeks' time,' he said, sipping his glass of milky tea. 'Once he's here he will need to see what you have built so that he knows how big the package should be.'

'Will we find out what the target is?' Nadesan asked. It had been something that had been bothering him. He wanted to make sure that he was able to transport the bomb without running into any roadblocks. The military had been particularly active since the insurgent uprising and they often set up impromptu checkpoints and closed roads without any warning.

'I would think so,' Deva said. 'If not him then someone else will. I am not going to worry about it too much. It's up to them to tell us what the target is.'

'What about the general?' Nadesan asked. 'I found out where the hospital is.'

'That's good,' Deva said approvingly. 'Tell me where it is.'

Nadesan gave Deva the address which he wrote down on the palm of his hand. 'The place is well guarded by the army,' he said. 'I have driven past it a couple of times and it won't be easy to get into the building.'

'Don't worry,' Deva said, studying the address. 'I'll get Kumar to take a good look at the place.'

'Why don't we target the general instead of just waiting?'

'No' Deva said, shaking his head. 'We have to wait! We'll get our instructions soon.'

Nadesan was getting very impatient. He felt that the longer he stayed in the city his luck would eventually run out. Just yesterday a black dog had run across a junction in front of the three-wheeler making him brake in shock. The dog had turned and looked at Nadesan malevolently, his eyes gleaming in the harsh street lights. Nadesan shivered just thinking about it. As a child, his parents used to tell him that Mahasona, the most feared demon in the island, used the apparition of a black dog to show himself. That night he had found it impossible to sleep, his mind full of the dog's snarling face.

'I hope it's soon,' Nadesan said uneasily. 'This waiting is very difficult.'

'Just continue to do what you normally do,' Deva said. 'Don't break your routine. We'll come to you when it's time.'

Nadesan knew he didn't have a choice. If he stayed he would always be expected to do their bidding. They didn't know what he wanted ... not really. They thought he wanted to avenge his wife and son. They didn't know that he had always wanted to join them.

The thought of running crossed his mind. He had saved enough money to live for a while. He could take the three-wheeler with him. He could go south and avoid the hills. Drive to the next town, then the next. Find work. Save some money. He could do it. But that would not bring back his family.

Nadesan fingered the locket around his neck. No! He would remain and finish what he came to do.

There seemed to be more soldiers on the street than normal when Nadesan drove back to Wattala after dropping a woman and her shopping bags near the Hendala town centre. His eyes narrowed at heavily armed soldiers stopping people at random, questioning them and examining their bags.

His normal route back to the petrol station took him past a Police checkpoint. He thought about trying to avoid the area but dismissed the idea immediately. He had nothing to hide and his identification had held up to hundreds of checks. He would try to use the opportunity to find out what was going on.

Nadesan stopped behind a queue of vehicles waiting to get through the checkpoint. The policemen were searching every vehicle, getting the drivers to open their boots and looking into parcels and shopping bags. Nadesan had never seen them at this time before, not at this checkpoint and only late at night.

The traffic crawled forward, the drivers behind Nadesan tooting their horns in irritation, not understanding what the delay was.

Nadesan finally pulled up to the red and white striped barrels. In addition to the two policemen normally on duty, two armed soldiers with their automatic rifles across their chests, stood alertly watching the road from behind the barrier. A policeman who had checked Nadesan many times in the past motioned Nadesan to get off the three-wheeler.

'What's going on,' Nadesan asked. 'This delay will make it difficult for me to find enough fares for the day.'

'Stop talking and show me your ID,' the policemen growled at Nadesan. 'I am tired of everyone complaining.'

Nadesan handed over his ID, glancing at the closest soldier who was staring at him impassively. The policeman glanced cursorily at the ID card before handing it over. He knew who Nadesan was, he had even got Nadesan to drive him back to the Police station one day when it was raining.

The policeman bent over the three-wheeler checking behind and under the seats. 'What are you looking for?' Nadesan asked.

'There's been a tip-off of another attack,' the policeman grumbled. 'We've been ordered to check every vehicle for bombs.'

Nadesan's blood ran cold at the policeman's words. To his paranoid mind it was too much of a coincidence that the Police had received a tip off just before the bomb maker was going to arrive in the city. He stood there in stunned silence wondering what he should do.

'You can go,' said the policeman, gesturing impatiently for Nadesan to get back into the vehicle. He had already turned his attention to the next vehicle when Nadesan drove the three-wheeler away.

The closer Nadesan got to the city, the more Police and soldiers he could see. Some were even going to every building, talking to the occupants who had gathered in the street.

Nadesan panicked. If the safe house was searched, they would find the box that had been delivered from the north. He needed to do something about it. When he drove up to the junction, instead of turning left and driving into the petrol station, Nadesan turned right into the street where the safe house was located. He breathed a sigh of relief. The street was empty. The Police were concentrating on the shops and businesses on the main road and had not started checking the side streets.

Nadesan parked the vehicle on the street a few doors down and hurried to the wooden door knocking on it loudly. He saw the curtain move and the bolts being withdrawn. Deva's face peered out at him, angrily.

'What are you doing here,' he said harshly. 'You should know better than anyone how risky that is.'

Nadesan pushed past him into the shadowy room. Kumar was standing at the entrance to the back hallway.

'The Police have got a tip off that an attack is imminent,' Nadesan said, speaking quickly, his eyes darting around the room. 'They are stopping all vehicles on the street. I also saw people being searched … their packages. They know what's going to happen.'

'Calm down, calm down,' Deva said, putting his hand on Nadesan's shoulder. 'How could they have found out?' he asked. 'Only the three of us know about it.'

'I don't know,' he said. 'Maybe the information came from somewhere else, from the north.' Nadesan started to calm down and think a bit more clearly. 'Yes, yes, that makes sense. They obviously don't know where we are.'

Deva nodded. 'See, I told you,' he said. 'They don't know.'

Nadesan shook his head. 'But that does not mean anything. There are hundreds of Police and soldiers on the streets and they are going from building to building talking to the people. I have never seen anything like it. We have to get rid of that box and what's in it.'

Deva tried reason with Nadesan. 'If it's like that outside they won't risk sending the bomb maker,' he said thoughtfully. 'He's too valuable an asset. It'll just mean that the whole mission will get cancelled or delayed.'

What Deva was saying made sense to Nadesan. But there was still the problem of hiding what was in the box. 'Let's open the box and see what's inside,' he said.

Deva nodded and walked into the hallway leading to the back. The wooden box had been pushed into a corner of the back room under a pile of clothing.

Deva pushed the clothing away with his hand. It was a square box made to look like a tea chest. It was made out of inch thick plywood, held at the edges with metal strips riveted metal to the sheets.

Kumar handed Deva a metal bar which he used to lever up the lid. The chest was full of straw. Nadesan watched over Deva's shoulder as he pushed the straw aside revealing what was underneath. What he saw did not make any sense to Nadesan. There were metal boxes of various sizes and shapes with foreign writing on them.

Deva turned and looked at Kumar. 'You've had some training in bomb making, haven't you?' he asked. Kumar nodded his head and stepped forward, kneeling by the chest. He gingerly lifted a small flat tin, the size of a cigarette pack, out of its bed of straw. A set of wires hung from two small holes drilled into the base of the device.

'This is an electrical detonator,' he said, turning the device in his hand and examining it carefully. 'It needs to be wired to a series of batteries and a timer.' Nadesan had been trained to handle explosives but every bomb he had been trained on had already been assembled. He had watched the bomb maker in Batticaloa construct the car bomb with its electronic switch but the old man had not talked much and it was left up to Nadesan to figure out what he was doing.

Kumar put the timing device on the ground, reaching back into the tea chest. He pulled out what looked like a portable radio.

'This looks like a transmitter which sets off a radio-controlled detonator,' he explained. 'I don't know much about them.' He dived back into the box and after rummaging around pulled out a couple of packages wrapped in a waxy paper. He gingerly unwrapped one package which contained long silvery tubes which looked like cigar cases.

'Acid time fuses,' he said. 'You poke this end into the explosive, break the top seal and run like hell.'

At the bottom of the box was a tightly-wrapped, brown paper package packed carefully in the straw. He lifted it up and hefted it in his hand. 'It's feels like a plastic explosive,' he said. 'About two kilos, I think.'

Nadesan tore off the brown paper exposing clear plastic bag. The explosive was packed like a long, thin sausage and coiled around in a concentric circle. Nadesan rummaged around the box moving the straw around but other than a reel of detonation cord, he could not find anything else.

Nadesan stared at the contents of the box lying on the ground. They did not look like much but when wired together and armed, the explosive power they would generate would cause a scene like the one he had witnessed from the train at the central bus station.

Nadesan was getting anxious. He had already been here too long. He didn't know whether the Police had started searching the side streets yet.

'We have to get these away from here,' he said. 'We don't have much time. I'll take the package and the two sets of detonators and hide them amongst all the junk at the station. You get rid of the chest and the radio-controlled thing.'

'It won't matter. If they come here we're in trouble,' he said. 'We have weapons and ammunition that can't be moved. We're stuck with them for the moment.'

Nadesan looked at Deva in dismay. 'I didn't think about that,' he said. Moving the weapons and ammunition in the safe house would not be possible with the Police and military presence on the street. 'Ok, at least let's get the explosives away from here.'

Deva nodded and gave Nadesan a cloth bag from a pile of clothes in the corner of the room. 'Here, use this.'

The packages all fit into the bag which Nadesan hefted on his shoulder. He hurried to the door and looked out through the window. It was empty.

Deva grabbed his arm before he stepped outside. 'I know who the target is,' he said, pulling Nadesan closer. 'It's the Minister for National Security.'

Nadesan felt confused for a moment. 'What about the general in the military hospital?' he asked, looking at Deva questioningly. 'I told you where it is.'

'You go after the Minister,' Deva said decisively. 'We'll take the general.'

Deva released his arm and placed a folded piece of paper into Nadesan's hand. 'This is his home address.' He smacked Nadesan's shoulder. 'Good luck!'

Nadesan looked at the note before putting it in his pocket. It had the man's name and an address in Cinnamon Gardens. It wasn't some public place. Nadesan felt a sense of immediate relief which disappeared as quickly as it appeared. The Minister would be well protected in his home, and what about his family?

Nadesan nodded distractedly at Deva and stepped out onto the street. Other than a woman hanging clothes about four houses down, the street was empty.

Nadesan hurried to the three-wheeler and with the cloth bag clamped tightly between his legs drove back up the street, crossing the junction without incident. He parked the three-wheeler in its normal spot and hurried into the room he slept in, hiding the cloth bag under the pile of junk in the corner. He panted nervously, his heart beating hard against his chest. He would wait until it was dark and find a better spot to hide the bag.

CHAPTER THIRTY-SEVEN

The sound of knocking woke Tilak from a fitful sleep. He lay still for a moment, gathering his thoughts before reluctantly opening his eyes. The sparse bedroom in the officer's quarters was bathed in a soft light spilling through light cotton curtains which did nothing to stop the sound of beeping horns and traffic outside the window. The knocking grew insistent as he swung his legs off the bed and unlatched the room door.

'Message for you, sir.' The duty orderly handed him a folded note before saluting and walking down the corridor. Tilak, grunted and closed the door, sitting back down on the bed, his mind still foggy from sleep. He had gone to bed late after spending the evening with Amanthi. Sleep had evaded him for a while. His mind churned with thoughts and emotions, one following the other in quick succession.

The evening had started well! Amanthi had been late and kissed him when they met, rolling her eyes playfully as he tried to draw her close. They had ordered their meal and while they ate, talked about their jobs and how the Indian Peace Accord would affect the country and what they were doing. Amanthi was charming and even flirtatious at times but as the evening passed, her mood seemed to retreat and become somewhat subdued. Tilak realized that something was clearly bothering her. This was the first time that he had ever seen her unhappy and it troubled him deeply.

Tilak decided to say something after a long silence. 'You seem a bit distracted!'

Amanthi sighed, 'I am okay, I guess.' She glanced at him before raising the cup of coffee she held to her lips. She seemed uncharacteristically reluctant to look at him in the eye.

Tilak leaned back in his chair, studying her face as she sipped her coffee. He knew enough about women not to believe that for a moment. 'You guess?'

Amanthi raised her head, her puckered brow tightening her face as she looked at Tilak straight in the eye. 'We shouldn't see each other for a while! The words were forced, coming out like bullets from a gun. Everything about her posture and expression tightened, as she was suddenly aware of some danger.

For a moment Tilak hadn't understood what she meant. But alarmed by the change that had come over Amanthi, he sat forward in his chair.

'What do you mean?' His voice sounded hoarse, even harsh to his ears.

'I mean we shouldn't be seeing each other so often. This, … you, have become a distraction and it's affecting my work.'

Tilak felt confused. What does she mean? Meeting Amanthi had been one of the best things that had happened to him and he couldn't comprehend why she didn't want to see him anymore.

'What happened? Why don't you want to see me again?'

Amanthi reached out and grasped his hand, squeezing it firmly. 'I am not saying we cannot see each other. We just need to do it less often.'

Tilak's mind started to clear. She's not saying we cannot meet. He could feel his heart thudding against his chest. But why?

'I still don't understand!'

'My job in the burn unit requires my total commitment and focus,' Amanthi said soothingly still holding onto his hand. 'It has all changed since I met you and it's affecting my work.' Tilak tried to cut through the emotions that were crowding out his rational mind and make some sense of what Amanthi had said.

'Look Tilak, I've known from that first time I met you that you were the most attractive man I met in a long time. You're strong and you make me feel at ease, feel very special really. But we just need to cool things down a bit.' She looked at him compassionately, seeming understanding what he must be feeling. 'I have already been pulled up by Dr Perera and don't like it. What makes it worse is I knew she is right.

'What did she say?'

'She has noticed that I am not concentrating on what I am doing.' Amanthi shrugged. 'The work I am doing is too important to even make a small mistake.'

Tilak could clearly see that she was waiting to see how he would react. The shock of what he was hearing had begun to wear off and he began to think more clearly. He consoled himself with two thoughts. The first was that she was not saying their relationship was over. And the other was that he had to be careful not to say anything that'll drive her away. I need to be unselfish. I have too much to lose. He took a deep breath.

'I think I understand,' he said, not really meaning it. 'I won't put any demands on you! I'll wait until you want to see me again … if you want to see me that is?'

'No, you mustn't think that,' Amanthi protested, as she offered comfort to him.

Tilak felt a pang of disappointment, but there was something else too. A bittersweet realization that the two of them had found something special in one another. He would just have to be patient.

Amanthi had declined his invitation to visit a nightclub and had kissed him goodbye when he dropped her off at her home. He had lain awake for what seemed like hours before he finally dropped off to sleep.

Tilak suddenly remembered the message slip he clutched in his hand. He read the message, tilting the piece of paper to catch the light coming from the window. The message was brief. There was some sort of an emergency underway and they wanted him at the operations centre right away. It hadn't take him long to have a quick shower, throw some clothes on and grab a sandwich on his way out, but however much he tried, he couldn't shake the feeling that there was something missing.

The special branch corridors and offices were already a nest of harsh and total confusion when Tilak walked through the door. The ringing of telephones, rising voices and the harsh sound of radio static mingled and coalesced among the police bureaucrats, sleek in their clean shirts and pressed trousers. Technicians were kept busy hoisting a mass of cables and wires, attaching the computers and transmitters that would secure instant access to the field teams being dispatched to various parts of the city.

The commander nervously paced among the rooms, querying and instructing the occupants to greater activity while waving an unlit cigarette jutting out of his fingers like a miniature baton.

He saw Tilak come in and waved to him from across the room. 'It's about time you got in.' The commander's raised voice rose above the clamour. 'I want Chandra and you in my office right away.'

Tilak nodded. The commander was unshaven and he looked like he had slept in his clothes.

Must have been an all-nighter, Tilak thought to himself. He went looking for Chandra. He found him in the small canteen at the rear of the building sipping from a plastic cup.

Chandra grunted when he saw Tilak. 'The boss is looking for you,' Chandra said, before raising the cup to his lips again.

'I know,' Tilak responded. 'He jumped on me as I walked in the door. He looks like he's been here all night. What's going on?'

Chandra shrugged. 'I heard that they are close to uncovering another Tiger cell … maybe the one which controls the other cells.'

Tilak paused for a moment, thinking about what Chandra had said. It would explain the frenetic activity. Finding and cutting off the head of the beast in the city would be very high on the priority list of all the security service branches responsible for the safety of the city. The service which could shut it down would reap great rewards.

Chandra drained his cup in a final swallow and followed Tilak out of the room.

The commander was talking on the phone but waved them into his room. 'Do we know what name he is using?' the commander bellowed into the mouthpiece. 'Where is he hiding? I want more information about him. We cannot let him get away again.'

He listened for a moment. 'I don't care how you get it … just get it by tonight.' He smashed the phone back into its cradle. 'Bloody idiots,' he said.

Tilak smiled to himself at the commander's reaction. Tilak realized that the commander was always impatient, loud and perpetually angry. But he was always brutally honest.

'What's going on,' Tilak asked, tentatively. 'I've never known it to be so busy.'

'We have been investigating the recent bus bombing in Maradana,' the commander said irritably. 'It was unusual because the bus was almost empty. There were two dead, a Tamil man and a woman. A few passengers were injured but the bombing did not feel right. The target should have been something more significant, not just a half- empty bus.'

Tilak glanced at Chandra who lounged against the door. 'So, what have you found out?' Tilak had never known the man to get excited or flustered about anything. And the commander seemed to let him do his own thing. Not for the first time Tilak wondered what relationship the two of them had shared previously.

'It turns out we just got lucky'. The commander paused, looking at the two of them. 'We now know that the two who were killed were moving the bomb somewhere and it went off, perhaps by accident but who knows. We traced the identity of the Tamil couple to a militant cell operating out of Batticaloa and raided the place yesterday. We found a stash of weapons and bomb making materials and captured a man who turned out to be the bomb maker.'

Satisfaction shone on the commander's face. 'It turns out he was the one who had built the central bus station and the Maradana bus bombs … and he has been working on another.'

The commander moved over to a large map pinned on the wall. He tapped on a location circled in red on the map. 'Under interrogation, he revealed the location of a safe house here in Wattala. This information was corroborated by the militant informer we now have in the east thanks to you two.' He considered the cigarette still clutched in his hand like he didn't know it was there.

'We are moving teams into position to raid the place tonight,' he said, shuffling papers around his desk until he found a lighter. The commander slumped on his seat and lit the cigarette, inhaling deeply. 'I want you both there.'

Tilak nodded. 'I heard you on the phone talking about someone ...' he said. 'Who is it you were asking about?'

'We have received information that the man who set off the central bus station bomb is still in the city. The bastard could be anywhere ...' the commander swore, 'chances are we will catch him in one of these safe houses if we know what he looks like. I have asked our people in Batticaloa for a description of the man. I hope to have it by this evening.'

Tilak looked at Chandra who stared back at him stony-faced. It would not be easy to pinpoint one man in a city the size of Colombo. It would require a huge police and military effort.

'We cannot screw this up,' the commander murmured to himself.

Tilak understood what the commander was saying. Failure was not an option. Reputations could be damaged, perhaps even destroyed.

*

The streets of the city were silent and dark. It was almost eleven thirty and the very large Police and military presence in the city had driven many of its inhabitants indoors. Only the occasional person hurrying home from a late-night shift broke the stillness of the night. Young khaki-clad soldiers wearing green berets, their rifles strapped across their chests with the barrels hanging down, stood at every street corner watching their vehicle pass.

Tilak listened to the hum of the powerful Land Rover engine as Chandra drove through an affluent area of large, white colonial mansions surrounded by walled tropical gardens. Large trees lined the wide streets, their branches touching overhead creating the impression of driving through a dark tunnel.

They were driving to meet the person coordinating the search for the militant cell in the northern part of the city. Home to many small industries, warehouses and Colombo's biggest slums, most of the militant safe houses that were discovered in the city came from this area.

Tilak stared alertly at the road ahead, wary of being flagged down by one of the many army patrols that roamed the city at night. The military vehicle they were in gave them some form of immunity to being stopped and questioned but the threat of the militant cell in the city had everybody's nerves on edge.

'We'll have to show our passes here,' Chandra said, glancing at Tilak.

They were in the sprawling suburb of Grandpass, a collection of ramshackle shantytowns and commercial buildings covered with billboards of every size and description.

The two bridges which were the main gateway to the city from the north and central parts of the country were heavily guarded by both the Police and the army. Chandra drove up the old bridge, with its elevated causeway spanning a large area of slums. On either side of the road a jumble of corrugated-iron roofs fell towards the banks of the fast running Kelaniya river. Two checkpoints, one at each end of the bridge were covered by sandbagged, corrugated-iron sentry posts out of which protruded the menacing barrels of heavy machine guns.

Chandra lowered his headlights and flicked on the interior light of the Land Rover as he slowly drove up to the barrier. The checkpoint was manned by members of the Special Task Force. The troopers looked alert, studying the occupants of the vehicle warily as it cruised to a stop.

'Paper's.' The trooper bent at the waist and looked into the Land Rover, scanning the interior of the vehicle before stepping back.

Chandra glanced at Tilak, who handed his new set of papers across.

'We're both from Special Branch,' Chandra said, handing their papers to the trooper. The trooper scanned both sets of papers before handing them back, motioning for the barrier to be raised. The scene was repeated at the other end of the long bridge where army soldiers manned the checkpoint.

Chandra took the Negombo Road and turned into the Wattala Police Station located near the bridge over the old Dutch Canal. The search was being coordinated by a Superintendent of Police who had control of a vast collection of Police and military units. Chandra dressed in civilian clothes, acknowledged the senior officer by coming to attention.

'Lieutenant Dassanayake reporting as ordered. This is sergeant Munasinghe.'

The Superintendent looked stressed as he frowned at the two men irritably. 'I've been wondering when you were going to show up,' he said. 'We have men moving into position right now and will kick off the operation at dawn.'

'Where exactly is the house?' Tilak asked, ignoring the man's complaint. His orders were to report to the Superintendent at the Wattala Police Station by midnight.

The Superintendent moved over to a large map pinned on the wall. He tapped on a location circled in red on the map. 'It's here.'

Tilak and Chandra walked up to the map and looked at it. The address marked on the map was in a small narrow street leading off a junction on the old Negombo Road. The area was a rabbit warren of low income housing built during the 1930's by private landowners for laborers who were engaged in the processing and shipment of tea and rubber from the thriving plantation industry.

'Hmm, have you sent anyone to take look at the place,' he asked. 'It's pretty congested and there may be other exits.'

'Yes,' the officer nodded. 'We have, but there's nothing much to see. We have cordoned off the area and will hold everyone within that circle for questioning.'

Tilak looked around interestedly. It was not the first time he had been in a military operations room. Men dressed in khaki and camouflaged military fatigues huddled over radio's and maps, while others hurried in and out of the room carrying messages and attending to other duties.

Chandra walked over to where Tilak was standing. 'They seem to have it covered,' he said looking around.

Tilak nodded. 'I think we'll stay here and wait for the operation to end. It doesn't make sense going over there. We'll see the big picture here.'

Tilak and Chandra walked over to the room that served as the kitchen. They prepared steaming hot glasses of tea for themselves and went outside the Police station, sitting on a wooden bench in front of the building.

The sky was partially covered by dark clouds that loomed ominously in the west. It had hardly rained that day. Tilak wondered what Amanthi would be doing … whether she was also looking up at the sky like he was. She was never far from his thoughts.

A light breeze rustled the leaves on the bushes separating the Police station from the road bringing with it the smell of rain. Chandra looked down at his watch. It was after four in the morning. He hadn't realized they had been sitting outside for over two hours.

'We should go in now,' he said. 'It's after four and the operation will be getting underway soon.'

The Police station was quiet. Like it had taken a deep breath and was waiting to release it once the operation was over. Hushed voices spoke into radios as teams moved into position.

The Superintendent was studying the map, standing where they had left him earlier. He was startled when Chandra spoke. 'Are we still on schedule?'

The Superintendent turned. 'Yes, yes. We are ready,' he said. 'I was just going over the team assignments to make sure I haven't missed anything.'

Chandra nodded. It was refreshing to see a senior officer pay so much attention to detail. The countdown clock on the wall read thirty minutes when the Superintendent gave the order to begin the operation.

Blocking forces started moving into position, closing off streets wooden barricades and metal barrels filled with sand. Traffic was diverted creating an island where nothing other than stray dogs wandered. As the minutes ticked down, the assault team moved into position on the street. The plan was to blow open the door and throw in two stun grenades before entering the house.

The seconds ticked down to zero and the blast of the door being breached could be heard over the radio.

'They're in,' the Superintendent said, bending over the radio operator like he wanted to get closer to the action. Two more loud cracks and then the sound of gunfire.

The countdown clock read plus seven minutes when a voice came over the radio. 'Mission complete. Two Tigers down. Both dead. No casualties.'

The Superintendent straightened and smacked one hand into the other. 'Bloody good work.' He looked around the room. 'Don't relax for one minute,' he said. 'We don't know how many were in the house. Make sure that all the blocking teams follow their orders.'

He turned and looked at Chandra. 'I am going over. You can follow in your vehicle.' Chandra and Tilak followed the Superintendent who almost ran out of the room. It would be a feather in his cap if he'd taken the militant cell down cleanly.

CHAPTER THIRTY-EIGHT

Amanthi hunched down in the chair at her desk, tucking her feet under her. She cradled a mug of sweetened tea she had made at the canteen.

The phone had rung, waking her from a deep sleep leaving her disoriented and groggy. The voice on the phone informed her that a 'Red Alert' had been declared in the city and that the Emergency Response Team had been placed on standby.

Amanthi had found it difficult to fall asleep the previous night, her mind going over and over her evening with Tilak. She had felt very confused. She was so committed to her work at the hospital that she had felt compelled to tell Tilak that they needed to see each other less, that it was affecting her concentration, her work. But when they had met at the restaurant, her resolve cracked. She got lost in the moment, enjoying the feeling of pure happiness that almost over whelmed her when he held her in his arms and kissed her. It was a feeling that she'd never experienced before and it scared her. It took most of the evening for her to find the courage and tell him that they should meet less often. Her resolve almost cracked again when she saw the uncertainty in his eyes and reached out for his hand. But she had steeled herself with the thought that she should not think of herself, that there were countless women …children, and men, who needed her total focus and commitment.

Amanthi had woken up with a strange feeling that she had made a significant change in her life. A transformation that would shape her life from that moment on.

The driver who picked her up was not the regular ERT driver she was used to. He was a middle-aged man with greying hair whom Amanthi had seen before driving one of the hospital ambulances. He had picked up Nelum and Shanthi on his way and the three of them sat around Amanthi's office grumbling about being woken up so early.

The Tigers had launched a bombing campaign in the city and red alerts were being declared in the city almost daily. Dr Perera had decided that the Emergency Response Team would remain at the Burn Unit until specifically requested to attend an emergency. They would not go out on call where they had to wait for something to happen. They had communicated their displeasure of hanging around street corners while raids were conducted by the security forces. Amanthi had run two training courses for army medics on immediate burn care and she felt comfortable that the victims would be attended to correctly until the emergency response team would get there.

Amanthi had gone to the private military hospital the previous evening before meeting Tilak to review the General's condition. Even though she would be late for her date with Tilak, she knew it was the right thing to do.

The thick hospital walls were about three metres high and a strong metal gate protected its entrance. The electric gates slid open and two soldiers with automatic rifles, wearing body armor and battle dress uniform, stepped outside as the ambulance entered the hospital compound.

The ambulance was searched by two other soldiers in a walled in area behind the entrance, before a second gate opened and they were allowed into the compound.

The two-story hospital building about thirty metres at the end of a curved driveway, was a recent construction. The property was originally the site of a colonial mansion used by a European ambassador as his residence. Armed soldiers patrolled the well-lit grounds which were shaded by enormous flame trees. The building, with its white stone façade had big arches behind which a wide veranda could be seen.

The atrium lobby inside the wide entrance held a high semicircular desk behind which sat a receptionist dressed in army uniform. She looked at Amanthi inquiringly.

'I am from the Burn Unit of the General Hospital,' Amanthi said. 'Dr. Karunaratne requested I check on one of your patients.'

The receptionist nodded and picked up a phone. After speaking into it she replaced the handset and pointed to a sofa and a set of chairs.

'Please wait there,' she said. 'Someone will come and meet you.'

Before Amanthi had taken a few steps, a youngish-looking army officer wearing a white coat walked briskly into the lobby. 'I am Dr Gunasena,' he said, extending his hand. 'I have been expecting you. Thank you for coming.'

Amanthi had met the Doctor assigned to look after the General but this was someone she had not seen before. 'Where's Dr Fernando? Isn't he in charge of this case?'

'Dr Fernando has been called away on an emergency,' Dr Gunasena said. 'He asked me to meet with you.' The doctor smiled and pointed to the corridor he had emerged from. 'Please come this way.'

Amanthi nodded and moved in the direction the doctor was pointing. The hospital didn't have the smell she had grown used to at the general hospital. Everything smelt brand new and she was surprised at how lavishly it was supplied. Some of the equipment lying in the corridor were still in their shrink-wrapped boxes waiting to be unpacked.

'How's he been responding to his treatment?' As Amanthi had suspected, the general trauma from the explosives were more serious than the burns. He had lost a lot of blood and even though they had pumped him with many bags of blood it had taken them almost forty-eight hours to stabilize him so he could be transferred.

'His vital signs are strong and we expect full recovery from his wounds,' the doctor said. 'The reason we wanted you to see him is about his burns. We don't have as much experience treating severe burns and wanted your prognosis.'

The general was located in a room towards the rear of the first floor. He was unconscious or seemed to be. His head was huge, his face bright red from burns to his face. He was lying on his back, one bandaged arm suspended by a sling from an overhead rail. His neck and upper body was swathed in bandages and a tube ran down his throat. Other tubes and wires hooked him up to a battery of pumps and monitors.

Amanthi's practiced eyes were immediately drawn to the monitor next to his bed. The patient's blood pressure was holding steady and his pulse looked strong. She stepped up to his bed and bent over him using all her senses to gather information. Dr Gunasena did not speak and waited patiently for Amanthi to complete her observation.

'Are his dressings being changed twice a day?' she asked. The second dressing change of the day usually took place in the late afternoon or early evening.

'Yes, they are,' the doctor said.

'Any signs of infection? Amanthi asked. It was during a dressing change that a patient was examined for signs of infection and healing.

The doctor shook his head while reading from the file he was carrying. 'There's nothing on his chart and his blood tests have come back clean.'

'Good,' Amanthi nodded and stepped back from the bed. 'Could I look at his file please?'

Amanthi slowly leafed through the thick file, going back to the day the general was brought into the military hospital. Everything looked in order but Amanthi was painfully aware that it could take six months to a year to properly train a nurse to look after a burn victim. The hands-on care and the close observation it entails are among the reasons why bedside nurses know their patients better than anyone else.

'I am going to send one of my nurses to do a dressing change with the patient,' she said looking at Dr Gunasena. 'Everything looks in order but only during a dressing change can you really tell what is going on under all that.'

Dr Gunasena smiled and nodded. 'I was hoping you would suggest that.

I would be more comfortable knowing an experienced nurse has taken a good look,' he said. 'None of the Doctors at this hospital have treated anything this complex before. We have spoken to the Medical Director requesting that we be assigned to spend time with you at the burn unit.'

Amanthi glanced at Dr Gunasena before speaking. 'I am sure it can be arranged,' she said. 'Dr. Perera will welcome it. She wants to maintain a national register of doctors and nurses who can handle severe burns for any major emergency like the one we had at the central bus station.'

*

Amanthi cradled her mug and took a sip. The drink had got cold but she was too lazy to get a refill. She stretched her aching body on the chair and looked at Nelum who stared back at her sleepily.

'I need you to go to the military hospital today and supervise a bandage change,' she said. 'I was there last evening and promised to send someone.'

'Why?' Nelum asked. 'Is there a problem?'

'No! I don't think so but I want to make sure.' Amanthi said. 'I want to make sure those army nurses we trained are not taking any shortcuts and you'll be able to assess the state of the general's wounds.'

Nelum nodded without saying anything. Amanthi remembered that she needed to tell Dr Perera what the army doctor had said about being assigned to the burn unit.

CHAPTER THIRTY-NINE

Nadesan woke to the sound of the three explosions. For a moment, he thought he was dreaming but the sound of gunfire was unmistakable. He jumped up from the mat he was sleeping on and hurried outside the store room. From where he stood it looked surreal. The fluorescent lights above the petrol station cast their yellow glow onto groups of heavily armed men dressed in camouflaged uniforms. Their attention was focused on the road that led to the safe house. None of them were looking his way.

A chill ran through Nadesan's body. The safe house has been raided he thought. His mind was racing. They would be looking for him next.

Nadesan moved into the shadow of the storeroom and looked around. There was no one watching him. Lights were coming on in the buildings around him and people were coming onto the street wondering what was going on.

I need to get away from here, he thought, but where?

Getting on his three-wheeler and driving away was not an option. He would be stopped and questioned before he even left the petrol station. Staying in his room was dangerous. The Police were bound to do a thorough check of the area and he would have to explain his presence. His only option was to hide somewhere. But where?

The hideaway in the warehouse roof was only two streets away. They would not find him there but he had to be careful no one saw him climb into the building. He would remain there until he felt safe to come out.

Nadesan ran into his room and grabbed a gunny bag into which he stuffed a half empty bottle of water and another empty bottle. He would fill them with water outside. He always had a packet of biscuits sitting by his mat which he threw into the bag along with a couple of sarongs and a shirt. He had slept bare bodied so he slipped on a shirt and put his cash and ID card into the pocket. He was ready.

There was a tap outside the room that he used to wash the three-wheelers. Nadesan used it to fill both bottles with water. While filling the bottles he remembered the package of explosives and the detonators he had brought from the safe house. He had hidden them in the old three-wheeler he was planning to use. It was with dozens of other vehicles, right at the back of the lot. He couldn't think of a better place to leave it. If they found the package, then it was fate that led them to him. He was not destined to do what he had planned. He would find a way to get away and try to lead a normal life.

Hefting the cloth bag on his shoulder, Nadesan walked onto the road at the rear of the station. He would leave the package where it was and come back for it later. He tried not to look back but couldn't. There seemed to be more soldiers on the street. Officers were shouting orders and a Police Jeep and a military Land Rover turned into the petrol station. Two men got out of the vehicle, one looked around and saw Nadesan.

Nadesan didn't wait a moment longer. He put his head down and disappeared round the bend. It was not more than fifteen minutes since the attack on the safe house had begun.

*

Nadesan crouched in the warehouse ceiling looking through the gap between the roofing tiles and the supporting wall. He fiddled with the locket around his neck nervously. There were Police and army personnel everywhere. His body was trembling with anxiety and fright. He'd been almost caught again. He took a sip of water from a bottle, letting the moisture trickle down his parched throat.

What should I do now? He was tired of running, tired of having to look over his shoulder. Tired of the endless checkpoints and questions. Tired of living on the edge. There was nowhere to run to anymore. Nadesan took stock of what he had. A little bit of money, a few clothes and nothing much else.

Nadesan reached into his pocket and pulled out the ID card and the money he had stuffed into his pocket. His face stared at him from the card but if the Police had learned the name he was using it would do him no good. He noticed a folded piece of paper with the rupee notes he had pulled out. He opened the crunched paper and smoothed it. He squinted at the small writing and read what was written. For a moment, he couldn't understand what it was, then he remembered. It was the piece of paper Deva had stuffed into his pocket the day he had picked up the explosives. It was the address of the Minister.

It was like a weight had been lifted from his shoulders. He had forgotten he had it. For a brief instance, he felt a sense of disappointment that it wasn't the general, but he shrugged it off. It would be a difficult to even get close to the officer.

Nadesan concentrated on what was needed. He had loaded the fully-fuelled three-wheeler with the explosives. The detonators were in the compartment. He fought a sense of panic when he realized that he would have to arm the bomb. Would I be able to do it? He tried to remember what Kumar had told him about the electronic detonator. He would have to buy a couple of batteries and it would have to be wired to a timing device. Too complicated. He would use the acid time fuses! Kumar had said to push one end into the explosive and twist the other end. That sounded easy enough.

The more he thought about it, the more he realized that he was running out of time. He had to assume that his identification was known by now and that it would be circulated to all the checkpoints and roadblocks in the city. The explosives hidden in the three-wheeler may be discovered, which would mean he couldn't complete his mission. He had to act right away, right now before it was too late.

CHAPTER FORTY

It was a chaotic scene when Chandra turned the Land Rover into the petrol station at the junction leading to the street where the safe house was raided. Tilak got out of the vehicle and looked around. There were dozens of heavily armed Police troopers, grouped into squads, being briefed by two officers. A man carrying a bag on his shoulder, stared at him from the back of the petrol station before disappearing around the corner.

The Superintendent spoke to the two officers and walked purposefully across the junction followed by an officer and a squad of armed Police troopers. Tilak and Chandra followed them turning into the street.

The row of narrow, dilapidated houses on each side of the street had common walls, the front door and window of each just an arm's length away from the road. The militant safe house was about a hundred and fifty metres away, easily identified by a group of heavily armed men dressed in ballistic vests and helmets standing outside. Men in plain clothes moved purposefully in and out of the building as the Superintendent marched up to the door.

'Where's the OIC,' he barked at one of the men. 'Find him and bring him here.'

People from neighbouring houses were huddled around their doorways looking onto the street. It looked like a mixed community of people which was common to the towns and villages along the coast. A few houses had Christian symbols over their doorway and one had a black, multi-armed statue of a Hindu God in a niche on the front wall. A Muslim family, distinct by the hijab the woman wore, peered out from a house a few doors down.

A man dressed in camouflaged green fatigues hurried out of the building. He walked over to the Superintendent and saluted. 'I am sorry sir, he said. 'I was not informed you were coming.'

The Superintendent waved at him dismissively. 'Never mind, Inspector,' he said impatiently. 'Did we get them all?

'There were two men in the house,' the Inspector said. 'They're both dead.' He shrugged his shoulders apologetically at the Superintendent. 'They both had weapons and my boys had to take them out.'

'So, the information we got was accurate,' the Superintendent smiled. 'It was the militant safe house.' The Superintendent pushed past him and entered the house. Chandra and Tilak followed the Inspector who hurried after the Superintendent.

The shattered front door lay to one side of the room. Two scorch marks from the exploding stun grenades were clearly visible on the concrete floor. The bodies of the two men were in a back room accessed by a corridor. A Russian AK-47, easily identified by its curved magazine lay next to one of the men. A Colt 45 pistol was the only other weapon Tilak could see in the room.

Tilak studied the two men. They were both dressed in ordinary clothes, one was older than the other. The bodies had been searched and the contents of their pockets heaped in a small pile next to them. A crushed cigarette packet, loose change, a few small denomination notes and what looked like a receipt. Tilak looked around the sparsely furnished room. A sleeping cot and an assortment of clothing occupied three corners. Two AK-47 rifles leant against one of the walls. On a wooden tea chest in the middle of the room, an oil lamp, its glass shattered in pieces, still smouldered. There was another room with a single cot and two boxes filled with grenades and ammunition piled in one corner. A kitchen at the back had a wooden cabinet and chest. A kerosene cooker sat on a low table next to a metal fuel can.

'There are four cots and only two men,' Chandra said looking at Tilak. 'It looks like we missed the other two.'

Tilak nodded looking around the room. Something didn't look right. The tea chest. It looked out of place. What was it doing here? He walked up to the square box and lifted the kerosene lamp, placing it on the floor. He lifted the wooden lid which was not fastened and looked inside. The tea chest was filled with loosely packed straw. He reached in and after rummaging around pulled out a portable, battery operated radio. Tilak placed it on the floor and reached in again, pulling out a square black box about the size of two packs of cigarettes.

'It's a VHS radio transmitter and detonator,' he said, turning the device in his hands. He had seen them being used before.

Tilak turned the tea chest over and dumped its contents on the floor. Other than the straw there was nothing else in it. 'The explosives would have been in here,' he shrugged. 'Perhaps it's hidden somewhere.'

Chandra shook his head. 'I don't think we'll find anything more. We'll have the place searched but whoever was here has taken them.'

The Superintendent had been listening to the two of them talk, his face getting dark with anger. He turned and stormed out of the room closely followed by the Inspector. He wouldn't be looking forward to reporting that they had missed two of the Tigers.

Tilak left Chandra talking to one of the men from the forensics team. He stepped onto the road looking up and down the street. The people on the street would not be going anywhere that day. They would all have to be questioned. He walked away from the house further into the housing estate. The whole row of houses stretching down the road as far as the old Dutch Canal looked the same.

As he turned he saw the Muslim woman he had noticed before gesturing for him to come over. The woman was middle aged. Deep creases lined her weather-beaten face. A blue cloth was pulled over her grey hair.

The woman looked up and down the road before leaning forward conspiratorially. 'There was a man who came to that house on Monday,' she said, 'in a three-wheeler. He came empty handed but left with a bag on his shoulder. He was in a big hurry.'

'What did he look like?' Tilak asked. 'Is he from around here?'

'I've seen him before,' she nodded. 'He came to this house once I think … before the rains,' she said. 'There were a number of them who come and go from there although I haven't seen the woman for a while. He wasn't staying here I think. Are they the terrorists everyone is searching for?'

Tilak nodded. 'Yes, they are. You said you've seen the man before. Where else have you seen him?'

The woman clutched at her hijab at a gust of wind that blew up the street. 'I've seen him working at the petrol station,' she said, 'on the main road.'

Tilak looked up the street and saw that Chandra had come out onto the road. He waved him over. 'This woman has seen a man driving a three-wheeler leave the house,' he said. 'He's not one of the normal occupants.'

'A three-wheeler,' Chandra said. 'Isn't there a yard full of three-wheelers at that petrol station we parked at?'

'She says he works there,' Tilak said. 'But we won't find him there.' Chandra looked at him strangely. 'When we drove up a little while ago, I saw a man carrying a bag on his shoulder leaving the station at the back. I only saw him for a moment but it must have been the man.'

'How many people lived there,' Tilak asked the woman.

'Only two, I think,' she said, looking nervously over her shoulder. 'There were two others, a man and a young woman but I have not seen them for a few weeks.'

Tilak looked at Chandra. 'We better pass that information on,' he said. 'Maybe there were only two of them staying here.'

Tilak thanked the woman for her help and after talking to the Inspector in Charge, walked with Chandra onto the main street. He was convinced they would not find the man who had driven the three-wheeler. He wouldn't be easy to find.

The search of the petrol station revealed nothing. The station owner confirmed that a man was living in the storeroom at the rear of the station and that he was a Muslim.

'I've seen his ID card,' he insisted. 'His name is Basheer. He's from Maligawatte.'

'What's his family name,' Chandra asked. He doubted that it was the man's real name but the Police could make enquiries to identify the source of the forged identification.

'Mahroof I think,' the station owner responded. 'I've got it written down somewhere. Let me get it for you.' He hurried off towards the station office.

Tilak walked to the rear of the property. Chandra came out of the storeroom. He shook his head. 'There's nothing there. It looks like he left in a hurry.'

Chandra studied the layout of the petrol station thoughtfully. On one side stood the pumps for both petrol and diesel. The silvery, above ground storage tanks stood next to each other at one corner of the yard. A building, it's bricks painted white held a small office on one side and an open garage with a hydraulic lift on the other. The storeroom at the back where the man had slept was neat and tidy. A small toilet with a wash basin and a squatting pan was the only other structure in the premises. To the left of the petrol station, a large open space was crammed with about fifty three-wheelers of different shapes and sizes. Some were dismantled and looked like they had been cannibalized for their parts.

'His name was Basheer Mahroof from Maligawatte.' The petrol station owner had followed Tilak to the rear of the station. 'He's a good mechanic. He cleaned and repaired all the three-wheelers for me. This is the one he used,' he said pointing to a well-maintained machine sitting next to the storeroom.

The three-wheeler that the man used had offered no clues. The Police would take the machine in and dust it for fingerprints but that would not help in the overall hunt for the bomber.

Tilak walked back to the Land Rover with Chandra. 'Ok, I've seen enough. Let's get back to HQ. I'll get the bomb squad to check all those three-wheelers. He may have hidden the explosives in that mess. That's what I would have done.'

Tilak stared across the sea of tin and board shanties, their roofs glistening in the early morning light. The view from the Kelaniya Bridge always reminded him of how crowded the city really was. Once a part of the flood plain of the Kelani Ganga, the Dutch had built canals and widened the mouth of the river to drain the swampy land. The land had quickly filled up with villagers who came from the interior to find jobs and get better education for their children.

The soldiers manning the roadblocks on either side of the bridge were alert as the Land Rover crawled along the congested lane that led up to the barrier. A quick glance at their credentials and they were waved through, accelerating down the slope into a wide boulevard leading towards the city. Tilak had offered to drive. He felt tired, not having slept at all, but he was alert, his mind going over what had happened that morning.

It was proving very hard to catch this bomber. The man was responsible for the central bus station bombing that had killed over a hundred people. And he had been linked to the Maradana bomb blast through the terrorist cell he was operating in. He had almost been caught in the raid at a safe house in Grandpass and now he was on the run again.

What was frustrating was that although they had a good description of the man, they did not know his real name and what his target was. He had to give the bomber kudos for impersonating a Muslim and living away from the safe house. The man was obviously intelligent and would be difficult to find.

The commander was not so impressed. His lips were a thin slash, his eyes pinched and red with repressed anger. 'How the hell did you manage to let him get away?' he asked incredulously. He spoke with deliberate purpose, like a boxer throwing punches. 'I just can't believe it. He will go to ground again until he is ready.'

'We have his name and description and we know how he plans to approach his target,' Tilak said, not letting the officer get on his high horse. 'That's more than we had this morning.'

'Yes, you do have that,' the commander conceded reluctantly. 'But this red alert will have to be lifted soon. It's crippling the city and the government. I predict they'll lift it before tomorrow morning which means we're back to square one.'

Tilak shrugged. It was not within his control. 'I am not sure what more we can do at the moment,' he said. 'The name he is using and his description is being circulated and if he attempts to come into the city he'll be caught.'

The commander strode to the map on his wall. 'He'll be hiding somewhere in this area,' he said, drawing a circle from the Kelani Ganga to the international airport in Katunayake. 'We'll have to lockdown this area and find him.'

'Not so easy to do,' Tilak said. 'There are fishing hamlets all along that coastline. They don't like the Police or the army coming in to their areas. I lived in one for over two years and I know how they think. If you want their help, you'll have to talk to each of the local crime bosses. They usually know what's going on in their area.'

The commander looked at Tilak thoughtfully. 'Hmm, I forgot that your family have a business in the area. I'll raise it at the JOC briefing this evening. In the meantime, an urgent assignment has come up,' he said. 'Security has been increased for all the VIPs and I want you both back at the Ministers house right away.'

Tilak looked at the commander incredulously. 'You want us to go back and play nursemaid again? Can't you give us something more important to do? There's a bomber on the loose.'

The commander inspected him, his look as intent as a cobra eyeing his prey. 'This is important. There's a red alert for a man driving a three-wheeler filled with explosives. They don't know what his target is so everyone is getting their protection detail doubled. We are running out of men so there's no choice. One good thing is that everyone on the A-list has been told to remain indoors and not move around the city. The President has enforced the request so it will be followed. The Minister will remain at his home with his family.'

Tilak had a dozen responses but remained silent. The commander had never looked more serious, or more tightly focused.

Tilak left the building with Chandra. 'I can't believe they are doing this to us,' he muttered getting into the Land Rover. But at least he could keep his dinner date with Amanthi on Friday.

The Minister for National Security lived in the affluent suburb of Cinnamon Gardens and they arrived at the laneway leading off the main road within a few minutes.

Tilak had been here many times before. He'd always believed that it would be very difficult to target the Minister's home. The surprisingly modest house the Minister lived in was located behind the family ancestral home which fronted the road. The old colonial villa looked neglected, it's front garden full of overgrown bushes and enormous trees which shaded the house from the rays of the sun. Clearly the Minister's father still occupied the property and the old man refused to have anything done on it, preferring to live alone and in the past.

The Minister's house could only be approached down a laneway which ran beside the family property. The entrance to the lane was guarded by two armed soldiers and Tilak knew another two were stationed at the end of the lane at the entrance to the Minister's home. The lane was blocked by two red and white striped oil barrels filled with sand allowing only pedestrian access.

Chandra parked their vehicle across the road from the laneway and they crossed the busy one-way street filled with vehicles of all types. Tilak waved his credentials at the two young soldiers who were watching them approach.

'We're from Special Branch,' he said to the nervous soldiers. 'We've been assigned to the Minister and will be hanging around out here for a while. Just do your jobs and ignore us.'

Tilak left Chandra with the soldiers and walked down the lane to the Minister's house. He introduced himself to the man in charge of the protection detail who seemed relieved to see Tilak.

'It's good you're here,' he said. 'We've not been able to move from our positions since the red alert was issued this morning. I'll be able to rotate my men now.' He looked behind him hearing voices. The Minister and his family were out in the garden sitting under a tree having lunch. 'The Minister's wife has organized lunch for everyone. We'll wait until the family has eaten.'

CHAPTER FORTY-ONE

People had come out from their homes after sunrise, clustering around the Police barricades and peering down the street towards the safe house.

Nadesan watched the petrol station owner talking to a group of three-wheel drivers. He wished he could hear what was being said but couldn't risk being spotted by the station owner. The three-wheel drivers were obviously angry, waving their hands in the air. Some were even wagging their fingers in the owner's face. A group of them broke away and walked to the tea stand at the corner. Nadesan followed them, his head down hoping that they would not notice him.

Nadesan could hear snatches of conversation over the sound of the growing traffic. '... checking them would take all day.' '... waiting for the bomb squad ...' 'They will release them one by one ...'

He had heard enough. Nadesan hurried back towards the petrol station. He needed to get to the three-wheeler with the explosives. It was hidden amongst a bunch of old three-wheelers at the back of the property near the wall, behind the two front rows of machines that were rented out every day. But he needed to be careful. The station owner would hear the vehicle being started. He had no choice but to push the heavy machine out.

Nadesan waited until the station owner went into his office and closed the door. One by one the crowd of drivers left the station yard until it was almost empty. Nadesan darted past the storeroom he slept in and walked behind the outhouse, along the fence to the last row of vehicles. He could not see the front of the yard so he knew that he would be out of sight to anyone looking in his direction.

The three-wheeler almost fell over when Nadesan pushed it off its stand. Gripping the handlebars tightly, Nadesan negotiated the narrow space, having to stop twice to move other three-wheelers out of the way so that he could get through. Sweat poured off him in streams as the effort of pushing the heavy machine started to wear him down. He concentrated hard on what he was doing, pushing everything else from his mind.

Finally, he was on the street. He pushed the vehicle along the pavement, ignoring the curses directed at him by pedestrians trying to squeeze past. When he was a few doors away from the petrol station he got into the machine and started it. The four-stroke engine purred into life. Nadesan drove off the pavement onto the road, immediately getting off the main road and turning towards the beach where a labyrinth of narrow lanes and sandy tracks used by the fishing communities along the coast would buy him time to think.

It was clear to Nadesan that he needed to abandon the three-wheeler. They would not let one into the city without it being properly searched. And if they did he had no doubt they would find the explosives under the driver's seat.

That left him with only two options. Forget the whole idea and try and live a normal life. But what was a normal life without his wife and child? The thought of giving up filled him with despair. Everything he had endured over the past few months was for nothing. And he had not avenged the deaths of his beautiful wife and son.

No, I only have one option, he thought.

Nadesan had parked the three-wheeler in a grove of coconut trees behind an abandoned building not more than a hundred paces from the beach. He dragged a number of fallen branches over the vehicle which hid it from the path that wound through the trees. It would be discovered if someone came into the coconut grove but for the moment he felt safe.

The package of explosives was rectangular and flat, just two fingers wide. It weighed about two kilos. Nadesan tore his spare sarong into long strips of cloth. He took off his shirt. He was bare bodied, his dark brown skin glistening with sweat. He pressed the package of explosives onto his stomach, pushing the edges in so they curved slightly. He tied the package tightly to his body using three of the long strips of cloth.

Nadesan put his shirt back on and buttoned the front, looking down at himself. The package fitting perfectly over his flat stomach. The shirt bulged slightly making him look slightly overweight. He could move his arms quite freely. He adjusted one of the cloth straps that was biting into his skin and walked around the vehicle making sure that the package would not move. Smiling to himself, he picked up two of the acid time fuses which had the number two on them. He pushed them into the explosives, one on either side of his body. All it required was to twist the top of one of the aluminium tubes and the bomb was armed and would detonate in two minutes. He was ready.

The sound of voices from the beach galvanized him into action. Without even looking back, Nadesan walked through the coconut grove to the lane which wound its way through the fishing village. There were people moving around but no one spared him a second glance. He was just another anonymous face walking through the village.

Nadesan's confidence grew as he crossed the old Dutch Canal with its fleet of fishing boats. The fishermen used the canal as a harbor to anchor their boats during the day. The entrance to the canal was at the mouth of the Kelani Ganga which gave them easy access to the sea.

The main road was congested with traffic, the Police and military presence still very much in evidence. Every three-wheeler was being stopped and searched much to the annoyance of the drivers. One of the drivers was angry and his voice could clearly be heard over the traffic.

'This is the fifth time I've been stopped and searched,' he yelled at the policeman who had signalled him to stop. 'How can I make any money to feed my family.'

Nadesan was glad that he was not driving the three-wheeler. He started walking towards the city, blending into the crowd. He would look for a bus to take him into the city, to the place where his target lived.

The government-run bus looked crowded. All the seats were taken, the people at the windows hanging their heads and arms out to catch some fresh air. A young man with a sheaf of folded currency wrapped around his middle finger, stood near the door issuing tickets. He shouted at the commuters standing on the centre aisle to move back towards the rear of the bus. Those getting on the bus pushed forward until those on the bus were gradually pushed back until they could go no further.

Nadesan was very conscious of the explosives strapped to his body. He tried to protect the package as much as he could, with both his arms, but eventually had to give up when he found that he was wedged between two people in the middle of the bus, unable to move.

The bus approached the new Kelani bridge leading into the city. The traffic moved forward at a snail's pace in the mounting heat. The bus finally stopped at the checkpoint. An armed soldier with sweat stains under his arm reached up and took the papers the driver handed down to him. Other soldiers walked along the sides of the bus, examining the passengers through the grimy windows. No attempt was made to ask the passengers to get out.

Nadesan breathed a sigh of relief when the bus jolted forward once again passing the tall smoke stacks of the Kelanitissa power station on the south bank of the river belching heated steam a hundred metres into the air. He had caught the 104 bus from Wattala to Bambalapitiya which would take him through the heart of the city. He would get out opposite the Thurstan College cricket grounds and walk the rest of the way.

The bus partially emptied as it drove down Baseline road which split the city in two. He was familiar with where he was going, having dropped and picked up passengers from the Colombo university campus and the many colleges and schools in the area.

As he approached the bus stop, Nadesan felt a sense of peace. The thought of being captured still terrified him but he knew that he would not let himself fail again. He would finally complete what he had set out to do so many months ago.

*

Nadesan walked down Flower Road feeling out of place. The road was filled with chauffeur-driven cars and the women on the streets were dressed in expensive clothes which his family would have only dreamt of owning. He had driven hundreds of times down this road in his three-wheeler but felt exposed and vulnerable walking on the street.

For a moment, he felt that he was being followed but it was much subtler than that. It was a feeling, a sense that he was being looked at that making the hairs stand up at the back of his neck. The feeling was so strong that he turned and looked behind him but didn't see anyone following him.

Nadesan's stomach was churning. The opening to a narrow alley next to a busy three-story building on the opposite side of the street gave him an idea. He remembered what he'd been taught about being followed and shaking a tail and suddenly dashed across the road, avoiding an oncoming SUV and a taxi who had to slow down at his sudden appearance. The taxi driver tooted his horn and yelled something at him out of his open window. Nadesan ignored him and disappeared into the narrow-cobbled alley lined with garbage bins. Concrete walls towered on both sides only broken by entranceways shuttered tightly with steel lined doors.

Nadesan quivered in surprise when a door clanged open. A bare-bodied, dark skinned man in his twenties, dressed in shorts and an apron, carrying a black plastic bag in both hands appeared in the doorway. The man's eyes widened when he made eye contact with Nadesan and his mouth opened a fraction, but then he clamped it shut and threw the bag into an open garbage bin before hurrying back into the building.

Nadesan walked deeper into the alley and looked around carefully to see whether he was being followed. The street he'd left was busy but there was no sign of anyone. He was starting to wonder if he had imagined it. The alley opened out at the end to a dusty vacant lot with a huge mango tree in the corner. It dominated the whole space. Three shiny new cars were parked under its spreading branches, next to an entranceway barely visible on the other side. He walked across the open space resisting the urge to look over his shoulder. The wide entrance to the lot led to a narrow lane which emptied to a side street. Nadesan hurried down to the corner, losing himself in a crowd of teenage school children standing at a bus stop. The teenagers, all dressed in white uniforms, ignored Nadesan as he rushed past them, his head down not wanting to catch anyone's eyes.

*

Nadesan was confused. He chewed the inside of his lip as he contemplated the location. The address on the note was a rundown colonial building set back from the road. The building old and neglected. A driveway, accessed by two closed gates, curved in a semi-circle under the colonnaded front porch which was partly obscured by overgrown bushes. Dark streaks of water stains and oily grime ran down its once whitewashed walls. It didn't rate a second glance but it was the target he'd been given.

The morning congestion was well underway. The traffic was thick with sleek modern cars sharing the road with busses, lorries and the ever-present three-wheelers. Office workers and school children skipped nimbly across the busy road courting death with every step they took.

Horns blared as a police car, it's lights flashing, followed by a large, black Pajero, cut across two lanes of traffic and turned towards a narrow laneway next to the property. The police car pulled up next to the lane and stopped, allowing the Pajero to slow down and enter the laneway. About ten metres down the lane, two barrels blocked access to the narrow entrance. Out from the shadow of the bushes a soldier stepped into view. He was dressed in fatigues which made him difficult to spot. The soldier turned and spoke to someone Nadesan couldn't see, then stepped out and moved aside one of the barrels.

Nadesan realized that the target must be someone important and lived down the laneway. The soldier he saw was dressed in army fatigues, like those he had seen in Batticaloa. If his target was being protected by the Special Task Force it would make it very difficult.

The laneway was hemmed in with overhanging branches from the surrounding trees and bushes and from where Nadesan was standing he couldn't see much down the narrow space. Nadesan tried to appear casual. He didn't want to draw any attention to himself by trying to cross the road in front of the watchful soldier.

Nadesan was gloomy and sullen. He drew a deep breath. He didn't know how to overcome this latest challenge. How would he be able to get past the guards? Then he remembered the black Pajero. It had tinted windows which had prevented him from looking inside. Was the person he was supposed to kill in the vehicle? It would be much easier to blow it up rather than try and get past the guards. The Pajero had slowed down almost opposite him and there would be enough time to throw himself at the vehicle and set off the bomb. But how did he know whether the person he was supposed to kill was in it? What if his family was with him?

Nadesan looked around cautiously. There were many people going about their business but no one paid any attention to him. A woman wearing a sari and carrying a child in her arms, brushed past him unexpectedly, intent on crossing the road. Nadesan glanced at her uneasily. He needed to think this through so he continued to walk up the road towards a junction ahead of him. He turned right at the junction and walked towards Viharamahadevi Park. He sometimes parked his three-wheeler at its entrance and lay on the grass. The park named after a famous Sinhalese queen, was the largest park in the city and was always full of people. He would try and find a place to hide amongst its many trees and bushes and come back to his target in the morning.

CHAPTER FORTY-TWO

Tilak was feeling slightly apprehensive, but at the same time elated. He had just spoken to Amanthi on the phone. Although the call was brief, he could sense that she was worried about him and that made him feel good.

They had been at the Minister's house since noon and Tilak's eyes were beginning to droop in the heat. The Ford was parked under a large flame tree which shaded it from the hot afternoon sun but it did nothing to keep the hot humid air from spilling into the vehicle.

Chandra had stepped out onto the pavement and leant against the side of the vehicle. A police siren sounded and he turned to watch the driver skilfully manoeuvre his vehicle through the light traffic. The normal rush when parents picked up their kids from school had died down and the momentary lull was only a precursor to the evening rush hour which was just around the corner.

The lights turned to red and motorbikes maneuverered their way to the front of the traffic, revving their engines, impatient for the light to change. People cut across the pedestrian crossing, intent on getting to the other side before the light changed. All around, Mercedes and BMWs with their tinted windows, children from wealthy families' safe inside, being driven home after school. Tilak studied the pedestrians through the dancing heat as they moved purposefully on the pavements. They had been warned by the head of the protection detail that a three-wheeler had been found, abandoned and empty, and that the bomber was probably on foot.

Chandra leaned in through the open window. 'I am going to use the toilet,' he said. 'Do you want anything to drink?'

Tilak shook his head. 'No, thanks. I'm fine.' He watched as Chandra crossed the road, nimbly avoiding a delivery man riding a motor cycle.

Four teenage school girls in white uniforms from the girls' school just up the road, walked past giggling and looking over their shoulder at three young teenage boys also dressed in white, calling out to them. Tilak smiled, remembering his days at Royal College less than a kilometre up the road. The three boys were probably from his old alma mater doing what he'd done to the girls from Ladies College those many years ago.

His eyes narrowed as he saw a man stepping purposefully towards the vehicle. The man's attention was focused across the street at the old colonial home partly obscured from the road by overgrown bushes and the low hanging branches. There was something about him that did not look right.

Tilak watched attentively as he slowed and walked past, staring intently at the property across the street. The man did not notice Tilak sitting in the car. Ordinarily Tilak would not have paid any attention to the man. He looked just like anyone you would find in the city suburbs but he looked out of place in this affluent neighbourhood. Why was he here?

The man was dark skinned, in his mid-thirties. He was wearing a crumpled white shirt which stretched across his belly. His sarong was tied low around his hips and he was not wearing anything on his feet. Tilak had caught a glimpse of the man at the petrol station but he was thin. Not like this man.

Tilak kept watching him as he wandered down the street and disappeared. He wished that Chandra was with him so that they could have questioned the man. But he was not carrying anything and didn't look like a threat. But Tilak still felt uneasy. The man looked rough, he had the air of a criminal about him. Tilak had seen enough of them in prison not to recognize it. Chandra walked across the road back to the car. Tilak opened the door and joined him on the pavement, looking up the road towards where the man had disappeared.

'What's wrong,' Chandra asked, alerted by Tilak's tense posture.

Tilak glanced at Chandra and stared back up the road. 'There was this man who walked past just a few minutes ago,' he said. 'He didn't look right. He was very interested in the house although he was not carrying anything.'

'Do you think he's the man we are looking for?' Chandra asked.

Tilak shook his head. 'I'm not sure. He could be scoping out the place and will come back tonight. I don't know. I saw someone at the petrol station but it wasn't the same man.'

'What did he look like,' Chandra asked.

'The man at the petrol station carried a bag,' he said. 'And was quite slim. The man I just saw was not carrying anything and had a big belly. It wasn't the same man.'

Chandra's eyes narrowed. 'Are you sure?' he asked Tilak. 'We have heard reports of people being trained as suicide bombers. Could he have been wearing an explosive device on his body which made him look fat?'

Tilak tried hard to create an image of the man he saw in his mind. He had been wearing a shirt which was too tight for him. Could it be a bomb?

'I'm not sure,' he said finally. 'But it's possible, I guess. The only way to make sure is to find him.'

'Yeah,' Chandra nodded. 'What did he look like?' Tilak described the man to him.

'He should be easy to spot. You better warn the guards and the protection detail. I'll wander down the road and keep my eyes open.'

Chandra strode rapidly in the direction the man had gone.

Tilak felt devastated. Had he let the bomber get away from under his nose? Tilak crossed the road on which traffic was steadily increasing as the evening rush hour drew near. He warned the two soldiers on duty and hurried down the laneway to report to the head of the protection detail.

The plain clothed officer did not hesitate when hearing what Tilak said. He reached for the radio transmitter on his hip.

'Possible sighting of the bomber on Flower Road,' he snapped. The communication device had a wire running into an earpiece. A microphone was attached to his lapel. 'Activate Plan B.'

There was a burst of activity as the officer directed his men to secure the Minister and his family and called in a possible sighting of the bomber. He listened and turned to Tilak.

'They're sending help,' he said. 'I'll remain here. See if you can find him.'

Tilak nodded and ran back up the laneway to the main road. The evening had suddenly got more interesting.

*

The response to the sighting had been swift. Flower Road had been blocked off by two army trucks at each end while heavily armed soldiers directed the rush hour traffic away from the minister's home. Rush hour commuters, plainly angry by the closure of a major road leading out of the city, blew their horns and argued with the soldiers to let them through.

A group of plain clothes and security force officers gathered around a police car blocking the entrance to the laneway. A detailed map of the surrounding area was spread open on the car bonnet. It showed every road, every property, every building, storm drain and culvert for a square kilometre. Orders were being barked into hand-held radios directing armed squads to seal off roads, while reinforcements were being requested to begin a house to house search of the area.

Tilak studied the map on the bonnet of the car, wondering what he would be doing if he was the bomber. If he was on foot, he would try to find a place to hide. He'd feel exposed walking on the street. But where?

On the map, the green expanse of the large park a few hundred metres away attracted his attention. I would go there, he thought to himself. He would hide in the bushes and try and approach the target again. Either in the night or in the morning.

'What are you thinking?' Chandra asked. He'd been talking to the search coordinator whose name was Silva.

'If I were in his shoes, I'd be hiding here,' Tilak said, tapping the map. 'There are a lot of places to hide in the park and no one goes there after dark.'

Chandra nodded thoughtfully. 'Yes, I agree. We'll throw up a cordon 'round the area and search it.' He turned to Silva. 'We think he may be hiding in the park. We need to surround the park with men and search it thoroughly. We'll need more men to do that. Whom do we have to talk to?'

Tilak left the group of men who were poring over the map. He wondered what was driving the bomber to push himself so hard. He had met people before, who, like the bomber, would go to extremes to fight for a cause or redress some form of injustice to themselves or their loved ones. He wondered if it was the case here.

Chandra walked up to him. 'They're organizing for the park to be cordoned off. It's going to take a little while to get the units in position. I want to leave the vehicle here and walk over there. You okay with that?' Tilak nodded.

It was getting dark when they reached the park boundary. Roads around the park had been blocked off causing chaos in the city. Vehicles diverted down secondary roads and lanes moved at a snail's pace and the discordant sound of irate drivers sitting on their car horns drowned out any other noise.

The stone pillar of the Cenotaph War Memorial anchored one corner of the urban park. Built by the British to honor both the Sri Lankan and European servicemen living in Ceylon who died in the two world wars, the tall stone monolith dwarfed the surrounding trees, its carved stone crown gleaming in the rays of the setting sun. To the right of the Cenotaph was the Public Library, it's dark modern architecture in stark contrast to the rest of the buildings surrounding the perimeter of the park.

Tilak and Chandra walked along the wide pavement, looking into the park through the steel fence that surrounded it. There were people in the park, couples wandering around or sitting on the grass with their heads close together. Others striding purposefully across the open spaces using the park as a short cut to get to the other side.

Large trees and clumps of flowering plants and bushes restricted their view of the centre of the park which was getting difficult to see in the gathering darkness.

CHAPTER FORTY-THREE

The flashing blue of the police lights cut a path through the deserted roads passing junctions manned by heavily armed soldiers. The city had been in lockdown for almost forty-eight hours while the security forces searched for a bomber who had managed to evade capture during a special branch raid on a safe house.

That much Amanthi had been able to glean from her conversation with Dr Perera. The head of the burn unit was well connected and usually had her finger on the pulse. She had insisted on the police escort when the emergency response ambulance was requested at the park.

'Don't take any chances,' she warned Amanthi. 'The man they are looking for is the one who caused the central bus station bombing. He has proven very difficult to catch. I really don't want to send you out but the minister insisted.'

Dark clouds built up over the city and the wind picked up. Back in the ambulance, Amanthi huddled on the front seat looking out. They had parked near Viharamahadevi Park where it would be easy to respond to an emergency anywhere in the city.

Amanthi stared morosely out of the window, wondering what was happening to her life. The endless round of bombing and emergencies were beginning to take a toll. She wondered how Dr Perera was able to handle the stress of working on burnt and battered bodies and the long work hours without seemingly being affected.

Rain had swept down the open boulevard earlier, beating down with a heavy drumming noise on the roof of the ambulance.

Amanthi was grateful having met Tilak but she realized that their relationship was fraught with danger and could end at any time. He was a soldier fighting a secret war and anything could happen to him. She shuddered at the thought of him being caught up in the violence and being hurt, or even worse. She wondered whether she'd done the right thing by asking him not to see her. She didn't want to think about it.

The ambulance was hot and stuffy, the late evening sun shining directly into her face as it dipped behind the buildings in front of her. Amanthi opened the door and got out, stretching her legs. She felt hungry and reached into the vehicle, pulling out a newspaper wrapped parcel. Nelum had walked down into the park and bought some food from a food vendor many hours ago. Amanthi had not been hungry then and had put aside the parcel. She was ready to eat it now.

The road still steamed from the passing tropical shower, the air feeling humid and sticky as Amanthi walked to a bench under a street lamp. It was situated next to a large sign showing directions to various parts of the museum enclosure where a few large artefacts, that could not be stored in the imposing museum building, were scattered among the trees. The bench was well shaded from the setting sun by a clump of large bushes.

The most wonderful odor, spicy and rich with the promise of curried meat arose when she opened the parcel of food. She felt her mouth fill with moisture as she placed the package on her lap and took a spoonful of the aromatic mixture. The parcel which had been baking in the sun in the ambulance, was warm and tasted wonderful. She didn't realize how hungry she was as she ate every morsel in the food parcel, sighing with pleasure.

After throwing the remnants of the parcel into a refuse bin, Amanthi rinsed her mouth, bending over a garden tap that was used to water the lush property. She straightened, stretching her back to work out the kinks and pulled out a cigarette from her coat pocket which she lit with great relish.

The sun was setting fast and long shadows stretched across the boulevard where the ambulance was parked. The rear doors to the vehicle were open letting fresh air in.

CHAPTER FORTY-FOUR

Sore and aching, Nadesan hid behind the balustraded staircase looking out into the extensive gardens. A large banyan tree obscured his view of the road opposite the building.

The open park had made him nervous. The trees and bushes were trimmed back and sparse, not providing any concealment. The popular park normally filled with couples sitting together was almost empty. Nadesan relieved himself in the public toilet, washing his hands and feet in a tap outside the building. The owner of a food cart next to a children's playground was packing up for the night and was glad to sell the remaining food in his cart to Nadesan for half the price.

Nadesan walked outside the park. Across the wide boulevard was the Colombo museum. He had often dropped off and picked up tourists who visited the place. Once he was asked to wait and he had wandered around the sprawling, two-storey, colonial building with its wide-open balconies. It was the ideal place to spend the night. He could easily hide in the museum's many nooks and crannies. No one came to the building at night and he could easily avoid the watchman who wandered through its external corridors in the late evening, reminding visitors that the building was closing for the night.

He had just crossed the road when he heard the sound of heavy vehicles. He felt a clawing fear in his guts as he watched a military truck turn into the boulevard and stop, disgorging over a dozen armed soldiers. Nadesan retreated further back into the bushes. More military vehicles turned in blocking off both ends of the wide avenue. The boulevard quickly filled up with policemen and heavily armed soldiers. Their attention focused in the park.

All the activity made him very nervous. They must be looking for him? But how did they know where he was? If they spotted him he wouldn't have a chance to escape.

Nadesan looked around. Large trees dominated the area he was in. Thoughts skipped through his mind. He didn't know what to do. He felt exposed. He knew he didn't have long before someone spotted him.

An ambulance parked on the road between the museum and the park caught his attention. A woman dressed in a white coat stood next to a large sign near the vehicle, smoking a cigarette. Her attention was focused on the activity across the street. The roar of truck engines increased, as more and more vehicles disgorged dozens of armed men in combat fatigues. Officers shouted commands and the soldiers started to cordon off the area.

Nadesan felt physically sick. He had come this far and it was all going to end. He closed his eyes. An image of his wife and son lying lifeless at the bus stand entered his mind. His breath choked and tears came into his eyes. He was going to let them down again. He was not with them when they died, and here he was, unable to avenge their deaths.

Nadesan shook himself, rubbing his eyes with the back of his hand. He took a deep breath. The image of his family had given him what he lacked … some courage. He would not face them like this. He would avenge them before he died.

The ambulance gave him an idea. He had to get out of sight. He'd use it to get away from here.

Nadesan closed on the woman through the bushes. Her attention was still focused on the activity in front of her. He took the last few steps quickly, clutching her arm. With his other hand, he grabbed the woman's hair, yanking her head back.

CHAPTER FORTY-FIVE

Amanthi blew out a stream of smoke and watched as the smoke drifted to the stars. What a beautiful night it was. The clouds danced playfully in front of the moon causing shadows across the road. The muted hum of traffic added a familiar backdrop to the evening.

A disturbance at the beginning of the boulevard next to the cenotaph caught her attention. A police jeep followed by a military truck was disgorging heavily armed soldiers, some of whom walked across the busy intersection stopping traffic. At the opposite end of the boulevard, Amanthi could see more military vehicles and soon the area was full of heavily armed police and soldiers dressed in combat fatigues.

Something was wrong. Amanthi could sense it when people behaved in a certain way and these many soldiers had to mean something was seriously wrong. She bent and stubbed the half-smoked cigarette on the ground, placing the stub in the cigarette carton she carried in her pocket. She straightened her back, working the kinks out with her fingers when she sensed something behind her. Before she could turn she felt herself being grabbed, her head yanked back violently. The sudden attack took her completely by surprise. Her breath caught in her throat, she whimpered in shock.

A man's face appeared just inches from hers. He was dark and unshaven, smelling of stale sweat. His eyes were cold and hard. He looked into her eyes.

'Don't speak, don't move, don't do anything unless I say so. I am carrying a bomb and will kill you if you don't listen to me.' The man yanked her hair hard to make sure she understood.

Amanthi nodded. The sudden shock of being attacked had made her speechless. Her breath caught in her throat and her heart pounded against her ribcage.

The man's eyes flickered away from her looking over her shoulder. She felt his grip tighten as he lowered his body, pulling her down with him. They stayed like that for a moment and she felt herself being dragged backwards into the bushes.

'You're hurting me,' she whimpered. The pain in her head from her hair being pulled brought tears to her eyes.

'Shhh, keep quiet,' the man snarled, twisting her head so he could look into her face. Amanthi could see a look of intensity, almost of terror in his eyes.

The grip on her hair loosened. 'Listen to me. I am not going to hurt you. I just want to get away from them.'

She began to shake, her legs felt weak she could hardly stand. Terrified as she was, Amanthi managed to nod her head. The man pushed her to her knees and crouched next to her. In the gathering twilight, they would not easily be seen.

The man who was dressed in a white shirt and sarong, peered through the leaves across the wide boulevard. The area across the street was swarming with men, their attention focused into the park. None of them were looking their way.

Amanthi felt the man relax his grip on her hair. 'Who are you?' the man demanded. 'What are you doing here?'

Amanthi's mouth had dried up. She felt light-headed. She swallowed before answering. 'I am from the general hospital,' she croaked. '... the emergency response unit.'

'Are you a doctor?' the man demanded.

Amanthi nodded without saying anything. The man stared at her. His eyes glinted with intelligence and purpose.

Amanthi 's hands were still shaking, but the initial shock at being attacked was wearing off. She could feel the tension as the adrenaline began pumping around her body. She tried to control her breathing. She needed to be calm, to think.

Amanthi closed her eyes trying to focus. Often when she worked on a badly burned victim, the extent of the burns and wounds the patient was suffering would almost overwhelm her. She had learned over time to control the emotional side of her consciousness, to shut everything out and focus on the job she was doing.

Amanthi felt a sense of foreboding. Was this the bomber everyone was looking for? The thought came unbidden into her mind. What did he want with her?

The man's grip tightened as a series of loud commands drifted across the wide boulevard. Darkness had come quickly as it did in this part of the world. Dull yellow light from the streetlamps barely penetrated the inky blackness that surrounded them. They would not be seen in the bushes unless someone shone a spotlight on them.

Waves of panic engulfed her. She wondered whether Tilak was anywhere close. But how would he find out? No one knew that she had been grabbed by the bomber. She studied the man from the corner of her eye. It was difficult to say but he looked like he was in his thirties. He wore a dirty sarong and a shirt that was tight across his body. A plastic bag dangled from his left wrist.

If he was the bomber, where was the bomb?

Amanthi could hear the blood pounding in her ears as she suddenly realized that the man must be wearing it on his body.

She had felt something pressing against her lower back and had thought it was the man's belly. If she could break free from his grasp, she might be able to put enough of space between them not to be affected by the blast.

Would he blow himself up in the middle of the park? What good would that do?

Amanthi wanted to understand the motivation behind the man's actions. In her experience of dealing with people who tried to kill themselves, she had come to realize that many of them were driven by anger and hopelessness.

Maybe if she could get him to talk about what drove him to take such an extreme measure she could persuade him to let her go.

'Why are you doing this?' Amanthi asked him in Tamil. The man stared at Amanthi. 'You speak Tamil!'

'Yes,' Amanthi said. 'My mothers' from south India.'

The man shook his head and looked away from her. Amanthi felt she had won a small victory when she felt him release her hair.

'Don't do anything stupid,' he said, gripping her arm tightly.

Amanthi took a few deep breaths, filling her lungs with oxygen. As her strength returned, her courage did too. Amanthi stared at the man. He looked like a wounded man or someone who had undergone some terrible suffering. His brows were knitted, his lips compressed, his eyes feverish. There was a restlessness in his movements but he did not look to her as a threat. He was agitated about something but he didn't have an air of violence about him. During her time at the general hospital she had seen enough of men, and women, for whom violence was second nature. It showed on their faces and by their actions. This man didn't! He looked more like … like a miserable but ordinary person.

She felt strangely calm. 'What's your name?' she asked. Her throat was so dry that the words came out harsh and croaky.

'What?' the man hadn't understood what Amanthi had asked. He stared at her for a moment before scanning the surrounding park.

'What's your name?' she repeated. 'My name's Amanthi,'

The man glared at Amanthi, his fingers digging into her skin. 'Do you always ask so many questions?'

Amanthi swallowed hard but was relieved that the man was engaging with her. It was important to get him talking, she knew. She had trained as a psychiatrist as part of her medical training and he was a troubled person. Once they began communicating she'd be able to calm him down. 'I am a doctor,' she shrugged. 'We are trained to ask questions.'

The man shook his head in irritation and continued to look through the bushes at the activity on the street. The light from the streetlamp cast a glow across his face.

'Tell me what happened to you?' she persisted. 'Did you lose someone?'

The man took a sharp intake of breath, staring at her in surprise. 'How did you know?' The answer came out involuntarily and he looked annoyed at himself. He compressed his lips in a thin line. 'What do you care?' he said looking at her angrily. 'You're just one of them.'

'I am not,' Amanthi said emphatically. 'Would I look after people who are burned if I am?' Shaking her head with conviction she pressed. 'You may not think so, but I'm just like you; someone trying to survive in a crazy, mixed up world. As a doctor, I must deal with the consequences of your actions. Men, women, children … you think that's an easy thing?'

Amanthi had been in many situations where distraught friends and relatives of burn victims needed to be calmed and thinking rationally for her to get information about what had happened. She decided she'd used the same tactic on this man.

'Tell me why you're doing this.'

The man closed his eyes for a moment, his face grimacing as he relived some painful memory.

'They killed my wife and son,' he said, tears filling his eyes. 'He was only five years old.' The raw emotion in his voice shocked Amanthi.

'Who killed them?' Amanthi asked gently. She could see that the man was devastated about what had happened.

'The army,' he said angrily. 'They opened fire on the street.'

Amanthi shook her head in disbelief. 'That's terrible,' she said, quietly. She was beginning to understand what drove this man.

'They were innocent … they were innocent,' the man's face crumpled as he lowered his head and sobbed.

Amanthi felt a sense of sympathy for the man, but it was tempered by the knowledge that he had already killed many people and could do so again. She doubted that he had ever spoken to anyone about his suffering and being so consumed with grief had lost all sense of compassion.

'So, you're going to kill others' wives and children in revenge?' she asked. 'How can that be the answer?'

The man flinched as if being struck and bent his head in despair. 'I don't want to live anymore,' he said. 'And I don't know what to do.'

'What's that going to achieve?' she asked. 'I have seen people burn themselves terribly because at the time they were consumed with anger or with grief. While I can understand what drove them to doing it, what I cannot understand is what they have achieved. Only more suffering and a life of humiliation and pain.'

'Why don't you give yourself up?' she asked. 'You seem like a decent man. I am sure you don't want to kill more innocent people.'

'No,' he said vehemently, shaking his head. 'I won't allow myself to be captured and tortured. I'd rather kill myself.'

Amanthi recoiled in surprise at the intensity of the man's response. It came as a horrific realization to her that he had decided his fate long ago and that he was not going to change his mind. She stared at the man as she pondered her next move. Help was just across the street but how was she going to be able to break free of his grasp.

The man suddenly stiffened, inhaling sharply through his teeth. He tightened his grip, moving back further into the bushes and pulling Amanthi with him. Amanthi wondered what had spooked him and twisted her head to look in the direction he was staring. Through the leaves, Amanthi watched as two soldiers sauntered up to the ambulance. They were dressed in combat fatigues and carried automatic rifles, which hung down their sides.

One of the soldiers spoke to the ambulance driver through the open window. The soldier straightened and looked around, turning his head in a half-circle. He shook his head and leant down, talking to the driver. The rear door to the ambulance opened and Nelum got out. She spoke with the two soldiers and pointed to the bench where Amanthi had sat and had her meal.

'There're looking for me,' Amanthi whispered. She heard the wheeze of his breathing as the man shifted nervously, his grip tightening on her arm.

'Why don't you give yourself up without hurting anymore people?' she asked. 'You don't look the type of person who wants to hurt anyone.'

The man turned and moved deeper into the bushes dragging Amanthi with him. She thought about resisting, trying to make it difficult for him to keep her with him. She could lose herself in the bushes and try and hide from him but before she made up her mind, they were out in the open.

A crumbling brick wall ran the length of the museum garden blocking their progress. The man pulled Amanthi to a section of the wall which gave them a foothold to clamber over. The man moved deeper into the garden, towards the imposing white building which gleamed in the dark. The garden, shaded by enormous banyan trees spread out around them, empty in the moonlight.

A balustraded wall enclosing a lush flower garden lay adjacent to the museum. The man dragged Amanthi towards the pillared entrance, anxiously looking around for any movement. The man gripped Amanthi's arm as he pushed her up the two steps into the raised garden. A narrow brick footpath crisscrossed the garden ending in steps leading up to a wide verandah. The man crouched and pulled Amanthi down next to him after taking a few steps into the garden.

From their vantage point, they could remain hidden and look across the open expanse of the garden without being spotted.

The minutes slipped by. The man sat next to Amanthi, watching and listening for any signs of life from around the building.

The silence unnerved her. Even the distant sound of traffic had died away completely. Where would she go if she managed to escape? The sound of voices calling out to one another drifted over the wall. They came from the direction of the road.

Amanthi felt the man loosen his grip as he tried to look through the gap in the balustrade wall at where the voices were coming from. It was the moment she had been waiting for. She wrenched her arm from his grasp and rolled away.

'No, don't!' The man reached out to grab her but lost his balance, falling on his side.

Amanthi jumped to her feet and turned to run. Her foot slipped on the moss-coated bricks, throwing her forward. She put out her left hand to cushion her fall but crashed head-first into an ornate pillar flanking the footpath.

CHAPTER FORTY-SIX

Tilak shook his head. He had to focus on finding the man he'd seen earlier. If he had only acted sooner and questioned him. He had heard of suicide bombers who blew up vehicles. Who would have thought they would resort to wearing explosives on their bodies?

The search in the park had not found the bomber. Despite three sweeps of the area, they had only found stray dogs and an old beggar who was sleeping under the slide in the children's playground.

It was long after midnight when Tilak and Chandra walked up to the command post which had been set up at the Cenotaph. Lightening flashed across the sky and thunder rumbled in the distance, coming closer with every sound. Tilak could feel a sense of gloom in the men around him. They had been searching for this bomber for many days and he had proven very elusive.

'He must be around here somewhere,' an army captain argued. 'How far could he have gone. I think we should widen the search area.'

Tilak walked up to Chandra. 'What's going on?'

The army captain seeing Tilak stuck out his hand. 'Hi, I am Mohan,' he said. 'I am the military coordinator.'

Tilak nodded, introducing himself. After introductions all around, Tilak and Chandra moved away from the huddle of officers who were discussing how to redeploy their search teams.

'The man's disappeared again,' Tilak said, shaking his head. 'He's proving to be quite resourceful.'

'He won't be far,' Chandra said. 'I can understand why he chose not to stay here. There aren't many places to hide.'

'So, what are you thinking?' Chandra asked Tilak.

'I think the captain is right,' Tilak said, gesturing to the group at the command post. 'Extending the search area is a good idea.'

They studied the park. It was hemmed in by four major boulevards, lined on one side by buildings of various shapes and sizes. The Colombo Town Hall with its neo-colonial design anchored one end of the park. Headquarters of the Colombo Municipal Council and the office of the Mayor of Colombo, it had a twenty-four-hour security presence. The National Museum sprawled across the base of the park across a wide boulevard, surrounded by large open gardens shaded by enormous banyan trees. Only occupied during the day it would have many places in which to hide.

'The museum and that bunch of buildings over there are all empty for the night,' Tilak said, pointing across the boulevard. 'That's where I would start looking.'

The two of them started walking towards the rear of the museum compound. Opened by the British in 1877 as a museum, the structure held some of the most valuable national and cultural artefacts in the country.

Tilak noticed an ambulance parked on the boulevard next to the museum.

He wondered what it was doing there at this time of the night.

As they got closer, he saw two soldiers talking to the driver. A nurse got out of the ambulance and joined the men, pointing towards the museum grounds. Tilak increased his pace … maybe they had seen something.

The ambulance had the logo of the Colombo General Hospital with a sign that said Emergency Response Unit.

'What's going on here?' Tilak addressed the group, surprising them. They all turned to look at him.

'The Doctor who was with them is gone,' one of the soldiers answered. 'She was out here a moment ago but seems to have disappeared.'

'What are you doing out here?' Tilak asked the nurse who looked vaguely familiar.

'We're first responders from the burn unit in case a bomb goes off,' said the nurse.

Tilak realized where he had seen the nurse. She had been one of the nurses with Amanthi when she attended to Saman.

'You attended to my soldier in Batticaloa with Doctor Amanthi,' he said, smiling at the nurse. 'Is she here with you?'

'Yes, she's here somewhere,' said the nurse, recognition lighting up her face. She looked around. 'The doctor stepped out to get some fresh air and to smoke a cigarette, I think.'

Tilak walked around the ambulance, looking for Amanthi but he couldn't see any sign of her.

'I don't see her,' he said. 'Do you know where she went?'

'She was sitting there not long ago,' the driver said pointing towards the park bench. 'But I don't know where she is.'

Tilak felt his heart beat faster as he began to walk towards the bench.

Chandra followed with the ambulance driver.

'Have you seen anyone around here this evening?' he asked over his shoulder. 'A man in a white sarong and shirt?'

'No,' the driver said. 'There was no one until the soldiers came.'

There was the lingering smell of cigarette smoke near the bench, but no sign of Amanthi. Tilak peered into the dark bushes behind the park bench. Irrational thoughts swirled through his mind. He started trembling and his knees felt weak. A sense of helplessness came over him.

Don't panic, Tilak told himself, trying hard to suppress the feeling. Amanthi must have just been here … she couldn't be far. He bit his lip hard, glancing at Chandra who looked back at him, concern etched on his face.

Tilak turned to the soldiers who had followed them. 'One of you stay with the ambulance.' he ordered, 'The other report to those officers that we have a missing doctor. Tell them that we need the building surrounded right away. Warn them that the two of us are going into the garden to look for her.'

Tilak tugged his handgun from the holster on his hip and clicked off the safety. Without waiting for Chandra to follow he plunged recklessly into the bushes behind the bench, his eyes scanning the darkness for anything out of the ordinary.

The large thicket of bushes separating the museum gardens from the road was dark and dense. Unseen branches smacked against his face as he moved deeper into the greenery. In the shadowy darkness, his mind played tricks making him feel he was in the jungle. His anguish slowly diminished, replaced by a cold fury. His military training asserted itself, making him slow down and begin to use his senses.

There was nothing in the bushes just behind the park bench that caught his attention. The head-high leafy barrier was not more than a few metres wide. Tilak suddenly found himself in front of a waist-high, brick wall which separated him from a grassy lawn which circled the sprawling building. The museum stretched out in front of him, it's white walls gleaming in the moonlight. Dark shadows from the large banyan trees scattered about the garden made Tilak pause, his eyes trying to pierce the darkness and spot any movement.

Chandra moved silently next to him. 'He would have taken her to the museum,' he said confidently. 'That's what I would have done. It's too open around here.'

Tilak nodded in agreement. He studied the rambling building trying to figure out where the man would have taken Amanthi. The night was relatively quiet with the muted sound of distant traffic. Only the bark of shouted commands from the soldiers in the park behind him broke the stillness of the night.

Tilak jumped the wall and walked towards the museum, his eyes scanning the surrounding area. A low balustraded wall surrounding a flower garden abutted a wing of the museum building. A flicker of movement caught the edge of his vision making him turn his head sharply to the right. He stared at the spot he thought he'd seen something but nothing moved. He changed direction, gesturing to Chandra to follow him. He was convinced he'd seen something.

The enclosed flower garden they approached was two steps higher than the rest of the surrounding area. The balustraded cement wall was streaked with dirt, it's surface pitted with age.

Tilak reached the wall, looking over it into the raised enclosure. The enclosed garden held a collection of tired looking rose bushes clearly visible in the moonlight. He instinctively looked-for places where danger could be lurking, running his eyes along the dark shadows under the balustraded walls. Tilak's eyes were drawn to a shape on the ground, lying next to a pillar. It looked like a pile of clothes but something made him pause and look closer. He could barely make out the shape of a person, face down on the footpath. As he watched, the person moved, rolling to the side and attempting to get up.

'She's here!' Tilak yelled as he vaulted over the low balustrade into the flower garden shoving through a row of rose bushes onto the gravel footpath. Tilak heard Chandra's footsteps on the footpath behind him as he reached Amanthi who was seated on the ground, her head between her knees.

CHAPTER FORTY-SEVEN

Amanthi didn't know where she was. Her jaw hurt and her head throbbed. She felt physically and emotionally drained. She tried to open her eyes. Why was she laying on the ground? Amanthi tried to push herself up but a sharp pain from her left wrist prevented her. Rolling to her side, she used her elbows and right hand to push herself up until she was in a sitting position. Her head felt as if it were enveloped in cotton. She put her head down on her knees, cushioning it with her arms.

'Amanthi, are you okay?' A voice called, sounding distant. She tried to ignore it, but the tone was insistent. She looked up and blinked. Tilak was staring at her, a worried look on his face.

Amanthi stared at him blankly. What is he doing here? How did he find me?

She tried to say something but she couldn't form the words. Her mind seemed to be swimming in thickened honey.

Tilak had a stricken expression on his face. He knelt next to her, bending his head and looking into her eyes. He glanced up and snapped out a command. 'Give me your canteen.'

A hand appeared holding a metal flask. Tilak fumbled with the screw top, finally wrenching it open. Supporting her head with his arm, he held the aluminium container to her lips.

Amanthi raised her head and took a small sip. She felt a surge of nausea. She lowered her head, the bile from her stomach threatening to overwhelm her.

Tilak cradled her, supporting her upper body. 'Take another sip.'

Amanthi swallowed and raised her head, allowing him to hold the canteen to her lips. Water dribbled down her lips as Tilak tilted the container. She took a sip and swallowed. The water was cool, filling her parched mouth and throat with moisture. The nausea retreated and she immediately felt better.

Tilak saw the change in her expression. He held the container to her lips allowing her to take another sip. 'What happened?'

Amanthi shook her head, trying to clear the wooziness. 'I slipped on the bricks and fell,' she said. 'I hit my head on the pillar.' She reached up and touched the side of her face which felt tender. 'What are you doing here?'

Tilak sat back on his haunches. 'We are looking for a man we suspect is a suicide bomber,' he said, looking around. 'We think he's hiding somewhere around here.'

Amanthi sat up straighter. The small enclosed garden next to the museum was busy with activity. A tall man dressed in civilian clothes was directing armed soldiers in pairs to various parts of the museum compound.

'He was here,' she said. 'I spoke to him.'

The expression on Tilak's face and the sound of his voice changed suddenly. 'The bomber? You saw him?' he asked abruptly.

'Yes,' Amanthi said. 'He grabbed me and brought me here.'

Tilak grabbed her by the shoulders, his face an angry mask. 'Did he hurt you? Where did he go?' Amanthi was shocked by the intensity on Tilak's face 'No… No, she said. 'He didn't hurt me. He's not who you think he is.'

Tilak pulled her into his arms, hugging her tightly. Amanthi could feel his heart thumping against her chest. 'We have to find him!' Tilak growled into her ear. 'He's too dangerous. He must be found. Where did he go?'

Amanthi had never seen Tilak this way before. It scared her. 'I don't know,' she said, pushing him away. 'He was here when I fell.' Amanthi pushed herself back against the wall and dragged herself to her feet, using the pillar for support.

She felt dizzy for a moment but it passed.

Tilak let her go as she steadied herself. He looked around and motioned to the man in civilian clothes who had come closer and was watching them. 'He was here. He must be hiding somewhere around here. Get the men to surround the building. We'll have to search it.'

Tilak looked at Amanthi. 'Was he carrying anything?' he asked. 'Like around his waist?'

Amanthi nodded weakly. The effort made her head hurt. 'He has a bomb strapped to him,' she said. 'His wife and son were killed by the army and he wants revenge.'

Voices raised in concern just outside the museum garden made them both turn and look in that direction.

'Doctor, doctor, are you alright?' Nelum, followed by the ambulance driver, ran into the garden. A soldier hurried after them.

'Yes, yes, I am fine. I had a fall and hit my head.'

Amanthi put out her hand which Nelum grasped between her own. She looked anxiously into Amanthi's face before putting her arm around Amanthi's shoulder, supporting her.

'You need to be examined,' Nelum insisted. 'Are you okay to walk back?'

Tilak was watching as more soldiers deployed around the building. He stepped up to Amanthi and grasped her arm gently. 'I have to go now,' he said. 'Go with your nurse. I will see you later.'

Amanthi shook her head. 'I am coming with you,' she said, reaching for the canteen that Tilak still held in his hand. She took a long swallow of the cool water. 'I am okay now.' Her head still ached where it had hit the ground, but she felt much stronger, the fuzziness in her head had disappeared.

'Are you sure?' Tilak glanced at Nelum before responding. Amanthi saw Nelum shake her head but she didn't care.

'I am fine,' she said determinedly, shaking herself out of Nelum's grasp. 'I think I can talk him into giving himself up. The poor man lost his wife and child and is driven by revenge. He is not a terrorist.'

Tilak kept watching Amanthi. She could see that he was not convinced. 'Please,' she said, stepping up to him and placing her hand on his chest.

CHAPTER FORTY-EIGHT

Nadesan didn't know what to do. He stood in a darkened corner on the first-floor verandah, watching for any movement in the bushes. He realized that it was a mistake trying to take the Doctor hostage and to try and escape by using the ambulance. His heart had almost stopped when he saw the doctor crash headfirst into the stone pillar. He had admired her spirit, and knowing that she was a doctor, he had not intended to harm her. He had checked her to make sure she was alive. She was clearly unconscious; her ashen coloured face had unnerved him. Thinking that she had killed herself, he was relieved when he found that she was still breathing. He felt a sense of remorse when he looked down at her. She had awakened something in him which he thought he had lost.

Nadesan shook his head to clear it. Making sure that the doctor was okay had cost him valuable minutes. There were soldiers just across those bushes and he needed to find a place to hide until morning. It was time to go to ground again. Nadesan scurried around the corner, towards the front of the building making sure he kept away from the balustraded wall.

A wide staircase leading to the second floor made him pause. The upper floor would provide some cover as he felt completely exposed where he was. Looking around to see if he was being observed, Nadesan scrambled up the stairs which led to an open landing. A corridor with elegant columns looking out into the garden stretched away on both sides. Doors and windows shuttered for the night opened onto the wide passageway which surrounded the building.

An empty alcove at the back of the museum provided a place for him to sit and rest. He was feeling the effort of the previous twenty-four hours beginning to catch up with him. But he was not ready to give up. A plastic bag with bread rolls and a bottle of aerated water were at his feet but he didn't feel like eating.

Voices called out from the garden where he had left the doctor. The soldiers must have found her. Nadesan felt the familiar hatred well up inside of him. He despised the soldiers who had taken away everything he loved but for the first time it was tempered with a voice of reason. He hated them for their arrogance and conceit, for their racism and their air of superiority. But the doctor was right. His anger was against the soldiers who had killed his wife and son. Why had he allowed himself to become like them and kill innocent people?

Nadesan was struck by a sudden wave of fear and found himself cursing his decision to come to the museum. He sighed! He would have to move soon otherwise he would be trapped

The museum had shut for the night but he tried to open each set of doors he came across just in case one wasn't locked.

A tall wooden ladder lying on its side in the corridor made him look up at the ceiling. The outline of a trap door gave him an idea. Would he be able to climb onto the roof and draw up the ladder behind him? It would be the perfect place to hide.

Nadesan lifted the heavy ladder with difficulty, wedging it against the architrave around the trapdoor entrance. The trapdoor opened easily and he found himself on a flat area running around the iron corrugated roof of the museum. A short balustrade concealed the walkway from view. Drawing up the ladder was not easy but he finally sat down, breathing hard and in a bath of sweat, with the ladder resting beside him.

Nadesan crawled over and shut the trapdoor, falling on his back in relief. The roof was quiet and eerie, the moonlight falling across the dark green expanse leaving no shadows. Smart new office buildings across a wide avenue to the east, towered above the museum, their windows dark and lifeless at this time of the night.

He'd stay here until it was safe.

CHAPTER FORTY-NINE

The size of the sprawling two storey building became more evident as they drew closer, it's many open galleries and courtyards would make it difficult to search.

Tilak leant against the root of a banyan tree studying the enormous white washed building which had begun to glow in the early morning light. A hard knot of fury was growing in his stomach, threatening to overwhelm him when he thought about what had happened to Amanthi. They had been lucky that the bomber had let her go. He had proven to be an elusive prey, using the city like a jungle to hide from the security forces. They must find him and stop him before he did any more damage.

He had refused to let Amanthi come with them although he had almost given into her pleas. He made up his mind when he saw her frown and quickly looked away from the brightly illuminated museum building.

'I am sorry but I cannot risk it,' he said emphatically, shaking his head. 'You're showing signs of being concussed and need to be checked out properly.'

He turned to the two soldiers who were standing at the entrance to the garden. 'Take them back to the ambulance and remain there until you're relieved,' he ordered.

Tilak could still picture the look on Amanthi's face when she was walking away with the nurse.

'I don't think any soldiers will be allowed inside,' Chandra said, bringing him back to the present. 'The Curator will have a fit. We'll have to get the museum staff to search the building.'

By the time they walked around the building, the entire area had been cordoned off by troops who had been redeployed from the park. Chandra walked up to the officer directing the search operation. 'We'll have to get the Curator to open the museum,' he said. 'I don't think we should have anyone tramping through the building without someone from the museum being present. There are too many valuable items in there.'

The officer nodded. 'Yes, I agree. I've already sent someone to wake him up.

We'll check the outside of the building but leave the inside alone for now.'

The sky was brightening rapidly by the time the army tracked down the curator and brought him to the museum. Tilak joined the others standing by the front entrance to the building.

The man was in his late fifties with a head full of white hair. He was wearing neatly ironed shirt and trousers, his feet enclosed in leather moccasins. His eyes, framed by round rimless glasses, stared out from under his bushy white eyebrows.

'We're closed today,' he grumbled, looking around at the heavily armed soldiers surrounding the museum. 'What do you want me to do?'

Tilak had been taught at school that the museum was closed on Friday. The Curator got the watchman to open the front doors of the museum. They entered the museum's musty interior filled with relics from the country's impressively long history.

'We should check for any signs of forced entry,' the Curator said. 'We just replaced all the locks and unless the man is a skilled locksmith, the only way he could get in would be by breaking in.'

They split up into pairs, one pair accompanied by the Curator and the other by the watchman. Chandra and Tilak followed the watchman as he trudged along the western side of the building, checking on every door and window for signs of forced entry. Tilak looked around the museum thinking how easy it would be for someone to hide amongst the hundreds of cabinets and objects laid out in the different galleries.

Not finding any signs of forced entry on the ground floor, they walked up the double staircase to the second-floor galleries leaving the two soldiers to continue searching the ground floor. Tilak couldn't help but look at some of the displays. He had come to the museum as a child and remembered how impressed he'd been with what he had seen. In one of the upper rooms a skeleton of an enormous blue whale hung from the ceiling over rows of dusty display cases filled with puppets of all kinds. It was one of the most bizarre sights he had ever seen.

The second floor had no signs of forced entry and they gathered at the top of the main staircase to plan what to do next.

'It's going to be a massive job to search every room in this place,' Chandra said, looking around. 'At least there is no sign of forced entry.'

'What about the roof,' Tilak asked. 'Is there a way of getting up there from outside.'

'Yes,' said the Curator. 'We have to send people up there often to clear the gutters. They get blocked by leaves and other debris and the water overflows into the top floor.'

The Curator walked to the eastern side of the building and opened a door leading to the large balustraded balcony which surrounded the museum.

'There's a trapdoor up there,' he said pointing to a rectangular shape on the ceiling. He looked around. 'That's strange,' he said. 'There's normally a ladder lying here which we use to climb up. The Curator looked at the watchman. 'Has it been taken away?' he asked.

The watchman shrugged. 'No, it was here last evening when I did my rounds.'

The four of them looked at each other. The bomber had to be hiding on the roof. He was trapped up there but they needed to get him down without blowing the museum up.

'Is this the only way onto the roof?' asked Chandra.

The Curator nodded. 'Yes, as far as I know. But you could get up there from the ground if you have a very long ladder. But we don't have one.'

'Is there another ladder we can use to get to the trapdoor?' Tilak asked the Curator.

The Curator shook his head. 'We have two stepladders that we use in the museum to hang the exhibits,' he said. 'They might be tall enough to just get you up there.'

'Wait a minute,' Chandra said. 'We can't just go barging on to the roof. We don't know what he will do if we startle him.' He looked up at the ceiling. 'We don't even know which part of the roof he is hiding in. In fact, he could be listening to us right now.'

Tilak nodded. 'Let's go downstairs and talk to the coordinator.' He glanced at Chandra.

'Why don't you stay here in case he makes a move?'

Chandra nodded his head in agreement, moving to the side where he could watch the trapdoor.

Tilak could think of at least one way to get at the bomber but decided to remain quiet for the moment. Let's see what they'd come up with.

CHAPTER FIFTY

Nadesan stirred to the sound of dogs barking. He had lain restlessly all night, every sound magnified a thousand times. Sleep had eluded him His mind restless with thoughts that started so quickly before the previous one ended. He shifted uncomfortably, his body aching from laying on the hard floor and the previous day's exertions. The morning was hot and humid and sweat was beginning to gather on his brow. Perspiration had soaked his grubby shirt overnight and it clung to him like a second skin. He noticed that one of the sleeves had a long tear in it but couldn't remember when he had torn it.

Nadesan remembered every detail of the previous day and found himself confronted with so many obstacles, that he knew the end was near. The most terrible recollection was that he'd failed again. He was tired of running, of hiding, of facing the shame of what he'd done every time hour of the day. The words of the doctor kept echoing in his mind. 'So, you're going to kill others' wives and children in revenge?' she had asked. 'How can that be the answer?'

Nadesan felt a sudden loathing at what he'd become. It was not the way he'd been brought up. From deep within his tortured mind a thought struggled free. Ahimsa is not cowardice, it's wisdom. It was something his father had said to him many times. That respect for all living things and avoidance of violence towards others should be the driving force in his life. But by giving into the hate that had consumed him, he had abandoned the Hindu principles he had grown up with, dishonouring his family in the process.

Nadesan dejectedly realized that he had hardly thought about his father or his mother since he had come to Colombo. It saddened him thinking of the person he'd become.

Voices drifted from below him. Nadesan scrambled to the trapdoor trying to listen to what was being said. The voices were muffled and they seemed to be arguing about something.

Had they discovered where he was hiding? He tried to hear what was being said but could not make out any words. He was glad that he had pulled up the heavy ladder and pulled it across the trapdoor which would make it impossible to open from underneath.

He saw the package of explosives which lay next to the trap door. Last night, he'd removed his sweat soaked shirt and untied the wet strips of cloth holding the bomb which had given him instant relief from the chaffing under his arms. The two detonators lay on top of explosives.

Nadesan couldn't remember pulling them out. Did I do that? He was suddenly overwhelmed with confusion and shook his mind trying to think clearly. It would be so easy to activate the bomb and blow up the building and himself in the process. He could no longer hear any voices below him. It was very early in the day and he wondered what the men were up to. The sound of barking dogs took on a more urgent quality as Nadesan crawled along the narrow platform, looking through the short squat columns of the balustrade. The extensive garden was empty on the east but he felt a cold stab of fear race through his heart when he saw the road in front of the museum full of Police and military vehicles.

Nadesan drew his head back in dismay. They had found him. Nadesan didn't know how they had tracked him to the museum but he didn't care! He had failed ... again. He was not going to get away from them this time.

The frustration, the dread, the wretchedness and worry finally peaked. I have failed again. It was a monstrous torment.

Nadesan sat down heavily, his knees drawn up against his chest. He rocked back and forth as he listened to the officers barking commands at the soldiers who surrounded the building.

The thought of being captured sent a shiver down his spine. He felt weak and alone, tired of all the running. A sense of sadness overcame him, tears streaming down his face as his thoughts returned again and again to his dead wife and son. He closed his eyes and remembered the time that his world had fallen apart. One minute they were happy. How quickly it had changed and so much had happened in the months since then. He relived the pain of his wife and son's deaths and he sobbed as it still affected him as deeply as it ever had.

Nadesan opened his eyes and shrugged off the bad memories with an almost physical effort. He tried to remember the good times they had and the love they had shared. What am I waiting for? He had wanted to go to his family as somebody who had avenged their deaths but he realized that it was wrong. The doctor was right. It's time to stop. He roused himself suddenly, as if waking up, and felt a sense of peace overcoming him. He would join them now. It was time.

Nadesan reached for the locket around his neck. It was taken from the thaali he had given his wife. He remembered brushing aside the long strands of Radika's hair and knotting the holy thread around her neck during the Hindu marriage ceremony. Worn for the long life of the husband, its significance was not lost to Nadesan as his fingers fumbled with the clasp, managing to open the piece of gold jewellery without dropping its contents. The locket held a tiny photograph of his wife taken on their wedding day. Nestled in the locket was a small capsule filled with cyanide.

Nadesan grasped the tiny object in his fingers and raised it to his lips. He felt at peace. It was the right thing to do. He stared at the photograph of his wife, so pure and innocent, who had been taken from him so violently. Nadesan said a small prayer under his breath asking for her forgiveness for not avenging her. Holding her face in his gaze he placed the capsule in his mouth, biting down on it firmly.

CHAPTER FIFTY-ONE

An untidy line of black and yellow three-wheelers was parked outside the restaurant when they pulled up at the curb. Tilak helped Amanthi up the wide stairs leading to the restaurant entrance. He had picked her up from her home after leaving a message that he would come by in the evening to give her an update.

It was late in the evening when he had finally got home that day. They had found the body of the bomber on the roof of the museum after using the fire department's mobile ladder unit. Examination of the museum rooftop from a nearby office building had shown a man laying by the balustrade overlooking the front portico of the museum. By his posture and lack of movement it had been determined that the man was not alive. Two army snipers from buildings on opposite sides of the museums had their sights trained on the man with instructions to take a head shot only if the man showed any signs of movement. But it was an unnecessary precaution. The man was dead by his own hand. The explosives and the detonators had been recovered and the city had slowly come back to normal.

Tilak still remembered how he had felt when he had heard that Amanthi had gone missing. He looked at her carefully when she came to the door to greet him, looking for any signs that she had been traumatized by what had happened to her. He had come directly from Army HQ and was in his uniform.

Amanthi watched him staring at her with a slight frown on her face. Tilak remembered the first time they had met. She had always been able to read him like a book.

The ground was still wet after a late evening shower and small pools of water had gathered as they climbed the steps to the restaurant.

The restaurant was built in the colonial style, square in structure with a low red tiled roof set around an inner cobbled courtyard lit by flickering lanterns. All around the edge of the courtyard were colourful bougainvillea and frangipani bushes with an ancient fig tree occupying the centre. It served Sri Lankan food cooked in the traditional village style. The cooked food was displayed on rough earthenware pots which sat on clay platforms on which hot coals were piled to keep the food warm. The different dishes each person picked were served onto banana leaves held in flat wicker plates and brought to the table by the waiters.

Amanthi had hardly spoken during dinner, answering Tilak's questions in monosyllables and not initiating any conversation on her own. Tilak began to sense her mood and wondered whether she was mad at him for not letting her go with him into the museum.

'You've been very quiet,' he said. 'Have I done anything to upset you?'

Amanthi shook her head. 'No, no,' she said. 'I am sorry to be like this. I still cannot it out of my mind. Tell me what happened after you left me.'

Tilak had wanted the evening to be different. To be about them but he realized that she wanted to talk about what took place that night at the museum.

'Let's order coffee and I'll tell you about it.'

Tilak felt Amanthi's eyes on him as the waiter took the order from him. He sat back in his chair and sighed. He was still feeling the effects of the hunt for the bomber and the investigation that followed. He'd not got much sleep in the last few days.

Amanthi stared across the table at him expectantly.

'Preliminary reports say that the man had died from cyanide poisoning,' Tilak said, shrugging. 'We have known for a while that the militants all carry cyanide capsules around their neck and use it to avoid being captured.'

Amanthi nodded at Tilak. 'Is that what happened?' she asked thoughtfully. 'I should have guessed he might do something like that. I wonder what made him change his mind about blowing himself up. He wanted to take revenge after his family were killed, I could see that very clearly.'

'Maybe it was something you said to him?' Tilak looked at her questioningly. 'You've never talked about what actually happened when he grabbed you. Did you try and talk him out of killing himself?'

'I was more concerned about staying alive,' Amanthi's eyes flashed as she responded to his question. 'And anyway, it was the death of his wife and child which were driving him. Were you able to find out anything about the incident?'

Tilak marvelled at Amanthi, her even tone, her calm eyes and how relaxed she looked. It came as a sudden realization that he knew very little about this woman. He knew her name and what she did for a living but very little about her passions, her strengths and weaknesses, her innermost thoughts and desires. What he was absolutely sure about was that he wanted to learn more.

Tilak shook his head. 'We're working on it,' he said. 'There were a number of civilians killed in a crossfire earlier this year and I have asked for the report, but you know how these things are.' Tilak paused, steepling his hands and looked at her. 'But what does it matter now anyway?' he shrugged. 'He's dead and we prevented another massacre.'

Amanthi looked at him with her calm, penetrating eyes. 'You think that's the end of it all?' she asked abruptly. 'If we treat these people like animals there will be many more like him.'

Tilak was taken aback by her response. There was an edge to what she said. He went quiet as the waiter threaded his way through the tables towards them with their coffee order.

Amanthi studied Tilak as he sipped on the hot beverage. Her coffee lay untouched in front of her. 'You are wondering whether the incident that night and the death of that man has affected me somehow?' she asked, her eyes narrowing as she waited for his response.

Tilak nodded cautiously. It was a side of Amanthi he had not seen before. He wondered whether the nights events had affected her in some way.

'It's not that it's affected me in any strange way,' she said calmly, almost reading his mind. 'It's more a realization that all these people who are affected by the war; those who are burnt and maimed, all the bomb victims who are brought to the hospital … to me, for treatment …. all this could be avoided. It's ultimately what we are doing to them that's causing all this. They don't have to suffer this way.'

Tilak felt the blood rush to his face. He stared at Amanthi like he was seeing her for the first time.

'What do you expect me to do?' Tilak asked, throwing his hands up. 'It's not that I am in any position to help them.' His voice sounded unusually harsh to his ears.

Amanthi cocked her head at him. 'Surely you're more intelligent than that. All I am saying is that we are creating a generation of Tamil youth who are growing up with hate in their hearts.'

Tilak realized that he had over-reacted to her comment. He smiled at her apologetically. 'I am sorry!' he said. 'I understand what you are trying to say, but they shouldn't go around blowing people up.'

Amanthi pursed her lips and looked at him. 'Yes, it's not the answer. I agree,' she said. 'But what about those soldiers who killed his family? Were they ever brought to justice? Or was that all swept under the carpet and the incident forgotten?'

Tilak shrugged. 'There's a war going on if you haven't noticed,' he said. 'Innocent people get killed.'

Amanthi leaned forward, her eyes flashing angrily. 'Damn you, Tilak,' she snapped, waving her arm at him. 'You're just like the bloody rest of them. Is that how you justify what you did to that woman in Kataragama? How can you kill someone like that or was it okay because she was supposed to be an insurgent?'

Tilak tried to ignore her angry outburst but her words cut deeply. 'I paid for what I did,' he said defensively. 'All I am saying is I'd rather it not happen, but I can understand how it does.'

'I'd thought that you'd learned a lesson after what you went through.' There was a hard edge to her voice he had never heard before and he realized that he would have to tread very carefully.

Amanthi was sitting back in her chair glaring at him. Tilak suddenly realized that she saw him as a part of the problem and was sorry that he was in his uniform. Tilak could sense that he was on dangerous ground, that he might lose her completely if he said the wrong thing.

Tilak held up his hands placatingly. 'Yes, I agree,' he said carefully. 'I am being an idiot by not taking this seriously. I can see that you're upset and I need to understand what is it you want from me.'

Tilak felt dishearteningly alone. Amanthi was the one person whom he had felt he could confide in, someone who understood him. But now he wasn't so sure. He still couldn't understand what Amanthi wanted from him. It wasn't that he was in a position to do anything. Or was he?

Amanthi hadn't moved. She stared at him without blinking. Tilak didn't know what she was looking for. He tried to appear contrite, telling himself not to say anything. But he knew that nothing he could say was going to fix this.

CHAPTER FIFTY-TWO

Amanthi leaned back on the chair and stared at Tilak. Her whole body felt tense, her fists clenched tight. It came as a complete surprise that she felt so emotional about what had happened. She had always prided herself in remaining calm and professional in everything she did.

Amanthi was frustrated about how much she didn't know. It was her blind acceptance of the illusion of normality while all this was going on in the country that troubled her even more. It had been upsetting her from the moment she had heard the bomber's story. Of course, she had heard stories whispered by the nurses about Tamil civilians being shot and killed by the security forces, but she had always believed that they were terrorists and there was nothing wrong. She shook her head in disbelief at her own naivety. How could you hate a person for who he was? You could hate a person for what he did, but why did she feel guilty about the bomber? Was there something wrong with her, was something missing? She realized that she had been on edge since the incident happened and had put it down to working long hours. She wondered whether she was suffering from some form of anxiety disorder. She breathed out slowly, letting her hands relax.

Tilak continued to talk but the words didn't register. She had felt a bitter, helpless anger when he had refused to let her go with him. However, by thinking about it more rationally later the next morning, she understood why he'd done it. But she couldn't get the image of his angry face out of her mind.

Amanthi realized that the bomber's death had affected her more than she had thought and regretted having snapped at Tilak.

She really didn't blame him for what happened, but he was part of the problem, in fact they were both part of the problem. She chewed her lip, thoughts tumbling through her head.

Tilak had stopped talking and was watching her closely. They sat looking at each other for several minutes without speaking. Amanthi looked away first but Tilak wasn't going to let her get away that easily.

'What's going on, Amanthi?' he asked. 'It's obvious that something is bothering you. Do you want to talk about it?'

Amanthi shook her head slowly. 'I am sorry for what I said earlier,' she said. 'It wasn't fair. I had no idea of what you have to go through when people are trying to kill you. But meeting that man has affected me more than I thought,' Amanthi admitted. 'When the bombs were going off I felt nothing but revulsion for the people doing it. But now...'

Amanthi rubbed her face with the palm of her hand. 'I have very mixed emotions right now. I have only seen the horror; just one side of it really...only what happens after the bombs go off. He has opened my mind to why ordinary people go to such extremes. I just cannot imagine what it must have been like for that man to go through what he has been through. It had changed him into what he became.'

Amanthi shook her head and stared down at the table. 'Even though it hurts me to say it …. while I cannot sympathize with him for what he has done … I certainly can understand why he did it.' Amanthi felt a rush of sadness remembering how the man talked about his dead wife and child and wondered how she would feel if she lost a loved one. Would she react the same way?

Amanthi looked at her wrist watch wishing that the time would pass more quickly. She suddenly felt that it was a mistake going out for dinner so soon.

Tilak leaned forward, a small frown creasing his forehead.

'I think I understand what you are feeling but I don't want this to affect us,' he said placatingly. 'He may have had very good reasons for what he did but I am a soldier and I have a duty to perform. I know I have done some bad things in the past that I am not proud of, but I am changing and I am not the same person I used to be.'

Amanthi nodded, her mind still not totally focused on the present. She shook her head trying to clear her thoughts. 'It was a mistake for us to meet so soon after what happened,' she said looking at him. 'I want to go home, take some time off from work and think about that night. I may even go away somewhere far from all this. I need a break really badly.'

'I can get some time off and come with you,' Tilak was unsure whether it was the right thing to ask but he knew that she needed someone to talk to.

'No,' Amanthi said. 'I need to spend some time alone. Thanks for offering. I'll let you know when I get back.'

Her answer appeared to have satisfied Tilak, but she could see that he was still uncomfortable with what had happened. They didn't talk about it again. She left the restaurant with him and let him drop her off at her home. Amanthi kissed him on the lips making sure that there was no resentment in the air. But it was a quiet goodbye. Their eyes weren't meeting as much as before, their gestures seemed perfunctory.

Tilak waved goodbye to her as he drove off and Amanthi wondered whether they would see each other again.

~

ABOUT THE AUTHOR

Roderic Grigson was born in Colombo, Sri Lanka where he was educated and lived till he was twenty-one. Rod's family were Burghers, descendants of the Portuguese, Dutch and British colonials who ruled the island nation for 450 years. With no prospects in the former British colony of Ceylon that had become a socialist state run by Sinhalese nationals, he left the country of his birth with a few dollars in his pocket and entered the United States on a tourist visa. He found work at the United Nations Secretariat in New York where he worked for the next twelve years. After studying information technology at New York University, he volunteered and joined the United Nations Peacekeeping Forces in Egypt and Lebanon, serving on the Suez Canal during the signing of the Israel Egypt Peace Accord and in South Lebanon during the Lebanese Civil War. After spending two years in the field, Rod came back to New York in 1980 and joined the UN Technological Innovations team. He spent the next six years helping develop and implementing office information systems in six languages in UN regional offices around the world. Rod migrated with his wife to Australia in 1986 where he became a senior executive for a global IT company.

Recently retired, *After the Flames* is Rod's second book. His first book *Sacred Tears* was released in 2014 and is available for purchase on Amazon.